DARK LADY

books by Michael Baldwin include

poetry
KING HORN
THE BURIED GOD
DEATH ON A LIVE WIRE
HOW CHAS EGGET LOST HIS WAY IN A CREATION MYTH
HOB
SNOOK

autobiography
GRANDAD WITH SNAILS
IN STEP WITH A GOAT

fiction
MIRACLEJACK
THE GAMECOCK
THE GREAT CHAM
THE CELLAR
A WORLD OF MEN
THERE'S A WAR ON
EXIT WOUNDS
HOLOFERNES
RATGAME
SEBASTIAN (short stories)
UNDERNEATH (short stories)
THE RAPE OF OC
THE FIRST MRS WORDSWORTH

DARK LADY

Michael Baldwin

LITTLE, BROWN AND COMPANY

A *Little, Brown* Book

First published in Great Britain in 1998
by Little, Brown and Company

Copyright © Michael Baldwin 1998

The moral right of the author has been asserted.

A CIP catalogue record for this book
is available from the British Library.

ISBN 0 316 64066 2

Typeset in Century Old Style by
Palimpsest Book Production Limited,
Polmont, Stirlingshire
Printed and bound in Great Britain by
Creative Print and Design Wales, Ebbw Vale

Little, Brown and Company (UK)
Brettenham House
Lancaster Place
London WC2E 7EN

For Ted and Carol

Two loves I have of comfort and despair,
Which like two spirits do suggest me still,
The better angel is a man right fair:
The worser spirit a woman coloured ill.
To win me soon to hell my female evil
Tempteth my better angel from my side,
And would corrupt my saint to be a devil,
Wooing his purity with her foul pride.
And whether that my angel be turned fiend,
Suspect I may, yet not directly tell,
But being both from me both to each friend,
I guess one angel in another's hell.
Yet this shall I ne'er know, but live in doubt
Till my bad angel fire my good one out.

William Shakespeare, 'Sonnet 144'

... evill disposed men, who forgetting they were borne of
women, nourished of women, and that if it were not by
the meanes of women, they would be quite extinguished
out of the world, and a finall ende of them all, doe like
Vipers deface the wombes wherein they were bred, onely
to give way and utterance to their want of discretion and
goodnesse ...

Mistris Æmilia Lanyer (Wife to Captaine
Alphonso Lanier, Servant to the King's Majestie),
Salve Deus Rex Ivdaeorum

Down from the waist they are centaurs,
Though women all above:
But to the girdle do the gods inherit,
Beneath is all the fiends';
There's hell, there's darkness, there's the sulphurous pit,
Burning, scalding, stench, consumption.

William Shakespeare, *King Lear*: Act IV, Scene 6

... it pleased our Lord and Saviour Jesus Christ, without the assistance of man, beeing free from originall and all other sinnes, from the time of his conception, till the houre of his death, to be begotten of a woman, borne of a woman, nourished of a woman, obedient to a woman; and that he healed women, pardoned women, comforted women; yea, even when he was in his greatest agonie and bloodie sweat, going to be crucified, and also in the last houre of his death, took care to dispose of a woman, sent a woman to declare his most glorious resurrection to the rest of his Disciples.

Mistris Æmilia Lanyer, op. cit.

She has outlasted all man-uses,
As was her first resolve:
Happy and idle as a port
After the sea's recession ...

Robert Graves, 'The Great-grandmother'

ONE

Frustration was getting the better of Lord Chamberlain Hunsdon. He began to sweat. His crotch stank like a sick horse. The breath of a sick horse, at the least.

He advanced his boot and wriggled his stockinged foot inside it. The boot was hardly the item for a man of his rank to be wearing in the forenoon – not in London and secure inside his own most secret house and love nest. Not indoors and on a steamy day in Autumn.

His Emilia crouched very close to it, exactly as he insisted. She was naked, again as required, and hating to be so. Her body trembled in a heady mixture of what he took to be fear and desire, emotions which ran very close together in women. He prayed even now, and out of love, that she might once more begin her monthly bleed. Sweet Heaven, if only God's mother could make it so!

He gazed down on her back and saw that it was good. He watched her spine with its ripples and rungs, its delicious *wriggles*. He eyed her neck and the soft curls of her hair, which was darker than proper, blacker than its own shadow. He saw the peeping undersides of her toes where they stole timidly in and out from beneath the crouching hemispheres of her bottom.

Her flesh gave off that magic incense of hers. Did she bring it on with oils or old-fashioned sorcery? She smelled like spiced mull and freshly baked cake-dough – no, better than that, like

1

the herb garden in his house in nearby Blackfriars. Her whole body was as clean as a kitchen, even her most private skin. It was what had won him to her in the first place – fifty-year-old man to sixteen-year-old woman – that and certain other gifts too distracting to remember now, seven years on. No, he wouldn't be led astray by them, even though his tally stick was standing proud as a pikestaff at the high-port-and-push, and would doubtless prance higher still if it weren't sheathed and in its holster.

His tiny Emilia, his jewel of ruby and jet. What an inconsiderate black-haired little bitch! He couldn't bear what her womanhood was doing to him. He hated her calendar of interrupted months, the whole unnecessary engine of parturition. The Creator had designed the female beast as helper and handmaiden. Why had he spoiled His own creation and frustrated His servant man with genesis? Children should come forth as Adam had come, from breath and stones. Men would make less of them and love them the more. And this dear creature would be the more wholesome for it.

Woman was made for the going into, not the coming out of. That comforting inlet of hers was devised for the easing of grown men and the enlightenment of privileged schoolboys. It wasn't for babes to use as a sally port, with their mewling and puking ways. It was much too cunning a creation. As for those other, nastier issues, what a threatening little wound it could be!

He kicked her gently, then wept a tear at her suppliant form – a disgusting waterdrop he dashed away as soon as he saw her take heart from it. Poor sweet Emilia. He must murder her tonight, or arrange for her to be some other man's possession and plaything. Murder seemed the most likely, he loved her so much. Emilia, who for seven years had been his toy, his dream and his rest. Seven years. He wept a little more, but not excessively: he wasn't a weeping man. Perhaps it was no more than six. Even so, only his wife had lasted him longer and now looked like outliving him altogether, though she – praise God – was in Northumberland with his tiresome daughters, when she could keep them there and they weren't with the Queen as ladies-in-waiting.

The girl stirred herself, as if to get up. He pushed his boot into her back to prevent the move. This side of her was bewildering enough. If he glimpsed any more he would be vanquished.

'My lord,' she murmured, 'sweetest lord Harry,' all this entirely without permission to open her mouth. 'Dear lord, I have knelt long enough. Pray grant me leave to lay myself down and *wallow* for a little.' She turned up her face and grinned at him, in spite of her tears.

He refused to laugh. He didn't seek entertainment, and anyway the witticism wasn't her own. It was that damn'd dead poet's, whatever the villain's name was. She read and wrote too many verses, and too much other nonsense besides. He kicked her, hard. She mustn't cite *that* fool. He kicked her again, then stamped down to take some of the spring out of her tongue. The fellow had been cheeking a man he must not remember, and in the presence of a royal personage Henry Carey Lord Hunsdon had schooled himself never to mention and, if possible, totally forget.

His rage nearly knocked her over, so great was the downward pressure in his leg. Thank God he hadn't sent her sprawling and left her woman-sweets uppermost. A breast would be enough to bewitch him beyond recovery; as for her little wedge of horsetail and polypody, that gallimaufry of bride-whisker and bottom-grass all bedewed like the cushions of maidenhair, clubmoss and hart's tongue in his own herb garden, praise be she had the wit to keep her limbs crossed and all glimpses hidden. He couldn't bear to see it.

Even so he drooled and dribbled at the thought of it. His mouth made water intolerably at the memory of her tiny basil plot and privet. How he recalled her darling pussy-willow in all of its moods and during several of his own, from cannon-ramming ramrod-breaking lust to the tinier to-and-fro inchings and itchings of courtly consummation and carnal chit-chat.

She stirred again, and he quietened her with his boot. His recollections of her beauty were much too vigorous for him to allow her to intrude upon them in person.

Let her not get up. Let her not rise. He couldn't pin her down

3

anymore. His head was swimming with heated blood, and almost more engorged than his pikestaff. Whatever his loins said in the matter, his mind told him he mustn't let her dance for him. Her dancing was like her singing, sheerest venereal witchcraft and mummery. She'd even captivated his cousin the Queen by it, and Elizabeth was not much given to women.

There, he couldn't keep his boots on after all. Nor much else either. He lifted her face with his foot beneath her chin, rolled her on to her back, peeled off his stockings and felt her belly with his naked toe. He stamped on her there hard. 'Drop the child,' he said. 'Or tonight I shall trample you with my boots on. *And* send others to do likewise.'

'My lord, you cannot use me thus. I am commanded to play before the Queen this day.'

'And who commands you so?'

'You, Harry.'

'Never again, my love. Not unless you void yourself of your belly.'

She cried openly now. Warrior though he was, he joined her in tears. He was the one who was suffering the most. Suffering is a man's emotion. Women have little sense of tragedy, even high-born women, and Emilia Bassano certainly wasn't one of those.

He lifted her towards a more comfortable place, parting the bedcurtains and stepping towards a nest of such sweetness a lesser man would have fainted. 'You should not have conceived,' he scolded. 'Or, if conceived, retained. I do believe this swelling is a deliberate insult to me.'

'You have other bastards, my lord.'

'Yes, but mares. All but one, and him in Berwick. I made his mother promise to bite his bollocks off or put him in the Church. I think she's done both. He's a bishop now.' He tightened his arms about her. 'I dare not wait to see how this one falls out. When I do this thing to a woman for pleasure I always make males.'

'What's another Tudor, more or less?' she asked, much too pertly considering her circumstance. 'You're only Her Majesty's cousin, Harry.' She wriggled, deliciously.

4

He moved his hands to her neck. It might be the best and simplest way. Surely she knew or guessed? Everyone else did.

Squeezing might do it. Squeezing or pincers of fire. Her body was moist with fear, her thighs dry and reluctant – this in spite of the fact that women respond well to rape. Still he mustn't be rough with her yet, not till tonight. He owed her his love. He made love to her consolingly, his thumbs firm against the vein in her throat.

She muttered, protestingly. She was liquorice now, liquor and liquorice and lickerish. His prick was huge, and his body an increasing hill. It was like lying under a bull. As for his breath, it was great enough to fill a barn and infect the hay.

~

As soon as he'd finished consoling her he left the bed. The anguish she'd caused him would have to be mended later. She'd put him in a temper even so. He bawled for her to rouse herself up and fetch him his clothes.

She stayed behind the hangings and whined against walking naked. Or he thought that was what she said. He couldn't hear her through the bed-curtains, what with her sulky voice and his own bad ear. He fingered it for wax and tried clearing his nostrils. 'Too many mulls and too much black powder,' he grumbled to himself, then shouted through the draperies, 'No need to talk back at me! I'd as lief lie with a mute dummerer as a woman with a thorn on her tongue!' She'd soon cheer herself up, once he fell to cracking a joke or two.

She'd peeped her nose out at last, so he made her find his garments: his boots and doublet by the foot-cushion, his shirt inside her sheets – and a damned sweaty tale they told his nostrils!

She delayed over one of his nether stockings and didn't offer him much of a smile when she'd found it, so he told her to take her chamber pot from its stool, then kneel herself down in front and hold it up for him. Again he wouldn't let her hide herself by as much as a petticoat. 'No need to whinge and cringe, madam. Your private women and other people are all down below, and

5

your skin's so moody brown you might as well be lurking in blackest midnight! I'm eclipsed each time I'm into you.'

He was piddling more and more copiously since coming down from the Borders. He went on staling like a packman's ass. 'Not speaking to me, Emilia? Every man to his humour, and the devil take all women!' His waters smelled stronger than mouldy biscuit or a bear's piss in the ring. A soothsayer could doubtless read marvels from them – they were cloudy with all manner of omens. 'Still keeping mute, my little rook-eye? What a mumbudget you are!' He thought of drying himself in her hair, but the gesture was on the common side, for her if not for him. It would be all right for clanswomen and the wives of rebels – first his prick then his sword – but less than appropriate for his leman who danced before the Queen.

He was done with himself at last. He put his cockerel away and tied up the strings. 'Call someone to be rid of this,' he instructed. 'Keep yourself as privy as you like, and as voiceless. But naked, mind. I may have a want or so left.' He watched her shout for Maria her personal woman, then hide inside the bed again. 'Not for your comfort, neither,' he told the curtains. 'Your bum is in need of my belt. I have to scourge the mother to reach the child.' This was a fine jest, and it quite recovered his good humour.

When Maria came in, he decided to be pleasant. 'Your mistress sends more waters down her cut than the whole Fleet River and Drain.'

The girl could scarcely balance the pot – she was fearful of spilling it over. 'Indeed, my Lord.'

'You should gargle with some,' he said. 'Aye, and rub it well in behind the ear! It's sovereign against the plague. And keep yourself a cupful against the smallpox.' The other pox it could do nothing for. Nor the clap, judging by his itch. He would have to cook his bones again, or waste time riding to Bath.

She was gone on the instant. A pleasing girl, not averse to a subtlety or so. Emilia was one of the few pretty women he knew who liked to have other fair faces about her. She was all sweetness when she chose to be. Again he felt a pang of anguish at the thought of being rid of her. He paced about.

∼

Lord Chamberlain Hunsdon did not inspect his house in Bishops-gate very often, even when he was in London. But a man needs to take an inventory of his possessions from time to time, and there are items too precious to be checked by letter or left to a servant, particularly one with time on his hands and an itch in his cod.

Emilia Bassano was such an item. He was accustomed to having her visit him, accompany him about the realm on the Queen's business, to be produced as his fancy's scabbard and ornament at all manner of festivals, but in general to be stowed like a doll in his baggage. Yet here, in Bishopsgate, she was mistress of his house. He needed to check her *in situ* where she queened it among his *lares* and *penates* – 'queened' it was the word. He needed to count his sheets and number his cushions – and *sniff* them too, not least for other men's odours.

Emilia recovered from her sulk and decided to be cheeky. 'That horse-minding fellow is sending me messages again,' she called from her bed. Still as bare as a trout, and as brown too, she pulled back the drapes and added, 'I speak of the one who writes the masques for young Southampton, and the entertainments for your sister and cousin. That countryman from Stratford with his foreign way of talking.'

'If you mean my cousin the Queen then you'd better say so and give majesty its title.' He spoke seriously, and saw how she pouted at the danger in his voice. He did not joke about his cousin Elizabeth. Being Mary Boleyn's son, and thus the child of one of her father's paramours was sensitive enough. The possibility that King Henry might have gone on visiting his mother after marrying her off was a speculation so common that he did his best to avoid it altogether. Only a fool would boast of being a male Tudor, especially in the hearing of anyone ready to carry the story to the Queen. She did not take kindly to fools of that sort, and was prompt to set their heads on poles, with their bollock-bags and cullions in their mouths if need be. So he was plain Harry Carey – to christen him Henry had been a stupid proclamation of his likely parenthood by his whorish mother and cuckolded father – and an exaggeratedly obedient servant of the Crown. Elizabeth trusted and needed him. That was why he was now Lord Chamberlain Hunsdon and Keeper of the Eastern Marches. It was also why his own paramour and plaything was accepted at Court. He couldn't have the silly bitch making jokes about a subject he'd spent the better part of fifty years avoiding. Especially now she claimed to be with child. Suppose she bore him a longtailed bastard for evil tongues to claim as the grandson of Henry the Eighth? He'd have thought she'd have more sense.

He again came near to throttling her. He probably would have done so if he weren't stricken by his need to visit the pot once more. He shouted downstairs for the girl, and told her to bring him a second jordan as well, if the pantry could run to another. When she came in, with one in brass and the one from the closed stool which was in pewter, he snatched them from her and said, 'It's my turn now. Your mistress has had her easement. Now it's only the old man who stands here, full of stale water. You'd best leave him to it.' He set about relieving himself, this time without help from Emilia. He was so angry with her, he'd have beaten her brains out with the pewter jar if she'd stood close enough to his outfall.

She'd got herself with child by him too often. He could scarcely come at her with any pleasure before she was missing and swelling like a milch heifer. He'd never known a young thing so fertile, whether cow or kitten. Generally, to speak true, she managed to shake herself free of all his impedimenta before they were more than slime in her rattle-bag. She'd learned any number of quaint tricks from her mother, and possibly from other witches too, for she'd been orphaned young. It was women's business, never his own. This time she'd chosen to bother him with the matter. *And* confess she was about to send him a note of hand round the corner to Blackfriars. A woman who can write is ten times more risky than one who merely has a tongue. By God, he ought to pull her fingers out by the roots, as well as set a red-hot spoon in her mouth. She'd have to start

8

bleeding, or he'd bring her blood on for her. Whether she did it by magic or moonlight was no concern of his. He mightn't be able to shine on her sundial, but he knew how to leave his shadow in her bed. And his hoofprint too, if need be.

~

He'd been in a reverie for some time. Such a state can proceed from rage or old age, or – according to the poets – the planets. For himself he did nothing by the stars save plant the herbs in his garden. His wits were wandering in direct consequence of unlatching himself for the jordan, he well knew that. Beside the purling of cool waters a man may be in ecstasy, and when they flow warm or even hot he comes close to delirium. At the very least he calls upon God and dreams of his doctor. He'd better ask the leech for an ear-trumpet while he was about it. What was she chattering about?

'I speak of Master William Shakespeare,' she was saying. 'The bumpkin pursues me with letters.' She had dressed herself without his permission, and was handing him wine, while wrinkling her nose in disgust at the contents of her pewter pride and bed-cup.

By God, a man ought not to be treated with such contempt, especially one of his rank and breeding. 'Master What?' he asked, 'Master Which and Who?'

'Shakespeare – the country boy from Warwickshire.'

'"Boy"? He's a middle-aged man of nigh on thirty.'

'He's old enough to have holes in his face and something approaching a beard, I grant you, my Lord Harry. And he has the arrogance too. He has the presumption to pen those toys and trifles that make me stand aside from my place before Her Majesty.'

'Your belly will stand you aside, if you swan it up with any more stuffing.' There, that was enough of that. 'I doubt he's as pretty a piece as you, or that he sings so sweet.'

He could swear her skin grew lighter when she smiled. Except for her black hair and eyebrows, and the dark wire of her privy *mons musae et veneris* which only he and a few pismires and

9

bed feathers knew about, she might almost be as English as her mother when she let her teeth shine through.

'Other matters have dripped from his pen, you tell me?'

'Letters, my Harry.'

'So long as you write him none. Otherwise I shall have him hanged. And you as well, I daresay.'

She laughed, as if he merely threatened in jest. 'I'm told you hanged eight hundred men in Northumberland, my Lord.'

'Not all by my own hand.'

'Some in hemp, some in straw, some in hot chains. But as for hanging me—'

'If I don't hang you, the Queen will. Clear out your belly with a toasting iron and guard your tongue.'

She tried to be pert again, so his fingers caught at her throat, then lower, back and front, unfastening what he could find, lifting and pushing aside. He needed her to her bed again, and intended to have her there without entreaty.

She wrinkled her nose at the unstowed pewter on her centre floor. Strange how they all thought they could behave like great ladies, this one most of all, when they were born no better than kittens under the milkmaid's stool.

He waited until he was firmly home, though scarcely dry, before saying, 'Don't think to play the Queen with me, madam.' Though the Good Lord God on His Topmost Throne knew cousin Elizabeth was coarse enough. The Boleyn daughters must have been a ribald crew, judging by what children had come out of them.

He grunted and truffled about her and over her for less time than it takes to seethe a quick egg, finished as best he could, then whispered tenderly in her ear, 'It hurts me to share you with a husband.'

'My lord knows I have no husband.' She was panting, more from the weight of him than from pleasure.

'More's the pity, mistress. I must find you one.'

'Let it be a badel, then. A hermaphrodite or a eunuch. Or one whose hunger is for boys only.'

He seized her again with a whoop of joy. Men of his age

10

weren't supposed to be able to manage such an extension of their will – not three times running, not normal healthy fellows with wholesome members well-wrapped in lint. Save his wasn't healthy, was it? It was puffed up and vengeful with the clap, as if his rod were scalded with sunburn – aye, *and* the rooster that sat on it. That was the *primum mobile* that kept his imagination in such an everlasting itch and twirl. It was well known (and written) that a gallant with the clap could do it and do it till his forepiece exploded or plain fell off. His own discharge was lustrous in consequence. One day he would compose verses on it, whole roundels and roundelays, when the Queen left him enough time. His culverin might be painful with excess gunpowder about the touch hole but – by God! – when it fired, it was shotted with quicksilver!

She squeaked, not from joy. Well, a woman must learn to sweeten her wind and protect her waters, a witch-woman especially, or what's necromancy for?

'Get rid of that belly,' he told her tenderly. 'If you can't, madam, and I can't come up with a fool to play husband, then 'fore God and every King Christian I'll take out my dirk and cut it from you.'

TWO

Emilia Bassano's doll's house of a dwelling was at the bridge end of Bishopsgate Street, so Lord Chamberlain Hunsdon brought his doll by river to the Palace of Whitehall. He did not command his own boatmen, not for this – gossip carries far by water. Instead he summoned a horse-minder to call him a waterfly from among the best, a fellow with a clean pole and straight teeth; and – better still – a boat that had cloths and rugs, and was tidy beneath the thwarts.

'It's not big enough for the Queen's Majesty,' he murmured to Emilia. 'It lacks the girth of your royal barge, but it will serve well enough for a great lady or a nobleman's dandle and tearsheet.' This was domestic chaff, and he kept his voice down. It brought blood to her cheeks just the same. For the crowd in general, he shouted as he handed her in, 'I'm not floating upstream in an onion basket, still less a kettle that's been steaming shrimps.'

The watermen laughed at this. There were already two sets of them with balanced oars, and the waterfly shouted for more when he saw what he had to carry. They all kept their eyes down and their minds on their hands, or they did when he'd boxed their ears.

Lord Hunsdon sat with his back to the prow, so he could watch the fly. He called Emilia forward a little away from being splashed by the pole, but the fly only needed it to steer and perhaps later to moor. Even so she felt a kind of coldness on her back, whether from the drip of water or the chill of being looked at she couldn't tell. She was used to being seen. She lived to be watched and heard, but her body carried bruises she hoped were all laced and buttoned under. When a woman sits stiffly before such a seed-rake and furrow-comb as Harry Carey Lord Hunsdon, no one supposes he's been kicking her. It's assumed she's been ridden to the bone. Men think so, anyway, lewd men like these. Women might paint a different picture.

The tide was still pushing, so they went upstream fast on the flood. This was a brutish experience, though brisk. The tide carried the City back on itself, all its waste, all its discharge, all its fishtails and eggshells and poisoned rats. For the first half mile the Thames smelled like a jordan, its scent as rancid as the stream with which the old brute had just despoiled her privy pot.

She dare not think this might be the last time she'd make the journey in her lord's company. She would not, could not consider such an outcome. How else would she be received at Court? Her young body had dropped more childlings and tadpoles to be sold to witches or fed to the street dogs than even the Queen of Sheba's after her ceremony with the goats and devils. Either a spell would ease her, or her apothecary's best philtre. If not, she'd lie in a salt bath all week and drink hot oil and brimstone. Surely the old lecher would allow her a week? Like all the rest of his kind, he seemed to think that a homuncle that took him half a gasp in the making could be coughed out of her just as easily. Only a week in the sulphur, dear Lord. If that failed she would call up her dead mother's familiars and enrol her housewomen in a great Sabbat, but she hoped there'd be no need of such a festival. Infants can be aborted without recourse to necromantic excesses. Or so Doctor John Dee, the Queen's own physician and astrologer, had long ago advised her in a letter from Scotland. Dear old man. He'd made it clear in the selfsame note of hand that he desired her mightily, and thought her body would be the most perfect altar-table for some of his most sacramental aspirations.

'What do you think of, Mistress Bassano?'

Lord Hunsdon was being formal now, as a man should be

before waterflies and boatmen. Why was it that her suitors were only these old men? When could she have a man in his prime, a nobleman of one-and-twenty, say? Or a youth of sixteen, a cleanness without a beard, who could bring her a body that had never broken sweat or wind.

'Lady, I asked you—'

Indeed he had. But the truth could never be part of her answer. 'I was thinking of the stars, my lord: all their configurations, all their signs, all their Heavenly conjunctions.'

'A woman should hold only to the moon, my love. It's brighter and closer to hand!'

Dear God, he even cracked jokes to hireling watermen about her condition – why else were the lewd fellows laughing?

'You speak truth, my lord. The moon should occupy us women, we who are poets even more so.' He always mocked her verses. 'The sun is reserved for you huntsmen and soldiers.'

He smiled his acknowledgement, and the watermen grunted.

God, how the fellows stank, especially now the breeze was setting across the tide. If only an engine might be devised, a kind of windmill or canon, to blow a young woman upstream without these everlasting reminders of armpit and gummed-up legging. To travel on the Thames with even half a crew was like floating round an ale-house jakes in a mouldy coffin. Use a solitary oarsman in a halfpenny skiff and he only pulled harder and sweated the more.

Emilia glanced round at their gasping faces. She ignored their stained thighs, the unseemly holes in their britches and gaskins. She travelled through their air, and that was tribulation enough.

It was demeaning to be carried towards her destiny by creatures of the mud such as these. Their bones were no better than cattle-cake. They were nothing but earth and water. She knew what she was, and how much she was worth. The Lord Chamberlain had told her so. Several great ladies had confirmed it. She was a radiant being. She glowed so much that she'd tanned her own loveliness from within. She was an angel of fire.

The little barge arrived at the Court Steps, which lesser

mortals called Whitehall Stair. She was handed out, and stepped up gently. Her bruises might glow, but the old fool's brutality merely reminded her of what she was. She was the Queen of Light, about to tread upon the marble pavement of Heaven.

There would be another Queen there, but the Queen of Light would once more win her approval. She would make Her Majesty a present. She would bring her the Music of the Spheres.

$\sim$

Night was closing in when Emilia and Lord Chamberlain Hunsdon stood in the gated carriageway of the Royal Court. The year was well advanced, and these bright skies would quickly give way to shadow. There were horn lanterns overhead, and cressets flared on the columns of the facing doors, making the gathering twilight seem even darker than it was. The Evening Star was bright across the waters through the arched stair at her back.

She viewed this planet with foreboding. It was her own lamp of love that shone there, but she was enough of an astrologer to determine other matters besides. Venus was a female denied the rights of her sex, no less than the heavenly Goddess had been denied by Adonis her limp and unwilling boy. She was robbed of her femininity by astrologer and grammarian alike. They called her Hesperus in the evening – a pretty name, but masculine. Then they didn't think she was Venus either, did they, those learned men? They thought she was Lucifer, the evil bringer of the fruit of Light-before-Darkness. This was how most of them viewed women anyway, all such scholars being eunuchs, pederasts or priests, and not much interested in females for their loins' sake.

Fires were being lit inside the palace, and the other fine houses nearby. These weren't the daylong coals kept a-smoulder for cooking, but the flames of evening cheer. Emilia could smell elm, chestnut and ash, the local woods. The ash as always was slow to burn, and a trifle unsavoury on the nose and in the throat. Must she sing in such a frowst as these fires would send about the rafters?

The fools were burning sycamore too. They were lighting coffin wood. She crossed herself quickly. She had little faith in Jesus Christ, in spite of her popish blood, but she crossed herself and hated herself for doing it. She distrusted the signs of God's followers, preferring to rely on the stars, which kept perfect time and printed all truths in the heavens, even in daytime when she couldn't see them.

Lord Hunsdon tugged her sleeve to hurry her forward. 'Why do we loiter, lady? I'm not the man to turn aside and piss against the brickwork, especially in the forecourts of Her Majesty!'

He urged her ahead, through the sculptured archway in the west wall. As she went with him she amused herself with her own thoughts, to keep her lips parted and her face alight. She wondered just how the Lord Chamberlain's floodgates had been able to sustain his tide for so long. It must be a full two hours by any sundial or column clock since old foulmouth Harry Carey had deigned to unlatch himself for a widdle, and that after drinking several quarts of her hot wine. He must have lost it in sweat, she decided, or passed it down his leg like a tree. She smiled at the faces that drew back from their progress, those that merely nodded their respect to Harry, those that glanced up at her under their hair after proffering them both a deep bow and flourish.

There were people everywhere, men in the main, none of them dressed as costly-dull as Lord Hunsdon, none of their few ladies – they were mostly of title – dressed as opulently as Emilia was. The Lord Chamberlain was not an ostentatious man. He carried his boast on his arm, whether it was his sword or a pretty woman. 'You know me by my blade or my scabbard,' he joked as a young man bumped into her, then drew back to see who she walked with. It was a demeaning jest, like so many of Harry Carey's asides. She must remind herself that tomorrow he might have cast her out from beneath his contempt.

They moved towards the Great Hall, but made little progress. The world was here by the hundred.

Emilia's owner and keeper was, as Lord Chamberlain, used to controlling gatherings like these. He was Lord Neat and Tidy, the Great Duke of Gravitas and Dignitas. Let no man scramble for a place before Her Majesty, not while Harry Carey was at Court. He saw to it that men grouped themselves about the Queen first according to their rank and toilet water, then with regard to their loyalty and capacity to interest her.

Today, the Lord Chamberlain was being neglectful. His mind was clearly on other things. Among these doubtless came Emilia herself, but even a pride like hers could draw little comfort from the fact.

Normally he would press forward and nudge the Queen to command her, and the Court would await in delight the very witty little entertainment of music and rhyme she would lay before it. This evening was different. Something had come about that the Lord Chamberlain was not yet privy to. An emergency beyond his control was engaging the world's attention.

This was irking. Worse was Emilia's clear impression that there would be no moment for her to shine tonight. She was being eclipsed here.

She would have to goad the Lord Chamberlian into action. 'You told me I was sent for and commanded,' she hissed. She was a woman used to making herself plain. In a moment she would sulk. He knew this mood in her, and hated it, but he could do nothing about it now. She might be Harry Carey's dog, but a man demeans himself by kicking his cur in public. This is a secret well known to whelps and women, so she was cheeky. 'Well, my lord,' she added, saying nothing and everything in a word.

'Patience, lady. I shall draw you out in a while.'

As a father leads his horse aside so he may thrash it unseen by his children?

'I thought my Lord Chamberlain was Master of the Revels?'

'I shall draw you out,' he repeated crossly. 'When Her Majesty is at ease with herself I shall draw you out.'

Out of what, she wondered. They were surrounded by a forest of flesh and all manner of fabrics from silk to fustian, their way towards the Queen – or wherever she was supposed to be – blocked by head hair and shoulder ruffs. There was no place to pass or press. She stood behind people built by their tailors and barbers. The world had its back turned. She saw its purpose in its buttocks.

'What's the buzz?' she heard someone ask.

'Noon,' was what she heard in reply. 'The Queen stood on the river bank and glimpsed a ripple in the water, then fancied she heard a pebble splash from a distant shore.'

At noon, when the sun was at its highest, Emilia was sniffing the Lord Chamberlain's boot then his prick. She had been suffocating in the freight of him. Seemingly at much the same noon the Queen had taken alarm at whispers of a treason or a foreign plot, or both. She wanted all her people here. No one dared be absent, and those who did not normally consider themselves her people hurried to become so.

'Where's Cecil?' she heard Hunsdon mutter to himself. 'Where's my Lord Burghley? Is he with the Queen?'

William Cecil, Lord Burghley, was one of Elizabeth's two spycatchers, and by some held to be spycatcher-in-chief, so it was a pertinent question.

'He's about the old lady's business.' Lord Harry had picked upon young Henry Wriothesley, Earl of Southampton and Cecil's ward. The young man was bored: bored by the Court; bored by the press of people; bored by the subject of the question, who'd bored him since childhood; bored most of all at having to frame an answer to a man almost as powerful as his own protector, and by repute twice as violent. He smiled upon Emilia, though, in spite of a reputed lack of interest in woman or any animal else that wore that awful space between its legs, that gulf of sighs that every young nobleman's dynasty was in such a hurry to crowd him into, the well into which he was supposed to toss his halfpennies and hear the darkness rumble with lineage.

Emilia watched him carefully, just the same. He was a beautiful young creature, paler than ewe's milk. Surely no man had fastened up his hair like that for him? It had been arranged in a dangling knot that hid half his face, and caught him coyly downlooking at the splendour of his own clothes, which were all silk-and-silver, his codpiece most of all. This was vast but geometrical, delicately ornate with gemmed ribbons and

19

spherical buttons of pearl, and not a braggadocio more. It was like a woman's sewing-box, bright with warnings telling her not to prick her fingers. His legs, if she could let her eyes sink below an object of such beauty, his legs were as straight as a pair of boating poles, and as coolly slender. What a sweetness he was, what a girl child's puppet-doll compared with old Henry Carey. Emilia stole one last look at his cod, as if she could read his brains in it, then stored the whole man away for future use.

'Not for you,' her own master growled. 'The poet Marlowe hangs from his lordship's postern, and your Master Shagspeare would too, if he weren't so stiffly fixed upon women.'

Someone had found the old man a drink, but nothing for her. Today was a time when rank gained the only courtesy, not that liquor was important to Emilia. Nor to Lord Hunsdon – his veins were already full of it. He'd been offered a cup of bastard, or some other muscadel, and stood sipping and pretending to enjoy it as if it weren't a woman's drink and likely to set worms in his teeth, never mind his culverin.

It did nothing for his talk. Was that young Essex, another ward of Lord Burghley's, and Southampton's cousin? What was the old brute saying? 'Aye, a *bona roba*, a *bona roba*, as you say, and as such not for the marriage bed! She's skewered with such a pox we're all likely to drop dead of it, if we don't stop quanting her, and straightway leap overboard!'

For a moment she thought they were talking of her, but of course they weren't. Harry Carey would never belittle himself by berating anything he owned, not in those terms. She wanted to ask them how it was their women could catch such diseases, unless their men hadn't first gathered them in the stews. But it wasn't a subject for herself to meddle with, not before noblemen so exalted. She knew when to pretend to know her place.

Now my lords Essex and Southampton, young Robert Devereux and Henry Wriothesley, were gossiping to the Lord Chamberlain about hawks, as if there were no more pressing matters afoot for Her Majesty and herself to be setting upon.

Emilia listened briefly to the men's chit-chat about haggards, lannerets, tercels, Barbaries and tassells, before plunging towards absolute despair. Her lord spoke of trifles like these as if her likely fate was of no importance to him. How could a man be so careless about his kept woman? She knew the answer, even as she asked herself the question. Women were plentiful. They were half of humankind, and cost nothing to find and no great gentleness to keep. A fine horse and a swift hound were expensive; and a hawk took years to train and frequently damaged itself. Women were everywhere, with no special wants in the way of food, and with nothing but time on their hands.

~

Emilia could stand very little of this talk. Even if a woman is no more than the gawgaw a man tucks between his conceit and his codpiece, she will soon lose even this nest and vantage-point if she seems content to stay there. As that great witch Margaret Johnson, her mother, told her when she lay dying, 'A man needs to itch. When he itches he will scratch. If he does not itch, he will grow forgetful.' She decided to make Henry Carey itch.

She eased her way gently towards the front of things. She saw no point in pushing herself into a circle of brainless chatterers arguing about hawks even if one of them was Devereux of Essex and another that angel the young Earl of Southampton. Her place was near the Queen, and among those who valued her.

Moving between shoulder ruffs was easy enough for her, even though the world's bumbarts and hipbones were staunchly jammed together, if not plain tangled up in front of her. Men startle to find a woman's breath at their ear; and a woman goes the more gently in passing, for she makes the sweeter breeze.

Her woman had oiled her body, and those oils had been full of nutmeg and citron. She passed among men with a presence. They stepped back from her path because they longed to press themselves against her – she knew what paradoxes pricked these popinjays ahead and held them rooted at one and the same time. She knew them all. She was amused also to know that Lord Hunsdon followed her.

She hurried the more. If he caught up with her, he would try to lead her by the hand. She was moving so fast among those who had been still for so long that she created her own stir. She became what she always was, a buzz of interest.

Men lusted after her. She knew that and despised them for it. She couldn't walk into a room and curtsy without smelling a rising steam of masculinity. In a minute or two their heated incense would lose its powers to disguise the filth of their bodies. She would be assailed by the stench of rancid crotch. Hunsdon might as well be stuffing his prick into her face, as this morning and so often. She retched at the thought of it. It made for an interesting smile. She was wearing this expression of happy disgust when she stood near the Queen and gazed full on Her Majesty.

The Queen was what she always was, an old painted woman with holes in her teeth and holes where her teeth should be. There were candles placed carefully to her right and left. These burned at eye-level so they cast no shadow beneath her lashes or her chin. They hid what was worse in her countenance and imparted a glow to her hair redder than a wild dawn or sunset, according to the viewer's sex and inclination. The candles could do nothing for her teeth. These were beyond illumination.

A pity Her Royal Majesty's gaze fell upon Emilia's face, and noted its sickened smile and glimpsed the possibility that it was her teeth that were being looked at by a young and beautiful woman whose own mouth was slightly parted with her tongue retching or even clicking as if the royal teeth were being counted. A very great pity. Emilia averted her gaze. Her Majesty did not.

One does not look away from the Queen. Or look at her either, if one is a woman. Emilia made herself aware of this.

And what, she asked herself, was Queen Elizabeth doing amid such a press of nobility? She was watching it watch her, and seeking to draw conclusions from men's eyes. She had been doing this for some hours, receiving assurances in public, ambassadors as they might find her, taking information from everyone and advice from anyone foolish enough to offer it. Waiting for catastrophe had first made her thirsty, and then rendered her hungry. She had called for refreshment and was

22

now pushing comfort into her mouth. It wasn't a meal time. Indeed a banquet had been called for later and was likely to be cancelled.

She eyed Emilia in slow recollection while she nominated, and had someone polish, a Kentish apple. This filled her head with noise and bad temper. She took a small loaf of cake and bit it. This she chewed at then spat out. 'If that's Heston flour, then I'm a creature of the sea.'

Nobody laughed. Mermaids and all such manifestations of virginity were not to be scoffed at.

'It was grown and ground as the finest corn in Middlesex, ma'am.'

'It's an ill bread, for it wasn't bred at all. Middlesex describes it perfectly, for I tell you plain it was begotten by a eunuch on a hermaphrodite or some other badel.' Her eye returned to Emilia. 'I don't know how that woman pours herself so often into a foreign skin,' she observed. 'Where's her trainer and keeper? Where's my cousin Harry of Hunsdon?'

Emilia had hurried too fast ahead, and stood herself too far forward. She tried to be back again, to wherever her lord was standing.

'Where is the Lord Chamberlain? Are you skulking, Harry?'

'No, Your Majesty. I wait upon your wants of me, and so do all of us.'

'Come out and show yourself, then, at least by the tip of your beard. By God, your house-fellows have left it badly, your house-fellows, your cup-fellows, your barber, or some woman.' Again with a darting glance at Emilia, 'Your face looks like a cooked lettuce.'

'It has been called many things, Majesty, but never so prettily.'

'Well, I can see your front is in flavour, cousin. Honest fair, what do you say to that?'

'As to my beard's flavour, ma'am, I cannot answer you. I have not chewed upon it today. As to being fair, I'll leave that to your Highness' own judgement, which is beyond equal. As for being honest, by which your Majesty means plain-Jack honourable, I'll confess I know only one meaning of that word, and that is to be faithful to my Queen in all matters, high and little. Your Majesty knows that already. My face may be a wild salad, but men may eat it without fear of poison – that you may well trust.'

'So what of this treason and this damned foreign cabbala?'

'If there is treason, ma'am, my Lord Burghley will roast it out. I know of no more capable or curious a cook in these matters. He can show you treason, ma'am, with its ankles slotted, its cullions cut for whitebreads, and only salt in its guts.'

'Treason does not taste so bad now, I grant you, cousin. Not after my Lord Burghley's assurances. Not after filling my stomach with these honey cakes and this small ale. But what of those foreigners?'

'Think nothing of them, your Majesty. We that have charge of your armies in the field will make short work of them.'

'They have more men than us. Spain is stuffed full of tall fellows, no matter how many we drown. And now they compound with France once again, who breeds more good horsemen in the field than summer makes flies round a bullock's arse – indeed, round a whole flock of the beasts.'

'If they outnumber us but three to one, we shall send them blackberrying, madam, and whistle while we do it. If they come at us in bigger numbers than that—'

'More than the grains in a trencher of salt, Harry, there's my fear. More numerous than the hairs on a Kern's front or, aye, up their women's plaid.'

'Ma'am, I've inspected both of them a-plenty, and that's not so many.' Lord Hundson allowed the Court ample time to show its appreciation at this, before saying, 'If our enemies grow in so great a number before us, then your Majesty must join us in the field as when I showed you Tilbury. Do our men but see you on horseback, Royal Lady, and they'll cut a path and thoroughfare through the legions of Hell, no matter how numerous. They'll even eat those monsters that growl from beyond the Styx with fire in their teeth and soot on their tails.'

'Enough of your damned Latin, and all that fable. I call those creatures chimney-sweeps, cousin.'

'They'll be no taller than sweeps when your soldiers have finished with them – Spanish ones, Majesty and Queen of our All.'

There was a great deal of shouting then, and lifting of feathers and other bonnets, a flourish of wrists both limp and sturdy. The Court, being full, was filled with more than courtiers. There were men who could wrestle a horse, or push a pike and swing a backsword as well as whirr up a fuse till it was flowing bright for the arquebus. They cheered loud and long, and laughed afterwards at the filth that fell from the cousins' mouths, for Mary Boleyn had been a broadly spoken woman, and her sister Anne was like to have proved even fouler if the axe hadn't shortened her tongue.

This was likely to be a fine gathering to play to, and swifter too than normal to appreciate a witty recital. Emilia glowed at last, and no longer from the imprint of Lord Hunsdon's toe.

'Then what now, Harry Carey? What now, my cousin? You have brought our woes to a halt and hiatus. What will you do for our womanly anxiety beyond such a service of spirit? Tell me, Lord Chamberlain. Be our Monarch of Wit, rule our revels and be their Master!'

'Music, my lady. Music to begin with, music and then perhaps a further divertissement. Tomorrow we shall bring you a recitative of English valour, and command our players and our dancers to show you a dumbshow of scarves and blades. I have been speaking to young Wriothesley here, and the Earl tells me he has that fellow Shagspeare to command. You already value him, and prize him for what he is – midway between a wag and a wit. Let him devise you some piece of pith and fancy, and let us smile with you, Highness.'

'You speak of music. My musicians have been deafening us all day, what with their high and low woods, the one sounding as if their bowels themselves were singing for us, the other as if they tuned their very fundaments. No, I'll no more of them, nor of their damned cases of viols, which sound no better than what they are, which is catgut.'

Emilia was glad not to compete with the court musicians.

They deadened the air with their playing, with their dirgeful toys, doleful dreams, their spiritual rests, their endless mathematical divisions on a ground. It was as if they learned their notes from the abacus and the astrolabe instead of from the Muses of Melody and Song.

Not that she could be done with them so easily. No sooner did the royal eyes fall upon her, blind-seeming and opaque in their shadowless sockets, than several of the court buskers came and stood close about her, preening themselves for Her Majesty's closer inspection. Whether they were on the way to or from the gallery she had no way of knowing. She tried to curtsy low, but her body was sore and she was tangled in their instruments. Their leader, a damnable Italianate Frenchman from Rouen, stood himself in front of her, as if he were the string-puller and she were his marionette. He had his heels on her toes and his bum towards her face – what was the coxcomb's name? Lanier, Master Alfonso Lanier, formerly of some foreign gutter, now of the royal pleasure.

Emilia was deft to extricate herself from that press of fakers, but her face was hot by the time she had swirled aside and stooped in another curtsy and flounce. Lord Hunsdon clapped his hands and bad the rabble make room for her.

'Whom do you applaud, cousin?'

'I applaud nothing and no one, your Royal Highness, save your own wisdom and light, which I take to be part of your trinity.'

'But you clapped your hands.'

'I did so but to make ground for one of my retinue – Emilia Bassano, your servant, ma'am.'

'The time is too charged for such a one.'

'She is all amusement and amazement, Highness.'

'I speak of today's climate, which is frowsty with treason, cousin. She's a damnable Frenchwoman with an Italian name.'

Emilia heard Lanier chuckle not half a fiddle-bow away.

'She's English, ma'am.'

'She's a foreign chanteuse and warbler, Cousin Harry. I'll tolerate her fiddle-diddling and all such scrapings on the viol and tappings on the virginals, but I'll have none of her singing aloud – not today. For all I know or any man can advise me, her verses may be in cipher and the pattern for a damned rebellion. I'll not sit and swallow such a fare, not with my bread and apple. The flour tastes like ratsbane as it is.'

'Her father was that Baptista Bassano who played before your majesty's own father, and was loved and protected by him. He was an Italian, for sure, but her mother was an Englishwoman.'

'She should have kept her legs closed, cousin. There are some English virgins who can, especially when threatened with a foreign marriage. We have had more proposals from foreigners than she has had lumps of meat on her knife, or good porridge in her pitcher. I do abhor all such foreign placket tenters and woman-swyvers. Speak not of Diegos or such like Italians to me!'

Her Majesty's witticisms were greeted first with grunts, then gasps of approval, then drowned out entirely by huge roars of delight that left poor Emilia nowhere.

'Music!' Lord Hunsdon snapped. 'Music, and by all instruments, and much of it!' He did something brisk with his fingers like a conjuror setting fruit on barren trees.

Emilia was swept aside by a rush of fiddlers in their scamper to move towards the heaven, or at least the haven, of the minstrel's gallery. This was a matter of stairs in the wall, and much scraping of small and large kettles and tables, and the general panting upwards of shaums, curtals, sackbuts and the like, and then four full cases of viols from the largest to the littlest.

'Lady, I am sorry for your much mismanagement.' It was their leader again, Alfonso Lanier, twice as foreign as she was because neither top nor bottom of him was English. He even dressed in those broad-striped slops beloved of Frenchmen and worse, that made him look like a clown or a lady's ape in pantaloon britches. 'Tomorrow we shall hear you, perhaps?' Then he was gone, leaving her with that servile smile of his, which moistened his eye and gave a most unseemly twist to the hair that sprouted from his top lip.

She would have said something curt, but Lord Hunsdon drew her aside.

27

Emilia gazed towards the minstrels' gallery. People did not normally regard what went on there, but she had clearly tangled eye-beams long enough with the Queen's Majesty, and was like to have her gaze poked from her head for impudence if she went on much longer.

There were Master Lanier and his silly musicians. They stroked their viols, they wriggled their ruffs and their elbows, and generally fidgeted about on high like so many squirrels in a nest.

They made a deft, mellow note together like angels making water. She amused herself briefly with this thought, and at the sight of Lanier most of all. He played the alto viol with a long draw of the bow and a most unnecessary flourish, to emphasize the pace of the music and his own importance.

Then he stood aside, above and apart from the rest, his eye still fastened on hers from his place against the painted ceiling among the branches of the rafters. He was holding a sackbut now, as if to show his versatility to her, or to Her Majesty or to God. What a fool he was. His lips puckered softly on the stem of the sackbut. For all the world the pink little creases and tucks in his face made his features resemble the bum of a seraph at stool. What an idiot. What a coxcomb.

Then she was through with laughing to herself, finished with smiling. She had to stand there and wait until the Queen was done with listening and the sound no longer scalded her ears like so much aquavit. Then she must be taken home – either to be thrown away or to have her body kicked and her belly and bowels ransacked with flame.

To make matters worse, someone left the shadows behind the great door, then stepped away again when he saw Lord Hunsdon. It was that upstart Shakespeare, who had recently minded horses but now stood between her and Her Majesty's grace.

He was not dressed like a man, now she glimpsed him full on. Nothing about him was to the point or entire. He looked like a printer's devil or a boy that larks for coal, but older and sadder than both. To think that he wrote her letters! She'd touch no more of them, not from such sooty hands.

THREE

There was to be no barge for the return journey.

Two men were waiting for Lord Hunsdon at the head of Whitehall Stairs. There was something menacing about them, so much so that Emilia feared they might be footpads or cutnecks, and caught at her protector's arm.

Lord Hunsdon shrugged her off, but not to make room for his sword. He stood aside and watched while one of the fellows tucked her elbows together from behind, as if she were a goose for the plucking, while the other dropped a hooded cloak over her head. They bundled her down the stairs and into a boat scarcely wider than a Dutchman's foot.

The thing rocked and canted, righted itself as they forced Emilia to sit down, then skidded away across tide and stream. It left the mooring so abruptly she thought Hunsdon had been left behind. Then she heard his breath, its wheezing and snuffling away like so many wordless curses. 'My lord,' she protested. 'I—'

'Be still, madam. I am here yet.'

'If we weren't afloat, my lord, I'd have thought I was against a frosty tree full of pigeons, your lungs are so scratchy!'

One of the men chuckled. The other had his work cut out to hold her, and said and did nothing. He gathered the cloak tighter about her face, until she thought she was to be smothered and cast into the tide. He crouched on the thwart behind her and pinched his knees round her waist, as if she were a lamb at the shearing.

The cloak was of some dark woollen material, not coarse, and it smelled of woman, woman's perfume, woman's breath, woman's fear. Emilia did not accompany the Lord Chamberlain everywhere he went, and she realized he had other playthings, other female toys and sweets he was used to smuggling downriver like this, presumably to his Blackfriars' house. She might be unique in his affections, but she wasn't alone. These men, who were clearly his henchmen, were practised in abduction, and the Lord knew what other villainies besides.

She had never been allowed in Blackfriars, nor in the Lord Chamberlain's country retreat at Holborn where he mewed up his hawks and kennelled his dogs and stabled his horses. Now the certainty that she was being taken to one or the other, most likely to Blackfriars, grew on her as soon as she was able to force her head up inside the hood of the cloak that muffled her, and wriggle it to and fro until her face unpinched the aperture and she could peer out.

The skiff was slanted across the stream and headed towards the outfall of the Fleet River. With one fellow pulling both oars, and Lord Hunsdon standing at the stern but not deigning to steer, they drifted past the Bridewell and then the Fleet confluent which was agush with recent rain. The sculler backed water with his right hand and nosed the tiny craft hard against Blackfriars steps, with a jolt that set Hunsdon cursing – never very hard to achieve.

An old woman of some forty years was waiting there, her scarred face bleak in the light of a horn lantern that flared above the mark-pole of the jetty. She stooped quickly, and pulled the boat alongside as deftly and as easily as if she were picking up crabs or crab-apples and dropping them into her apron.

'Where's Bess?'

'To Bishopsgate on foot, my lord, to dismiss the servants.'

'Aye, this night's work will need no peepers, nor stealers about with candles.'

The woman chuckled, and stepped aboard the skiff, which was almost up to the gunwales in the flood.

So Emilia's women – and her man Peter – had been sent

away, and these fellows and two women were to accompany her to her own house and practise horrors upon her. Bess was still unknown, but this one was all bone like a man, and knelt across from Emilia on a facing thwart. 'My name's Malk,' she said, 'and I ain't milk.' She smelled of vinegar, and unscented body, and fat from the roast. She treated Emilia as if she were a fellow servant, and one like herself of the basest kind, a scourer or scully.

The boat was so low in the water that objects adrift on the tide seemed unnecessarily close, eye to eye almost. So it was that Emilia saw a dead dog float by, its bowels torn out by rats between its legs to leave a great cavern. High chested, and inflated by death, it went past her gaze like a damaged galleon trailing bits of itself, cordage, and sail and spar. Its stench almost outdid Malk for a minute.

'You ever chewed on dog?' Malk asked. 'I'm told it's got a thin taste.'

Difficult to see her mouth in the fitful light of passing stern lanterns, but her smile didn't promise much in the way of teeth.

Nobody said anything more, till they grated ashore just upstream from the bridge. Then Malk said, 'Well, my Lady, we'll have to see if we can rat *your* guts out of you, just as his lordship requires.'

'Dog or bitch, I didn't notice, did you?' the man who held her said, again bagging her up in the cloak.

'Dog nor bitch, they all come to it in the end,' the rower muttered, missing the point entirely.

So they brought her ashore, too choked to struggle, and carried her to her own house, like a mandrake root in a bag. If she was a woman, they didn't notice. She would come to it in the end.

∽

An angel she was. She shone bright. And when she didn't shine she glowed. Tonight the Queen had struck a spark of rage in her and she'd gone flaring forth into the darkness with himself following at a timid distance.

31

He knew how to approach a woman, but an angel fettered by the Lord Chamberlain to entertain Her Majesty? Will hung back a little. Such a one he dare not touch. Not without her nod of encouragement and a wink that said she'd be secret. The rest it would be his pleasure to manage, God's precious blood, it would!

Each time he dipped his pen in ink, her face rose up before him. It gazed up from each folio sheet. By Saint Meg, he could think of a better sheet to have it on!

He must not, dare not follow her. A man who's run away from his wife does not have time for a woman, and this one was clearly no pet nor plaything. He came here to make his fortune, not to . . . He must . . . he *dare* not do this thing, yet he trod just a cobble behind her. He tiptoed inside the echo of her very footsteps.

Gone. Within an instant of touching, she was taken from him. Surrounded. An *ambuscado*, and him without a blade to flourish. No sooner did his angel shine than she was extinguished. Will drew back into himself. His shadow must not reach them!

An *ambuscado*? Worse. At the very edge of darkness, which he took to be water, one of Lord Hunsdon's villainous flies caught her by the pinions, while another threw a cloak over her head, as if she was a hawk to be jessed or a parrot to be hooded.

Comparisons! She was gone, and himself too frightened to follow.

A boatman with a back-skull offered his services.

Will looked the boat over carefully, and told him to dowse his lantern. Like most of his trade, he carried his lamp on a pole. It did nothing for navigation, and served only to light the faces of all who travelled by it.

'Sirrah, I could not see my way across a puddle without my light.'

'I would have you follow that skiff over there. Let its lantern serve to guide you, but hang a good bowshot backwards of it, and seek to remain unseen.'

'I know of no bowshots. Nor ever drew bow in my life. I'm an arquebus man when the militia calls me.'

'And a fine liar too. They only call gentlemen into the Honourable Artillery.'

'I'm a-spin-the-fuse-man, I promise you. I know how to ram the powder and blush the flame.'

'Well stay behind as far as the best ball or pebblestone will carry – say two hundred paces. Hurry, man!'

'I have no acquaintance with distances. I've never walked above ten steps in all my born years.'

'All carriage and chair, I take it? And a fine string of Barbaries else!' Will never boarded a flyboat without an argument. Some he lost. Some he did not win. He was surprised when this one ended.

They were across the tide in an instant, and going much too fast, with a terrible drip from the back-skull. The fellow was lifting so much water he might just as well have been quanting. Will let him hurry on.

The other craft was hard to follow, perhaps because it hung close in, against boats that were moored in the slack.

He was surprised when it put in at Blackfriars. 'Hang back here in the offing a little. Keep her in darkness here. Otherwise be still. Tongueless and still.'

'Yes, lordship.'

'I said to hang back and keep her here.'

'I'm being still, lordship, just as you promised me. It's the river that moves. I can't learn a way of stopping it.'

'Hush!'

Will saw the woman step aboard Emilia's skiff. He saw her crouch knee to knee against his poor hooded darling.

Woman? She was the Devil's midwife if ever he saw one, some abortive witch whose practice was the bringing out of babes by foul means or fouler – a winkle-picker of the female shell, whether by curse, caustic or needle. It was a hanging offence to meddle with nature. Will wondered why the Lord Chamberlain had need of such a one. The old rogue could still cock a leg, no doubt of that, but surely not with his Emilia, who was the Queen's possession quite as much as his own. Aye, she belonged to Court and Crown: surely not cock a leg with Emilia, not on her, upon her? It simply could never be so, between such a radiant Beauty and so ancient an old Beast.

Nor was it, he knew. He told the fly to front up the tide a little, that was it, back, back, back, so they were abaft the Lord Chamberlain's vessel now it put off again.

They were much too close, but his way had been chosen. He must stay the course.

Only a fool follows a man by water. And to follow by water *and in the dark* a warrior who carries his sword hanging free, and goes with a pair of villainous well-armed flies who could back oars on the instant and carve a man by the bollocks for presumption, or hold him nose first under the tide – well, that takes a special kind of fool indeed.

Especially when the warrior he follows is a nobleman who can command a retinue of half-a-dozen hundred and call others in by the thousand simply by coughing and crying 'hem!' Yes, only a fool.

Save Will Shakespeare wasn't interested in the noble warrior himself. It was his chattel he coveted, his sweet angel of a woman who was hooded and perhaps near to death. And he followed not merely as a fool, but as a lover. And as he himself knew better than any, a lover is more foolish than fools are. A love is three times an idiot.

To know she was bound for destruction and not be able to lift a finger to save her! It was worse than seeing a brother swinging on the gallow chats, more fearsome by far than witnessing the hangman drop his noose round the shoulders of your dearest friend.

Yesterday she was a dream, a distant longing. Tonight she was all his love. He ached for her now.

∾

It was but a step to go, and the way was not dangerous. True the two women were on foot and in the dark, but one had her head in a cloak and the other was scarcely female, such a creature of sinew and gristle she was, and spreading her odour all before her and about like a tub of old fish, some of

34

it sun-dried, some merely rotten. Not even a gull would have touched her.

Lord Hunsdon walked sword in hand, as if to strike out the eyes of any man who dared recognize him, but the sinister little group passed nobody and nothing, neither watchman, bawd nor packhorse. He had no need of his sword in this thoroughfare, nor ever would. Perhaps he flourished it to show his anger. In any event, his two fellows carried staves, and their belts were full of blades. They wore nothing long enough to fence with, but were well-equipped for murder. Emilia knew this each time she was pressed against by the man who muffled her from behind. It was like being chased by a slaughterer's apron, he was stuck with so much iron, or being bumped by a basket of knives.

This fellow steered her by the hood and neck till her face struck against the timbers of a door. Lord Hunsdon beat against this until it was opened. Emilia guessed it was her own, from the distance and direction, but none of her own people answered it.

'Ah, Bess. Is everything snug?'

This woman did not smell, or not enough to outshine Malk. 'Aye, my lord. I paid them their ale money, as you said, and bad them sit in the George until noon tomorrow.'

'Right, then. Do you two fetch her in, and make her in all ways ready. Gilbert and Mould, you pair of ferrets to secure the windows above and below – *muffle* them, mind: blind all this dwelling's lights and stutter them close – then keep the doors until I call you. If the Watch comes, use my name. If a neighbour stirs, break his head. I shall be private here. If the moon shows her face, throw a sack on it.'

'Yes, my lord. We'll poke it by the eye and drown it.'

The two fellows went their ways, laughing and joking, leaving Emilia free at last of the hood that stifled her. She blinked in the sudden glare of candlelight, and drew back from the immediate effronteries that were offered her.

The woman Bess was a clean thing, but big with it, her hands and forearms both candle-white and as scrubbed as any cook's table. She was more wholesome to have about one than Malk, and this was Emilia's only good fortune that evening, for about her she proposed to be.

She caught Emilia one-handed by the nape, and bared her breasts with a single sweep of her free hand. 'She's late, my lord. Well late for improvement, and more than far gone. This is not a month, my Lord Hunsdon, nor even two. Look at those circlets on her bubs. We're talking half a calendar here, if not the greater part of her belly's almanac!'

'So what can you do? By Heaven, how the sweet fool has lied to me!'

'Wring her neck most likely, sir. That would be the kindest way. Has she ever had child before?' Her hand was all about Emilia's belly now, deftly over and under, and finally most intimate and sly. 'Have you ever had issue before?'

Poor Emilia was pained by her fingertip, then by her hand and fist. She wanted to spit at her, but knew that such a gesture would neither avail nor become her.

'She's scarcely more than a virgin, my lord, and as tight and coy as any ten-week pullet. I'll need a much bigger hole than that to shake her insides down in one piece for you, and anything else will kill her. Best throttle her and be done. You'll be out of your misery in a minute, Lord Hunsdon, and there'll be nothing of the noise and mess!'

His lordship took Emilia away from Bess then, kissed her and rearranged her clothes.

She thought he was going to turn her loose. She was mistaken. He snapped his fingers for Malk and said, 'I'm fond of this young woman, fond as foolish may be. So I'll not have her dead if life may be kept in her. That being said, take her above and fetch the child from her bowels.'

It was Malk's turn to come closer now. Without her cloak she spread such a fume all about that Emilia almost fainted to breathe it in.

Malk handled her as crudely as Bess had done, before saying, 'We've a trick or two to fetch maggots from wells – yes, and some to shake costard-apples from branches.' She dragged at Emilia's arm.

Bess was more gentle, but drew her towards the stairs just the same. 'First we must search her loop and knot-hole with a bodkin, subtle as sly may be. Then, if needs be, with a hot bone.'

'Lamb's leg nor ox makes no difference,' Malk shrilled. 'I'll go and test the embers in her women's oven.' She gave Emilia an odorous shove and stomped off towards the kitchen.

Emilia had been educated of late by the Countess of Kent, then reared for Court by her master and keeper the Lord Chamberlain like any sop-fed lap hound. Her father Baptista came from a hard school of blade and buckler, and her mother from harder still. She refused to have this ill-treatment from scullions and other such denizens of the scrubbing-block, and fetched Bess's face a hard blow with the flat of her hand. Her hand hurt, and Bess laughed at her as if she were a tiny child. She struck again.

Bess did nothing but grin, 'A-mercy, mistress. You don't want to go knocking at my old chin. I've got a smile as strong men has bent their fingers on – yea, and broke their knuckles.'

Malk, or someone who shed an identical must, had returned from the kitchen and caught her from behind, folding her arm into the small of her back, and then up between her shoulder blades as if she were an urchin caught thieving sprats.

Urchins can be lifted almost to anywhere on a folded arm, and grown men likewise. Emilia found herself bent, then panged and bounced upstairs by Malk's grip on her wrist. She seemed to float towards her own bedchamber as if impelled by nothing more than the pain in her elbow and shoulder bones and Malk's chuckle, which was inhuman, and as divorced from the woman's chest and throat as a hen's croak in the yard is from its crop and wattle.

Bess had already shown herself quick with clothing, whether it was to be unfastened by ribbons or buttons, or rent straight down from the breast and the limbs.

Emilia was aware of pain, hard fingers, and of kicking out against flesh and air before floating between the two women's hands and inside a great coldness. She was in her own chamber, where no fire had been lit or warming-pan laid. She kicked and struggled at the heart of a cruel frost, which as soon as the pain in her arm slackened she knew to be the chill of her own nudity. She had known she was being undressed and, in a frenzy of fight, she hadn't cared. Her rage had made her behave like a child in a tantrum, screaming and kicking while being carried to her bed. Now, and unlike the child, she knew that she had no defences. The room might be hers, but it was a place without love.

Nor did they lay her on her bed. She had a small table against the window, where she and Maria her maid could spread out her dresses and check their hems and their stitching. It had already been dragged to the middle of the room, and on this they flung her face up, with Bess pressing her legs apart as if her flesh was no more than a garment waiting to have its seams unpicked.

Malk knew more ways to hold a woman than one. She twisted her fist in Emilia's hair and hauled on it tight.

Emilia Bassano had been ill-used many times in her life, but never like this. She tried, as it happened to her, to say her own name, to remember it even, for Christ's was long since forgotten, and God's – though she called it – gave answer only in these women's chuckles, their cackles, their foul words, the panting dryness of their breath.

She called on Henry Carey Lord Hunsdon as her Keeper and Protector. He had ordained her and made her and brought her to what she was, so she screamed to him, but again her cries got her nothing but mirth. The Lord Chamberlain might be her God, but just like the other God he was no longer in this room.

In the absence of God, and the temporary absence of man, she found herself given over to these women's curiosity. As they examined her, entered her with finger and fingernail, explored her, turning her body this way and that as if it were a glove to be pulled inside out and its stitching examined, she heard someone passing water in her jordan or joint stool just as Lord Hunsdon had done – one of the men, one of the women. She heard the sound repeated several times and knew she was in fiery torment, for Doctor John Dee and her mother had both taught her that whereas the angels do no such thing, having neither the need nor the necessary organs of micturation, the demons – and such like particles of the Inferno and the smouldering gulf – piss all the time, their own water being the only fountains they can play with in the parched landscape of Hell.

Malk had discovered a bone suitable to her science and art, or perhaps it was a pastry pin or a great needle. Whatever it was, the pain was intense and to no purpose. In so far as her body held an intelligence beyond these sharp rays of sensation, Emilia was convinced that she remained clenched upon her child more stubbornly than an oyster on its pearl. She began to rejoice for it. She thought her own spark had been extinguished. Now she felt it rekindle for the sake of her unborn child. Its life was no longer a burden to her so much as a piece of herself, an expression of grit.

Then the men came in. She felt no shame to be seen thus, nor to be handled by them. Pain brings its own values and eclipses all others.

One of the men used his hand offensively, then withdrew it with a curse. It was as if Emilia had bitten him or her sex had breathed fire. Certainly her rage was great enough. It was as if the child inside her struck out.

She found so much hope in this that her head cleared enough to see it was no such matter. Lord Hunsdon had entered the room and seized the fellow by the scruff and pulled him backwards.

'Enough,' he said.

'She can give no more, and take it neither,' Bess said. 'It's like I foretold, my lord. I'm near to killing her but to no avail. Her upper channels is like a stoppered puncheon. I can neither push her guts in nor spill them out.'

'I thank you for your art,' he muttered. Lord Hunsdon spoke hoarsely.

'Strangle her in this towel, my lord. Or knot her head in a damp blanket. You'll not kill the child without putting an end to the mother.'

'I thank you both,' Lord Hunsdon said. 'It's a dangerous service you do me, and danger has its rewards.'

The two women bent themselves and curtsied after their fashion, and his lordship busied himself by whispering in one of his fellow's ear. 'Take these people downstairs,' he said, 'and give them this, and see they are well cared for.'

He gave the man money and nodded to him. Strange, Emilia thought, to fee one servant to pay another. She crept to her bed and stole a coverlet about her, and watched the two women lead the men down her stairs.

'For shame, my lord.'

'Shame is in Heaven, Emilia. Or in Hell. Priests tell me that is a crowded place.'

She heard hoofs in the street, the walking tread of several horses even at this late hour. She couldn't think what they might presage. Their irons were muffled in some way, or they were curiously shod. They pattered gently nearer, moving at no more than 'pace', and making an eerie note with their hoof-fall, like dice on a board or the tapping of bones.

They came close, and then stopped. They were halted at her door. Did their riders mean evil to her? Was she to be tormented further, or simply taken off?

Again she forced herself from the bed, scarcely able to part the curtains. They touched her like whips now, so damaged she was.

She leant towards her window and looked downwards through the coarse glass. She wanted to glimpse a freedom where breezes were, and cats walked. Instead she saw something else. A packman stood against her front door, with a string of three horses. Their hoofs were bound in canvas, as sometimes – in gentle streets – they silence the nags that draw a fever-cart.

Lord Hunsdon's two men emerged from the house. They carried a bundle. They carried it with some difficulty. It was about the size of a bale of sheep's wool, but heavier, and with an inner stiffness. They nodded to the packman, who helped them lift it atop the saddle, where it perched awkwardly. As they struggled to strap it down it began to leak.

The men quarrelled and discussed, then Gilbert and Mould came back in again. She heard their steps on the stone floor beneath her. Of Malk and Bess she heard nothing.

The pair were outside once more, again burdened. This time

the bundle was long, like a rolled mat. It was heavier than a mat, though, and sagged in the middle.

Emilia gazed downwards and shuddered. It does not need two men to lift a rug out of doors. A boy – or a housemaid – can carry it tucked beneath the arm or balanced across the shoulder.

This bundle also began to leak, in ways that made its contents all too plain to her.

She wasn't of the fainting kind, or she thought she wasn't. She found herself sitting on – no, *missing* – a chair. It should have been by her window table, but both had been moved so that torments could be visited upon her.

The memory of these, then the horror that she was witnessing in the street beneath her window were dashed aside by the shock that had robbed her of her legs. '*Three* beasts of burden, my lord Harry? *Three?*'

'It could be I only needed one,' he agreed. 'I *may* come to want five.' He had drawn his sword and made the blade sing in the air like a saw beneath the bow. He touched its point to her throat. 'Who goes home?' he asked. 'Who, and where, and how many? How many of my children go home?'

She rose breathlessly to her feet. 'Malk – is Malk your—?' She retched at the thought, and at many pains else.

'A man can be stoutly served by bastards,' he said. 'By other men's as well as his own. But they need to be trodden beneath the bed and kept out of sight.' He caught hold of her, lifted her and said, 'I do not send any offspring of mine away folded across packhorses. Nor will I serve you or yours so.' He kissed her, a memory of former courtesies she was far from receiving graciously. 'Pah!' he said. 'Your breath stinks of fear.'

'Aye, my lord. I've been drinking a dead woman's air.'

'Well, sweeten yourself before the Watch calls another midnight. I must make haste to marry you off. You *lied* to me about your term, my Emilia. Lied to *me!*'

'Scarcely, sir. I have delayed a little with the truth, that is all.'

'So you say. And so our Bible tells it. Woman is all lies.'

'Hardly, sir. It is simply that the truth brings us poor creatures

41

more damage than it can to men.' She tried a final appeal to him. Let him grant her a little time, she pleaded, just a trifle more time. It was all she had prayed for in the boat to Whitehall, all she ever needed. Time for another trip to the apothecary. Time for a letter to Doctor Dee. Time for a lunar spell. She caressed his sleeve. 'I have a love for you, my lord, a great love and a great need. But the love is greater than the need. That is why I cogged and cheated you concerning my monthly heat, Lord Harry.' He was holding her clear of the floor, as if she were a child. 'I pray you grant me a little hope.' She struggled to be free of him.

'Aye, madam.' He set her down and pushed her away. 'But your belly rides upon a dial's point, not upon the stationer's almanac.' He sank his boot into her lower stomach. He kicked her there again, as if this morning's exercise were yet to be grunted through, and Eternity no more than a great circle.

She accepted his blows and his boots because these were the only reprieve he offered her.

He kicked her once more, conscious of the aches of his age, and aware even more of his own patience and generosity towards her.

Nothing. He looked for the first outpouring of blood. Not a trickle, not a stain. He couldn't even make her pass water.

If he kicked any harder, or kicked her much more, he might kill her. All in all it seemed the best way. Her death would cure everything. He kicked as brutally as he could, and this was much less than he would. He ached.

He couldn't kill her. He loved her too much. He must try thrashing her back. 'Beat their backs by the lower ribs,' his old nurse had told him. 'Beat their backs. They always miscarry then. Beat their backs below the shoulder blade.'

He drubbed her with the flat of his scabbarded sword, and her spasms started.

Encouraged, he beat her some more. Then he stopped. She wasn't miscarrying.

Even now she wasn't choking on the clench of birth. She was giving him nothing. She was sobbing with pain and laughing at the same time, but holding the cries within herself. She

retreated on to the bed and protected herself in the wrap-
pings again.

Laughing? Laughing at him? He returned to her in a frenzy,
beating her all over, rolling her off the bed, kicking her along
the floor, tearing at her bare breasts with his hands, twisting
the dark muscle of her thigh as if rending a crab. He could break
nothing from her, not a clot of blood, not a stillborn child, not
a gasp of anguish.

She was trying to speak to him, but her mouth wouldn't
shape the word. He knew the word without her saying it. It
was 'why'?

Because of the Queen, he wanted to say. *Because you mustn't
have a child that would be related to the Queen . . .*

Now she cried indeed. She cried at the ridiculousness of so
much anguish. And as soon as she got her brain round that
disgusting coil and tangle she laughed also. She laughed aloud.
She scorned him and cried out at one and the same time. 'Yes,'
she said. '*Your* child *and* the Queen's relative. Well, I'll keep it
quiet, my lord. I'll keep it hidden. Because it's *my* child also, and
I want him to live.'

Surely there was tenderness in those words? Tenderness for
the man who had created her and brought her so much fame
and fortune, and touched her with such love?

Surely there was. Yet, if there was, he had no need of it. He
was hardly the man to catch his needs from a woman. His needs
were his own, and he was himself. Her trembling nakedness must
find its place in his night as earlier it had in his day. She belonged
to him. She would remain his until his great excommunication
fell upon her. He knew the lusts of the wild. When the hind
is with calf the stag still reminds himself that her body is his
territory.

She saw what was in his mind and began to plead with him
– ever an exciting thing in woman.

Because of her nudity, because of her bruised skin and the
pleasure he had taken in darkening it, and because of the value
he placed in this his most intimate possession, he knew he must
have her.

If his mind was in doubt, he had to consider the tribute to her beauty and extension of his will and persuasion that even now was bursting from between his legs.

The sheets were fresh, too, now he thought to drop her among them. She kept good women and they dried sweet herbs and bright lavender, and one of them had changed the odours of the bed since his morning's exultation.

'No!' she was saying, and singing very prettily, 'Please my lord! Please, Harry!' – he supposed because of the trivial pains old Bess and Malk the Fish had caused her. Well, they were dead and done now. She was revenged, so let her take comfort! Besides, his little 'lume' as the Scots called it (though by God and all the heroes of Troy *his* wasn't little) had a soft tip designed by the Almighty Manshaper to bring healing and easement to every delicacy of her underside.

'No' was all she could think of saying to all this, but her throat was so dry with whatever occupies women that he could scarcely make out what she said. She did gasp his name again, and that was pretty to hear, though familiar to him.

He was inside her for a long time, pausing only to lean outwards and sip a little wine. Watching Bess at work upon her, then Malk, had been a thirsty business, and he must drink to it. Otherwise, he did not neglect his little darling. Not a bit of it. He did not scant or slacken.

He did everything a woman should want, or hope to expect. She made no further sound. She gave him nothing. It was like raining briefly in a desert. She gave him nothing at all except ingratitude. She behaved as if she was too bruised to enjoy it.

He couldn't have that. He decided to cheer her up – not an easy task, with his mind on other matters, principally the delights of her flesh when she chose to be delightful, and how to share these with a husband.

'You're not bruised, Emilia,' he whispered into the convoluted curls by her ear, these being nearest. 'You're merely dark within the depths of your skin. Yes!' And here he kissed the ear itself, making a noise like an organ pipe or the thick string on a harp.

'Were I a poet or some such species of verse-smith, I should undoubtedly term you dark. "Dark" is the label that most fairly comprises you. If I were in my rhymstering mood and about to afix a codicil to your bum, "dark" would be uppermost in all my terminations!'

He wriggled himself about, just to be certain he was still inside her. She protested neither in pleasure nor pain. She moved her head aside when he blew into her ear, and so confirmed she was alive, if only a little.

'Bruises do not show upon you,' he gloated. 'You're like a bullace or a plum – we must give your flesh time to ripen!' Not a giggle. Never a word. 'Old man Bassano must have dipped his prick in pitch before he got you. Unless your mother kept a bucket of tar in her hatching barrel!'

'Do not speak of her so!' An answer at last.

He shifted his legs, he rolled his stomach around her and congratulated himself for persevering. 'She must have kept the darkness somewhere,' he said reasonably. 'Most women have a little coal underneath their mizzen somewhere. Aye, or further aft than that. It's a fact of ships and nature.'

Seeing the pain in her eye struggle with a blushful refusal to weep made his own mainmast stiffen inside her keel and crowd on the gallants, royals and even skysails, so great was his bliss in her. 'Old Baptista must have come at the lady backwards,' he affirmed. 'It's a well-known Italianate trick of all such peoples.' He spasmed and threw her away from underneath him in the same savage moment of ownership and rejection. She was his and always his, yet he might claim her no longer. 'He must have planted you up your mother's coalbins, my sweet. He got you among the old lady's bavins and faggots and not inside the mouth of the angels.' He dried himself on her sheet, and was surprised to find blood, but it wasn't that blood. 'I knew old Baptista Bassano, and once went to that ancient lady your mother for a cure.' He passed over the fact of his being older than both of them, even then. 'Neither of them were Turkomen or Blackamoors. You must have been a child of the breech rather than the canon's mouth!'

She smiled at this, but to herself, the way some women will when they're storing an insult to remember you by.

'Well,' he said, grunting his way out of bed and reassured to find he'd scarcely removed any of his clothing before feeling impelled to comfort her, 'Well, I suppose I must be off to discover you a husband.'

'It is still pitch dark, my lord.'

'Aye, but the cats are afoot. I'll not find you a pitch black husband, never fear. I already have an honest fellow in mind.'

'Is he a nobleman, my lord?'

'I cannot blemish a good man's shield and reverse the bar on his blazon by leaving my bastards in his cradle, or not unless he lends me his wife and the lady is willing.' Seeing the piteous look in her eyes, he said, 'I am minded towards a good honest man, and delicate with it.'

'Landed, my lord? And gentry?'

'As to lands, he shall have this house. I know my own way into it, and such is my love and generosity towards you. As to his station, I'd say his rank is gentleman.' He leant down and kissed her. 'A little lower on Mondays, but by saints' days rising to gentleman.'

She did not kiss him back, even from anxiety, so he kissed her again. 'You'll be all right,' he said kindly. 'I shall bring him to you tonight, and he'll not notice a thing. With a darkness like yours a bruise can only serve to lighten your skin.'

His breath, as always, was made tender with onions. He had chewed one from the kitchen, while watching Malk and Bess at work upon her. Downstairs he found himself another, to take the smell of death from his nose.

～

Will knew her house. Had he not addressed letters there, delivered them even by his own hand at least twice, as if he were the slightest of ha'penny porters and not what he was, which was nothing?

He walked up Bishopsgate slowly, shielding his approach behind the pack-string. Here was an odd thing, a fellow who led horses with smuggled hoof. He wondered what crime was afoot.

When they halted at the very door, his brains were abuzz with foreboding. He walked on. He'd already seen Emilia bound about as if for the embalming and burial. Were these to fetch her off?

And why so many horses? Was the woman to be reduced to bloodied parcels? Why else were these men and that woman about her? It was rumoured that great ones like the Lord Chamberlain kept their own torturers and executioners. Burghley certainly did, and not all the ugly tales about Walsingham could be lies. Hunsdon himself had butchered and broken men by the hundred on the Borders – and women too. Why not here?

He stopped, turned, and approached her house from above, wondering how he dared. He should have kept walking north-wards to the end of the street. Save that the city barway was closed for nightfall, Bishopsgate led on to the open fields. He could have been in the countryside in ten minutes. Three days' walking would have seen him home in Stratford. There were none who cut throats in Stratford, save a few once a year, always promptly hanged each Assizes.

He stole nearer the pack animals. He could hear a woman sob, cry out at least. The sound could be coming from anywhere. The world is full of women who scream and sob.

Then he saw Hunsdon's pair of footpads. Flies or whatever kind of villains they were, they were stooping with a bundle. The bundle was of a size to be a corpse. A woman's corpse for sure, with a corpse's spillage of air.

They had made away with her as the night's events had promised him. His poor dead love. What folly had her sweetness committed that she should deserve such an ending? Emilia. He drew nearer.

Not much closer. The men came out again. They bore a second corpse, much as they had the former. It was certainly a death they bore. It made death's noises. It had death's leak.

He pressed himself into the shadow between house and house.

47

They had butchered Emilia Bassano *and* then the woman from the boat who would certainly have witnessed the act.

No need to reason the need. He saw no reason in it. The fact itself was too ugly for thinking.

Then he saw Emilia alive. Her face was at a window beneath the eaves, its shape distorted by the pebble. She was not herself, but she moved her head and he was certain. A lover is always sure. She was lit by taper-flame or firelight, her face broken into tiny parcels by the bubble of the pane.

She was pallid in spite of the colour of her skin, white as candlewax, fainter than a ghost, but alive, alive.

The men were outside again. The packman turned his string, and led his load back towards the river. The others followed after.

Two corpses. Was Emilia a part of it? She had disappeared from the glass so he could no longer examine her.

She had looked in such a bother, she seemed hardly to have got off with her life. The problem was too much for him. She was alive. She was there to be loved. Knowing this, after his hour of dread, was better than love itself.

FOUR

Once the Lord Chamberlain had gone, Emilia tore some pieces of rag, such as women use, and staunched herself with oil. Then she called her mother's name several times, summoning her both by 'Margaret' and 'Mistress Johnson'.

Her mother would not appear to her. Emilia lacked the will to light tapers and encourage her face to manifest itself in their smoke. Nor was there a decent fire, so she was unable to read the dead woman's eyes among the embers. Without smoke or fire, Emilia dare not shout her mother's witch name into the darkness, even though this would have been certain to bring her.

She crouched still naked on her bed and sobbed, 'Mother, mother,' as if she were a child. She could let the tears run properly now she was alone. She felt a great comfort just by calling out in this way. Her recent bruises began to glow, while the ones she had received that morning settled into an ache, and her body was suffused in a great flame, until the pain was so intense she was forced to scream aloud. She called only for her mother, and lay there while her agony filled the room. Her bed curtains could not hold it. Her torment was everywhere. It even pushed against the rafters with each shudder of her heart.

Calling on her mother so persistently was enough. As soon as her suffering reached the topmost window glass, and the black beams by the fire, she saw a spider's web against the ceiling in the ingle-corner which she had never noticed before. Her ache made it tremble . . . As soon as she saw the web tremble from her mother's invisible presence in the room, and the spider run out, so did her pain pull itself free of her bruised limbs and stomach and the fragile tubes of her bones. It dragged itself away from her as her mother commanded it. It stayed beneath the roof and still threatened, but it left her.

She touched her stomach and reassured herself that her child was still there. Then she fell asleep.

She was awakened almost at once by a loud crash, and the sound of water spilling. She sat up in bed and peered into the darkness.

A woman was muttering in distress beyond her door.

'Maria!'

'Mistress Bassano, are you alive?' Maria stole through the door, carrying a candle. 'I thought you would be dead, what with those coystrils my lord had bring you here. And the women, my poor thing! I hid above and heard them pulling you inside out.'

'I thought my lord sent you away.'

'He had her send us away, that Bess-by-night. She paid us off to the George. The other two went, but I stole in by the back. She *frightened* me, by Cock, she did. As fierce a harpy as ever I hope to light upon.'

'Amen, Maria.'

'The other's no better than a common polecat, mistress, by Cock and Pie she is! Though what with the smell on her, I doubt if there'd be many with ha'pence enough to put her trade to good use. She'd need to be laid on a cold night and in a strong wind.'

'Indeed.'

'And by a lazar whose nose was gone off. It's a wonder you're not dead and done, Mistress Emilia. By Cock, I thought it was your ghost lay here, bawling and squawling to its mother.'

This came close to cheek, and she couldn't have that. 'You're wet, Maria.' The girl was soaked about the hem as if she'd been wading in puddles.

'Yea, Miss' Emilia, drenched in those harpies' piss. I thought at first it was my Lord Hunsdon's, but it lacks the smell and the savour of a titled gentleman's. I heard them at it all night. They did nothing but make you scream then get so excited they had to drench in your joint stool. They'd stood it there in the dark where it doesn't belong, and now I've just kicked it over.'

Emilia's pains were forgotten now, lifted away from her by her mother's intercession and left against the rafters.

It could be she lost her hurts in Maria's account of her accident. The girl's words brought a vile flood of memories and disgust with them, as if everything putrid and spiteful about her time with Lord Hunsdon was awash before her.

'By all the Saints of Darkness, Maria! Those evil women have dragged my privy pot into my counting room and used it there!'

'I'm sorry, Mistress Emilia.'

'Now it has been spilled in my own most private place, where my secret thoughts are!' She wanted to add that a woman has no privacy elsewhere, not once a man has pushed himself into her bed.

There was no need. Maria already knew this, and saw how much she was defiled. 'I'll fetch cloths and water, Miss Emilia, and burn pine gum. By Cock and Our Lady of Nazareth, I'll soon make way with the filth of these women.'

'No, Maria. Set me lights about the house above and below, and let us have beeswax more than tallow if the kitchen stock will let us. Oh, and blow on some embers and carry new fires to every hearth. We shall enjoy some good yellow flame.'

'Mistress.'

'Then bring me a mop and keg – I'll clean this matter myself. It will bring my soul expiation.'

Maria nodded in gratitude, though she pretended to protest.

Emilia swept her aside. 'When you have done that, and before you rinse and hang out your skirts and petticoats, find me some fresh rushes, if we have any – I mean flooring, not tapers.'

'Aye, Mistress Emilia.'

'Or a rug will do. And clean lavender. Set me some in a dish, and burn a handful in this room and the next!'

She waited for Maria to come back then set about her own sorry task in her counting room.

As she cleared the mess and cleansed her utensils, she felt the aches return. She kept on. The stool and its pewter ornament, its hangings and stud-holes for soap and ointments – all these were the visible tokens of her breeding and rank. No wonder that Bess and that Malk, polecat and mackerel that they were, had been so prompt to despoil them.

Maria came back to her. The house was glowing now, and the hearths cackled with flame. Everywhere she looked there were coxcombs of brightness and wonder.

Emilia lay reeds on her damp floor – not many, just enough to let the draught blow free between them. Then she spread her rug on top. 'I have cleansed the pewter and all such pieces, Maria. Now I would have you scour it, then make it sweet with some French spirit.'

She waited till the girl had lugged all her pieces away, then she knelt on her sweetened floor. 'Now, mother,' she said. Her aches were again forgotten.

It was a thrice times terrible spell those harpies had cast by pissing in her privy pot, and thrice times three they had turned it back on themselves by leaving it where it could be kicked in the dark. They had immediately been strangled downstairs, almost on Lord Hunsdon's whim. She had seen their leaking bodies placed across packhorses and carried away like sides of beef – no, like woolpacks to the dye. She wondered whether to retrieve their souls but decided they were much too menial for her purposes. She had no service for them. But their curse still clung there for her prompt ill-use. The curse of their stinking water remained. She would send it where it belonged. 'Maria!' she called.

The girl came upstairs at once. She was willing in all things, and had been prompt to study the art.

'Kneel here, Maria. Kneel and take my hands palm-downwards. Do not leave touch of me till I tell you, but speak if you will. Our force is in our holding together and in the nature of things. No word is wise enough to set nature aside, to change what is already clenched in the stones or written in the stars.'

'No, my mistress.'

'It was a terrible spell you prepared for us by kicking that pot. You spilled the waters of dead women, you spilled them while they were yet warm from their bodies and their bodies were not yet cold.'

'*Dead*, Miss Emilia?'

'Lord Hunsdon's a powerful man, and all of a rush to act. Now do not leave go my hand! We have a circle running.'

'Aye, Emilia. My head's in the eddy. I can sense the whirl-pool.'

'You have spilled these wild women's blood, Henry Carey, as you had them try to quell my child. You and your hirelings have stopped their hearts, but their curse was left here to wait for you. You'll not outlive these your creatures long. I have spoken in threes, and their curse is made in threes. I shall give you three years more, Henry of Hunsdon.'

Emilia was ecstatic. Maria trembled like a woman in a fit and seizure. Poor girl, she could not let go of Emilia's hands for a long time.

～

Emilia would have carried her to bed for the comfort of her, women being sweeter than men and softer than warming-pans, but she had words to attend to. She kissed the girl in gratitude, freed herself from her hands, and went to stand at her counting desk.

Here she found the six letters from Master Shakespeare, bound in pink tape. She had told Lord Hunsdon of one, and he had taken no interest. She did not think she had lied, any more than she had about the months she'd been carrying. It's well known among men that women cannot count or otherwise do sums, and she felt it best to let the fools continue in error, even at the price of being held ignorant.

She did not read Master Shakespeare's importunities. True she had seen him at Court so her heart might find a place for him on that account if no other. But he lacked rank or fame, and she knew he lodged cheaply. Lord Hunsdon said he wrote plays, but the Plague had been all about London for most of two years, so no plays were publicly given; and what good could a man do in private? He was rumoured to be scratching at a poem, but she doubted if a countryman could be much good with rhyme, certainly not as sweet as herself.

She took down her leather-bound folio of accounts. Her figuring was neat, the items precise down to the last quart of vinegar or the purchase of firestone and soda. She did not turn to her sums, not this time.

Interleaved among her household lists she kept her magic records, which were largely an account of her life, which was mostly her love and as such all rage. She read: 'His pryke is the youngest thinge about him and that hes seen some fifty yeeres, each of hem comprised of God knows what number of maggoty winters and further tally of pestylent sommers.'

The memory of the old brute almost crippled her afresh. She did not yield easily to torment, and thought to compose a verse or endite a tune in dots, but her quill had grown rotten from being left overlong in the ink. It wanted trimming and splitting afresh. No, it needed further provision from a kindly goose. She threw it down, so it lay in its own blot on the paper, much as Lord Hunsdon left his foulness in her bed. She called Maria close to her, to wash and bind up her bruises. The pain was gone but its signature remained.

She did not lie or sit, but stood leaning against her desk as Maria worked. Maria, being her personal woman, decided to read round the blot as she did so. 'You should write your hate in a code,' she advised, 'hide every truth in a cipher.'

Emilia sighed. 'My lord fries over a slow coal all men who keep their almanacs by code; I thought you knew that? So does the Queen require him.'

'And this is preferable?' The girl had found the bruising on Emilia's lower back.

'I'm told my lord Burghley has a rack kept specially tuned for fools who think in ciphers.' Emilia smiled. 'Besides, Maria, this is not hate I write. It's my words of love. I should be proud of those.'

'Yes, mistress, proud indeed. They speak volumes. So long as you do not name him.'

'As you say.' Where her skin was broken, so did it burn. The girl worked in dock leaf and witchhazel, then with pine gum steeped in honey and oil. It was not as effective as a great spell, but it took the pain.

'Praise God you have a dark skin.'

'Praise Old Cock, as you say. Only cuts show up on me, and even they light my flesh no more than a cloudy sunset.'

She clung hard to her desk and propped herself against it. Now Maria had bound up her hurts, she could give her mind back to magic, and force the tired pen to carry. She wrote: 'He shows it to me often, and bids me taste it when I will, which is never, though it is sweeter farre than the rest of him, being the briefer to coddle in a scented cloth . . .'

She retched, and added, 'That is just to telle of his pricke. I'll not thinke on the rest of him, which uncovers like the wrapping from a hamme, a maggoty herring from the souse or the store of those who ripen cheeses in a clout . . .'

She began to sob, what with the pain of her disgust, and the love. She could smell his rage everywhere about her. His body never left her. It fouled the air like a cheap candle. Her soul cried for beeswax. Her nose was full of sour tallow.

Indeed, the old brute had not only beaten her, he had used her to exhaustion. ''Tis a great fire we have burning at last, my Maria.'

'Aye, mistress.'

'As I have written today, so shall you take it and burn it. For, as a man goes up my chimney, so shall all word of him be taken by flame up to Hell.'

'Hell is *down* there, Mistress Emilia. Pardon my correcting you, but that's as the priests tell us.'

'You'll get no wisdom from priests, Maria. And such is as I always taught you. Hell must be *above* the flames, girl, never below, or how is its cooking done? Here, let me add a curse or two more: "He hath plumbed, plumb-lined and plummeted me to the bottome of my wit's well, yea to my verray bottome. I need only gaze upon the gentleman's nose for everything queynt about me to tickle!"'

Maria giggled and carried the pages to the fire. 'Bless you for teaching me how to read and endite, Lady Emilia – for so should you be – but I'll never pen a thought as sweet as yours.'

'Is he burning in Hell?'

'He's risen to the stars, but with soot in his teeth, I promise you. But he's no *gentleman*. Lord Hunsdon is a *lord*. It stands in accord to name and reason. You can't burn the man without setting spark to the *lord*, or you'll miss the pith and point of him.'

'He's a bastard, Maria, a cock-outside-the-blanket bastard. If I told you whose, then both our necks would be cut till our bloods emptied.'

Aye, he was a bastard, with no more rank in Heaven than her own child would have. She called the girl to follow after, and crept painfully into bed.

~

She was awakened to a great commotion downstairs. The servants were back, so it must be gone noon, if there were any truth, obedience or honour in them. Servants never make noise, not unless they are bidden to laugh or whipped till they cry, so she could only conclude Harry of Hunsdon was downstairs for some reason of patronage or other. He liked to look at his property, drink with his people-hired-by-her-hand but his own purse-by-proxy, and in general fart in company rather than alone. Well, the house hadn't moved overnight, he would climb upon her bed when he wanted to, and piss when he chose. She saw no reason to be courteous over ale, mull or sack. She had been booted about the loins and fisted against the brains. She could take no thought of circumstance or consequence. The child trembled inside her belly or some lesser miracle beckoned. Maria was still a tiny globe of warmth, a veritable slumbering atomy. She clung to the girl and fell back to sleep.

Praise be that neither woman slept naked, though that was the fashion in rooms that could afford a fire laid. Praise the same

God also that their hems were not risen up nor their necklines adroop or otherwise made immodest by sleep.

The bed curtains were snatched back, then coverlet, blanket and sheet thrown towards the windows as if stun-sails were being hoisted or the room being seasoned for a romp and a rape, both of them always being near to the Lord Chamberlain's designs.

'There she is, Master Lanier! No – better! There *they are*! I wish I could offer you a brace of sisters or an otherwise matched pair.'

'My lord—'

'The one with coal eyes and ringlets of cypresses is the lady in question. Waking or sleeping, she is beauty's own self, if hardly the Queen, though I daresay she comes close to Sheba! And rare among women she chooses beauty in others. She has pretty maids aplenty, so there's no need to blink in this house, Master Lanier, and little time to yawn.'

'Sir, I do not know about Queens, though I gaze on your cousin Her Majesty often. All I know is this lady. She plays on the virginal like an angel, my lord.'

'Aye, Alfonso, and so do you long to place your fingers on hers. I know you Italians.'

'I'm from Rouen, my lord.'

Dreadful enough to be caught napping, and with her maid. Quite beyond nature to realize she was to be given in marriage to a French fiddler – the very fellow who made eyes at her daily in Court, and who was leering in her direction and rolling his oggle at her as recently as yesterday. The fellow had even commiserated with her for her public humiliation. Was this a wedding of convenience or a diabolical jest?

Emilia rose stiffly up on her couch and stood knee-deep in its box of feathers like a Venus arising from the sea. 'My lord, and you, sir, you must take yourself from my chamber and give my maid leave to attire herself. As for mine own case, I know not whether you would have her bring me my gown or show me as I am, like a heifer at the fair. I take it we're talking of buying and selling, my lord?'

Lord Hunsdon bowed and led Master Lanier away and through the door. He was back on the instant, and lifting her one-handed from the bed, with his fingers over her shoulder and his thumb beneath her collar-bone. She had thought she was all bruises, but he'd found a fresh segment to fasten on. 'No, madam,' he hissed, 'not buying and selling!' He slapped her, as one might a horse, but only a fool strikes a horse on the mouth. 'Not buying and selling, more your giving and taking. You're damaged goods, my dear. Your hold has been breached and broken, and you're water-damaged about the keel. There's no way I can sell you, or even rent you at a price.'

She smiled at him ever so sweetly and fell to combing her hair. He would be dead in three years – she had already killed him. And as to her love for him, it had changed into a blackened parchment and been sent up the chimney last night. Her hair crackled.

She found herself a dress she had worn before the Queen. Its hem was trodden and slightly torn, and that was a nice touch.

Lord Hunsdon took one step towards her. 'Emilia,' he began. His voice faltered.

'Fetch Master Lanier to me, my lord. Or my maids will drop him into a wine cup, where the poor little man will undoubtedly drown.'

'Aye, mistress. But let me first sing his praises to you.'

'Tell me about his back, my lord, and the furnishings in his codpiece. They are all I care about, and they need not be much to suit me better than yours.'

Hunsdon blanched. She had hurt Henry Carey into his bones, but he was not the man to give a woman best, particularly when he still owned her key. He nodded and left her, returning with the silly little Frenchman almost at once.

Lanier stood beside him and regarded her uneasily.

'There she is, Master Lanier, and I say she is comely. There's many a gallop to be had from her, I promise you. As for the colour of her skin, well, there's some who call the maraschino cherry black and some who call it fair—'

'Fair, my lord, most fair and passing lovely.'

'I'm glad we agree. Now you know me for a plain jack. Harry Carey's a power in the land, praise God's Light and the Queen's sweetness and majesty. When I stand by a man, then you can count on it I mean to do him good, both in his purse and his pride.'

'I do so count on it, my lord.'

'Will you take this woman off me as a gift? I aim to furnish her with a dot and a dowry.'

'I'll take her for herself, my lord, though being but a poor musician—'

'How clearly we each know the other. Now here's the extent of it. I'll furnish you with a wedding and the pomp of a feast, as well as those other considerations I spoke of—'

'My lord.'

Emilia decided to find herself a chair. She saw no need to find anything for the men. That would be like asking the horse to nail its own shoe.

She was amused to see Lanier couldn't keep his eyes from her.

My Lord Hunsdon, on the other hand, daren't look in her direction at all. 'For the minute she's to continue in this house, so here you many hang up your harp and cast off your shoe – my name will be a protection to you both.'

'Your lordship is most kind.'

'The lady already holds the key, if you take my meaning, and I'd have you take hold of it now. We shall proceed to weddings anon, or even more immediate than that, and sharper than anything known in the science of sundials. That being said, there is a hot moon a ticking like a tower clock. I insist you enter into possession at once.'

'My lord.'

'You are to admit to no parley, but take hold of her this night.'

'My lord, I scarcely—'

'Nothing scarcely, Master Lanier. I want her swyved by a good man, and her lily-pads served with his dewfall a-plenty. I shall require that man to stuff his ramrod into the cannon's mouth and send it home with a good charge, if you conceive me.'

'Aye, my lord.'

All of this as if she were no more than the trench engine they spoke about or a mare in the mating pen waiting to be bruised by the stallion's hoofs. Well, she'd been bruised enough.

'Speaking of cannons, we may send you a-soldiering, Master Lanier, do you hear me? There's very little advancement to be had from music, but for a man who stands where deeper notes are sounded, there's credit aplenty, if you conceive me. A gentleman rushes upon the enemy in hopes to be made a knight. I would have Mistress Bassano here be married to a knight, wouldn't you? Sir Alfonso Lanier sounds very pretty to an English ear. Foreign, of course, but Sir Alfonso and Lady Lanier, now that could cut a dash in the world.'

'My lord.'

'But to the business at once. I shall listen to your report in the morning, and beg your leave to seek the lady's account of this night as well.' He gave Emilia a thwack with his open hand, much as he might send a mare across the pasture, striking her so hard he almost knocked her off her chair. She winced as the blow fell among her entire fret and stretchwire of bruises.

'So *to* her, Master Lanier. Into the piece's mouth. Send your rammer up her muzzle and drive your wadding home, aye, and in with the powder.'

She laughed aloud at this. She laughed as she knew a whore might laugh, so on that account she amused herself only briefly.

It was sweet to see him suffering so.

FIVE

She watched Alfonso Lanier move about her kitchen. He did so with an air of complete satisfaction, proud to discover how much it was he owned.

He was correct and firm in his dealings with her two women, affable with Peter Rudkin, her man, and lofty towards the scullery girl, who was grateful for his condescension.

He had come here looking for wine. He was neither lordly enough to clap his hands and bid someone fetch him a quartern jug of the best muskatt, nor servile enough to go without drinking any. Lord Hunsdon had provided himself with some excellent grape in this place, none of it calculated to enable a man to satisfy his own best intentions. She was amused to see her betrothed sipping so much of the stuff. He was like any fiddler, particularly a French one: he would be dead of the spot before he reached thirty, and so good riddance to him.

He appeared to notice her for the first time, though his eyes had not left her from the moment she entered the kitchen. 'Madam,' he said, or he might have said, 'Madame' as the French do, he had such a damnable thickness of tongue. Then he bowed very low for everyone to admire him, while holding his wine steadily out to one side. 'Madam,' he went on, still not straightening his leg, 'Now you behold and may perceive me all.'

'Aye, sir. I perceive all of your all, of your bowing and scraping at the least. I have heard your scraping at Court, and melancholy

61

music you made there, and now I see you bowing to me. I doubt that any fiddler can show me more, whether he be knave or gentleman.'

He stood up, his face suffused and contorted, she couldn't tell whether from stooping so long or because of what she had just said. 'There is one viol I *will* show, Madame Emilia. It will not be like any you have seen, nor will the case I take it from.'

He held out his jugless hand for her and, when she did not clasp it, snapped its thumb and forefinger at her imperiously.

She could not shame him in front of her people – it would serve only to shame herself. She did not take his hand but walked past him and led him upstairs.

In her chamber she said, 'You play very fast with me, Master Lanier.'

'My lord bad me be brisk.'

She did not even glance her contempt at him. To show her contempt would be to notice him. He struggled to unfasten her clothing, and she refused to notice even that. This was easier for her than it would have been yesterday. The hands of all manner of ruffians had been on her since then.

She stood naked by the bed she had so recently been surprised in sleeping with Maria. Maria – bless the girl – had stolen back to straighten the sheets and rearrange the curtains.

She felt his eyes on her. They were amber rather than brown and somewhat moist. She did not allow herself to meet them, but she could feel them slipping about her, high and then low and then high again.

He desired her. To be desired is the kindest form of persuasion, if not always the sweetest.

'I would have you throw water on yourself, madame, both above and below. I do this to myself often. We French set great store by bodily cleanliness.'

'So do we women, sir. You may sniff I am as clean as my womanhood makes me.'

'This I must believe of you.' He caught her hand and held it, turning her this way and that about with it like a puppet-master, him still fully clad, she stark naked.

'Love me,' she consented at last. 'I'll give you everything I can give a man.'

'And what will that be?' He tried to undress himself one handed, finding she had no desire to help him.

'What will that *be*, Emilia?'

What I can give everyone else, she thought. My Lord Hunsdon's clap. She escaped him into the pavilion of her bed and arranged herself there.

She was round bellied with the child, but round bellied was fashionable. No wonder her previous owner hadn't noticed.

Master Lanier parted the curtains and crept head first into the tent, naked at last, but keen to keep his body concealed. He was all in all, from what little she could glimpse of him, a better piece of forked flesh than the Lord Chamberlain.

She smiled encouragingly. Silly little Frenchman. Fancy having a voice like that stuck in her ear all night, not to say the face that made it. She must give him something to make him sleep.

He allowed his body to settle about her, no easy matter since she remained sitting. His flesh was cold. Perhaps he had being throwing more water on it.

'Emilia,' he breathed.

It amused her to be twined up in a man who confined himself to the poetry of her name. 'Emilia,' he sighed once more, then 'Emilia' as he grew more certain of the refrain.

Being desired, and by a young man, was passably rousing, much more so than being kicked. It was comparable to riding a horse, she decided, and almost as sweet as doing nothing.

She watched him inspect his viol – did he call it that? – with the same air of satisfaction he had worn yesterday while contemplating the instrument he named it after. *Bass* viol, indeed. She prayed he wouldn't be so stupid with it as he'd appeared when performing on the sackbut, or was it the shaum or the drums? She sighed. 'Master Alfonso,' she breathed in her turn. 'Master Lanier.' He needn't expect her to be more vocal than that!

He sat himself against her in a cunning knot of legs as if he were Adam in the painting that shows him giving birth to Eve instead of being robbed of a rib.

She eyed what he hoped to be offering her. Why not? She watched his principal item of conceit, his French speaking knob-headed wattle-hued cockaloram, slide in and out of her, watched rather than felt. Her inner flesh had healed quickly enough, but not totally. Mercifully she was numb. Thanks to her mother's intercession and the operation of her own sublunar conjurings, she felt nothing. Yes, she did. Now she did. She felt an uncontrollable spasm coming on. What she felt was the beginnings of a yawn.

He smiled at her tenderly. It was his way of encouraging himself. She tried not to loathe him, and in truth she could not loathe him. What she loathed was everything he was and did. She loathed his grunting and blunt-ended thick-headed thrusting. His butting and buff-buff-buffing. It was like having a billy-goat inside her.

He was beginning to smell like a billy-goat too, in spite of throwing water on himself. The fust of rut agitated his unbearable foreignness and wafted it up her nostrils with every sniff and snuff. Her nostrils, *his* sniff and snuff. He was giving himself sweaty armpits with all this spending of wine-laden wind. Even the orange peel he chewed for his breath was revolting. It gave him pink teeth, save where they were black beyond mending.

'Ah, my little, *litt-le* Emilia. How it pleases me to pleasure you. How it – *eases* me.'

Dare a mere man talk to her like this? She was hardly born to tolerate such a thing: a man without a title, a mere Jack Nothing, and his little cod and cowcumber a nothing at the end of nothing. She might have tolerated a knight, a demon, a daemon, an angel – yes, preferably an angel, though a devil would do, if his claws were clipped and he had a kind enough tail. Not a not-stop non-stop in-and-out jiggling fiddler. Would he were a flute-player. He might have fingered her stops to a better tune. Oh – when – would – he give over mooing and mowing and learn that night-time and feather beds were designed by God and by man for sleeping?

She decided to moo a little herself, or at least to reward him with a breath. She managed one almost at once, and threaded it through her teeth in imitation of a sigh. It seemed the simplest way to bring him to a conclusion.

Or so he concluded, and did so conclude, and threw her away with a loud shout of satisfaction.

As she crept from the bed towards a receptacle of polished pewter that was once more truly her own, she noticed Master Lanier had retained the wine jug in his hand – retained it or regained it: he was a fellow of such exquisite balance and dexterity she could not be certain he had ever put it down.

Wine rather than contentment encompassed Master Lanier's sleep, but he did sleep, and rather soon. Emilia's own body still needed the comfort of her bed, and she discovered a corner of it that no corner of the Frenchman had crept into. Here she bestowed herself and here she slept.

'Well, Master Lanier, and have you swyved her?'

Henry of Hunsdon's voice was loud as always, but she was glad to detect the envy in it, as it stirred her from her dream of a gentler Eden.

She woke to find that daylight had broken somewhat brutally into her chamber and so had the Lord Chamberlain, both of them being equally familiar with the way.

Emilia saw no need to stretch any part of herself beyond the curtain, and Alfonso was gradual to wake though prompt to attend his lordship once his wits returned to him.

The poor man was naked and not even dressed in a dash of water. 'I attend you, my lord. I attend,' he bleated, while hopping desperately about inside the curtains in search of something, most possibly his dignity. 'I attend you.'

'Fetch your body up out of the well, good Alfonso, and show yourself. Come, sir, a horseman must never be caught at toil in the trench, as the good poet says. *Disentangle* your manhood, sir. Pull your harrow free of her furrow.'

Lord Hunsdon was only moderate at Latin, but had read enough to furnish his tongue with all manner of similar smut as Emilia knew only too well. It was the hurt in his voice that delighted her most, though. Every syllable he uttered was its own kind of torture to him. She wondered what kind of sleep he had had last night, and with whom.

Master Lanier was not at all apt in this situation. A naked man is but a paltry thing, especially when his wit can do no more than dangle and its coy little ruff is ruched and smeared with the dews of its own exertion. 'My lord, I beg you excuse me a moment. I am in need of my garments.'

'I can see your shirt and your slops. Here!' Lord Hunsdon's hand thrust them in through the curtain. 'As for your hose and other pretty feathers, the whole chamber is strewn with cast-offs, both male and female, just like a whore's anteroom. A set of squirrels could not make me a greater filth, breaking nuts. No, nor pigeons with their bowels loose with cherries!'

'My lord, do but grant me an instant. There is wine in the kitchen.'

'It is my wine, you idiot! You need to be a man to drink that. It's a cock-shriveller to any coystril else!'

Master Lanier, being a man, stole forth without even saluting her wakening with a kiss.

'There, Alfonso. You'd look better in shoes, and with less corns on your feet, but all in all I must say you're a very pretty fellow.'

'My lord.'

'Have you swyved her?'

'As you commanded, Lord Hunsdon.'

'Back and forth, and up and down, all as a Frenchman does. And did her maids and her man steal a glimpse of you above and about her?'

'I know not about their eyes, my lord, mine own were so transported. But their ears must have furnished them an adequate testimony. And even were they stone-deaf they'd have felt the ground quake underfoot, for I made the street rattle – yea, slates fell off and thatches loosened all over Blackfriars, my lord.'

Emilia beamed her face forth at this point. Before she

withdrew it through the curtains, she was pleased to see how sickened the old man looked.

'I doubt not they heard us at Whitehall, my lord. I made her sing so sweet I daresay my band of musicians struck up in accompaniment.'

'That will be all, Lanier, provided the deed has been witnessed. I can see her child has acquired a fine swinking father.'

She heard Master Alfonso's back being clapped or his face smacked. Lord Hunsdon was hasty with his hands.

Then she heard the Queen's Chamberlain speak more softly, 'I must bring you away with me now, until we can arrange a wedding, which shall be soon. I promise you that your banquet will not be made of air, Alfonso.'

'My lord.'

'Now, if you will give me leave to speak with the lady a little.' He waited for Master Lanier's answer, but clearly heard nothing. 'There is wine in the kitchen.'

She did not hear her betrothed take his leave of the situation. He must have stolen forth shoes in hand. All she could hope was that the poor fool had wit enough to dress his feet before showing himself before her people downstairs.

How to present herself to her late love and continuing possessor was a more delicate matter. Normally she would hate any disorder in the dress, her current nudity even more so. Yet, in this instance . . .

She stole forth to greet the Lord Chamberlain with her body wrapped in one of the flaxen sheets from her bed. It was not entirely unsmeared.

'My Lord Hunsdon.' She yawned. 'You must forgive me looking like a bag-pudding, my lord, but I am entirely as you have designed me.' She yawned again, and dropped him a deep curtsy, letting slip the sheet and allowing him to glimpse any part of her he felt strong enough to look at. She forced her body as low as she could, in spite of her great hatch of ripening bruises, the pain in her groin, the ache in her backbone. 'This is farewell, then? I do thank you and congratulate you on the choice of my new consort.'

Farewells clearly troubled him. 'Farewell to your days at Court, forsooth and for certain. Whether it is farewell to our other heaven—'

'What heaven is that, my lord?'

'Our love bed, of course – *this*!'

'No!' She leapt up as if she were a tumbler, and his 'this' was a cymbal and her cue. 'No, Harry Carey. There'll be no love for you in any bed of mine. Nor was there ever, you fond old man.'

'Take a care, Emilia.'

'Your child is in my belly. What will you do – go back on your word to furnish me with a dot and good Master Lanier with our dwelling and a pension? Or will you strangle me again, and club me hereafter?'

'I offered you my boot as a physic, Emilia. All I did for you was in love, even as far as scabbarding your back.'

'If Mistress Malk and Madam Bess and those other varlets were emblems of your love, my lord, you must give me leave to dress myself in your hate. I shall be safer there.'

A man does not part the legs of women without sometimes being forced to listen to their tongues. So his lordship's expression seemed to say, and wearied by the exercise of patience could be presumed to add that their message was ever wayward. Having let a little of his tolerance and understanding light upon her, Lord Hunsdon said aloud, 'Lady, I beg you to preserve a little truth between us. Is there, *was* there no love?'

She stood forward and spat at him. This was a gesture that her mother would not have encouraged her in, and her teacher the Countess of Kent even less. 'Forgive my sputter, my lord. You left me too weak to strike at you.'

'Aye, I'll forgive you your insolence, girl.'

'Then forgive me the truth also.' Legs open or closed, how she had waited for this. 'You've beaten me, you've kicked me half to death. So why should I lie about our great love?' She gave him time to savour the phrase, and saw his eyes prick with tears before adding, with as sweet a voice as pain could muster: 'Our

68

great love was an illusion, sir, a chimera. Oh, I daresay you took a little pleasure in my body, or so your old grunts and wheezes seemed to tell me. My body is, before all, *young*, and its heart, sir, *ungiven.*' Yes, she was wounding him now. 'Why should a young woman take any pleasure in an old hackle-back like you? You're all dry skin and scab – where there's not one there's the other, like a badly stitched quilt. Aye, and you're wrinkled like a quilt, too. I'd as soon lie in the coffin woollen as under a belly like yours. I'll not speak of the stink of you, nor the pox . . .' The Lord Chamberlain was in a rage now, and Emilia began to enjoy herself the more. 'You speak of loving me, by which you mean your skills at service, do you, my lord?' Oh, how fine it was to send back some of the disgust that comes with even the sweetest love – and theirs was never that. 'Well, sir, we women learn how to *pretend*, how to feign a sigh or so when our old tups and three-legged rams are overcome with grunting. And so I did pretend, having learned it from better men than you, *younger* men, sir, *young* men even better, and boys who are almost angels, and as such always the best' – oh, how sweet lies were, and how they became truths once their shafts struck home! – 'aye, and with a sweeter compulsion about the terses and dangleberries than you, and stiffer, and *sweeter* on the breath. And when they finish with me, sir, when they *come*, they do not heave me a squirt of old vomit, a spoonful of cess-water like the last lees in the firkin and fiery as stale-ale with clap . . . what they do is . . .' She thought he would strangle her now, or was he trying to break her neck? Well, she would die in bliss to know she'd thrown him into torment with her inventions . . . 'what they do is transport me into the bliss of Elysium,' she said.

Either her neck was shaking in his hands or his hands were shaking her neck until the red mists came. Fortunately, Master Lanier returned at that moment. He had breakfasted long enough on wine and sop, and now felt bold enough not to leave another man with his woman.

He tugged the Lord Chamberlain's elbow and shoulder. 'My lord, you have said your farewells long enough. Now I must say my own.'

'God hasn't made her your wife yet.'

'No, my lord, but I have. Our bodies have joined us well, she and I.'

Lord Hunsdon looked like thunder, but so does any cloud before it rains.

Her commoner, who was still short of being a gentleman, discovered he had a thought in his mouth. 'This lord loves you, I think, my Emilia.' Ever the courtier, he added, 'We are fortunate in that.' His accent was thick, his speech tender, tender, but he was only a man. He allowed her possessor to wave him away downstairs.

'Lady, you talk of angels and Elysium. I could have you hanged as a witch.'

'Yes, you could have me hanged. You have had me all ways else.'

'Ever the wit, Emilia, and always the fool. Well, I shall attend you at your wedding.'

'So long as you do not pretend to dance at it, sir.'

'Why, lady? Have we not danced, you and I?'

'Indeed, my lord, and worse it was to behold than a grotesque at a dumbshow. You were like a bear who thinks itself nimble enough to perch on the rail with the parrot.'

'Methinks you play the parrot too much, Emilia.'

It was a fine word to leave on. He shouldered his hurt and was gone.

~

She crept into her bed and cried. She would have died there, but she heard Maria calling her from her counting room, and now from outside the curtain.

'It's a note, Mistress Emilia, a letter done up in a waxed scroll. Before God, there's some fool who loves you. By Cock there is.'

The girl held a tiny scroll through the curtain. It was sealed, as she said, and tied with a fading ribbon. Otherwise it lacked all weight and substance, being paper not skin, and rolled up no bigger than a peascod or a knife handle.

Emilia knew the hand by now. It was Master Shakespeare's and probably his formal best, though scarcely ornate. It was too overused for that. She could scarcely bother to read it. His situation was well known, and scarcely to her advantage. Besides, love letters bored her.

A phrase or so leapt to her eye:

'Fore God, lady, you come between myself and my poem, which is all love. Fain would I write it in your heart, or at least speak to you . . .

Mistress Bassano, I thought there were only nine Muses – all the poets agree, but before God and Mount Helicon there are ten, and you are the most beautiful of them all . . .

Not Clio, not Euterpe, Calliope . . .

It was tedious stuff, and she let it fall about her pillow. Still, she would retrieve it later.

She settled back and reflected. Master Lanier, a fiddler. Master Will Shakespeare, a poet. Both of them under thirty years old, though clearly no longer young. She was gaining two middle-aged artists for the price of one ancient soldier and dotard. All in all, she didn't feel she was being offered enough.

SIX

Sweet lady, what a magical darkness she had. Her eyes were
as coals at the moment of flame. Men might say her colouring
was unfashionable, but Will knew her body for what it was.
He knew what he could see and sense of it, and each night he
touched on more. It was becoming his world. Her skin was like
a horn lantern, dusky yet full of its own light. It glowed upon
his pillow, preventing sleep.

Never was love such a sickness as this. Never was sickness so
sweet. Nightly her dream was forcing itself between his sheets.
Her dream of herself, not his dream of her. *He* did not dream
this dream, nor did he want it until it became numinous about
his bed then rumpled its way in beside him and became the flesh
of his own dream also, touchable yet not his to touch. He kissed
her mouth, her ears, laid his lips upon her eyelids as if sipping at
moths, then – like a lovesick boy – found he could go no further.
He placed his hand upon her breast only to singe his fingers and
feel the branch of his arm dissolve in smoke. He thought his fist
had been burned to charcoal, his bushel of manhood with it. He
woke, screaming he could write no more unless someone else
dipped a pen in the soot of him and drew his pain across the
paper. What a sorcery was hers! What devilish enchantment!

Once, as he lay with her dream in his arms, his hand slunk
towards the undoubted fact of her thigh, only to have it snatched
away, then his bed to be thrown about the room, the night
explode in a keg of gunpowder. He would have doubted the

truth of this, being a married man and experienced in the dreams of women, had he not sensed her all about him, and heard her giggling below his window in Silver Street. She eluded but never left him.

Then Mistress Mountjoy, his landlady, rushed in upon him to deliver him from witchcraft, half in and half out of her night-gown. He might have lost himself in consolation, save his love for Emilia was too pure for that, too single-minded anyway. It would brook no dilution, even with this foreign creature whose curves denoted an entire woman and who allowed herself to fall face downwards about him and across him and around him, sobbing and scolding, 'Oh, Master Shakespeare, you have been visited by succubi this night. Oh, Will! Will! Will!'

Will? He had will aplenty. No way he would surrender his body to his landlady. Paying the rent was hard enough. Besides, Emilia still giggled beneath the house, or somebody did, and he had his poem to finish, or forgo his young patron's faith in him.

He left Mistress Madame Mountjoy in his bed. She watched him like a cat till he crept downstairs and sought the jakes in the yard. The place was melancholy after rain, but then woman is not the only thing that reminds a man he is mortal. He pulled his nightshirt about him and returned to his chamber.

The Mountjoy was still in his bed. She still watched him. He turned to his poem and was defeated. He couldn't write with his head any more, or his heart. His poem was all thigh. It burst out of him.

Emilia, his sweet Mistress Bassano, was no longer between the sheets of his bed, she was naked upon his topmost sheaf of paper. She was Venus talking wickedness to the young earl his patron. She did not even hide herself between leaf and fold. She dared him direct. She—

> 'Fondling,' she saith, 'since I have hemm'd thee here,
> Within a circuit of this ivory pale,
> I'll be a park, and thou shalt be my deer;

74

Feed where thou wilt, on mountain or in dale:
  Graze on my lips; and if those hills be dry,
  Stray lower where the pleasant fountains lie.

'Within this limit is relief enough,
Sweet bottom-grass, and high delightful plain,
Round rising hillocks, brakes obscure and rough
To shelter thee from tempest and from rain;
  Then be my deer, since I am such a park;
  No dog shall rouse thee, tho' a thousand bark . . .'

He had written beyond this, or her dream had guided his lustful hand. He had progressed some several dozen stanzas more, but he could not read on or add a word further.

Here he was, standing upright and nib in finger, when the naked Mountjoy swarmed from his bed and caught hold of him in an exceedingly private manner. Trust these French ladies, not to mention whores, bawds and the owners of a man's lodgings! His stiffness, seen sideways on, was too much for her. Thanks be, she did not see the naked dream that lay between eye and page to extend him thus. She felt quickly past whatever he was wearing and did not even stop to fondle him. She held his hardness with both hands and clasped it close. She seized him like any miller's wife laying hold of a tally stick. After a quick appraisal with the well-oiled palm of her hand, she told him she had the very item to match it, and drew him towards his bed.

She was already naked and he was at most a quarter dressed. He tried to think of Emilia. He *did* think of Emilia. How could he do otherwise? The token the lady held him by was Emilia's own sweet thing – or it soon would be. Its stiffness was her very own doing. He tore at the Mountjoy's wrists, pushed gently against her breasts and more vigorously against her meaty shoulders. She laughed and drew him on. She had hold of the portion she held, and that – as any wrestler knows – is advantage enough.

She fell with him on to the bed, being careful not to damage him, but in truth he was so rigid she could have tied ships to it. He was so charged up he was in hopes of spending immediately and cheating sin by weeping through her fingers as coy as any mass-priest.

She was too quick for that, too steady-minded, too knowing. It was like lying with his wife Anne. He was inside her before he found time to ask what o'clock it was, or even what day he found himself in. It wasn't yet day. It was only halfway from night, and he was still buried within it.

What a curious sideways motion the lady had. He had no inkling she'd wanted this of him, not until his dream's visit, and now she was rocking beneath him like a cockle-boat when the tide turns.

'Master William,' she gasped. Then she added something in French, of which he had some, and she had more.

She was already at some high peak of sweaty delirium, sobbing and sighing, but still with this foreign rotation of the hips. His mind, unfortunately for him but miraculously for her, was on other things. He thought fleetingly of Anne, and felt too guilty to finish. He thought of his poem, which was intricate and placed him beyond termination. Yes, he thought of his poem more than Anne. He thought of his young patron a little, though – to be entirely honest – not much. Mostly he thought of Emilia Bassano.

It is perfectly acceptable to think of one woman while lying with another. The women themselves do not generally encourage it, but he had read a little Ovid, and knew it was done. But if a man thinks of *keeping* himself chaste and pure for one woman while treading another lady's deck and steering her galliass into the storm ... if he swears to himself he must remain *faithful*, that *this*, however blissful, is not the appropriate *it*, why his fuse may stay burning by the hour. What he would prefer not to do at all, he ends up by doing better than not badly. He ends up by doing it much too well. The pair of them can tug their oars to and fro across the sea and then ocean without him once hearing the holy bells, still less the breakers roaring in his ears as he comes to white water.

'Master Shakespeare,' she gasped, 'you've a good back.' She had already cried testimony to the fact some ten or a dozen times by now. 'A remarkable back!' She took an hour or so to conclude this. 'I think they only half-named you, though. It isn't a dart you brandish, Will, not a spear you shake, but a steel-headed pike or full red-hot lance you push in and out, in and out . . . then . . . back again . . . on guard!'

She was gasping so fetchingly, and praising him so prettily in-between, that his reluctance at last became uncorked and he lost the better part of his best vintage. No man can resist being praised for long, a poet even less, and an actor not at all, so it all had to come out in the end, or most of it, or some of it, every little droplet affording his assailant a further tremble of delight. By Cock and sweet Jesus, what wickedness had he done?

He leapt from his bed, and gazed upon his poem. Emilia was still there upon the scrubbed sheet. He heard her voice below the window. He must seek her out boldly and directly tonight or be lost in infidelity. Madame Mountjoy was too delectable a morsel to be easily ignored, and being French and a householder she was quite used to having all of her own way. Yes, he must seek the Bassano apparition in the flesh this night.

Meanwhile, the Mountjoy was working herself through his poem now, like yeast in a good dough.

> Till, breathless, he disjoin'd, and backwards drew
> The heavenly moisture, the sweet coral mouth,
> Whose precious taste her thirsty lips well knew,
> Whereon they surfeit, yet complain of drouth;
>   He with her plenty press'd, she faint with dearth,
>   (Their lips together glued) fall to the earth.
>
> And having felt the sweetness of the spoil,
> With blindfold fury she begins to forage;
> Her face doth reek and smoke, her blood doth boil,
> And careless lust stirs up a desperate courage;
>   Planting oblivion, beating reason back,
>   Forgetting shame's pure blush and honour's wrack.

To say her face did 'reek' was a trifle unjust. Madame Mountjoy's face, like the rest of her, smelled of live woman rather than dead flesh. It was her simple misfortune to compete with his Emilia; his Emilia was a dream and dreams are odourless. However

Hot, faint, and weary with her hard embracing,
Like a wild bird being tamed with too much handling . . .

She had handled him, faith! She'd wrung his cock-pheasant's neck and stuffed it straight into her catch-bag with the rest of him, toenails over tooth into a headlong embrace. As for kissing, she'd almost chewed his head off.

And here was her damnable body-breeze again. She had stolen from his bed, and once more seized his before from behind, this time to his manhood's positive harm and detriment, there being less of him to grab and nothing to hold on to, unless she plaited it between her fingertips like the end of a slippery rope.

This she did. 'Tee! hee!' she said. Or, 'Ho! ho! hollah!' – some such insulting foreign chuckle that even an English woman can manage when she's got a poor fellow to disadvantage. 'Tee! hee! ho!' and possibly, 'Tee! hee! ho – *heave*!' So saying she drew him irresistibly to his bed again. She wound him in and moored him there as if the bed was her own – as it was, in a sense.

Women were ever so. His wife Anne was always thus, in all of her disguises. A man can fight them to a standstill, leave them strewn about the counterpane in breathless exhaustion, but heaven forbid he should seek to retire from the field in triumph, with all drums beating if not all flags flying!

No sooner is his shoulderblade turned in their direction than they resurrect themselves like so many skeletons from the slaughter, and once they become the bones in the fable they find themselves parched for another fight. They have to prove to the victor that he is, in fact, the vanquished. They have to. They must. It – is – their – perpetual – sermon.

'I said it before, Will. You've a back as strong as an ash tree.'

The second he became man enough to undulate it she began to comb it with her finger ends and foot talons until it felt like

78

John Musshem's field under the big plough. No . . . more like chaff from the common being clawed by the tines and rakes of an entire village.

'I must return to my *Venus*—'

'I am your Venus this moment. Show me some common courtesy, if not another inch or two of respect.'

'I must return to my *Venus and Adonis*. My patron requires if of me early.'

'I am your patron *now*, Master Shakespeare. I am your poem and your ink horn. So dip your quill in me – *that's* the manner of it, and no need to trim it further! It's meagre enough already! . . . Now take good care not to slacken with me.' He took good care – her voice was pecking holes in his brain. 'I am your patroness, and the pattern of your entire soul. *Dieu!* What a sweat you are in. You must *practise*, Will. *That's* better . . . that's *much* better . . . *je te remercie pour* . . .'

He tried to slip from her embrace. He could not. Their bodies were joined by the one part of him that belonged to at least two women else, so he dare not damage it. Praise the Saints of hospitality he'd been diligent with the toothpick last night, for his tongue was in danger of being swallowed by her. She had hold of him by the ears while she spoke her sermon straight into the back of his throat. 'That Adonis of yours, *Master* Will, that young earl, he's altogether too *much* in your thoughts, I do think. You watch over him as if he were a *green*sick damsel, and you *dribbling* with *love* for her . . . and I *must* say I suspected you of very backward pretensions until you . . . *deigned* to let me talk to you this morning. And showed me you have a shot or two . . . in your . . . *poop* and *fore*castle still!' She choked on her pleasure a moment or so longer, then said, 'Now what does your poem say to that?'

'My poem thinks you speak in too many gasps and sighs, *Madame* Mountjoy, even for a lady from France. And gasps and sighs are but dots on the page!' He managed to extricate his various parts from wherever she'd put them, his tongue most of all, since speech lay uppermost, and place a kiss on her comely flesh, before adding, 'And dots will use all my paper up, so my

79

poem will have none of you.' He crept from her on his elbows. By Cock, he'd quenched her at last.

He had. By God, by Cock and Saint George, at the least, he had! But the beauteous temptress had taken her revenge. His landlady was *in* his poem. His landlady *was* his poem, to the last drop of sweat she'd accused him of. Sweet liar, fairest dissembler and cheat! His sweat was all hers. If a man plunges into a seawave he must expect to get wet.

Yes, Madame Mountjoy was his Venus. His patron, the young Henry Wriothesley, Earl of Southampton, was the undoubted Adonis. Together they made up his theme. But his Muse, his Muse was his Emilia. And his Emilia was not yet his.

Meanwhile, Mountjoy? Surely, no more, no more. He dare not set foot in her stirrup for at least a fortnight. And as for her saddle and crop – still less her crupper – they'd get no more wax for a month! By God, she wanted more! Naked as he was, he took up his pen and showed her he would not, could not, do any more by her. Enough was more than enough.

'Sweet boy,' she says, and drags at him again . . .

Sweet boy . . . ?

Dear Cupid, he had hives on his face, and lumps from the strawberry rash of childhood. And his beard outbristled the arse of a Welsh boar . . . yet this sweaty young Venus wanted him again. How would he ever see service with the lovely Emilia?

> Now is she in the very lists of love,
> Her champion mounted for the hot encounter:
> All is imaginary she doth prove,
> He will not manage her, although he mount her . . .

Indeed he will not. He has a great need to get his breath back, preferably before he seeks Emilia tonight.

SEVEN

Maria was an excellent parcel of possibilities. Emilia felt her all over and said, 'I shall need you in this, my Maria.'

'Yes, Emilia.'

'I intend it to be a huge enchantment, to free my child of Lord Hunsdon's clap. You will first see my dead mother, the witch Margaret Johnson. Coming from the grave, she will scarcely be pleasant to gaze upon! Yet you must look beyond the bone until you find the beauty of her.'

The girl trembled.

'If you stand and lie close to me, you need fear nothing, not even from my mother's murderous familiars.' Maria wriggled her body closer and closer.

Emilia kept her pretty constantly in her bed when Hunsdon, and now Lanier, weren't there to displace her comfort. Maria was round, and sweet, and warm, and affectionate. She had no pretences and she wore no prickles.

'It is essential we purify ourselves entirely, Maria. To be successful with conjuration, gramarye, and all the secret arts, you must be more spirituous than an angel. Do you follow me?'

'If you say so, Mistress Emilia.'

'To this end I shall purify you, and you me, as well as each of us ourselves. All other persons shall be excluded. I think we'll give the others some pennies for ale, just as that Bess did. This bedroom will be the best and most sacred place.'

No matter how often my Lord Brute has defiled it, she thought.

'Aye, Emilia.'

'Fetch water, then.' She pushed the girl through the curtains, and called after her, 'Oh, and fetch a clean chamber pot – don't look surprised, girl. It's for the devils to piss in.'

'Is my Lord Hunsdon such a devil?'

'No, child. He's just a diseased old man who can't hold his water.' Emilia rose and sprinkled salt on the floor, then thought she was being too easy with it, and scuffed it away against the bed. 'I've had a thought, Maria. Under the stairs there is a huge jar that stands on a cloth. Fetch that instead.'

The girl was too curious to start on her errand.

''Tis a basil pot, Emilia.'

'Throw the bush into the yard and wash away the soil. That was my mother's sacred jordan. The Devil has pissed in that pot, Maria, Old Nick Oddfellow himself and no-one else.'

'Are they so very full of the stuff then, these devils and imps and such like fiends?'

'Nick is, for he is their king. But all the infernal ones in general have a great thirst, because there's some that dwell among ice and some that live by fire, and as the demons drink so do their bladders weep.'

The girl rushed to obey her commands, then shivered, halted and called across her shoulder, 'They do say an icicle and a hot coal are the two things that will give even a frog a dry throat.'

Emilia shuddered too. 'Frog is an evil beast, Maria. Toad even more so. I'd rather have a blind worm to my bed, or a tailless lizard.'

The girl came back and caught her by the wrist. Her mistress must not say such things. Emilia was the sweetest woman. She was all delicacy and softness. Her limbs were like honeyed veal before it goes to make blancmange. And her bed was as you'd expect of her. There was no other bed like it. How could she talk of worms in such a heaven? Never mind its hangings, which were richer than an ostrich's tailfeathers. Nor its tassels and its cushions. Just to talk of its nestling place was enough to make an ordinary mortal swoon, so how could she speak of bringing lizards to it? It was stitched from snow-white linen, and other cloths so fine they might have been woven from clouds. There was none of your lumpy flax. Frogs and toads? She was glad her mistress was so much against them. The mattress was lined with downs so gentle that Maria could scarcely separate fluff from feather when she turned it, nor feel the stalk in them when she pinched the binding. 'You don't want no toads nor worms, nor anything else with tails, Emilia!'

'No, I want you about your errand, then here again with some jugs of water!'

While she was gone below, Emilia called to Peter Rudkin her man, and bade him go to the ale house, and take the cook and scullery girl with him.

'Is it a holy day, mistress?'

'Yes, and you'll find a rainbow in it if you walk far enough!'

As soon as Maria completed her journeys above and below, Emilia told her to set the Devil's pot by the window, and put jugs and bowls in the middle of the floor. Then she took her gown off and told the girl to do likewise.

'Your bruises are all vanished, Emilia.'

'My mother had her cat come and eat them. Stand very still, and take note of what I say.'

She took up her salt jar and made two circles of the stuff, pouring it clockwise about, one at each end of the room. 'When I tell you to stand in the circle, this is where you will stand.' She pointed to the one nearest to the bed. 'The other will be perilous with fire, and chasms, and – for all I know – crocodiles!'

The girl's mouth was once more agog, and her eyes fearful. Emilia felt awe at the trust of this innocent, and more than a little fearful on her own behalf. She could only do as her mother told her, and her mother was all truth. Just the same she decided to strengthen the boundaries of the circle with cloves of garlic, and sent the girl downstairs to fetch some, naked as she was.

When she came back, Emilia fortified her circles both with

the juice of garlic, and with its husks. 'Take care you never tread on this line, Maria, neither stepping in nor going out.' Then she caught hold of the girl and began to wash her from head to foot.

Being washed was new to Maria, both strange and unnatural. She cried out in protest, but Emilia smacked her once kindly, as a mother does a child, and as she soon would to her own, and said, 'Take care not to cleanse me from *your* bowl, and see I do not splash thee with waterdrops from mine!' She caught the girl across her knee and began to scrub at her private parts.

The girl giggled at this, but only while Emilia used a hand-cloth. When she used a husk, the way women do to remove loose skin, she was not so cheerful. 'Lord God a' mercy!' she squealed. She had so much to learn, but would not mind her tongue.

'Do not call upon God,' Emilia scolded, 'For the Old Man knows nothing of cleanness.'

'Only chastity, Emilia.'

'Chastity is a different thing. It's for nuns and poets. We of the Old Faith must understand how much our Master hates anything unclean, especially in the female.' She set the girl down, dried her, and inspected the result. She was less than pleased with what she saw. Maria, being new to the Art, needed work-a-plenty. 'God does not mind a dirty bosom or a moist toe,' she said. 'His own Son was bloody and a lot less than clean when the Romans killed him. Yet God took him straightway into Heaven.'

'Only his *soul*, Emilia. His soul was all spirit, and his spirit was doubtless pure.'

Emilia felt downcast to hear this chatter from the Usurper's religion. She almost changed her mind about using the girl, but she dare not face the demons by herself. Her mother had insisted they were best not met with alone. She silenced her by returning to her privities, which can never be spotless enough for the Dark One.

Maria suffered a most unseemly dab from the husk, which had begun bone dry and was very scratchy. It was so much like having her private parts scrubbed with a hedgehog that she screamed aloud, but added, 'I have *studied* this, Emilia! Jesus, I mean! His body did not go to Heaven until all those Marys had washed it and oiled it and – oh, mistress—'

'Now stop your tongue while I am preparing you for most excellent mysteries. Your God, as I say, does not mind a black toenail, or even a smudged forehead, not in men, anyway. You might say He is happy enough to leave our bodies and other bits completely alone, particularly those parts the priests tell us never to think on—'

'Frequently, Emilia, and by name.'

'Whereas Lord Satan cannot abide dirt, as I have said to you!'

Emilia was tired of talking. The truth was she felt numb with dread. She was not an adept. She was not her mother. She was uncertain about assuming her mother's power or summoning the dark forces which previously only her mother had courage to command. How dare she pretend?

Maria's body had been purified enough, she decided. It was glisteningly pink. Its soil, and even its shadows, had long since been banished, though troublesome to get rid of. Her mother had not warned her against the tediums of her art. She had to discover for herself that washing an acolyte could be as laborious as scrubbing the floor.

'Purify me quickly,' she commanded. 'All over, but quickly. All under, too!' What did she keep servants for?

Principally to admire her. The girl was again in awe at her naked body, and enchanted to find it so like her own, save for certain differences of colouring. Once she had discovered words to describe this similarity and ignore this difference, she praised Emilia's nudity in detail and at very great length.

Her breasts in particular amazed her. Being encouraged to soak them in water and dry them with a cloth was almost too much for her. She could ruin everything with her chatter, especially now, as she prepared to anoint the fundamentals of this rite's mystery.

Emilia was enraged to find herself so fearful in the presence of one who was so foolish. Another slap, this time to a damp buttock, brought the girl very promptly to a proper state of mind. 'Build the fire,' she commanded her, 'and wash your fingers afterwards. Then be quiet, my poor fool!'

Maria was good with instructions and almost perfect with fires. The room began to glow like a smithy.

'Now lay on holly twigs and branches of alder, turn and turn about, but always with enough alder to smother the holly.'

The room became bright, then full of a foul smoke in which fiends, hydra-headed serpents, and all manner of beasts began to suggest themselves, to Emilia's imagination at the least. There was even a giant grasshopper as big as a table. She would have ridden it to seek out her mother, if the smoke hadn't stitched her throat with a fit of coughing almost strong enough to abort the child from her belly – the boy child she was now quite determined to hold on to, the infant whose ceremony this was.

In her coughing, she saw that the giant grasshopper was a table indeed, the very table the dead women had strapped her on, but now growing hindlegs of smoke, its belly underlit by holly flame, which stabbed out from her fireplace turn and turn about with the dank fume of the alder branches.

Maria clapped her hands, impervious to smoke as any kitchen maid or scullery girl. 'This is a great glee, Emilia. It gives me more pleasure than Ox Night at the Fair!'

'Think well on that ox,' Emilia scolded. 'Recall how men baste the beast, and scourge it with meat-hooks and ladles!'

'Aye, Emilia.'

'And be mindful that they cut out its tongue.'

'I'm sorry, Emilia.'

She wondered whether to insist on 'Queen Emilia' – wasn't her mother 'Queen Margaret' once the Dark Powers were gathered to pay homage to her? A little thought prompted her it was early to claim the Infernal Coronet. Let those Beings she summoned be first to call her Queen, or Princess and Mistress. They would acknowledge her entitlement. Instead she told the girl to take herbs from her mother's box on the altar, and use them to sweeten the fire and its smoke.

Maria refused. She too was troubled by Emilia's table, claiming it was a pair of anthropophagi crouched nose to buttock, or a family of apes huddled in a ring. Emilia was already atremble, but she took up the box herself and scolded her towards the flames.

Music, she knew, was appropriate. She picked up a long pipe of reed her mother had given her, and began to play softly until the smoke obeyed her summons, withdrew across the room and stood itself high and grey as any tower in London.

She gathered the trembling Maria back into the ring, and took up the stone jar that had been her mother's last gift to her. It was Queen Margaret's swoon cream, the flying cream of the witches, the miraculous ointment that let you glimpse the Scroll of Life or killed you outright according to how much you used.

Again the girl had to wash her own hands. Emilia inspected her acolyte's nails and the skin that made her thumb-print, then dressed herself in one of her mother's white robes, Margaret Johnson's 'Cloak of Cobwebs'. She left the girl naked and shining, so she might light the way for devils and other such phantasmagoria when they issued from the smoky caverns of her fireplace.

Then she beat once on her tabor and stilled the flames. Drawing Maria to her she kissed her once on the forehead, then rubbed the inside of the girl's nostrils with her mother's unguent. The girl began to drool and croon, the stuff was so powerful, the more so when Emilia pinched the cream into her earlobes, where the flesh was soft, and pierced for ornamental hangings which Emilia now withdrew, leaving them like cherries that have been robbed of their stalk.

The girl was too drowsy drunk to giggle, still less to squirm, when Emilia stroked the magic grease into the crease of her elbow and the back of her knee. She wondered briefly whether to keep the girl earthbound, but her mother always insisted that young virgin witches should be encouraged to fly, so she stroked a fair measure more into the lips of her sex, which blotted it up like a drunkard takes wine. To send her sensibilities higher than the Pole Star, while keeping her fleshly integument somewhat closer to hand, Emilia anointed her right forefinger with the precious stuff and inserted it into the girl's fundament as far as the finger knuckle.

87

Maria was quite asleep. She began to dance, slowly and without music, but always within the circle. She made her own song as she did so, staring through the window-moulds and horn glass at the rising moon, which was rounder than Emilia's belly. She sang a little too, though the song did not progress. 'I am in that heaven,' she sang, 'I am in that heaven which is starry and infernal. I am drunk on sweetest syrup. I have supped the Devil's cream.'

Heaven was a contentious proposition, and Emilia nearly gagged her or strangled her as she uttered it. Her mother must have guided her to let the song run, for it became more and more appropriate. Emilia hadn't instructed the girl to sing so. She must have learned it from some fiend or other.

Time for Queen Emilia to use the ointment on herself if she was to stay ahead of circumstance. But which part of herself? There was the question. She contented herself with a nostril and an earlobe. She had no wish to fly. She needed to remain firmly planted, and with her feet inside the circle.

Even so, she inadvertently dropped some of the magic stuff on to her lip and thence on to her tongue, and felt her head slam shut at the power of it, as if her brain was being enclosed in a lump of coal.

> I am in that heaven,
> I am in that heaven which is starry and infernal,
> I am drunk on sweetest syrups:
> I have supped the Devil's dream.

What was that the fool girl was singing? The cream was now the dream, and the dream was the Devil's. Emilia was the one whose dream it was, thank the singer very much. She was the Queen who ruled her mother's universe.

She stepped boldly to the edge of the circle, and blew three notes on the reed pipe. The girl became as still as a stone statue at the first blast.

'Open your doors, O ye walls,' Emilia called to the furnace's fog. 'Open your doors and come forth, my mother's creatures!'

It was a bold moment, this, both awesome and beautiful; so it was a pity there were none to witness it, for Maria lay in a swoon deeper than death. Indeed, she might have been dead, save her limbs continued to tremble in spite of the heat.

'Come forth!' Emilia cried again, and out they all came, like a vision of Damnation itself, for this was a portion of Gehenna's wall she had conjured here, and built circle by circle from blocks of her own fire's smoke; and this was the Adamantine Gate itself she forced open with her mother's music and her own wild cries. To bring such creatures *out* when the Devil's portals were all marked *in* was a brilliant feat indeed. Her mother had instructed her in these things, but shown her never. Still, she must give credit where credit was due. Meanwhile, she rejoiced at being able to construct something upon which to rejoice. This was better than playing music to England's ugly Queen!

What a tribe they were, and what teeth they had, each mouth like a nest of nails whether it was used for hissing or kissing! Yet mostly they chewed and sucked, having tasted no blood and eaten no meat for their portion of Eternity, and now quick to take what they could. How she blessed the circle of salt and garlic, and her mother's inherited powers that kept them at bay. And how she cursed not having Lord Hunsdon's heart and lights to feed them on and keep them happy, his prick at least, then his cullion bag and both his bollocks slowly.

As it was they had nothing to eat save one another, which they did incessantly, or fed on air, guzzling the moonlight from the sky in puddle after puddle, like so many saucers of milk. And as they feasted, so did they clench and fuck.

Noah had not packed them away, nor stored them two by two. Neither Noah nor anyone else God loved. But it was in couples they came first. They swarmed from Hell's deepest hold, each of them glued together like the devils in any tapestry of sin.

There were crocodiles coupling with gigantic ants, basilisks crouched upon scorpions. A wasp the size of a deer sucked a three headed faun by each of her necks in turn while pleasuring her interminably with his sting, which was as long as any fletcher's dart and tipped like a bulrush in burrs and prickles.

There were beasts no one had seen – or not Emilia, nor heard her mother describe – sea-monsters that could float on air, whales and saw-fish, all of them mating or committing grosser acts. There were mermen and maids-from-the-mere, pleasured or being pleasured by turtles, and landcrabs and cuttles. But whether these creatures were made of smoke, hot coal or thin air, or were fresh from the abyss she had no way of knowing without leaving the charmed circle.

She clapped her hands. 'Cease your dance,' she commanded. 'My dream wants none of you!' They vanished on the instant, their revels all ended, as if their breasts, their buttocks, their beaks and stings and flukes were so many bubbles put up by washerwomen from a drubbing of bed-linen.

She wondered if Bess's soul and Malk's were available to her – revenge would be so sweet. For the moment she decided to tread safely and leave them in eternal damnation, where they might be reluctant to return, and she find herself powerless to compel them.

Her mother had bequeathed more terrible familiars, murderers both, and now *post mortem* slaves of her family and its running bloodline, seeded once more in her womb.

In 1563, six years before her parental maestro Baptista Bassano begat her upon the great witch her mother, two men had tried to kill him. They had been hired by others still unknown, save in the scroll of the years, but the two assassins themselves had been foiled, arrested and confessed on the rack, one of them after being stretched almost joint from joint. He gave his name as Marc Anthony, a lie if there ever was one, but he was clearly good for nothing but the town end, so was sentenced to perpetual banishment. He died on the way to France, and was buried at sea.

Henry Dingley was looser of tongue, so suffered little alteration to his length. He was sentenced to be whipped, and that to be good and hard, almost as complete as a flaying – this out of mercy, to keep his mind from what would follow. This was to have his ears cropped, and be exposed in the pillory.

The crowd scarcely responded to him, he was so limp and

generally undemonstrative after the rack and the whipping wire, so they pelted him with only a few dozen bricks or so, some stones, and a horseshoe which was several times retrieved and passed back among the most eager, it having the best carry.

He had no teeth to lose, and the horseshoe only found one eye, so he was reprieved after an hour or so, having failed to amuse the crowd with a single jest. His sentence was for life in the Bridewell, but no one lasts for long in there, what with the plague, the smallpox, the great flux and the rats, which can eat a chained felon much more nimbly than he can them. But it was the flux that did him, or so he'd told Emilia's mother. 'Either I burst my own bowels or drowned in another's – I'm less than clear, Queen Margaret.'

These were the slaves that appeared to her, once the phantas-mogoria had disappeared. Dingley was clad in russet, as if still from the cesspit, and his mouth was brown like a hound's that suffers from the disease of that name. But his one remaining eye was clear beneath its brow, because it had gazed on eternity's scroll and been burnished by the flames of Hell.

Marc Anthony was a sorrier case: a daddy longlegs of a man, he looked more stretched than a crane-fly, and he was wrapped in seaweed and a sail-maker's coffin, which in his case was nothing better than bad calico. Though he stood before her the better part of an hour, he never spoke word, for his mouth was full of fishes, and a lobster ate his tongue and very likely his brain.

It was Henry Dingley who uttered, his ears still dripping from the torturer's clippers, an eye hanging down on its stalk where the horseshoe had sought it from its nesting place. 'You summoned me, Mistress Johnson?'

'Do not address me false, you basest of knaves and vilest of all vile rogues. Know I am Mistress Bassano and Emilia your Queen, daughter of the mother you name.'

'Great she was and shall continue so.'

'Daughter of the mother you name and of the good Italian you sought to murder. So name me as I am.'

'Bassano is but mortal, Emilia my Queen. Tomorrow you are to become Mistress Lanier.'

'I have no plans to be wed so soon.' Was marriage to be rushed upon her like this?

'You want me to kill the man Lanier? Is that your instruction to me?'

'Talk no more of killing.' She felt a strange pity for the creature, so soon to return to Torment, though she knew such feelings were dangerous. 'Your ears are already cropped, and singed against the bleeding.' But still they bled and smelled of the hot iron on human flesh, which was the stench of the pit itself, being worse than a glowing poker thrust into lard. She breathed and swallowed, then said again, 'So talk no more of killing.'

'So how shall I talk, my Queen? You never summoned me before.'

'I had no need of you, fellow. Do not call me Queen.' And, true, her mother had warned her against letting any being call her that, whether ghost, apparition or revenant from the Dead, for thus they would seek to possess her and draw her back to Hades and beyond; even a man who drooled upon her pillow must not call a woman queen. Queen is a title she confers upon herself. 'Call me your Mistress and Possessor.'

'Aye, Mistress.'

'In return I shall bring you to me and grant you these respites from Hell.'

'Aye, Mistress and Possessor. So what will you have of me? Shall you step from out out your ring and let me pleasure you, while old Fish Head here does the same for that girl?'

'You try my patience, felon. I need you to protect my son.'

'What against?'

'The pox, fool. Or the clap. I have some such disease of old King Henry's in my bones.'

'Aye, Mistress. 'Tis the old King's. I know him well. And the smell of him. 'Tis the King's clap you have, not the pox. You have it from Henry of Hunsdon, his son the Lord Chamberlain. I can see it in the scroll of the Universe.'

'Then let it stay there. I don't want to wear it in my heart, or for my *fons* to corrupt my intended husband. He's a good, simple man, who has no need of the hot piss and pimple.'

'Let your child be whole, then.'

'Aye, my husband and my son. Let them be. My lovers, whenever God or Satan grant me them, must suffer as they will – it's a woman's only recompense for thanklessness. And as for myself—'

'You have a recipe of Queen Margaret's, the Ruler of the Witches, to keep you celery sweet.'

'Meanwhile, I demand my son be whole. I want a complete boy.'

'How do you know it will be a son?'

'Do not catechize me, felon.'

'Mistress, it is a son. I can read him in your stomach. He already has a fine tail on him, and a head full of music and dreams.'

'Will he live long?'

'Long enough, my mistress and possessor, but not as long as you.'

At this moment, Maria – or the flesh of Maria – started to her feet, sighed, and stepped from the ring, calling, 'Dingley, Master Dingley.'

Emilia tried to snatch her back, and ward off her father's murderers, but the moment she stepped from the ring the phantoms became invisible. Worse, the girl fell into another swoon, but in truth it was stronger than a fainting fit, she was in an ecstasy such as seizes green-sick maidens in their sleep, and it led her towards the bed. There the unseen infernals tumbled upon her, invisible but tangible, transparent yet wild with lecherous force. They thrust her deeply from before and behind. Such a squeal she set up, such an 'Oh, Master Dingley' and 'Oh, oh, Marc Anthony,' as she was transported between indignity and delirium by the pricks of malignant spectres, or by the libidinous Flying Ointment.

No time to rescue Maria, for the robe was clawed from her own back by a great breeze that gusted through the door, then the window was blown or thrown open.

93

Her skin was suddenly chill, and in that second she heard the Devil's pot being moved, feathery garments unfasten, and the jar being filled in a noisy stream.

Emilia had never doubted the Dark One was present, but now she heard him chuckle aloud and piddle into Margaret Johnson's pot, which was reserved only for him, passing waters he had guzzled from the fiery lake, asphaltus and molten pumice, hot blood and the dew distilled from sighs, dribbling on and on in acceptance of the honour the old witch had done to him by bequeathing the young witch his consecrated pot.

Then he stepped forward, and Emilia rushed to greet him, Great Satan himself.

'Master!' she cried.

~

Will was almost inside his lady's dwelling. Outside in his inky suit, inside in his astral cloak. Stark, with the storm between his teeth. His was a bold name. Let him brandish!

Night made the task too easy. He had only been inside by daylight before, delivering letters, verses. Now, with the moon bloating high, he proposed to deliver himself instead of a letter. Bru-ha-ha! and ... *flourish!* He would be his own poem, exact in every particular, a veritable rime royal.

What a magic place. Yes, magic. She was within.

The door was locked fast. He pushed. He did not knock. He pushed and pretended. He needed time for reflection.

He peered against her windows. They were damnably latched, shuttered tight. When he found a chink in the oak he saw the lower rooms were dark, save for firelight from the kitchen. There were no servants afoot – all highly suggestive. Her household should not be as modest as this. No household should be, not even his own in Stratford. Did such an emptiness betoken robbery, murder, rape? Only a few nights gone he had seen corpses carried from this place, corpses or other carcasses. Were her women lying about the floor with their necks cut or their brains beaten out? And where was *she*?

His own brain was out. It was like any lover's, stuffed with nonsense. His poem was doing it positive harm, so was his need to make plots full of ghastly misfortune. Madame Mountjoy had done him no good, either – or rather she had done him too much good, which always makes for empty-headedness or plain idiocy.

The rising moon was proof of this. It was, from where he stood in the inferior position, a pretty exact and exactly pretty copy of the French lady's breast, give or take a vein or two. He would, come the weekend, have that breast and that vein in a verse: the marmoreal mammary of his sweaty Venus! The moon itself had forced its way into poems far too many times already, so let it go!

Psst! Someone prowled about the house, on the outside from the sound of it. This was no ghost, nor mouse in the wainscot. Not a cut-purse, either. This was some swaggering keep-away and give-my-breath-room bully boy of a buckle-clinking swashbucklering hanger-rattler. Nothing sly about that man's footsteps. Nothing shy, neither. Will's hand fell to his sword. No sword. He touched his dagger instead. Then he thought better of it. It was blunt, and not even good for bragging. He'd carried better knives as a boy.

No need of it now. The footsteps stopped.

Meanwhile he heard voices, women's voices, water being poured in an upstairs room. Nobody was dead. Praise God for that! His lady was above and bathing, or being bathed. She would be at this moment, *naked*, entirely peeled or at least partially exposed to the moon. She would be a whole host of epithets, comparisons, most of them the wildest of hyperbole, all of them rinsing though his head in a pitcher full of hot blood to drown sweet reason. Bathing, with the water running over, and down, and dripping under, and . . . God's wounds! His brain was stuffed with the Mountjoy's gasps and dots!

The bold-footed peep-by-night had become a shadow. The shadow prowled closer, then was still. It was entirely still. It was a stout shadow, an assured shadow. Impossible, as is the way with shades, to tell if there was a man in it. He would need to step closer, much closer.

95

The splashing waters, the murmur of voices, seemed to interest the shadow almost as much as they consumed him.

To have a rival was intolerable. On the other hand, and on advisement, a rival the lady keeps locked out of doors presents no great challenge to a man.

Besides, it might only be a shadow. Excellent shadow. If a lover is to swoon – and lovers do so swoon, all the experts even Ovid and Catullus agree – if a lover is to swoon, he may as well flop about in company. And this shadow was company, and excellent company to boot!

Before God and all the virginities of St Ursula, he was swooning now! By the holy nun and her eleven thousand maidens as they were before the Huns dipped their pricks in them! He was overcome with the one taste of his Emilia his dream had failed to give him: a sweet tingling in the nose hole, an itch more fetching than a sneeze. .

Olfactory stimulation!

Oh, soft ecstasy – *delirium et tremens*!

From her window below the eaves came a most beautiful perfume. He smelled oils, unguents, ointments, and all the drowsy syrups of the East. He remembered her skin in bed. It was like breathing on fruit, but he had not known what fruit it was, since dreams have no smell. Now he knew. His Emilia smelled of every fruit in Eden, and one fruit most of all. The scent of apple-water was strong.

Too damned strong! The Snake was sure to follow.

Will heard a man walking quickly. There were others about, citizens along the street in a throng if not a swarm, but this one had left the strollers and was approaching boldly. He pushed Will aside, as if he had no right to be there, swaggered to the door and produced a key for it. He opened it, pushed it shut behind him with his heel and possibly his buttock, and could be heard bolting it up. Will knew his face. It was in his memory somewhere, as one who had features of very little account.

A window was opened beneath the eaves, and smoke stole out. First it came slight and then it billowed, changing from wispy halyards then serpents' tails to the canvas of a fully rigged ship.

Upstairs, a woman coughed. Somebody, another woman, moaned. A woman sang. A man spoke darkly, incoherently, like a prayer in Latin. Will heard exultant laughter, more coughing, murmuring, groaning, mumbling, then someone pissing at enormous length and from a manly height into a pot that began muffled and empty then changed its note as it filled. Twenty devils could not have done more nor a team of well-watered horses.

As Will moved in frustration against the door, a laugh floated from the window above. It was the man who laughed, not the women.

Will flinched, then examined the memory of that laugh, as lovers will. It stayed in his head, not because it continued to haunt him, but because the fellow carried on chuckling, guffawing, and generally ha-ha-ha-ing till the sound was pressed between his ears and leathered up like the blocks of a book. He'd know it all right. He knew it now, by rote and by heart.

It was foreign, strange in accent anyway, just as Old Nick himself might be supposed to sound, what with the soot in his chubs and his Egyptian blood. Will hated that laugh. It lasted a long time, even longer than the filling of the pot which was eternal, but midway through the laugh the window slammed shut, and that was the end of it. His Emilia was a prisoner up there, in a room full of sorcery and smoke! Worse, she was accompanied by a foreigner with a saucy, not to say salty way of walking. God's wounds! His memory came back to him at last. She and her chamber women were locked away with Alfonso Lanier, one of the Queen's musicians, a fellow who would unlace a bodice with any breath in it as deftly as he'd open a case of viols, and brisker too, bosoms having the less in the way of bridging and strings to damage!

'You have not seen me, Master Shakespeare!'

Dear sweet Apollo, Neptune and Mars! The Shadow had spoken! It was alive and knew him by name!

～

Great Satan laughed among the smoke. He continued his lordly pissing. He did not cough once, for the fume of Emilia's alder logs was as nothing compared with the frowst he sprang from.

Towards the end of his long transaction with her mother's pot, the hearth opened up in flame. Green holly flared. Ethereal oils exploded in sparks as they are wont to do, and ripped through the veils of darkness that separated Emilia from the nether world. She gazed into the furnace at the bottom of the universe, and saw the burning lake of asphalt upon which all Creation floats.

The Devil chuckled at this. He ceased his outflow and strode strongly towards her, catching her up in those awful talons. Was her life as his priestess at an end, or could she look towards a more ecstatic beginning?

Her mother had warned her about those crooked finger hooks of his. They could snatch flesh from bone and leave her in gobbets or with a few libidinous touches the Lord of Hades could transmute her corporeal being into nerveless ecstasy, and claim her as his very own. As she was. Ah, she *was*!

Even as the Great Beast seized her, so did he set her aside. But he brushed her cheek with a kiss and she smelled the smoke on him. His hand, just as deftly, explored her body, while he rejected her. Her limbs were naked beneath her mother's robe, and he touched them as if to make sure her womanish parts were correctly located about her – here a breast, and there the crease of buttocks and thigh – each of them separated by as much good flesh as was necessary.

'Ha!' he gloated, 'Ha! Ha! Ha!' while her ear was still close enough to his mouth to be deafened by such a clamour, 'So my wife and her pretty little maid are playing Greek tricks with one another!' The Devil tossed her away from him, chuckled and added, 'A man may sue for a separation and have *divortium legitimum* for this. And see both wenches hanged for sorcery – or in France, he may!'

The Man in Black had borrowed Master Lanier's voice to taunt her, and a very cunning stratagem it was. It chilled her to notice how well he could mimic her betrothed lover's every accent, from its foreign way of speaking to all its arrogant tricks and conceits of ownership.

Emilia examined her Master thoughtfully. He paid her scarcely any attention in return, but fastened his eye upon Maria's bewitching young body, bare as it was, and lying half in and half out of the bed curtains, her mouth winsomely ajar, her eye glazed, and with one hand guarding or giddying that part of herself that only midwives and priests dare think about.

'Look at that girl. She's drowsy with lust!'

'Not so.' Should she call him 'Master' or 'Alfonso'?

'Well, she's dribbling enough from something. Does she have fits, or *hysterica passio*?'

The notion that Alfonso might be the Devil himself, if this proved to be Master Lanier, was a hard one to let go of in all the circumstances. If he were, or if the Black Beast could assume the fiddler's form at will, then marriage to him might be counted as some sort of ennoblement. Let her not offend either of them.

'As I say, that Maria thing's drowsy with lust. I daren't think what you do to her.'

'Not so, Alfonso. She's bewitched.'

'Bewitched, and just a trifle bewitching.' He murmured a few words of French, some little aphorism she recognised about a just retribution being best when it is paid in kind, kissed Emilia by the smoky ear, and added, 'Well, I have here the very wand that shall unbewitch her!'

She had seen his fiddlestick before, from butt-end to nostril – had he not urged her to gaze upon it and adore it only a brief night ago? Now, as midnight approached them, it stood forth from beneath his jerkin at an angle that defied the Laws of Nature. It was a rod and discomfort of truly diabolical proportions, and might well have been borrowed from Black Satan's arsenal.

'You see what I hold?' he asked. 'You conceive how I am?'

'Oh yes, Master Lanier!' Especially now, with the light of the moon glinting full upon it, and lighting its swollen head and beaded eye to a most unholy glitter.

The idea of sitting upon it made her sore again to think of. She would be like a witch in those cautionary Tales of Torment, stretched open by inquisitorial demons then impaled on her own broomhandle.

'Put it away,' she wanted to cry, but she dare not – the respect she owed him for it being so recent. 'Put it away or sheath it somewhere else.'

'Aye,' he murmured, as if reading her mind. 'Aye, and *mais oui, madame.*'

At that moment her Alfonso proved himself to be the Devil indeed, and Emilia was glad enough to let him be so. Poor Maria, poor dear sweet child. She must watch over her in all things now. It takes a saint or a simpleton to deal with Old Nick, and she knew that in Maria she had both and must guard her accordingly. This was a wicked resolve, but entirely satisfactory.

Wicked but entirely satisfactory, yes, to witness her husband's bare bum going barumbarbilum up and down above the girl's thrashing limbs, though Emilia might feel differently when the ointment let go of her brain, for witch cream was intended to sanction general concupiscence, the deflowering of captive virgins, a woman's own daughters, and the robbing of passing strangers of their bloodlines and seedbags, and sometimes of their lives.

Really Maria was making a terrible fuss of protest, although still asleep or pretending to be. She was hopping about the bed, arms and legs bent backwards, like a great spider Emilia had once seen the young Princeling of Kent trying to stab with a daisy stalk.

Emilia must remember she was herself the Queen of Darkness, the girl's Queen at least.

She leant past the bobdancing head of the Frenchman and continued her intstruction of her acolyte. 'Of course darkness can sparkle, or it can when our Master makes it so. Look how the night dances with pinpricks of light.'

'Oh, it does, Emilia!' The girl croaked in her trance.

'Old foolish men – astrologers, dribblers on the astrolabe, and other faithless ones – old fellows without teeth call them stars, those sparkling pieces of darkness. They even claim they are there all the time. What ignorance, Maria, to fly in the teeth of visible truth. Whoever saw a star shine by daylight, I ask you?'

'Tut-tut-tut-turoo, Emilia. You speak nothing but the turooth!'

'No, by Old Saint Nick, it is night itself that shines. Sometimes it is so pure and cloudless, you can see it shine all over.'

Master Alfonso began to mumble and moan on his own account, his breath becoming shorter as his fiddle-faddling reached the high notes. '*Mon Dieu*, my Emilia,' he gasped, 'you're a poet . . . you put me in mind of my nation's Du Bellay and our own sweet Pierre de Ronsard . . . as for this little *poule de ménage* – "*Mignonne, allons voir si la rose . . .*"' Well, it was an invitation, wasn't it? Though, unlike Ronsard, he lacked breath to complete it.

Emilia didn't mind him speaking French, if only he wouldn't put so much effort into it.

~

So Will went peeping about, as lovers do, and guessed at everything that was to be guessed at, as lovers think they can. He wasn't the man to be fearful of voices from the shadows, any more than amazed by a dumb show of smoke and light in a woman's chamber overhead. He knew of the philosophers' quest, and the sacred stone. More, he had kissed the Rosy Cross. No, he feared nothing there. Master Alfonso was the spectre that troubled him.

As for the nearer ghost, he recognized a chance when he saw one, so he spoke to it boldly enough. 'My lord, I wish you good evening,' were the simplest words that came to mind, so he said them.

'And what, by Saint Poxis, are you doing, fellow?'

'I stand beneath a good woman's window, my Lord Chamberlain, and so do you.'

'Sir, I am not here.'

'That is a fact I can see most clearly, my lord, as well as swear to it upon Bible oath.'

'Better than on the rack, fellow. Now, were I to remain invisible in your eyes, you might see your way past me towards a great advantage.'

'My lord, I am but a player, though sometimes I pick up my

pen. Great though you are, this night you are a lesser man that I am.'

'Take care not to threaten me, little man.'

'This night you are a nothing, my lord, and I take that to be lesser than a little. I do not see you. Or if I do, I take you to be an illusion . . . and that is my best jest on you, my lord. Believe me, that jest is my only truth, and that truth is I do not see you.'

'And how long shall you remain blind, Will?'

'Till my lord bids me open my eyes. Will, in the meantime being a better word to call me by, as my lord divines.'

'And you will not speak?'

'My lord, I will not. I dare not, so I shall not.'

'Will, this is my own house we're on our knees before – is there not a sadness here? Speak to me of sadness. What of an old man's sadness?'

'Why sad, my lord? My lord loves the lute, and would play on it.'

'Aye.' The Lord Chamberlain's voice was thick with the night air. 'Aye, Master Shakespeare. And there you glimpse my woe. I would play upon that lute for evermore.'

'But my lord, you own her case already, and it's a fine one you put her in.'

'Aye, Will.' Again the old bully's voice betrayed him. 'But I've had to lay down another one beside her.'

'Another lute! A case of strings, my lord?'

'No, you fool. A husband. She's to be married in the morning. Did you not see the fellow saucy his way in? I came to pay her my last respects—'

'And to play an honest note or two?'

'The loon has already placed himself beside her – this night of all nights, when the bridegroom should never be.'

'True, my lord. He's a foul French fiddler. It's against all the courtesies of creed and beyond the use of nature for a husband to capture a young woman on the eve of their wedding!' Oh, poor Will, he was suffering all right, but he must offer what comfort he could. 'Women are rare strange creatures, my lord.'

'This one is rare and strange beyond belief.'

102

'They do less wrong than they're able, Lord Harry. Who's to say she has granted him suit.'

'He's *up* there, fool!'

'We're both married men, my lord Harry. A wise man knows a good woman can never do the wickedness our worst thoughts fasten on her.'

'True, Will. Yes, true.'

By Faith and Good Saint Charity, I only wish it were, he thought. By Cock and good Saint Gil.

There was an end to that rhyme, but he couldn't come to it. Instead he laughed, and his laugh hurt him. He clapped the Lord Chamberlain on his invisible shoulder and murmured, 'So she's to be married, my lord?'

'Aye, tomorrow. At Saint Botolph's, Bishopsgate. I've bought a shortening of the banns this very day.'

'Then we must take comfort. A woman is like a great tun or firkin. She's the more accessible for being broached.'

Lord Hunsdon chuckled at this, albeit sadly.

'And the safer for those who sip at her hereafter.'

EIGHT

The wedding was a bit of a come down after this, principally because it was performed by a priest and not a devil. Worse, it was to a man of inferior talents, a fellow who could do nothing but play music in a band of fiddlers and whose only other artifice was sticking himself in and out of women. True he could do this in an agreeable enough manner to the recipient if she was awake and willing, but dogs do it also, and goats can carry on with it for ever. And one thing she had noticed about bitches and doe goats is that they spend the better part of their lives running away from it. Geese and hens teach a similar lesson. Had the human female nothing to learn from them?

The problem with Alfonso Lanier, who was marrying her in a pair of leg-rags midway between slops and gaskins, was that he had spent the greater part of last night wagging his bottom up and down above the bridesmaid, who now had such a hole in her virginity as might more properly qualify her to be an invalid matron of honour. Drunk or sober, her little Frenchman knew where a woman kept it and consequently where to place his own. She must hope she was the only one who was *enceinte* after last night's little ceremony *and* free of Lord Hunsdon's clap (or was it pox?) for these afflictions do seem to be passed on very quickly. All she knew was – and here she sniffed delicately, a very pretty thing in a woman – all she knew was her own problem was entirely cleared up. Let her hope Lanier would not give it back to her again, or afflict young Maria who was still, fortunately, convinced she had lost her maidenhead to a crop-eared man. But base fellows do pass the clap around with that foining stick of theirs, base fellows and Lords Chamberlain too, like naughty boys shifting tadpoles from pond to pond.

Emilia had been brought up in what her mother called the Old Religion, and she knew it as the true faith. However, several of the priest's words seeped through her head, and she gazed at her new man to make sure he understood them. 'Holy Matrimony is an honourable estate . . . not to be taken in hand . . . wantonly, to satisfy men's carnal lusts and appetites, like brute beasts . . .' neither with herself or Maria, and certainly not again with one overlooking the other, or both conjoint. After all, it was ordained for a remedy against sin, and to avoid fornication . . . Yes, let Master Alfonso the pincushion pikeman take note! There was to be little or no fornication in her corner of the marriage, thank you, despite the pleasure she took in throwing it in Lord Henry's face.

She began to drift again. Margaret Johnson's Flying Ointment had the power to remove all emotion from any mortal situation, and marriage was nothing if not mortal. Maria sagged beside her, and they had to hold each other up like pikes at a piling of arms, but she knew they made an engaging image of virginity under siege and about to fall, and this too was appropriate if inexact.

Emilia, of course, had only taken one sniff of the stuff on her wedding evening. Whereas Maria, who carried posies beside her, had ingested the magic grease *per labras, per labia maxima et minora, per anum* as the Book of Cobwebs and sour old Albertus insisted, and quite possibly *per cuneum* entire, such was Emilia's terrified haste, one *cuniculum* in a swooning girl feeling much like the other to an alchemist still a long way short of *adepta* and *ipsissima*.

No wonder she thought she was tupped by Henry Dingley last night, with his one eye hanging over her shoulder and the other inside her ear; and by Marc Anthony who filled her mouth with fish and jellied eels; as well as by some dozens of devils else, and any number of firedrakes and crocodiles, Lanier having been at her as constantly between midnight and the seventh crowing of a very late cock that her woman-flesh was totally excoriated. Once he was near his final whinny and squeeze, and this was often, he was as unlikely to reconsider his lady's readiness as he was to break off a *crescendo jubilante* to tune his violin.

Hot mustard and crushed lemons could not have left her in a worse state than this nocturnal conjunction of witches' ointment and a saucy Frenchman. This made her presence at Emilia's side heroic. Her mistress knew she was worth cleaving to more than any other alliance she could ever make.

Emilia was aware that another stood beside her as well, *of* the party but not *in* it. This was her previous owner, Lord Hunsdon. She did not steal a single glance at him. She knew he was there. She could feel the heat of his sadness, which was pleasingly genuine and made the air all about them warm. He whinged and gasped like a horse coming up a slippery hill, and put out so much stale breath she was glad her bed was to be rid of him.

'Who giveth this woman to be married by this man?'

The Lord Chamberlain did not speak. He simply nudged her forward, as if to say, 'She is mine, priest. Conjoin her as you will.' But of course he did not say.

What he did do was interrupt the service with an aside to the bridegroom spoken across her head. 'Do what you like with her, Master Lanier, or to any woman else, provided it be with discretion. A very little of you will be enough for me, sir, I do promise you.'

Then, and in mid-ceremony and before the blessing of the rings, he dropped a silver piece on the clergyman's prayerbook, turned on his heel and left the church. The priest had been paid, and his duty by them all had been done, and as hurtfully as possible. She would have to consider later whether she had taken any harm from it. For the moment, her mother's ointment coddled her brain better than a good mull.

The Lord Chamberlain left noisily. His heels had wooden blocks in them, and St Botolph's floor was as loud as any other, being but stone with an underlay of dry corpses.

No sooner was he gone than Emilia became aware of others

stealing in at her back. She took little notice at the time. A wedding is a public ceremony, and she liked to be public. For sure the old man had left no sentinels in place, not once he'd strode away from his own indiscretion.

By now, Lanier had placed a ring on her finger, a foreign affair as big as a doorknocker or the padlock on a chastity belt, as in truth it was meant to be!

She paid little attention to the rest of the nuptial, nor to the eyes on her back. The old man's loss was no great matter to her, as she told herself over and over again.

Not of itself, said the bell. Not of itself. The problem was what it always had been. The venerable greybeard was her key to the Court, key to the Court. The bells were very sad about this. Her place with the Queen, place with the Queen.

～

Master Shakespeare had risen early, cleared his ears and his mouth, and washed his beard. Then he combed it with rosewater and soothed it with oil. A clean shirt would not go amiss, and he had one. His buckles, in general, could stay unpolished. This had long been his practice, and his belt and shoe fastenings had taken such a tarnish from the weather that a woman needed a keen eye to notice he wore them. A man can write the flaring line or he can dress himself. There's scant time for both. The paradox was that, like any forked animal, a poet needed his clothes.

He was up early because he could not sleep. He could not sleep because he had a rival for his lady's favour. He knew that the Lord Chamberlain kept her, but not till last night did he know what the old soldier used her for. After all, he was Her Majesty's Chamberlain. He owned all kinds of pretty pieces of flesh, maskers, masqueraders, dancers, musicians and any entertainers else who might soothe the Queen's impatience. He even possessed Master Shakespeare's self, though at second hand, through his patron Southampton. Will wasn't a fool, but he'd seen his Emilia as chaste, eternally chaste. He had a thimbleful or so of fancy, but not enough to encompass that venerable, pale and arthritic stag stalling above his youthful little darling of a darkling hind. What a damnably degenerate old ram to be poking away at such a sweet ewe.

Now there was the wedding. Never mind his words of comfort to the Lord Chamberlain. They were best forgotten. They'd tortured him to utter them. They were a torment to remember. How *could* he share his Emilia with another man, other *men*? His Emilia? *His* Emilia? How could he share?

Top and tail? Monday by Tuesday? Sunday by Saint's day? You take her body and I'll keep her soul? That least of all. All he could do was walk round the corner to St Botolph's, Bishopsgate. He wouldn't be the only man there, nor even the only one in a clean shirt.

As he sought to leave, Madame Mountjoy came into the room.

She was stepping very sedately for her, nose down and knees in air, like a horse at the trot. She was fully dressed, too, and showing her wit in every acre of her attire.

Will glanced at his landlady and breathed her in. Her perfume was drowsy beyond believing, and she was caparisoned *cap-a-pe*, or *cheveux-à-pied* as she'd call it through those burnished French teeth of hers. He took note of her from hair-ribbon to ankle, and saw she wore a wire-embroidered gown gold enough and vulgar enough for the Queen. Her teeth were brighter and her bosom infinitely to be preferred to Her Majesty's, so he stepped carefully away from her and made ready with his excuses.

She did not come in very far. She took a short step or two, very brisk and saucy, then made some sort of flounce and curtsy such as he'd never seen her in. 'My Lord of Southampton,' she said, in that up-in-the-nose voice of hers she was generally panting too hard to listen to. 'My lords, I await your will.'

The young earl giggled behind the door, seemed to decide he'd struck the wrong note, and changed it to a much less scornful basso-profundo before stepping inside from the stairs. 'A door above stairs is a poxy strange thing, Will,' he observed. 'For a door needs a wall. And walls above stairs there never were. But, I suppose, in a lodging house . . .' he glanced around as if he'd never seen one before, still less been inside this one.

Then he renewed his awareness of the voluminous Mountjoy, and soothed his forelock for her.

It refused to be soothed. Some scented barber or family milch-girl had trained it to stay across his face and look unruly. Nothing about him was unruly. He stood like a tapestry and walked sideways on so the world could have the best view of him. 'Madame Mountjoy,' he said, 'I do *not* impugn your calling.' He paused mischievously, as if considering just what her calling might be, but in truth the lad had nostrils too fine for sniffing bedsheets. 'Your Master Will here is stuffed so full of secrets you might think him some sort of embassage or spy like young Marlowe. Eh, Will?' He paused long enough for the name to sink in, then said, 'Did I tell you he's writing me a poem? Then so are you, eh, Will?'

Will did not enjoy talk of Marlowe. A patron may be liberal, but poets are thirsty men, especially poets with families and a landlady, and to keep two of them in ale might stretch the young earl's bounty too far. Well, if Christopher Marlowe was composing verses so was he. 'My lord, my poem grows apace.'

'Aye, it was growing all last night,' the Mountjoy said spitefully. She'd evidently been keeping his bed warm for him.

'Wine,' Will suggested to her, despairing of ever reaching the wedding. 'A jug and *two* cups,' he added as she retreated, hoping that a little arithmetic might lead to her subtraction from the scene.

'I don't want your wine, Will. Why don't we repair to some twelve-penny ordinary?'

'Only if you purchase the pudding, my lord.'

'I intend to, Will. And a flask to help it down.'

'I can offer us entertainment closer to hand that will cost you nothing.'

Whoever won this debate their direction was out-of-doors. Inevitably they met Madame Mountjoy on the stairs. She was not to be passed by easily, especially when supported by a maid who, as well as a jug of wine, was bearing noticeably more than two cups.

'Master Shakespeare persuades me to a wedding,' the young man explained diffidently.

Madame Mountjoy grew wider. She was a woman who could separate her breasts and block streets with them.

'My lord commands me,' Will said, his voice full of regret.

'Master Shakespeare is a player,' she answered. 'As for my lord, I dare not speak for him, young though he is.'

'True,' his lordship said, 'Thou must not speak for me.' His use of 'thou' was cutting. 'And as for Master Shakespeare, he is as thou sayest, a player, and such men are never sincere. He is also a poet.'

'He's a liar, my lord.'

'My point exactly, dear Mountjoy. Without a lie or two, how would a mere poet ever reach the close of a couplet?'

They stood two by two and stomach against stomach on the stair, like hens pressing one another for advantage. Unless the landlady abated a little they would never be able to go past her.

Wriothesley giggled, as he was wont to do, and took a cup from the maid. He poured a little wine into it, touched it to his lip, then held it out to the Mountjoy.

She could not refuse to take it.

The two men made their way downstairs.

Outside, Southampton said, 'I hate women like that, Will.'

The truth of the matter was that young Henry Wriothesley seemed to dislike all women equally. Madame Mountjoy wasn't evil, or ugly. She was simply a woman and nothing but a woman, and she made it difficult for men to ignore the fact. There was a lot of her inside that Toulouse gown of hers, and there would be even more of her when she took it off, as Will could testify.

'My mother wants me to wed one of the creatures.'

'Which one, Hal?'

'Any one. Almost anyone. This one, and she please.' He smiled at a girl trying to sell him a satchel of dried herbs. 'Any woman with bubs and a belly to her. Never mind her title. A pox on her family's blood. Just to see me get a country girl in milk will do for my mother. She thinks I'm some kind of baddle or barley-boy.'

111

'Fie, my lord.'

'It's not that I don't love them, Will. I love them all, maid and matron alike. But only in midwinter. In summer they smell too much of the grass.'

They turned out of Silver Street and strode towards Bishopsgate. The young earl looked much too fine for his surroundings, but the buzzers and mutton-sellers alike all stood back from him. His finery spoke of too much wealth and power to quarrel with by daylight. Besides, the older fellow he walked with looked like his staff-and-striker man. He carried no sword, did Will, but he wore a roughened face, and a beard with traces of weather in it. He could clearly break a back at wrestling.

The impression would have been dispelled for anyone who heard him say, 'My Lord Henry, I've a confession to make. Hal, I'm in love.'

'Not with Madame Tum back there!'

'No, not her.' His ears glowed a trifle, just the same.

'She, I think, is in love with you.'

'Because I know *you*, my lord. It makes me extremely fetching to her. No, my Hal. She's a great gift for loving, has my landlady. She loves all men equally.'

'Now you play words with me, Will. Let us play truths. Tell me which jade you fancy. Point me the bird in her bower.'

They were in Bishopsgate now, with St Botolph's almost at hand.

'She's in another man's bower, my lord. In his hand at the least, and very nigh to his bed-sheet.' He choked at the thought of it. 'I promised you entertainment, Hal. Though from me expect nothing more than a dumb show. She's halfway to being married.'

'You an old married man and her a newly-wed woman. Oh, my Will. And you my appointed exemplar. What *will* my mother say to you? And how shall I ever trust weddings myself?'

So they entered the church and stood gossiping through whatever remained of Emilia's wedding and Shakespeare's pain. He heard a bell ring. He saw his Emilia and met her eyes as she turned from the altar rail. He looked away, abashed and feeling an intensity of emotion he could not express to himself. The bell rang again, a solitary, mean-spirited bell. There was no carillon of praise. The bellringer felt as he did.

Looking down, he saw that a pigeon had fouled his clean shirt, a pigeon or some such temple-haunting bird with a crop full of berries.

They watched Lanier and his bride walk past.

'She is lovely, Will. True, I have seen prettier boys, especially in Cambridgeshire. But for a woman she is beautiful enough.'

'Aye.'

'Then you shall have her, Will. I give her to you this instant. She is already yours in your bed.'

'But how, my lord? For God's sake tell me which way to go.'

'You must write her a letter.'

'I write to her by the week, the day, sometimes by the very hour. My letters thunder against her indifference like balls from a siege cannon.'

'Write another letter, and I shall deliver it for you. It will amuse me to. I'm told she belongs to old Harry Hunsdon's seraglio.'

'I know nothing of that.'

'She is Hunsdon's. Rest on it. Your salmon has already been roached. She'll not mind being tickled again.' He squeezed Will's shoulder. 'What a laugh, eh! To pluck a feather from the old soldier's plume. Such a rich little darkling feather, too!'

'He's a difficult man, my lord. And he has the ear of her Majesty.'

'And there will be the fun of it – for *both* of us.' Wriothesley laughed and led Will from the church as if they were at their own wedding, and theirs was the triumph, and theirs the procession.

Outside, Will could see no sign of her, but the young earl was being serious for once, and there was no way to stop his talking.

'Harry of Hunsdon may not be the most powerful man in the realm. There are two or three more so, my guardian Burghley for one. There are even people closer to the Queen than the Lord Chamberlain, but' – he paused, as if delivering a truth so weighty

113

it should be wrapped in lead or lapped in rhyme – 'he is the only one she trusts, because he is the only man about her who is honest. And that makes him dangerous indeed.' Being serious made my lord laugh. 'I'll enjoy delivering your letter, Will.'

'I'll write it at once, my lord.'

'Tomorrow will be soon enough. We'll leave the poor fool to her nuptial. I promised us breakfast at the twelve-penny ordinary.'

'You promised us pie and wine.'

'What's wrong with a capon and tarts, eh? Then some wine, Will. Not a great deal of wine.'

'No, Hal, not a great deal.'

'Just a very great deal instead.'

NINE

Her wedding night neither amused nor entertained her. Monsieur Alfonso, the good Maître Lanier, was equal to any amorous task – she had already experienced his expertise as a love-doctor some evening or two earlier – but everything he did was as a swelling prologue to his own imperial theme. A woman can be beguiled too easily by a little expert plucking of her strings, sounding of her stops, and – yes – fingering of her notes and keys. Great can be her pleasure at being blown upon. To be treated as reverently as a man treats his lute or flute is a flattering thing. Yet it is always his own tune that is played, never hers.

She grew tired of all that as soon as he began. She left his bed – so recently her bed – on a passing pretence, and bolted herself into a further room. He followed her as soon as he found himself deserted for longer than the chiming of a water-clock. He beat upon the door. Let him beat. He might as well learn his place in her life was to be a menial one. They were married now.

'Emilia,' he pleaded. 'You are my wife.'

'I know,' she agreed. 'And you are nothing but my husband.'

'Then let me show myself to you.'

'I know your quality. I have already seen you with my maid.'

'Oh *that*, Emilia! You must dismiss her, then.'

'Certainly not. She's much too precious to me. *You* can vouch for how rare she is.'

'Come into our bed.'

'In a week or two, perhaps, when I have finished sulking.'

'Emilia!'

'Have you forgotten I'm with child?'

'The Lord Chamberlain's bastard.'

'Never, Alfonso. Will you have him pull your tongue out with tongs for saying such a thing? You were with me before my wedding night more than once – me, or my maid. My whole household will bear me witness. Now retire to our bed and try to remember our good times together.'

'I am a proud man, Emilia.'

'Not with our maid. Not anymore. I must insist you respect her person.'

'A man of extreme pride.'

'Go to, Alfonso. You are a base fellow.'

He heard her laugh to herself as if the room was full of demons. It probably was.

One of her worries was how to eat. Another was how to drink. Maître Lanier had his duties at Court, no doubt, and she would be able to lay in a good stock of cates and fancies while he attended to them.

Her greatest question was to do with Alfonso's possession of her bed chamber. That sacred temple of sacrifice held a number of items which were essential to her peace, her bed among them. More, it was here she had traced her magic circle, her charmed palisade of sea-salt and wild garlic to keep her safe against the sauciness of her fancy. Her mother's ointment was another item. She couldn't have her husband soothing that into his beard, or using it for other French tricks. God knows what would become of him if he used it on a pimple or spread it on a loaf.

Be that as it may, the night was dark. Somewhere above the cloud there staggered a drowsy moon a day beyond full. That moon was almost set, as well as going shawled, and the evening star had already proceeded her down to Hades.

'You summoned me, Great Queen?'

It was Dingley. One thought of Hades and the Furies were already unlocking Hell's door and letting the rascal out.

116

She prepared her ground swiftly, by means of the Lesser and then the Greater Pentagram.

Dingley giggled as she did so. Beyond observing to herself that a creature with his eye on his cheek shouldn't giggle, she harboured the fear that Marc Anthony could be loose as well. He might be close about, and have crept invisibly into her column of light. She completed the Endless Knot with her fingertip and bound it close about her, and decided she was safe.

'Slave,' she said, 'I did not send for thee. But as thou art forward, so shalt thou be useful. I saw two men at my wedding today. One of them was young, the other a long step from old.'

'I saw one poet in a clean shirt. I was aware of an earl's bastard.'

'Is Henry Wriothesley a—'

'The nobility are all bastards, my Queen. However, his title is safe, even though, just like your husband, he will one day marry a pudding stuffed with another man's child—'

'Peace, knave.'

'—having no stomach for puddings himself, nor possessing the plums to stuff them with.'

'Nonetheless he is a mighty man.'

'Many baddles are. It is one of Heaven's jokes, my lady.'

'Joke or not, I would have that young earl attend me here.'

'It is already destined. He will be here and at your suit.'

'Then answer me how I—'

The sinking moon fell beneath a cloud, and the tiny chamber became bathed with light. Master Dingley could stand none of it. He disappeared.

She sniffed. She smelled salty fish and seawater. She imagined seaweed and the tears of mermaids. Marc Anthony had been here as well.

She heard Maria whispering softly at the door, and let her in. 'How is my husband?' she asked.

'In a temper, Emilia. I peeped in, thinking to be assured of you. Instead I heard him mutter this was an accursed house, which had chambers with doors, and those doors with inner bars.'

'A door above stairs is an unusual but necessary invention, Maria. One day I doubt not all houses shall have them.'

She let her mind wander. The architecture of dreams was far too insubstantial a topic. She had a young earl to consider, a man of infinite power, no matter how much he was lacking in plums and other dried fruit.

~

Emilia was an impatient woman. Most people with servants find their lives overladen with time, and she was no exception.

Playing peek-a-boo and peep-bo with her husband passed an agreeable enough hour or so. Then when he left the house to journey to Court by one of the several ways open to him, she was able to repossess and fumigate her bed, and arrange for a couch to be provided in the small chamber she was now pleased to call her tiring-room.

If she was ever to use her own grand bed, then she would need to be rid of the Frenchman's smell in it. The turning of sheets would not suffice. Nor would the hanging of them from windows. The scullery maid, and just possibly Maria, would have to drub them clean at the pump every day, so that her canopied pavilion might be restored to its former glories, as the arena where she had encountered devils, the Lord Chamberlain and cousin of the Queen, and where her own maid might sleep with her clean and scentless as the Lamb of God.

This bed beating and sheet stripping, this darting in and out of chambers and hiding away in closets, were making an already impatient woman beside herself with anticipation. Had she not given Dingley his instructions a day ago?

There came a loud knocking on the street door. It was a bold knock, neither as clamorous as Lord Hunsdon's nor as sly as Master Shakespeare's. She listened to it once, then again in memory. It was no knock that she knew. All in all it was a loutish knock, but it had borrowed importance from somewhere.

Maria was not on hand to answer. The scullery girl was at the town pipe, up to her elbows in suds. Her man was quaffing farthing flagons at the halfpenny ale.

118

Cursed misfortune. She must answer her door herself. Even a two-piece *bona roba* has her woman and her turnkey. Yet now she had no one, and there was no help for it. She had ordered Dingley to provide the young earl to her door. She had called on Hell to speak for her. Now Hell must be answered.

She drew back the oak with as much grace as a woman may summon when opening her own door.

Henry Dingley stood there – she thought Henry Dingley. He looked freshly brushed and more like his younger self. He had clearly come from this side of the grave, or at least been lying a little less time in the marl and mud.

She regarded the fellow coldly. He smiled at her, and his teeth were much as before. His eye had been tucked back, but the resulting squint was scarcely an improvement. Surely it was himself?

'Mistress Lanier?'

'What is your business, fellow?' She could scarcely bring herself to speak to him. Were her devils set loose from the pit?

'Know me as the Earl of Southampton's man. He bids me make known his pleasure. My lord the earl will be with you in a quarter of an hour.'

His bow was a trifle stiff, and wormy about the joints. He grinned and stuck out his hand for a coin, but she was in her day gown and wore no purse at her girdle.

She shut the oak in his face. Whether he walked into the crowd or was lost into the thinnest air she could not tell.

She hurried to oil and perfume herself, then change her gown and improve her slippers. These little acts take time, and a woman's hair is a taller task altogether. She hurried through her preparations calmly, and soon Maria and the girl returned with clean linen, Maria to finish dressing her, the girl to strew lavender in the hallway and pour scented water beyond the front door.

Even so, the quarter of an hour took time. The young earl did not allow his life to be governed by sundials and steeple clocks. He measured most of the afternoon in yawns, and his mouth was often wide enough to swallow several quarter-hours end to end.

119

At last he was here. Or someone was here and drubbing on her oak with the ferule of a cane. His knock was nothing more than a fidget, like a bird pecking. Even so, Emilia chose to notice it and have Maria let him in.

He left two of his men out of doors, lolling around like dogs. Emilia received him in the room she called her solar. It was the only place below that was neither her kitchen nor her parlour.

She stayed sitting down as he entered the room. He noticed this fact with amusement. Beauty is its own rank. It makes its own rules. She was clearly certain she was beautiful.

'Southampton,' he said, since Maria was too tongue-tied to announce him. He was much more finely decked than Emilia, even though Hunsdon bought her gowns. He looked like a field of meadowsweet walking. Emilia had been brought up in the country and quite expected to hear the birds sing.

She told him so at once. ''Tis a fetching doublet you wear, my lord. Your needlewomen have stitched it with larksong.'

'You're a poet, Mistress Lanier. That's what Master Shakespeare tells me, and by Euterpe and Calliope he's right. I wonder do you serve Erato as sweetly as I've heard you mimic Polyhymnia on your harp?'

Never confess your ignorance to a prating fool. She smiled on him sweetly. 'At Court, my Lord?'

'Aye, in the Great Gallery of Whitehall Palace.'

Besides, he was so pretty.

A silence fell between them. The young man was not at a loss for words: he simply lacked a chair. Beauty might be bold, it might be saucy, but he refused to stand in its presence for ever.

Maria was swift to bring a winged seat and place cushions for him. She did this brusquely and perhaps over-noisily, for in the interval Mistress Lanier's man Peter returned from the alehouse, and the scullery girl could be heard scolding his beery breath. He began to gargle noisily in the kitchen.

Wriothesley smiled at the delicacy of this interlude, and Emilia acknowledged her people's *finesse* with pride.

'My lord,' she ventured, 'you must regard this household as

your own. My husband would expect me to offer you no less.'
She hitched her skirt about her ankles as if the cloth were royal
and concealed empires. 'May we ask what leads you to honour
us with your presence?'

'I bear a strange tale, Mistress Lanier; though it is, believe
me, the harbinger of glad tidings.'

'Then let us be strangers first, and become glad hereafter.'

'Indeed. I believe you saw a fellow of mine. Well, not of mine
own, you understand, and there's the strangeness. This fellow
has an eye that is less than an eye, and teeth as blank as the
gun-ports in a battery. It is several years since I have seen a
creature so brown about the gums, even at a bear-baiting.' His
lordship grimaced. 'There was something of the coffin-worm
about him, even so. He was whiter than the lime in a sepulchre. If
it had not been full daylight, his appearance would have thrown
me into a tremble.'

'If it's the fellow who came knocking on my door, my lord,
then I must second your description. I have looked on corpses
thrown out for the plague-cart, and I swear some of those have
appeared more healthy.'

'It was as a stranger that this vile fellow presented himself
to me. He would take no hire, not even a small ale, but he told
me he was sure I would have some errand for him.'

'And, my lord?'

'I had not, and then I did. This letter came into my hand from
an admirer of yours.'

She saw the handwriting and the ribbon and recognized them
with some disappointment. 'I thought only we poor women tied
up our packets in pink.'

'Women and poets, Mistress Lanier. And men who are deeply
in love with a woman.'

'He writes to me often, this poet of yours.' Still she did not
extend her hand to receive the letter, nor signal Maria to carry
it between them. 'I hope his verses come to a truer conclusion
line by line than his notes to me.'

'Master Shakespeare is a fine poet and a great wit. The Muses
smile upon him, and so do I. For he lives within my protection.'

'This Master Dingley, this fellow who touched his forelock to you, you say he came pat. Then why not send this note by him?'

'I preferred to have him announce my own embassage. Master Shakespeare is my dearest and most faithful friend. He lives within my affections as well as my bounty. As I gild his palm, so do I expect to find gold in his writings, for he is a great man.'

'And old, my lord. Even across the great divide that separates us at Court I have counted some six or seven grey hairs gleaming on his chin. Or perhaps he dribbles his soup and cannot carry it.'

'He is twenty-eight.'

'No natural beaver in his bristle? Then, 'fore God, my lord, the base fellow dribbles, as I say. Why do you propose me such a man?'

'Have a care, lady.'

'My lord, I will have a care. I do have a care. Your suit flatters me. You are my care. I want us to be friends, my lord. Normally I spend Master Shakespeare's dross in my fireplace' – her eye forbad Maria to contradict this lie – 'or else I give it to my women to read for their amusement. But since you have been gracious enough to bring it in person, I shall keep it in my embroidery basket to giggle over during the winter months.'

She beckoned Maria to bring her the note, and made some little show of reading it. Then waved the girl away, confident she would shut it up in her day book, along with the rest of the poet's letters. 'It is a fond *billet*, my lord, and – fond being halfway to foolish – I take the writer to be at least a quarter mad.'

'You will see him, as he begs?'

'My lord, were I to grant audience to every gentleman who writes to me thus, I should need to live in a palace by the river and have barges ferry my visitors to and fro.'

'You will see him, nonetheless. As he begs, and I insist.'

'"Insist" is a terrible word, my lord. Of course, if the great Earl of Southampton insists then Emilia Lanier must comply. But I do protest at "insist", my lord. Merely to have implored would have been to insist enough.'

'You are too kind.' The young man rose swiftly from his seat as if his time could be spent in better company. He had not discarded his cloak which was light and for show, much like his pointed clogs and his codpiece.

'And now, since I have granted your suit, perhaps you will give your servant leave to insist a little?'

He was already halfway to the outer door, where Peter at last waited in a passable shirt and a new jerkin.

'My lord of Southampton!'

It was a crass form of address, but her tone was so insolent it spun him about to face her.

'Perhaps you will bless this house with another visit, my lord? For I too have a suit to you, my lord, and to do with poetry, a suit no less urgent than Master Shakespeare's.'

'Indeed,' he said uncertainly.

'So tell that tart old poet he may visit me. He may visit me for as long as his young patron visits here also, turn and turn about. There is no need to tell him *that*, my lord.'

She was so arch, so challenging, so confusingly beautiful and – yes – so *womanly* that he almost retched. He felt it best to hurry outside.

His men waited at the door. So did the villain who had announced him. He gestured for the wretch to be offered some money.

'No coins, my lord. My purse is made of cobwebs.'

～

Emilia hurried to find her day-book, and Maria scurried after her.

'Yes, do, you poor green child! Read the fool's letter if you will.'

Emilia had no need to glance at it again. Master Shakespeare could write all the pretty sentences he pleased. She knew her own would always be prettier.

As now, for instance, quill in hand, and with her imagination dipped in honey: ''Fore God, he is such a flower! He can't be above twenty winters old, and his face is still unmown ... As

123

for his suit, he dresses like a clover field. His cloak is woven from marmalade. Sweet Venus give me leave to borrow him from the bees a little.'

Maria read over her shoulder, seeking instruction in the ways of women as she always did.

'Cock, mistress, you're a bold lady, by St Gil, you are. You're beginning to collect so many gentlemen, you'll soon have admirers sticking out of your person like pins from a cribbage block!'

'Admirers' was sensitively chosen. Anything more would have been saucy, not to say salty, and led to her ears being boxed.

Young Henry Wriothesley the second earl of Southampton was in no hurry to seek out Master Will Shakespeare, his melancholy friend, the poet and lover. Why should he be? The fond wretch had beguiled him into risking himself with a woman. A *woman*. Himself, Wriothesley, with one of those sweaty tangles of birth and death and other stratagems for slowing a young man's progress through life from a canter to a trot, and then a damned dreary amble.

And what a woman she was. Pert, forward, hoydenish, and with a strangely unfashionable colour to her skin. She wasn't natural, that much was certain. When Heaven was dishing the anatomies out, some angel or other had stitched her together from a darker piece of calico. She might be full grown, and cut large enough and bright enough to put him in mind of a tilting doll, but in truth she looked more like a child's cuddle-toy, and behaved like one. That's what she was, a moppet, with limbs all a-sprawl and manners to match. And then there was her smell, which was odd, devilish odd. Perfume was all right on boys – most of them needed a sprinkle or so – but on women, those nests of cut grass and bees in the gorse? Unnatural. That was the short answer. On this one doubly so. She stank as if she dipped herself in witch oil, some kind of juice of almonds like adders leak from their heads in summer. Some females made him retch – be damn'd if she hadn't already done that to him at her doorpost! But worse than retch, much worse, Mistress Lanier made him itch.

Will found him at the cockpit in Whitehall Palace. Southampton didn't keep fighting birds himself – the thought of hiring a fellow to look after them tired him immeasurably – but he liked a flutter or so. The birds' blood was such a sprightly hue. 'Look at that spike's eye,' he offered Will, as if to explain his presence there.

One of the cocks had an eye pecked out, and the blood-hole was making it frantic. It spun this way and that unable to balance.

'I see no eye, my lord. That's why the poor fool walks in circles; it's a noted confusion in the brains of chickens.'

'It's the colour he wears in place of his eye that takes me so. Did you ever see a painter find anything so rare? Rubies are duller. Well, I've lost my bet!'

The cock was down now and unreclaimed, spoiled beyond advantage. Its opponent stood on its neck and tore into its head, driven into a frenzy by the colour the earl found so beguiling.

'Cocky little morsels, birds. I suppose they're likely to be spry and sprightly, Will. It's in the name of the things, isn't it, cocks?'

The poet said nothing to contradict his friend, partly from habit, more because he had things on his mind.

'Proud as Punchinello, cock and hen alike. They put me in mind of that pullet of yours, the one who dwells in Bishopsgate!'

Will did not enjoy the expression, but he kept his own counsel.

'She's a pretty little piece of flesh, and certainly no *bona roba*, still less a *cunnus*, if your Latin's up to following me. But she's *enceinte*, Will, an unmistakable case of *gravida* and heavy with child.'

'Aye,' Will said miserably. 'I do believe there's a belly on her.'

'You must more than believe it. You must have faith in the matter. She's got a coney in her pot, if not a brace of Mad March Hares. Not that she'll go as far as March. She'll drop them tomorrow, if I've ever stood in a barnyard!'

Will hung his head – no, not that. His eye was fixed on the

cockerel's dying. For his love to be pregnant was too painful for him to comment upon.

'I wonder who's been yerking her?'

'Her husband.' He knew it was a lie even as he spoke it.

'Lanier? Nay, he's a prompt and prickly Frenchman, as would be brisk to unlatch himself. But he can't afford to fornicate, Will, still less to marry. No, he's been put up to this one, and being paid good coin to stay there. I wonder who by. Dare we make the obvious connection?'

Will refused to speculate. He had two powerful friends now, two of the most useful men in England. He had far too much good sense to betray one to the other.

TEN

His patron said she would see him, so Will sought her out boldly. That is he lurked about Bishopsgate until he saw Lanier leave the house, then knocked at her door.

His exchange with her man Peter did not proceed very well. They were both of them in new shirts, and Peter found that his own shirt confirmed his rank, whereas the other fellow's merely signalled presumption.

Maria it was who bore Will's message to Emilia where she rested downstairs among cushions. Rested and needed to rest. Flesh which seemed healed now ached with the emergence of a deeper bruising. Rubbing her that morning, her young maid had said, 'That old bear hath sowed blisters inside your bone, Emilia. Now, poor lady, all your roses flower.'

So, deep among cushions, Emilia determined that some man should pay for her discomfort, be he earl or husband.

'Your letter writer is here, mistress. He says you gave him leave to call.'

Master Shakespeare's presumption put her in a black fury. 'I gave and give no man leave,' she said roundly.

She spoke too late. The actor was not the man to delay an entrance unduly. He came in briskly, and bowed full as such fellows are wont to do, being trained to fawn and flourish.

'A pity, lady. My Muse has need of you.' He carried some half dozen folios of paper in his hand with not a blot upon them.

They were copies, and not his originals. 'Fie, fie, fond love,' he declaimed.

'Master Shakespeare,' she said. 'I do know your face as I do recognize your squeak, but neither have been presented to me. As to your words, I am not your love, and "fond" is a foolish impudence.'

'I do not speak those words from my heart, Mistress Lanier. I recite you my poem. My lord's poem, rather. It is, just this morning, finished.'

'So you write your lord poems which do not speak from your heart? What, I wonder, can the rest of us expect from you?'

He had no kind of answer to this, save a dogged will to proceed as planned. He flourished again, and hitched his voice into place with his clothes.

> 'Fie, fie, fond love, thou art as full of fear
> As one with treasure laden, hemmed with thieves;
> Trifles unwitnessed with eye or ear—'

'Heroics!' she scolded. She did not speak entirely to herself. The conceited fellow was using her own favourite measure, as if such numbers were there to be taken up by any idiot who thought he could chime a phrase or two. She let her brain listen on until she realized he had stopped short of stealing her very own *ottava rima*. The stanza lapsed off into a *sestain*, which was obviously the most his thin muse could manage.

She refused to follow the stuff. Perhaps if he'd begun at the beginning she might have, but thank Heaven and Hell that he hadn't. All she was listening to, without hearing a word of it, was the death of a beautiful boy, who was clearly the young earl his patron. He had a wound in his side that felt much like her own, save that her own was all over. She drowsed.

She dozed through twenty-eight stanzas until she came to herself on the twenty-ninth.

'Thus weary of the world, away she hies,
And yokes her silver doves, by whose swift aid
Their mistress, mounted, through the empty skies
In her light chariot quickly is conveyed,
   Holding their course to Paphos, where their queen
   Means to immure herself and not be seen.'

Her torment was at an end. The words were particularly suited to her, the last line above all. The fourth merely confirmed her opinion of the fellow, even so. It was so lame a crab could have written it – and drowned himself at its end. The rhyme was as sour as a standing pool.

The poet presented her with this final blast of fly-away-home from close to. He was leaning over her where she lolled among her cushions. This closeness, this loudness, these draughts of declamation were not what had awakened her.

What brought her to her senses was his bardic hand, which had given up sawing the air, and was now plucking at the comforter on her chest and trying to lift it as if it were the cloth on a joint of meat.

She gave his own verse back to him, full in the teeth it had sprung from:

'Fie, fie, fond love, thou art as full of fear
As one with treasure laden, hemmed with thieves;
Trifles unwitnessed with eye or ear
Thy coward heart with false bethinking grieves.'

She was a player herself in her way. She could remember lines, however base.

He didn't blink at this. He had already lifted her stomacher as if it were the lid on a chicken blancmange. He began to stroke her heart, and the breast and nipple above it, with a curious circular motion of his hand. Sometimes his palm touched her uplifted skin, sometimes it brushed the air above it. She found this immediately stirring to her fancy, naughty though it was.

129

'You are forward, Master Shakespeare. Forward and furtive with all.'

'I come when your husband is away at Court. Is that furtive or merely prudent?'

'It is nasty, deceitful and sly!'

'My letters have declared my love for you. My lord has declared my love. I have given letters daily into your own hand and into your maid's hand. My lord has given you my letter. I tell you boldly that I love you. I do not speak lightly or idly. What more do you want?'

This was a ridiculous question, but her mind was in no mood to answer it, such was the circular wizardry of his touch, which had now become all fingertips or perhaps merely mothwings a long way off. What his fingers discovered, what she discovered they discovered, was herself a lot more naked than at the start of the poem. She frowned into his face, which was nearer than almost anything else, and saw he wore a ring in his ear like a common lewd fellow, though there were other parts of him pleasing enough to finger, if doing so could form any part of her intention.

'You are forward, Master Shakespeare,' she scolded again, in a voice without weight. 'Oh, sir, you are bold, and, yes—'

His kisses were like dew settling, even on her bruises, and his weight upon her was no more than a warm quilt.

'—you are bold and, yes, saucy!'

They rolled about her cushions, then under and through them, in a number of geometries, for he was an inventive man and she loved to tumble and dance, a number of geometries and several anatomies, not all of them two backed. Clever as he was, he was not conceited with it, unlike Master Lanier. He was her lover, or was fast becoming so and against all her will, which was negligible however she contorted herself to summon it. Yes, he was her lover, and not some acrobat of the fiery lance, still less her scampering marmoset.

They did scamper though, and she did mope and mow, as Maria saw when she brought in a jug of wine, then watched to see her mistress came to no harm, till she assured herself Emilia was firmly in charge, and with her bruises quite out of mind, as if their petals were already shed, or flowers in another room.

So Maria stole away, and Emilia sought to praise him, or adore him, or at least adore herself, which was much the same thing, they were so close. 'Great harm can come to a woman,' she murmured, as if her guilt was talking to them both from a long way off. 'Great harm indeed.'

'You are married, mistress.'

'So my poor husband is to be fobbed off with your brat?'

'It could not be a brat, for half of it would be yours, lady.'

She kissed him for this, the first time she had offered a man affection since her father died. She regretted it instantly.

'No need to speak of being with a child, even so. God has already put this belly on you.' He stroked the child in her affectionately. It immediately kicked him for interrupting its sleep.

'Goats and monkeys, you talk of nothing but coupling.'

'And couplets, lady. But now I speak most particularly of love.'

Those hands became busy again, those fingers, those little draughts, those moths in their cage of light. He began to whisper. First his love was all declaration, now an exquisite dumb show, now soliloquy.

Poor Master Shakespeare. He told her he thought himself too old for her, too middle-aged, and true he was twenty-eight which was middle-aged indeed, and true his beard was fading a little and lacking somewhat in lustre like the autumn sun. But his body was sweet and his shaft sure. He had a pleasing wit, when he could remember it, and a most becoming servility. Sweet William, *old* William . . . She began to laugh, but only in pleasure. He was half the age of old Hunsdon, and that old devil would never think himself old while he had a prick to look for, and brain enough to recall where he'd left it, which was always to hand anyway.

Will was too full of her to notice her mind was straying. Too full of himself, also. He felt as joyous as a Summer sunset, after ale. He felt his way about her again. He simply did what his lord had given him permission for, and what he had an instinct to do. And Emilia, so suddenly his lady, she did not seem to mind at all.

So the minutes poured themselves out in sand and became hours – one hour at least, and in that hour time became eternal.

It could have stayed so. It very nearly did, but Will was a man and in these matters foolish. He turned her thoughts towards tomorrow and broke the spell. There was a moment between a kiss and caress when he chose to speak. His speeches were already wonderful to her, but in them she detected tiny chinks of light wherein she might glimpse another day.

'My queen,' he mused, and his lips were like a bee seeking honey. 'Queen Emilia, this is your kingdom, these cushions your throne.' His fingers traced the comely swellings of her body, which was softer to the touch than a newly born calf, plumper than it should be though in truth – so great was the wisdom that settled in her brow – it was scarcely plumper than a tadpole. 'I cannot believe my good fortune to be your slave and servant here. Here is my lady's crown.' His lips wove traceries on her brow, lattices of molten gold more noble than any diadem. 'And here her orb.' He handled her breast again, and with a delicacy that surpassed any man's touch, even Lanier's when he was being foul, French and sly. 'And here,' bringing his implement into view, which was firm again to perfection and considerably younger than the rest of him, '*here* is your rod and sceptre. For here, madam, you must rule, now your fate decrees you be privy and walk no more abroad.'

It was a fine speech, a *poetic* speech, but as with the serpent's dreaded coil there was a sting at the end of it.

'"Be privy"? "Walk no more abroad"? But Will, my life is all abroad. I long to be unprivy. My Muse inclines to Court again. Surely I may take her there?'

'The Court belongs to Lord Hunsdon, my lady. No person plays at Court, unless the Chamberlain commands it so.'

That a man should bring her body to such a bliss only to inflate her spirit with such a fear. 'But Will, I wish to show myself abroad. I must be at Court. Can you not get me there?'

'My love, I am but a player.'

'But a player who pens masques and plays. Have you no part for me?'

'Not till they let women play women, Emilia. And, as *you* know better than most, women are best played by boys. So that shall never be.'

She lost all interest in rods and sceptres at that point. Her sadness became a pout, and that pout grew near to a fury, though not with him. She kissed him once or twice more, but half-heartedly, to show it was the world she hated, and life and time.

Then she sprang from his arms, all naked as she was, and bad him put his ambition away.

'I love you, Emilia.'

'I have a love as well. A love and, before it, a want. I wish to sing again, and play before Her Majesty.' Some time later she gave him her fingers to kiss. 'Aye, my fond Will,' she murmured. 'Go to, my love. Go to.'

The silence was heavy rather than eloquent. He bowed, as a lover will. And left, as a lover must.

ELEVEN

Christopher Marlowe was a pretty man, a damned pretty man. Several people acknowledged the fact, mainly rakes, queans, punks, bitchery boys, and all such bare-arsed loiterers in brothels and hedgerows.

His prick was an ornament too, as many of the same would agree: well fed, well kept and well kempt, and about as long as an unshaven quill. Songs had been written to it, either Master Marlowe's own or something very like it.

Henry Wriothesley had heard about the implement, and heard men sing about it too, mainly the same lot of rakes, queans, punks and bitchery boys. He did, he frankly and freely admitted, keep company with such people. When a man cannot stand women, he shuns the company of men who love women. Will was an exception, of course, but Will had a wife who was far away. His lordship would never have to breathe her airs in a parlour, still less sniff the back of her hand while making little bows of politeness over it.

Now the silly fellow had found himself this Lanier moppet, this dell, drab and doxy, and he Southampton would lose his friend to her unless he could bring himself to treat her gently himself, as the witchery bitch demanded, and go creeping about her as coy as any pimp or apple-squire in a vaulting-house. Phaugh! What a callet! She'd already made him itch, and the vomit run from both sides of his mouth. Before God, she'd even brought the bile down his nose.

Now he sat at his Will's lusty and lustrous poem *Venus and Adonis*, and read its eleven hundred and ninety-four lines of accusation, its scoffing at his supposed impotence, and realized that his beloved Will had penned every one of them, all one hundred and ninety-nine stanzas of them, including their hundred and ninety-nine final couplets, for no more lofty a purpose than to please his mother.

Here was Madame Mountjoy, a lusty perspiring Venus trying to play High Cockle-oram with his own limp-wristed Adonis, a youth who was wont to lie naked in the embrace of the beautiful Goddess, with his cullies being tickled by her silky bottomgrass (as Will so delicately called it, being learned in rural lore) and not experience the least alteration to his willy-lily, or not even be able to bring the precious object to mind or mention.

Master Marlowe stood quietly behind him for all of five minutes while he had these thoughts. He wasn't jealous of Will's poem. He was contemptuous of it. He hadn't read it. He didn't need to. Shakespeare was a contemptible man. If Wriothesley of Southampton was minded to toss his coin around, Christopher Marlowe knew himself to be a more fitting recipient. He could offer a greater return between the sheets, whether of paper, parchment or bed-linen.

Even so, the young nobleman's reverie was becoming over-long. Master Marlowe was used to waiting on ambassadors, spies, foreign Kings, and similar eminences of pith and buzz. He had little time to spend on the likes of the Earl of Southampton, unless for amusement's sake.

The poet leant across the Southampton's shoulder and placed a folio on top of Will's.

Wriothesley gazed down and read

> Some swore he was a maid in man's attire,
> For in his looks were all that men desire . . .
> And such as knew he was a man would say,
> Leander, thou art made for amorous play.

It was another accusation, and from an accursed sodomite.

They wanted to label him one of them, and harvest him for their own.

'You wish for my encouragement in this case?' he asked. 'Or do you seek hire and salary for your Muse's pain?'

'Aye, my good lord.'

Marlowe's perfume sickened the air, some soapyish cherry-laden Turkish stuff he'd doubtless stolen from Walsingham's spy-pen at Scadbury in Kent.

'I'm writing it for you and you alone, my lord. I've signed it with this.'

And then the famous implement was out in plain air. Still behind his shoulder as he sat trying to read, Master Marlowe drew his prick along the side of Wriothesley's neck and let it kiss the lobe of his ear.

Wriothesley found the bile in his mouth this time. It was not a matter of tasting. It scalded his tongue. This time it was the sick that came down his nose.

He stood up, seeking a kerchief, a cloth, anything. When he could breathe, he said, 'There is a little coin in that box, angels more than groats, but not many of either.'

'Five angels, my lord.'

The famous implement stood rebuked. It stood, even so.

'They will bring you lodgings and a fine supper.'

'More than that, my lord. Much more.'

'Well, live at my expense a little. Let me peruse your poem in the meantime.'

'You flatter me, my lord.'

'And you flatter me, Master Marlowe. But I am not given that way. Mine is a more monkish trail than most men suppose.'

'We see the cut of your cloak, my lord, and assume you're a hunting monk at least.'

～

Her man Peter was overawed to find the Earl of Southampton on his doorstep. Peter himself was still in his moderately clean shirt. It was a shirt that made him feel confident and forward.

He did not feel confident when he glimpsed his lordship. He did not find himself forward in the least. Henry Wriothesley did not merely wear a clean shirt, he was all clean shirt. His shirt, like everything above it, was exquisitely embroidered in silk and silver. With the sun on his back, he shone like a cobweb on a broomhandle. Slight though he was, he was more substantial than that, as even Peter realized. More like a meadow on stilts, or a plum tree newly in blossom. 'My lord,' he muttered, when his voice came back to him. 'I shall tell my mistress.'

Maria had already told her.

'Fetch my lord of Southampton above,' Emilia called briskly, and hurried herself upstairs. She had no thought of receiving so mighty a personage in her parlour. Her cushions were in disarray from the flutterings of a less ethereal lover. The fabric, whether of Damask or Tulle or plain West Country matt was pocklemarked with lucubrations beneath her dignity to remember. Her rugs were no longer immaculate. She wrinkled her nose at the thought. Master Will was a lustful though lovely man. Wherever he'd propped her the furniture was spotted.

She was certain of one thing about Southampton, nobleman though he was. She knew he would do as an authoritative woman told him. With men he might be coltish and wild. Womankind was otherwise. Woman was mother. Emilia, with her belly bulging just a little and the rest of her in blossom and even fruit, intended to bend him to her will, whatever that might prove to be.

She arrived upstairs in a breathless rush, her heart not yet slowed from Master Will, and her chest all a pitter and a patter.

She drew back the curtains on her bed, and smoothed a cat from the coverlet. She had not seen the creature before. She knew it had never been created. It was black, darker than her own eyebrows and with eyes of apple-leaf green. Her mother giggled in the corner of the room, and the cat disappeared into the smoke of its own tail. Margaret Johnson was here to see everything was good, and the cat was quite clearly her puckrel. 'Hurry, my daughter!'

By the Dark Prince himself, she had to be quick. There wasn't a house in Bishopsgate, and possibly not in all London, where the bedrooms were higher above ground than the head of a tall man. So young Henry, lounging skyward behind her busy Maria, would already have his eyes above the floorboards in the anteroom. But she had her mother's help, and she had it without asking. She felt bold and slightly mad. She'd been successful in love once today, and the sundial in the yard was scarcely gone the forenoon. And the old witch was all about her, like a bat trapped in her hair.

What young Henry saw, once he'd recovered a little breath – and Maria was a delicate woman to follow after, as agreeable on the nose as an under-ripe costard or a bunch of spring flowers – what he saw was Emilia seated far back on a curtained bed. She did not loll or display. He saw nothing of a leg. She sat tall and upright like the Queen on her throne. Indeed, with her curtains all above her, she might well have been painted by Master Nicholas Hilliard or Marcus Gheeraerts. Henry was an authority on these matters, so it struck him that only Hilliard could have caught that saucy look of hers. There was no need to search the composition for symbols of virginity, whether riddling sieve or fan, because everything he knew about the lady told him there could be none.

Explaining why he'd come to her court was something of a difficulty for him. Explaining the matter to himself was hard enough. He solved his lack of words by bowing very low, thus establishing himself as her servant.

'Henry,' she said. 'My young lord.' She was only a year older than he was, but her voice had a depth to it even more pleasing than a boy's, and infinitely more disturbing than a choir of monks at pricksong. 'How well you keep your promise to your friend.' She moved swiftly down the bed, coming towards him in an impossibly disjointed slither as unnatural as an uncoiling serpent, and with every darting fold of herself full of the same surprises, revealing all of herself as she did so. Here were her legs, darting all about, one arm falling out of her gown, and – by sweet Saint Charity! – were these her breasts, like a tumbling

139

heap of apples? Surely she only had two, but even one was a shock, they were rolling this way and that, and, Heavens, they kept on coming to him!

The young earl was bemused enough already, what with his thoughts of painters, and women, and serpents, and his recent encounter with Master Marlowe. To his shock he found that the lady, having got up to him and all around him, drew him with her on to her throne. Which was a bed. Drew him on to and into her bed.

She threw herself upon him as directly as Master Marlowe had, with the promise of a poem in one hand and the rest of life in the other. He hadn't had time to mention this to Will, only the poem which was shared ground. He didn't see how he could speak frankly about Christopher Marlowe to anyone. For a man to point his prick at a man – for God and Jesus on His Cross, it was a damned vile accusation, goats and monkeys it was! By Saint Gil, to see the nave's *Punchinello Pulcino* staring eye to eye with him across a writing tablet without even so much as its cap on! He wanted to be sick again, without all this childish flurry on the bed, as so often with his mother. *Phaugh!*

The fact was he did not want that vileness, or any carnal contact, not with anyone of any sex whatsoever, not even a nursery wrestling match. Praise all the Saints in Heaven, his Will was not like that. They could be like lambs in the spring pastures, they could frisk and quaff, but there would never be that. Boys, of course. He had clung to boys in his time, principally when he was a boy himself. But Master Marlowe was no boy. God's abundance! Nor was Mistress Lanier.

Ah, what a clever lady she was. It was as if the sweet witch divined his deepest fears and perturbations. She had herself quite naked now, and there the thing was, all exposed, only as all the poets agree a man can never see much of it. But it was there, a quaint furry animal hidden between her legs, a lapin or shrew, or some such small deer. She knew, murmuring all about him as she was, how much he was frightened of it. Pleasing little witch – well, she was big really – she was his globe, his universe, so much of her was in his mouth, first one breast then the other, then ... then there was this other thing, this miraculous maze and honeycomb. He was becoming more and more acquainted with the monster, but unlike his encounter with Venus in his Will's poem, there were no dogs to eat his Adonis up, so when he refused to go in she forbore to eat him with it. Instead he heard her laughing, no not laughing, nothing *aloud*, he heard her smiling, and found he'd dribbled all over her fingers, dribbled? No, she was tugging at him freely now, to her great exultation and his very great pleasure. And afterwards, she lay kissing him and sucking breath from him, and generally breathing him up, until he found he wanted it again. She would not let that lower part of herself eat him, but they lay quite naked all afternoon, rubbing bodies together in that vast scented bed of hers that was like a cloud or a Queen's pavilion.

He tried to be sick again, then again, but he couldn't be, nor would his nose dribble or his bile run, even though he was itching all over. So why couldn't he retch? Why dare he not heave and vomit, as he liked to when in difficulty and distress? She had the top of herself in his mouth, that was why. This was a distraction stranger than his own tongue when singing, especially when he found the bottom of himself all undone, and discovered that her fingers were gentler than his own, or any man's else, though he'd feared they'd be horny from the fiddle-strings.

At some moment or other, the window grew dark.

When Maria came in with wine and candles, she found the young earl face down and asleep all over Maria's bed. He was occupying it entirely with outflung legs and arms, as if he couldn't bear to release his hold on any part of it, her mistress included.

Emilia was not there. She was at her day-book and writing desk. Maria stole to her shoulder and read her words with wonder. Her mistress had already taken possession of the young man, and was fixing him in her life with a great spell.

∼

She read, and was frightened to see such words in Emilia's set secretary hand:

Cullions small as walnuts, or peaches a quarter grown, and as furry soft and sensitive to hold, and yielding much more pleasure, at least to the touch . . .

Maria sobbed somewhat at this point. How could there be any pleasure in mortal man? Or was it because her own body had been invaded by immortals that she felt so uneasy: the long dead Marc Anthony with his mouthful of fish, and the loathsome Henry Dingley whose thigh-balls were doubtless without exception, but whose eyeballs – or one of them – hung on his cheek. She read on:

I sudded and soaped and lathered him, till my lord's lupin which had begun all sweetness now became as a rod or light from a clerestory window, and full of as much holy promise. I gazed at this object of joy, while my lord continued in a red-faced mutter and giggle gargle the way such boy-men and even girl-boys will once their small clothes are off and their parts naked.

It was indeed a thing of beauty, slimmer and longer than my Lord Hunsdon's, and not so foreign about the extensions as my husband Lanier's (though to be honest, I have scarcely inspected his. The French fiddler – dare I call him *Viol*ater? – is so damnably prompt to bury it inside me and wriggle it about until it is no more than a shadow of what it was when it entered me unseen).

I know not what to call such a lord's thing, or the thing of such a lord. The Scots have a word, that quondam court poet of theirs calling it a 'Willylily', or 'King William Lily', nowadays known by the lazy English as Willy . . .

By now I had scrubbed and tubbed and rub-a-dub-dubbed this wondrous thing overlong, and before I was aware of its predicament, it began to cough and retch and posset its noble ointment over my hand and in no small part about the tester and ceiling rafters as well.

This was a bad accident, and I do not disguise the fact that just as my lord had a candle, so did I have a sconce

to stand it in, and long could it have glowed there for the illumination of both of us, and my no small profit.
Eheu, fugaces, Postume, Postume
Labuntur anni.

I must wait for another chance tomorrow, for I do not think he will escape myself or my mother at all easily.

TWELVE

So now Emilia Lanier had four lovers, or three lovers and a husband, according to her humour. Sometimes, but only when a melancholy fit fell upon her, and her gall was sickened with black bile, she told herself she only had two lovers and a husband and a grumpy old possessor. Then one of the other two (or four) would entertain her with – or, preferably, *present* her with – something witty and kind; and she would think in large numbers again.

Lovers – and even husbands as she now arranged it – are creatures of the day. If Lanier was inconsiderate enough to be at home at night (and a royal musician and Gentleman-Guardian of Her Majesty's Revels could not often be so – Lord Chamberlain Hunsdon saw to that!) then she kept to her tiring room. It was narrow but comfortable, cabined, cribbed but not confined. But whether she lay there or in her own bed, she had the excellent Maria to keep her back warm. Every gravid woman of substance needs such a muppet and warming-pan to hold close to her back during the Autumn frosts and, if necessary – Cock and Saint Juste forfend, but if *necessary*! – to throw towards her husband should he tear aside the curtains unexpectedly, or be man enough to batter down her door.

The great days of her virginity were upon her now. The golden years were pressing to return. Her child – he could only be a son – her child grew more and more considerable by the hour. As he was considerable, so was he more and more considered.

Her belly, which was nothing more than a ripple beneath her

stomach, became a presence more insistent than her mother, more brutish even than Dingley. Not that she thought of it like that, still less of the child in it. The child, after all, was her own, and therefore a particle of herself.

She did allow herself to thicken a little. And having allowed herself she allowed it to be allowed that she had. Her belly began no bigger than a walnut, or so she told Will, who was experienced in such matters, being a countryman. But now, dare she confess it? Now it was a gourd. She would giggle at melon or any such similarity, and as for pumpkin she would scratch the eyes from the face of any man who suggested it, save for young Southampton who did suggest it indeed. He would lie with his head upon it, and her son – never her stomach, or its varied retorts and cisterns – would rumble in his ear.

Meanwhile her pumpkin, her mulberry tree in its shawl and apron, did keep her lovers at a respectable distance while providing her with a multitude of excuses to have them dance in attendance upon her. Her stomach developed a single need, which she allowed it to express in plurals. Errands. Men must run errands for it and run them quickly.

Henry Wriothesley, the young earl, was the lover who was less kept at bay by her belly than the rest of them. He *had* to return to her. He knew needs must. Although she was a woman, an hour or two in her company and lying close to her mountainous nudity was better than wrestling with a rhyme, and much kinder to the concentration than reading Thomas Nashe or Master Marlowe, both of them being after him for money. She could also bring him to bliss in a more wholehearted manner than those sweaty young monks at Cambridge. Women are accomplished at all forms of worship, and Emilia seemed to regard his cod's-roe and conger as if it were some kind of God, or at least the Tree of Life. God knows how she did whatever she did when she was close to it. She seemed to say prayers to it, with the result that it became full of divine sensations and felt almost everlastingly holy. No priest nor prelate had prayed to it before, but his little pagan did. She would have danced all about if it weren't for the belly on her.

'Oh Will, Will, Will,' he used to exclaim in self-reproach the moment the dusky witch laid a naked hand on his naked self. Then, 'Hang Will!' the second she brought her second hand to bear.

As for that little depth and entrance she hid between thigh and thigh but was ever keen to let him glimpse, it was, all in all, better than a hole in a cockerel's eye socket. He knew. He'd seen plenty of those.

He became more fond of the place the more he allowed himself to become fond of the child that lay beyond it. The young lord loved children: he was pretty much a child himself.

More and more he allowed her to encourage herself to encourage him to enter lightly in. There was no way he could be in there for ever, he reasoned, or imprisoned like a Greek sailor in the cave of the enchantress. The child and presence beyond the gap was his best protection against nightmare. Then once he was doing the thing, once he had done it – and how soon it was over! – he found it much more pleasurable than reading other men's poetry, and so much easier than writing his own. Yes, by Cock, he fell in love with the act. He couldn't, as it happened, wait for her to be free of the child, so he might fit his slim young white body against her slim young dark one. Nothing would eat him. He was confident now.

So what about Will? Damn Will for a little minute – *this* little minute, certainly. Damn him for another half hour, in fact, until Wriothesley was outside and resting on his horse. Will it was who had written about him as the impotent Adonis. The poem was already published and famous. It was dedicated to him. It might as well be dedicated to his codpiece! Everyone was sniggering about his unwilling implement. Everyone except his Emilia and the child who was her witness.

Southampton's mother and his mother's husband – whoever that was now; he couldn't keep up with them – had persuaded the cocky Shakespeare to pen a whole string of sonnets to set him towards jumping three-legged into a suitable woman. What had he just been handed?

147

From fairest creatures we desire increase,
That thereby beauty's rose might never die,
But as the riper should by time decease,
His tender heir might bear his memory.

It was beautiful stuff this. Southampton had read it to Emilia, and she had sworn she could scarcely write better herself. But what came next?

But thou contracted to thine own bright eyes,
Feed'st thy light's flame with self-substantial fuel,
Making a famine where abundance lies,
Thy self thy foe, to thy sweet self too cruel . . .

And, by God, what was this?

Within thine own bud buriest thy content,
And tender churl mak'st waste in niggarding.

Wanking, that's what it was about. Will was accusing him of tossing off. Just as this lovely fat milcher was moaning and bubbling about in his arms and he . . . a plague on you, Will! You should be here keeping me from her!

Emilia! Fairest dark Emilia! Where are your eyes? Closed in momentary bliss. She was thinking . . . who knows what she was thinking, perhaps that this masculine thing, this pike and pigstaff may be a damned ungracious object when there's a man on the end of it . . . but when there's a beautiful young earl?

~

Hunsdon allowed himself to overcome her once more. He did so infrequently, but one evening when he had arranged for Lanier to be away he sent Maria outside and told Lisbet the scullery maid to stay downstairs and advised the man Peter to drink ale in a distant tavern.

As for Emilia's stomach, he paid scant attention to it. If a wench wants to keep a cushion on her belly while she swyves, then let her have her cushion. He had one on his own now he couldn't get to horse so often. A brisk little war, preferably against the Scots or Irish, was what his belly wanted. Somewhere the roads were long and the killing good at the end of them. Rebels would do, but rebels weren't far enough away to get his belly down.

'You're fat, my lord.'

'Not as fat as you are. My implement's an inch or two short of being a halberd, I grant you. But it can still make its point on a level bed, even when I'm knocking my spike and spiggot into a great tun like yours.'

'You're a poet, Lord Harry.'

'Not me, you black whore. No need for me to be. I've bought you one of those already.'

The old man was ageing very rapidly during the autumn of 1592. There is nothing like the acquisition of a young lover to make an old and unwanted one appear increasingly ancient. At times, indeed, her body's geriatric intruder used to seem quite dead, in spite of his brutish gruntings and thrustings, both of which she strove to ignore while concentrating her mind on the Topmost Triangulum of the *Kabbala*, then her memories of *The Divine Pomander of Hermes Trismegistus*, recently sent to her by Doctor John Dee, still her admirer.

'There's a dreary look in your eye,' the Lord Chamberlain gasped, at his sticky end. 'I can still transport you, my squealing puppet.'

'Yes, my old poet.' Her repetition was becoming tiresome, even to her.

'You could still be rid of your encumbrance and come back to me.'

'My lord I am a married woman.'

'A husband is less than a tooth. I can have him drawn tonight, or send him abroad in a bottle. I did not speak of Master Lanier.' He dealt her stomach a fat smack of affection, and was irritated to feel the child kick back at him. 'I speak of this object.' He handled the dancing brat again.

'My child is almost born, Lord Harry. I could not be rid of it

149

even when it was no more than a wicked thought in that creased old skull of yours.'

'The babe is on its gallows tree,' he said shortly. 'When he drops you could strangle it in that cord they all wear. You could bear him dead. I know of a middlewoman with a handy tongue to certify so. She'll declare in your favour, and a couple of golden angels will buy her silence thereafter.'

She gathered her belly in front of herself and lifted it from her bed, since her old despoiler showed no signs of quitting it. 'No mere man planted this child in me,' she said firmly. 'You talk of angels, my lord, and similar nuggets of gold. Well, I met an angel of the fiery sort. It was such a one told me I was gravid. He told me my babe would be a boy and God's true heir.'

The Lord Chamberlain rose and dressed himself quickly. She had a look in her eyes that he'd encountered before, particularly among clanswomen when he'd set about drawing and quartering their husbands – aye, and cindering their bowels on a bonfire. It's the wild mad look that comes over the faces of deranged females before they run at you with a knife.

~

Will it was who was her kindest lover. After fitting his body gently to hers a few more times out of politeness, he knew the time had come to wait for her recovery. Soon her child would be born, and she would no longer be a circumference but a woman with whom he could reinvent geometries. Meanwhile, he was content to leave her contentment unruffled and run little errands for her, fetching flowers and fruit from all about; buying her a tiny locket in Silver Street so she could carry his picture next to her heart, but no likeness was ever painted, and who knows what a woman wears near her heart? Once he even rode into Kent for her, a full league away and on pathways paved with footpads, but he rode there just the same to fetch her a bag of fresh apples. That was poetry indeed.

Less to her fancy was his *Venus and Adonis*, now a printed book, and reprinted too. He gave her the poem and read it to her several times while she slept. It affected her dreams with its sweaty huffing and puffing and not-quite-buffing, then the attempts of that lard-thighed Venus to have her little earl for her own! The sound of the verses was very unpleasant. It was like listening to lovers on a noisy floor. And when that wild pig stuck its thing into Southampton's side it was more than she could bear.

Will's sonnets were much more to her liking. He read her a dozen or so of the ones he was writing at the insistence of the young earl's mother. Sonnets were preferable to *Venus and Adonis*, none of them lasting longer than a yawn. Their message nearly brought her a megrim on, or a miscarriage, even so. The noble lady wanted Will to persuade her son to marry some fertile cow of a countess. And, as if that wasn't bad enough, Will kept on stuffing the things with family jokes, like lights into a dish of tripe. Emilia didn't want to find her name was in one of them, and being fingered around by the young man's family and friends.

Meanwhile, he made amends by putting her (and his presumptuous self, of course) into a play to be given at Court and before the Queen's own Majesty, whatever that was. She hoped to act in it, but he reminded her she couldn't, being pregnant, though very like a boy in all ways else. *Love's Labour's Lost* it was called. No one could quarrel with the title!

Sweet Will. He would lie close to her, yet not with her, and certainly not upon her. He asked for nothing save that she should hear him recite. What woman could ask for more – save that he should shut up, and ride into Kent for apples?

~

Master Alphonso (as she preferred to spell it), Master Alfonso (as he himself often did), the Lanier who was her legal possessor (in the sight of the Christian God), was almost as much trouble in his way as old Lord Hunsdon in his.

For a start, he was the man in her house. For a finish, which came not very far behind the commencement of this inventory, the man he was was French. Such a one was not markedly different from an Englishman, possessing a like number of arms and legs and similar attributes, but he was more imaginative, passionate, demanding and argumentative. When he was denied these functions, as he always would be by a woman of character, he could become downright quarrelsome, especially when drunk on Lord Hunsdon's wine, which he consumed of jealous necessity, having so far failed to provide any of his own.

Frenchmen are in the main better grounded in Euclid and such like navigational rubbish than Englishmen. Their minds move in straight lines. They know the fastest way round a triangle, especially an amorous one. Nowadays, and nowanights especially, Alfonso Lanier did not bother to become imaginative, passionate, demanding or argumentative. Why waste time being downright quarrelsome when his energies were better spent on getting drunk? Sometimes Emilia did not even know he was in the house until she heard cups break in the kitchen, and maids giggle, and benches fall. She had this quarrel with Euclid, which she would one day explore in a letter to Doctor Dee. How was it that the famous Greek mathematician and philosopher could help a man proceed in straight lines – a difficult enough feat once one accepted what was commonly propounded, namely that the world was bent if not completely circular – how was it Euclidean man could walk in a straight line while not being able to remain on his own two feet while he did so?

Tonight was no exception to this eternal theorem. She heard liquid fall, pots break and oaths rise, and proceeded downstairs with all the show of breathless dignity that the child behind her belly button made prudent and inevitable.

Her kitchen resembled a potter's shed after the cats have been locked in. There were very few pots, but shards in abundance.

Drink never dealt gently with the Frenchman. When he was last at home, the wine had been brutal with him. Tonight, it was worse. The fume held total sway.

Emilia was reluctant to depose it. Her husband was flourishing a naked sword all over the kitchen and halfway across the parlour whenever the intervening doorway was not too narrow for him, slight little foreigner though he was. It wasn't one of those slim blades with baskets on the hilt such as gentlemen wear, or lords or coystrils in the ale house. It was a broad two-edged hacker, suitable for wood-chopping or bone-paring.

'*Master* Lanier!'

No use to call. He had his shoulder and sword-arm jammed into the parlour again. The blade winnowed the air with a flurry of sound like a windmill in a storm, or the wings of a giant bird. He fell in after it, and was almost caught up inside its breathless gyrations. Alive, just, and uncut, miraculously, he menaced her settles and cushions. Had her lovers been there he would have disembowelled them. If he could see them.

'*Master* Lanier, I say again.'

'"Captain", if you please madame.' He struggled to speak, spoke, and sobered appreciably once he found he had words that would obey him and a listener to them in consequence. 'Yes, I am to be a soldier now. The Lord Chamberlain has ordered me to follow on ahead of him to Ireland. As to the Earl of Southampton – you know, that young girl with the forelock? – he wants to send me even further.'

Emilia felt a warm surge of affection for the two men who were using their power to effect such a kindness on her behalf. Equally, she was a married woman and shortly to be a mother. She felt a lump in her throat, several lumps. Tears burst from her eyes. Her husband was being taken away from her. Her child wasn't his, any more than Mary's was Joseph's. Yet wouldn't Mary have wept if the old carpenter had been sent into Sumaria at such a time?

'My poor, brave husband. Isn't monsieur brave?'

'Captain, as I say.' He eyed the assembled servants, here as always to grin at him drunk, and wiped his blade very carefully on Peter's shirt before trying to unpick Maria's placket with it. It lacked enough point to be a stitch-hook, and he soon grew tired of this game, tried to sheathe his sword, missed, thought better of it and tossed the weapon to the floor. He was tired of being a soldier. A better game began to suggest itself to him.

Emilia always did her best to improve and ornament her household, especially now she had so many noblemen to her door and even inside. So it was that Lisbet the scullery girl had been encouraged to clean herself at the yard pump, including her hair and latterly her clothes. She chose this moment to come in with a change of candles.

She was revealed to be a comely young woman of fifteen or sixteen summers with a slim waist and swellings above and below. Some of these manifested a very brave vibration indeed, and dropped very pretty odours all about. She smelled partly of her own freshness – an excellent thing in woman – and partly of soap. Her face was admirably frank now she could see out of it, too.

Master Lanier had known his wife and tried her maid. Now he had been promoted he glimpsed further horizons. 'There are no personal servants in this house,' he observed. He stooped and picked up his sword as if to emphasise the point. 'No servants appropriate to a Gentleman of the Queen's Revels.'

'No, husband. We have none of that sort. Not until the Gentleman himself provides us with some.'

'Well, the almanac stands nigh on winter, and I have need of a lass with a loose back to soak my feet for me before the frosts come on. Send up that Lisbet, will you?'

'To soak your feet, husband?'

'We soldiering men have a great fear of chilblains.'

Never speak to a pregnant woman of washing. Nothing good will ever come of it. There and then in the kitchen, what with the shouting and the flourishing and the violent alarms, Emilia's waters broke.

THIRTEEN

~

What does a woman think about when her waters burst, her pains come on, she's never done this before, and she's surrounded by sword-waving drunks, a giggling Peter, and callow girls?

She thinks, albeit briefly, of death. Especially if the issue is to be, was, is about to be or could be regarded as a Tudor.

The Tudors were a doom-laden crew. Men who fussed with them died on the block. So did several of their women, including Lord Hunsdon's Aunt Anne, his cousin Elizabeth's mother. She fussed with the late King too hard and too often, so he was obliged to have the axeman separate her from his heart. God and Saint Nick, how poor Emilia's own heart panged! And her belly and lower back!

When they escaped the block the females died in childbed, but that was woman's lot anyway. It happened among the Howards, the Riches, the Sidneys and innumerable other wenches that History is much too selective to recognize. Any husband with half a shot in him could love his wife to death in no time at all. This dulled the First Elizabeth's appetite for marriage, and infected her poets with their endless thirst for variety.

All of these thoughts rushed into Emilia's mind, firstly in her kitchen then upstairs on her bed, where she waited for her night of anguish attended only by Maria and Lisbet and a hastily summoned midwife who reminded her of Malk – or was it Bess? – and who did things just as disagreeable.

In fact the birth was easy. Her son might be a Tudor but he flowed swiftly and joyously into the world. This was because he knew from their sighings, their whisperings, their chantings and chucklings, as well as their sleep-disturbing tappings on his carnal carapace, that he had any number of happy uncles who were eager to welcome him there. He gazed up into their faces and found he knew some of them better than well. These were the ones who had come a considerable way to meet him during the past few months.

~

A baptism was supposed to be a private affair, she thought, but in truth the better half of the world was there in St Botolph's, Bishopsgate. She might have been banished, but by admitting a gentleman or two to her bedchamber, plus a pair of noblemen, she was able to establish a court wherever she was. She was queen at her royal child's christening.

At the front of the church stood her own family and Captain Alphonso's, all intermingled. Her own family consisted of her sister Angela Holland and Joseph, her husband. The Laniers were a larger tribe, having flocked all together from Rouen to fasten on her husband's good fortune in becoming a royal musician. Innocent Lanier was Alphonso's only brother, but he was breeding so fast he was clearly hoping to become a widower as soon as possible. There were sisters Lanier everywhere, some of them with husbands. And children. Meanwhile, she clung to her husband, having scarcely got her legs together from childbearing, and scarcely able to stand upright. She mightn't have the Captain for much longer, not now he was going soldiering.

Lord Hunsdon spoke to them both, and the babe, from behind their backs. 'Too public a crowd,' he said. 'I expected something far more privy and close.' His hand brushed Lanier's ear, and startled the babe, all of whose early hours had been peaceful. 'Who told you to invite my fiddlers and the prettier portion of Her Majesty's court?'

Captain Lanier was in a rage at this, or – being French –

had taken more English ale than was good for his head. 'My lord,' he fumed. '*This* [or perhaps] *Ziss* is intolerable! Goats and monkeys!'

The priest silenced him by taking hold of the babe, who obliged them all by howling, then stopping on the instant. Neither Frenchmen nor babes cry goat to the Lord Chamberlain, not if they wish to retain their warrant, their royal commission, their freedom and sometimes their lives. Only Emilia smiled. Her keeper could widow her as soon as he liked, for all she cared.

'Too public a crowd, as I say.' He motioned the priest to stop stroking the babe's foreskin, a pretty enough mummery and sound-swaddle when practised by its mother, midwife or nurse, all of whom have need of their intervals of silence, but to his thinking unseemly in a man. 'Look who's behind us, will you? One of them's an epicene ninny-nanny, and if that's not bad enough, Lord Nanny has brought his friend.' Lord Hunsdon raised his voice. It was never happy at a growl, still less a whisper. 'And his friend is a spy and a fart-arsing bumboy. Shagspeare' – he sank his voice with an effort – 'Shagspeare I don't mind, so long as I don't have to be reminded of him.' Still muttering, he receded until he'd put a pillar or two between himself and anyone who might notice him. His retainers filled the church, picking their teeth or standing with their arms folded as such men do. Others of them, almost as many as the army of guardians he'd mustered to protect his cousin Elizabeth on her way to address her troops at Tilbury, stood outside holding horses in bunches of four, two to each hand as the fashion was, while their steeds did their best, as they always do, to lift the graveyard a little closer to the sun, bringing much needed nourishment as it happened to the mortal resting places of Emilia's parents, Margaret Johnson and Baptista Bassano, whose spirits hovered elsewhere, be it high or low.

Emilia was delirious with happiness at her keeper Hunsdon's words. So her young earl was there. But he'd brought a friend! Her heart plunged at once into the chalice of black bile that so easily follows upon birth. A friend! Turning coyly she saw Wriothesley clinging to – and laughing with – Christopher

Marlowe. *Christopher Marlowe!* He was a famous poet, even though her Will was overtaking him by leaps and bounds, and famous as a lover of men, though whether he did it to men as Lord Hunsdon suggested, or men did it to him, was a frequent topic of controversy and not to be pursued at a family time like this and among the stink of horses. Oh, black black bile! Oh, bitter cup! Melancholy indeed.

Her woes worsened. Master Marlowe said something to make Henry Wriothesley giggle. She didn't like to hear the young earl giggle. In so young a man it sounded like a cross between the whinny of a ticklish mare and a treble viol. She didn't like to hear it at all.

Still less did she wish to contemplate whatever it was Master Marlowe might have said to prompt such a note – vile old man of nearly thirty that he was! If it proved to be anything bad she might need Dingley's help, or even her mother's, to remove the ageing poet from her young lord's life.

Then the babe smiled at her, and she rather than her husband named it Henry after its father and grandfather. Henry Lanier, of course, Henri even. What else was she married for?

And what are christenings for, save to celebrate arrivals and contemplate departures? Deaths and Entrances, as somebody said or would doubtless say.

~

There was a brief feast a little lower down Bishopsgate to follow. Well, not so much a feast as a time when the canakins were encouraged to clink, though not among maids nor women in milk.

Master Shakespeare was not invited to this. How could he be? He was excellent company, in public and private, but how could he be? As for the young earl, he simply dared not present himself. That is, Emilia did not dare encourage the young man to present himself. He was *her* secret, the only secret she kept from everyone except the servants of her house.

Hunsdon did not allow Master now-known-as Captain Lanier to stay long either. The fellow was drinking too much of his wine and becoming proprietorial at every wink and nod, as if a man can presume to own a woman who is clearly owned by the Lord Chamberlain, whatever constraints may now have been marked on her title deed. Until the Captain was wafted abroad, until the flower of his genius was fairly planted in the shifting meadows of the ocean, he had a deal of business to attend to in the fiddlers' gallery at Whitehall; the Lord Chamberlain saw to that. And soon the Queen would be in Richmond, a long half day away up-river, then at Hatfield, Woodstock, or wherever he might suggest Her Majesty would be safe.

So the Captain received his marching orders, and Lord Chamberlain Hunsdon stormed upstairs to itemize the cushions and bed hangings, as was his wont.

Emilia glanced towards Maria, handed her the child, and followed him up. She needed to protect her magical places, and see he did not peep into her day-book.

He inspected her bed, moodily. 'That's a fool name to give him!'

'A fool name, but not a fool's name!'

'There you flatter me, mistress.'

'*You*, sir? Heavens above, sir, I did not name him after you. I named him after that great King Henry. Lord, sir, *no* need to strike me. I merely named the child after your uncle.'

'My *uncle*, yes, lady, and by *marriage*. My uncle, and no nearer to this child in blood than that!'

'Why should I think he'd be close in blood to anything of mine, sir? Lord, my Lord Hunsdon, I do now *conceive* you, as once before. This child is not yours, sir.' She began to laugh. 'What! My poor sweet babe Henry a twig of so mighty a tree? No, sir. Did I not tell you?' She had twisted this blade once, but the wound was ready for a further turn. 'Why, the very day I was married to my sweet Alphonso, my poor belly bled and emptied itself of every last reminder of you. It says much for the discretion of your kicking, sir, that I was quit of this your entire lineage.' She savoured his look. Even a strong man can be hurt by a woman on so intimate a matter, even when he knows she is telling him a lie. 'Why, sir, my *lord*, you must

159

never think this child is related to anyone you fancy yourself related to.'

'Lady, if this is so, the babe I saw baptised had only been in you a handful of weeks before it came gushing forth.'

'It is in all ways a miracle, my lord.'

'Madame, I take it we may resume?'

'Sir, I'm an honest woman, a married woman. I'm no *bona roba*, no *fornicatrix* or whatever you take me for. Besides, my lord, I do revere and most closely *dote* upon my Alfonso, even to the point of fondness. What a lover you found me, sir, and not merely a husband, but a highly accomplished gentleman in the lute and shawm.'

'*Silence*, madame.'

'I thought you and I were wont to have *times*, sir, but believe me they were but schoolboy practice, mere grunting in the tilt-yard compared with what I get up to with that Captain Alphonso you so kindly provided for me.' She found the Lord Chamberlain a little fresh wine. He could not tell if she was lying or not now, and well she knew it. 'He can pleasure me a whole winter bedtime sir, from dusk to cockcrow, so ardent is he. Aye, sir, a whole night long, then another night added to it end to end.'

'Mistress Lanier,' he grunted, 'I'll have you as I want you.' His mind went rushing beyond rhetoric in its pain, but he was never the man to be deflected by mere words.

'Lord, my Lord Harry! Lord and Lawks a' Mercy! You must not be so fierce with me, nor be angry at the comparison. Nay, strike me not, sir.' She ducked with all the skill of her long practice, but she could only move her head. The rest of her was being handled and knelt upon. She found herself fixed by his customary impetuosity. 'I mean you no discourtesy, in bed or out of it. I owe you much, sir. You are a mighty man, my lord, for one so advanced in years.'

'As I want you, mistress, so shall I have you.'

'Then I'll petition to your cousin the Queen, Harry. Is it a rape you think you'll make upon me? Fie, my lord, fie! I'm but recently birthed of a child, and not yet churched!'

He had her clothes about her neck by now, and his own clouts unfastened. 'No rape, mistress. You belong to me. As for that sweetness between your legs – hear how I flatter! – as for that little inglenook and chimney, as I am a man of tact and discretion, so shall I sweep it properly for you in your fiddler's absence.'

Emilia was a woman of many stratagems. She nodded eagerly at Lord Hunsdon's every word, then as an afterthought gazed towards his naked sinews, and let her gaze sink coyly a little lower.

Her coyness, her fear, her quiescence had always been powerful aphrodisiacs. She could calculate them to a fraction of a wink. So it was now.

As his resolve stiffened, so did she allow a smile to stray across her lips. Then she gave a sidelong glance at what his pride had planted for him, and began to giggle at it.

He adjusted his grip upon her. His pomp was considerable because of its several weeks of deprivation, but it did not enjoy what it heard next.

'Lor, sir! God-a-Cock, my lord! What do you call *that*?' She tittered then snorted with mirth, lost all control of herself and laughed aloud. She squirmed and wriggled with an amusement close to downright hysterics, and for far more time than any man in his advanced situation could continue to find convenient, any man of heart and passion that was.

His pomp was not at all meagre, not to start with, but it couldn't stand being laughed at, it couldn't stand it or stand at all.

She stopped herself long enough to be saddened by the fact, to express compassion even, and concern. Then she was laughing again. 'Why!' she trilled. 'Compared with Lanier's 'tis but a daisy stalk!'

~

Christopher Marlowe was a spy. Or, as the Lord Chamberlain put it, a spy abroad and a damned pillow-sneak and gossip at home. A pity the fellow had been at his bastard's baptism.

Lord Hunsdon had some experience of parenthood. He knew

it was never easy. A man tried to behave well, but the child never thanked him for being born. As for mothers, they were rarely appreciative, whatever he showed them in the way of affection and largesse.

Just who had Marlowe been speaking to? Was it Marlowe himself who'd spread the gossip, or that bitchy Southampton, his quean? And why had Emilia invited such people? Why invite sodomizers and catamites to a christening? It seemed like a plot, but he could find no sense in it. They were dangerous things, women, worse than bear-traps, and not just in bed. Even their friends were dangerous. If a man is to have a woman, he should have one without friends.

These thoughts did not come to the Lord Chamberlain at all easily. For several days now he had them all the time, and carefully assembled, but he had to be cautious when he was summoned to appear before the Queen, as he was now. He had to keep his wits about him and his ears pricked. Yet almost the first word she spoke brought his old fears about him like so many ghosts.

'Cousin Henry, there used to be a dark young woman who would sometimes play before us, and otherwise amuse us. Once we tried a pair of virginals together in the Queen's Gallery, she and I, and sweet notes we made.'

'You speak of one Bassano, Majesty. Emilia Bassano.' He wished she'd never been born.

'I speak of her whereabouts. Her name is well known to us already.'

'She keeps to a house in Bishopsgate. She was with child. Now she is without child, in that her lying-in is over, and her delivery safe.'

'We did hear and fear as much, cos. Rumour has an ugly mouth, methinks, and altogether too brutish for our ear.' The Queen was chewing an apple, one of her favourite Hestons, and the crunch of it in her mouth, her scrutinizing of it, her biting, gave the inquisition a peculiar resonance.

'Indeed, cousin Elizabeth.'

'You do own a house in Bishopsgate, methinks?'

'In Bishopsgate, in Blackfriars else, and in Holborn.'

'And a castle or six? We trust you own no part in this young woman's condition?'

'She is a married woman, cousin, married some several months to Alfonso Lanier, one of the chief architects of your Majesty's revels. You know Master Lanier – he's a brisk upstanding music master of Your Majesty's own household.'

'He'll have needed to be brisk, by all we hear. Since it can only be last Tuesday he first nodded to the woman.'

'Your Majesty jests with me.'

'If I jest, it is only by a sennight or so. Well, you are prudent, cousin. As you are loyal.'

'Cousin Elizabeth.' He knelt and kissed the hand she held out to him. So the worst was over. The skin on her fingers was ageing now, oiled and frog-like. 'They are but jesters and fiddlers. Why do we talk of them?'

'Foreigners, Cousin Harry. My God, how these serpents breed. You only have to place two of them in the same dunghill, and they are about it and each other like a pair of vipers. They do so fawn and dribble and writhe about.' She peered at him intently, then asked sharply, 'My speech pains you cousin?'

'No, Majesty, but it pains me to kneel overlong, no matter that kneeling be my station. I have bone-ague, as is audible, and a gout your Majesty's ears have heard make me cry aloud even in privy sessions.'

'We are not so young as we were, cousin. Nor so foolish.'

'No, Majesty. Nor so foolish. I am afflicted by another disease I dare scarcely mention, cousin Elizabeth. It keeps me from concupiscence, as do my old joints.'

'Sins of the fathers, Harry. It is fortunate I do not suffer it.'

'Most fortunate.'

'We must hope the child is also free. The child of the French fiddler, if you follow me.'

'They're a dissolute race, though he's an honest fellow.'

'You must rest your knees, Cousin Harry. Rise and rest your joints. Praise God you are beyond tiring them with one exercise we could name.'

'Praise God, madam.'

Lord Hunsdon took care to rise painfully, though he wasn't so crass as to hold himself by the back or squeeze his kidneys.

She eyed him kindly. It had been a dangerous episode, but they'd both made their points.

FOURTEEN

The Lord Chamberlain had a great need to see this Mistress Lanier the Queen had asked so many questions about. It was almost as great as his want to see Emilia herself, his own venereal witch who was waisted in a matron's girdle and manacled in another man's wedding ring.

Hunsdon rarely had need to put his politics before his prick, because his politics were known to be honest. But he couldn't let his prick do his thinking for him, not this time.

He dare not rush. Emilia Bassano was known to have been his possession, a toy he was prepared to share with Her Majesty's Court, his doll that could recite and play music, dance and sing. All that was changed. She was a mother now, and something of a woman. She belonged to Lanier, and the child could be presumed to be the Frenchman's only if Harry of Hunsdon stayed prudent. Otherwise the babe would become a ward in a dungeon, and his own life forfeit. How he fumed.

For the Queen's cousin to go riding off to Bishopsgate immediately after so painful an audience would be crass imbecility. So would it be to float or take a chair. He must wait his time. The world knew she was his plaything. He would be allowed to stray in her direction, but not with the urgency of a man involved in a plot. He must not appear to proceed anxiously. He dare not rush.

So he waited a day. He waited two. He questioned people loudly at Court about Captain Lanier's whereabouts. Then he

165

did not steal away into the night. He put his legs into clean stockings and chose himself a gaudy cloak. Then he splashed his ears and his beard with scented water like a man who means to fornicate.

~

Mistress Lanier did not mean to fornicate. It was her evening for asking favours. A woman may expect well of any favour she asks from a man when she's been kind to him. Most women know this universal truth almost from birth, and arrange their bedtimes accordingly.

A woman of spunk and spirit will sometimes go about matters another way. She will wait till she has humiliated a man completely, then pitch her demands sky high. The poor wretch will make haste to obey her, simply to show there is at least something he can do aright.

Emilia Lanier was such a one. Hardship had taught her to be a woman of spunk and spirit. 'My Lord Hunsdon,' she began – she led him towards her parlour rather than up her stairs, lest he grow dizzy at their height or out of breath from ascending – 'Harry, my love, I would ask you to unfasten yourself a little and be ready for me.' She smiled invitingly as he'd taught her to smile, and as tenderly as his nurse and mother. 'However, my lord and love, we must be mindful of the difficulty you found yourself in when you last sought to encounter me before my churching.'

'Mistress Emilia!' He made to stand up, then decided to wait his time. He knew more ways to set a horn on his little salamander than a whore could dream of. For the time being, there was his audience with the Queen to discuss.

'No, my love. We must consider the entire man, not just his ironing stick. There's more to a walk in the forest than picking roses, Lord Harry. When I see the ardour in those old eyes of yours, I only pray you are still able to see out of them as well as I peep in.' She approached him, but only briefly, to wipe his forehead as if to unblear his gaze. 'We must remember your heart has been beating more years almost than you have grey hairs on your head – if that's a possibility in nature – or pearls on your codpiece!'

Then, perhaps after the cat came into the room, perhaps just before, he raised his fist deliberately and struck her. It was a trick a bawd had taught him, a device every whore knows. He struck her again. He had no need of the lesson. Nor had she. Brutal men and some women already know it in their blood.

Her lip bled a little. He had snagged his hand on her tooth. He sucked his knuckle before saying, 'We can continue this discourse above, if you prefer, mistress.' He was, all in all, a brutal man, as she had reason to know, yet he was delicate enough to do his worse deeds in private.

'Above, my lord? Why above?' She did not intend to be one of the women who thrived on this sort of treatment. He struck her again, and she noticed the cat. It was not black. It was not her mother's puckrel and mim. It was Meldew, her principle rat-catcher. The animal froze in fear, the way they do, gathered itself and sprang back towards the doorway.

She rose swiftly to follow it. 'Above then, my lord.' Upstairs she could hope Margaret Johnson's cat would manifest itself and remind Lord Hunsdon of his former humiliation. Upstairs she could summon Dingley and Marc Anthony, and have the old wretch strangled in a towel, or spirited away and drowned in the Fleet sewer.

'Nay,' he said. 'It is late for above. You had your interval to choose above. Now we are below. 'Tis a fine cloth that gowns you, Emilia. A fine cloth with shrewd stitching.'

The listeners in the kitchen heard it tear long and slow like a sail rippling open on the first wind. There was no door to close.

'My lord, it is a Toulouse you yourself bought for me, though the stitching is by Maria.'

'Maria shall be your spider again. She must spin you a new web.' He continued to rend her clothes till she was quite naked. It takes a strong hand to split cloth.

'Please, my lord. It is time to put little Henry to my breast.'

'Time to put old Henry there you mean. He'll put himself to your breast – and your belly button to follow. I'll not be driven from your bottom grass by an infant.'

He eyed her, head to toe. Motherhood had changed her meat somewhat. Her breasts were finer and fuller. The blood was like a little ruby in her mouth-corner.

There was no denying the Lord Chamberlain this time, she could tell that. Either he had not drunk enough to disappoint himself, or he had drunk too much. 'The kitchen, Harry,' she gasped. 'My people are in the kitchen.'

'Then it's my backside they'll see. If we had mirrors you could confirm 'tis a noble vista they'll gaze upon.'

Later, a long hour later, she had to creep naked upstairs, with the Lord Chamberlain gripping fast to her hand. They were both out of breath, but gossips had told her that childbearing is bad for the wind.

She found that Maria had laid an underskirt ready on her bed, and hung a gown on the wire frame of herself. She began to dress.

'I'd have sported your oak, mistress. But your parlour has no door to close. You had best remember that, if you wish to be cheeky among your cushions again.'

'Aye, my lord. I'll remember.'

'Old men are impatient, lady. When they would jump, they had best jump at once.'

'Aye, my good lord.'

'Know better than to use my own stick to beat me with another time. I can horn myself anytime I choose to be ungentle with you. You do not enjoy that, I think.'

She did not answer.

'You've come to behave like a callet in a trugging house, since I married you off. These tricks will not do, Emilia!'

She must remember how the evening began. It began with her being a woman of spunk and spirit, determined to gain favours. The Lord Chamberlain had arranged her bedtime instead, but she must hold to her ambition even so.

Even when he said, 'If you've got yourself with child because of our little spurring hop just now, do not look to me to find you a second husband, mistress.'

~

She could not presume to plait his beard. He wore it too short. Sometimes he liked her to finger it a little, search it for knots. This evening he seemed irritated at her touch. She used to twist his eyebrows once. They were as bushy with old age, and grew long as any archbishop's. She saw he'd had them plucked. Her only benefactor and principal keeper was a changed man. She must not let herself be worried by the unexpected.

'My lord,' she began, easing herself over him.

'The Queen has had intelligence of the birth of your son. Her Majesty will not be beguiled by your falsehood of an immaculate conception, mistress. Tell your husband to guard his tongue.'

'Guard it? Why, my lord, should he not boast of it?'

'The Queen is a Tudor, Emilia. They can all count. I have never known a family so brisk with coin. Do not suppose they will be any less sure with months and days.'

'It is the Frenchman's child, Lord Harry. He will say it is even on the rack. He will say so because he is married to me. He has more honour to his little finger than you may find in the entire company of saints.'

'You're a witch, Emilia. Do not whisper sanctity to me.'

'Lanier has got enough honour in him to stuff a pie shop, my lord and love.' She kissed him, an act made slightly more bearable to her by the perfume in his beard. She still dare not approach his ears. They reminded her of a badger-warren, and with something of the same smell. 'Worry no more, my lord. Should Her Majesty's spies ever put me to the question, I will confess enough to protect your dignity, but profess nothing to endanger your life. Nor my child's.'

Yes, he could trust her to hold her tongue. He was ready for love again, but decided against spoiling his purse by the price of a second gown.

~

169

So she was dressed, and arrayed moreover in some of her best pendants and hair-studs, all of them provided by the Lord Chamberlain. He always enjoyed seeing her hang herself with his little bits of finery.

She clapped her hands and called for some more wine. The evening had begun with her needing to be explicit about certain matters near to her heart. She had not been able to humiliate the old brute, but she'd afforded him a deal of pleasure, after his fashion and according to his whim. As he had taken, now must he give.

'Now I am a married woman, my lord . . .'

He snorted at this, less from pain than amusement.

'Now my child is out and my belly flat from your frequent occupancy . . .'

He still wore a look, and she knew it well for what it was. It was the look of a man who knows he is being flattered for a purpose.

'Why do not you reintroduce me at Court, good my lord?'

He smiled at her. He smiled with her. He seized her hand and stroked her arm a little. This did nothing to gladden her spirits or quicken her desire. His skin was too old for that. It was like having a chicken perch there, and shuffle between wrist and elbow.

Meanwhile, he said nothing.

'Now that I have a husband, Lord Harry . . . Harry?'

'A husband – there you have it, my love. If I could introduce you with your husband. He to make music beside you, perhaps?'

She grimaced at that.

'Or to play a few soft notes while you gather what you endite?' His voice had sunk to a purr now. She could not move her arm. The cockerel slept on his perch.

'Yes, my love. I must produce you with Lanier. I must, and as I will, so shall it be Her Majesty's pleasure.'

She would have kissed him again, and meant it if the grip on her arm weren't so strong. 'So when the Captain returns from abroad . . . whenever that may be, though I fear that will be long . . .'

Desire was returning for a better reason now. Victory and triumph it was called. He had outmanoeuvred the enemy: now he was among their women. 'Take a care, Emilia. I'd not have you damage your apparel.'

If she took long enough undressing . . .

'Leave the gems at your ear. They'll give me something to chew on.'

There was no deflecting the old goat now. They gave him something to chew on.

A woman who cannot have what she desires still needs something to want. 'Master Shakespeare,' she said, as soon as Lord Hunsdon had finished his closest grunting and seemed ready to grunt again. 'Could you not do something for Master Shakespeare? Advance him, I mean?'

'He's advanced enough already.' He shifted himself a little and, yes, my Lord Hunsdon was once more advanced in no small fashion himself. 'He fishes unasked in my favourite pond.'

Some expressions are too hideous for virtue to contemplate. She let the current occupier of her flesh contemplate that fact by himself.

What struck him, after a due interval of pleasure, was that Master Shakespeare might come to bear on his relationship with his cousin the Queen. A woman with a husband was only a problem halved. But a woman with a husband and a lover was a problem disappeared. And the agreeable thing about Shagspeare – he still thought of him as the world did – the agreeable thing about Shagspeare was his humility. He wasn't some upstart fiddle-faddler to lord it in a man's house, drinking his wine and soiling his linen. As lovers go, and that should never be far, Master Shagspeare was perfection. He knew his place.

As for Emilia, she began to see herself in a much more pleasurable light. She was a benefactress now, a patroness. Without desiring this man's gift or that man's scope, she could advance his art. She would even let the Lord Chamberlain have a little bit more of his will of her. He was ageing fast, so it could never be much.

She congratulated herself, she exulted aloud, and he took it as the expression of another kind of pleasure. He was a disgusting old man, but disgusting old men always are.

~

Will had never had so much money in his life, and his life had not been entirely without money. His patron's largesse was all about him, his pleasure at *Love's Labour's Lost* as well as at having the most famous poem of the season dedicated to him, was considerable. For the young earl to clap his hands or cry 'Bravo!' would have been tedious, and very bad for his hair and the hang of his cloak, so it was much better done by gifts – coin in abundance, as well as a deal of, 'You're a frank, open and honest friend, Will. Just mention my name and ask the fellow to send his bill to me.' Then there was the success of the poem itself. It had already run through several printings, and at each of them the poet was able to put money in his purse.

Not that he was happy, not entirely happy. He had his beloved wife to consider. She was a long way away. This was quite the best place for a beloved wife and his children to be, but he still needed to consider her, along with young Susanna and the twins Hamnet and Judith, and the thought was often painful.

What was even more painful, exquisitely painful, was his love for Emilia. It was so exquisitely painful and painfully exquisite that he wouldn't be without it.

The pain was in the jealousy. He had to share her with the old stallion Hunsdon and put up with her being married to a younger French stud with a fancy name. The fact that the one was ancient and the other no more than convenient did not assuage his jealously the least little bit. He had *other* men to be jealous of, others to fret over and be joyously miserable about, his young patron and friend the Earl of Southampton among them. He wanted an answer to the Lord Chamberlain's question: why had young Wriothesley been at the christening? Why was he there, and why was Marlowe there? Christoper Marlowe was his rival for the Muse's hand and the earl's patronage. So what was Emilia to him, or he to Emilia? What?

He put this question to his friend when they next met. Southampton had been harder to find of late, and was often blushful and breathless when discovered.

'My lord, I did notice you at a baptism the other day.'

'And I did notice you, Will. We spoke, do you not remember?'

'I showed you a wedding, my lord, and it did entertain you. I am surprised you found such entertainment at a baptism. Let me be frank with you. Our friendship craves a little frankness. So let us be open about Mistress Lanier, with whom you know I am in love.'

'I did make the match, Will. Do you not remember?'

'What I remember most is that she is a woman, sir.'

'Will, she must not be mine. I wonder you dare make her yours. She is Lord Hunsdon's.'

'She is a woman, Hal.'

'She has the shape of a woman, I grant you, and a most appealing smell. Then there is her voice.'

'Aye, there's her voice.'

'She sings as well as any castrato. But, in truth, I know nothing of women, Will.'

They had ruffled petticoats enough. 'Therefore I'm writing these little poems for you.' Let him rustle some parchment instead.

'To persuade me towards the sex? I know my mother will thank you.'

'To persuade you to nothing, my lord. Most of all I seek to confirm you in your bachelorhood.'

He could trust him. They were friends. They adored one another. They were friends. He could trust him.

'Will, you must excuse me now.'

'My lord. When shall I see you, Hal?'

'Tomorrow, Will.'

～

Some things he dare not mention to Will Shakespeare, many things as it happened, though he regarded the older poet as his confidant, tutor and guide no less ardently than he was held to be patron and friend.

Mistress Emilia was one such secret, of course, but he scracely dare mention the dark enchantress to himself, let alone the upheaval she caused in his system of beliefs by means of the wickednesses and wonders she practised upon him, and encouraged him to try with her. Yes, he *loathed* women, but not his dark Emilia, not quite, not yet. She had made a man of him. Jack Spratt had supped on fat, but he mustn't think about it, or the sick would be down his nose again.

But Will would understand all this. If a man loves a woman he will understand his friend for loving her too. And having her. And lying about it. Or what does friendship mean?

What he could not tell Will – or Emilia come to that, though he told her altogether too much while she was all a-kiss and a-coax at him – what he dare not mention was his seduction by Christopher Marlowe. Seduction? No, rape would be truer, but the earl was predispositioned for that. That is why he had sent Will away too abruptly, for fear the two poets might meet in his lodgings, face to face.

It had begun much as before, the seduction or unresisted rape. Southampton had angels about him, money in all sorts of store, and his note of hand would always be good for the building of a playhouse, a church or a ship-of-war. But here was Master Marlowe, pen in fist so to speak, and clearly after meat rather than coin. He presented the matter so coyly, too:

'Nay, my lord, come young Henry, are you still a boy? Let us unbutton and be jolly and brisk.'

Southampton chose to see no help for it. He unbuttoned and Master Marlowe was brisk with him, too brisk, and coarse. The young earl was reminded of what he'd always known, that it was no sport for men of discrimination. Marlowe smelled like a goat and was brisk and brutish like a buck among his does and young nannies in the pen. Doing it with Mistress Lanier was infinitely to be preferred. That and having her do it to him.

After what Master Marlowe had done to him, including the toothmarks in his ear, as if the brute were a tomcat clinging to

174

his tail, after all that it was pleasing to bathe himself all over in a spiced rag and creep towards Mistress Lanier, nodding in on Will in passing to make sure the poet was at work with his pen and unlikely to want to play lover for at least an hour.

God, he used to place himself between her fingers. Now he was bold between her legs when his mood was firm enough and Jack Spratt's stomach was good.

FIFTEEN

Never mind the Plague. It doesn't afflict lovers. Three and perhaps four people were monstrously happy with one another all season, and even Master Lanier was not disappointed now he was a Captain and going beyond the sea. It is irksome for a man to be cuckolded in his own house every instant he turns his back on the place. The world sees an idiot whose wife is making a fool of him. But to be cheated when he travels in distant climes is an arrant villainy, and no one is demeaned by being the victim of villainy. Meanwhile, Alfonso allowed himself occasional use of Emilia, to keep his emotions in practice, and frequent hours with Lisbet, after he'd run through his scales. He gave little thought to either woman. He was waiting for the tide.

The happiness did not last long. The problem perhaps lay in Emilia's misuse of her mother's powers, more likely in her summoning of Dingley and his fishy accomplice without due scrutiny of the heavens. She supposed a fat moon and the fullness of her need to be enough. She presumed.

Her greatest mistake – she realized her error within a month of the commencement of this season of tranquil joy – lay in trusting her well-being to the kindness of men. Her men *were* kind, both her lords and her gentleman the famous poet, but in what ways were they kind? Only after their own needs and fashion.

Mars was in conjunction with Saturn, and Venus in opposition to her Sun, when Master William was untimely enough to be

177

approaching her front door just as the Lord Chamberlain came stepping out of it.

This could have been an ugly encounter, but men who have clasped hands in the dark can at least pass each other quietly by daylight.

Henry of Hunsdon was one of them. The Lord Chamberlain was smarting from his meeting with Emilia. He needed his confidant. 'She's *enceinte* again, Will. As gravid as a Sudbury sow. So what have you been doing to the lady?'

'I, my lord?' Hell's blackest pit, this was an ill tiding!

'Not "I, my lord?" Not to your friend. 'Tis more of your "aye, aye, my lord" that you should be telling me.'

'Nay, my lord. Not aye aye. I have been allowed to know but little of the lady. This I do swear.'

'Aye, but which little has she allowed you to know, Will? Swear to that! If a lusty young rake can come by the right little in a wench, then that little is more than enough.'

'So you may say, my lord.'

'And so I do. Ask any sparrow, Will. Nay, stop the next tomcat.'

'I do not have the necessary tongues my lord. My name is not Solomon.'

'Confess to me, Will. You've been converting Mistress Lanier's spy-hole into a postern and sally-port!'

'Not I, my Lord Hunsdon, as I continue to swear.'

''Tis you, Master Shakespeare. 'Tis you who've been planting pearls in the aforesaid oyster.'

Will allowed himself to smirk a little at this, and the smirk became a smile. Was he really to be a father again?

He stopped to eye himself in a puddle, all hose and long-legged nose though its mirror made him.

'We can't talk here. We'll take a jar of wine at the ordinary, and my fellows will see we're neither of us disturbed.'

Sitting moodily at table, and picking a capon's beak from the gravy in his pie, Will realized the Lord Chamberlain had stopped him going in to his love. He'd only wished to read her a sonnet, then sit knee to knee across those dull little verses of hers. He brooded about whatever it was that Harry of Hunsdon had been doing.

He found the old man's hand on his wrist. 'Did she never give you the clap?'

'My lord!'

'Or the pox or the fidge, or the Mad March Itch? Have you not had a pain in your pikestaff, or found the whole implement come out in blisters?'

'Impossible, my lord. She's—'

'She's a liar, Will. And she's caught so many tricks from her mother, she's grown more cunning than a fiddler's bitch – which, of course, she is.'

'My lord, I am bound to ask—'

'Who gave her this terrible affliction and handicap? My father did, young William.'

Will's head swam. How many lovers did his lady have, and was her taste exclusively for old men like himself, or older men like the Lord Chamberlain, or older men still as his father presumably was?

'Not directly, you understand Will. My father never knew Mistress Lanier in the flesh. Nor did I, Will.'

'My lord, I can scarce credit—'

'On my oath, Will. My hands have never touched the woman, any more than my daddy's did. My prick was the fiery villain on both our accounts, and that's such a negligible item we needn't think of it. So don't let's.'

Will was in a frenzy, a half-frenzy anyway. He would probably have cut Lord Hunsdon's throat, if he'd worn anything sharp enough to make a success of the task. Or seized the old brute by the neck and throttled him till his Adam's apple came out of his mouth, had the Lord Chamberlain not now sunk his voice to a serious whisper. 'Do you know Master Burbage?'

Of course Will knew James Burbage.

'He's minded to build himself a theatre and start up a company of players with myself as patron. The Lord Chamberlain's Men they'll be known as, or some such gee-gaw, provided it mentions me and makes Master Burbage some coin. He'll need a partner,

Will. I've told him it'll have to be you, even if I go surety for you.'

It is hard to stay enraged with a man when he offers you such an enormous slice of good fortune, indeed a whole haunch of fortune to be seized with both hands and gnawn to the bone.

'My lord, words would be but an imperfect expression of my joy.'

'They always are, Will. A pity some of you don't pay more attention to the fact. I think particular of Masters Greene and Nashe. Both of them are having their ears cut or their terminations stretched, and for nothing more than letting their pens run away with them. You'll never let me down like that, will you, Will?'

'Lord Hunsdon—'

'Burghley tells me he's had that Thomas Kyd on the rack since Quarter Day, and likely to keep at him. He was a tall man to start with. Now his slops and his doublet cover less timber than flags on a masthead. They scarce reach his knees or his elbows!'

No, he couldn't strangle Lord Chamberlain Hunsdon, especially when he said, 'You're the natural master of a troop of players, Will. The wretches will keep you well-employed.' Even when he added, 'You can't be at that Lanier woman all the time, y'know. You'll have to find some occupation while her husband's in residence – if he ever gets back from the Indies.'

Shakespeare had finished his pie. Always eat up a rich man's crust was the precept he lived by. Swallow and be grateful. There's no point in cheeking a man who can break you, and even less in presenting yourself as a churl to a Lord Chamberlain who could undoubtedly make you.

'Will you have Emilia back at Whitehall, my lord?'

'So she does insist, and so I shall try. But my cousin is against it, Will. Yet so I shall try.'

His lordship nodded to say he was departing, and looked for his cloak and sword.

Will watched him go. Their meeting had been full of good fortune, yet a lover will find pain in anything. His Emilia had the clap, his lordship said. Yet Will had nosed nothing of it, nor seen the least glimpse of the French Crown anywhere on her person. Her privities were more pure than the heart of a lily, everyone knew that. Oh, and she was with child, and perhaps the child was his.

When he sought out her house, he found her a trifle disappointed to see him. This was in spite of his new hose and fresh linen quite unnoticed by Lord Hunsdon. He did not mention her belly to her, nor Lord Hunsdon's undoubted slander of her fitness and health. It wouldn't be proper.

He told her about the Lord Chamberlain's Men instead.

'I know,' she said. 'Sweet love, I did arrange it for you. They spoke first of Thomas Dekker and then of Master Marlowe. But I showed them you are the man.'

No man need stay for kisses when his destiny is so clearly elsewhere.

~

He felt he should seek his Hal. That would be the kindest move, to let his patron know that his purse had earned him such an advancement. Pray God the young earl feel neither slighted nor offended by this new and unavoidable patronage. Pray God and praise Him.

He would give Hal some new sonnets first – there was plenty to amuse him there, and not a little to amaze him. He had also made a copy in his own hand, not by scribe, for the earl's mother. Then he would talk about his plans for *Lucrece*. Hal had only been vaguely engaged by his previous diversion about Venus, the raping Goddess. The *success* of the poem, the fame, the glory it had brought them, had also been an embarrassment to the young man in his current state of shilly-shally and dither. Will understood his reluctance to be tied in with the daughter of a suitable family. He was still young to be offered at the meat market, whether by his mother or his guardian Burghley, the Lord Treasurer. At least the new poem wouldn't present him as Adonis, the bashful youth. It wouldn't involve him at all, but if he *chose* to be Collatine the wronged husband he could be so, and if he wanted to regard himself as the raping Sextus Tarquin, so be it. Will allowed himself to smile. Lucretia had become his Adonis now. There was no way young Henry Wriothesley could see himself as the raped virgin herself. He congratulated himself on his choice of subject.

Only after he had presented his patron with all these gifts of fact and intention would he speak of becoming one of the Lord Chamberlain's men. It would be a ticklish moment, but Hal would congratulate him for it. It was but hire and salary, not reward.

His friendship for Hal Wriothesley, and Hal's for him, each of them the other's muse, that was his reward. He would show him the verse which said

> My love is strengthened though more weak in seeming,
> I love not less, though less the show appear,
> That love is merchandized, whose rich esteeming
> The owner's tongue doth publish everywhere . . .

It was a splendid sonnet, almost as bright as his new hose and his clean linen.

Back in his lodging, he and Madame Mountjoy inspected both of them carefully. When a woman who lusts after you knows you have another love, it is gentle to let her bring sugared water to your hair and scented cloth to your doublet. What she touches upon in your hose is another matter.

Poets are not apt to dine like gentlemen, especially when bidden to eat pie from a knife in an ordinary, but the linen he wore clean for Emilia was still clean, and his new hose still clung to his calves and knees. The Mountjoy was now above those cutlets and hinges, her damp cloth searching ever upwards for gravy splashes. She was in a fever about something, pausing dab by dab in a kind of ecstasy, whether out of admiration for his thighs, which were well-formed by walking, or by thinking on the earldom of her lodger's young friend, how could he tell?

It was a good moment, a saving moment, for Mountjoy himself to appear. The venerable Huguenot counted the damp patches on Will's legs upwards and towards the overhang, before observing dryly, 'My wife is something of a Platonist, 'Sieur Shakespeare.'

They laughed together, the men, at least one of them amused. Will offered wine, but the older man was stern in his refusal, as if it was already Lent. His face softened a little. He said, 'I am forming a taste for your London beer, my sir. But you cannot keep ale in a bedroom. Nor Plato, either, I think. He is on everyone's tongue, but nobody reads him.'

'Only the Wits,' Will agreed. 'I've got Edmund Spenser some-where.' He found the little book on his bed. 'You shall borrow it. That's where we're all getting it from.' It was only the *Daphnaïda*, and he knew it wouldn't do.

'Well, your rungs are dry now, Sir Shakespeare.'

Yes, he was fresher than new. Save that, compared to Hal, he would look like a tare in a poppy-field.

~

She was with child again. What a curse for a woman with plans to make. And whose was it? Was it Lanier's, the young earl's or Master Will's? Or conceivably – she chose the word carefully – Lord Hunsdon's, for the old brute had twice refused to be deflected. Wit was wasted on him, and scorn pierced him less than it would a hog or a porcupine.

'Master Shakespeare is your lover now,' he said, as he rose from the bed he had returned to almost as soon as Will left the house. She was expecting young Wriothesley, not Will, and certainly not the Lord Chamberlain twice in the same hour. Old Harry was dressed in almost no clothes at all, though somehow, by a miracle beyond any the witch Johnson could devise, still with his boots on.

'So you keep your spies about me, my lord.'

'Spies? If there's any such thing in the realm, then they're Burghley's, not mine. Hang about a woman's door? You'll not catch me at it, nor paying base fellows to do it for me. I was going out. He was coming in. I deflected him into an ordinary. Now Master Shakespeare and I have a pact.'

'My lord?'

'Aye, a pact. I pay and he plays.'

'Methinks you deal with me in too gross a fashion, my Lord Chamberlain.'

'I send you playthings. Why should you complain?'

She smiled. She did not complain. So everyone knew about everyone. Almost everyone. Young Henry Wriothesley, the Earl of Southampton, was her secret. What a beautiful secret he was, and with how many promises of tomorrow.

~

Henry, the third Earl, had recently taken a house in Canon Row. His mother the Countess had insisted on it. It was in the City of Westminster, close to Whitehall Palace, and there was no Plague to bother the good lady in Westminster. It was the Citizens of London that suffered from the buboes, but only the common people and women in childbirth. Noblemen and gentlemen were exempt, as were their horses and dogs, or that was their belief and prayer.

Will's step quickened as he entered the Row. The air smelled clean. He was away from all thought of infection.

There were half a dozen booted fellows lounging at Hal's door. They wore leather jerkins, and were belted with flat-bladed swords. Save for the swords, they looked like bum-bailiffs, and that would have been a sorry image indeed. Their sleeves were ornate for bailies, and their buckles burnished. Will recognized the yellow flounces above their sleeve-bands. They were wearing the Essex livery, and were clearly armed retainers, wearing leather above their blazons until the spring grew warmer.

So the mighty Earl of Essex was here, Hal's cousin and the Queen's new favourite. Will hesitated, but only for a moment. He wasn't the one to cough and cry 'hem!', then touch his forelock and stand back. He was friends with great ones on his own account.

There was a wake in progress, a wake or a rouse, or some kind of other gaudy. The house was full of drunken men and boisterous servants, with dusk not yet falling. There wasn't a woman in sight, certainly not Lady Heneage, the Countess.

She'd have boxed ears and emptied the house, and given her nephew Essex a good roasting. As for her son – where was the young earl?

No need to bang on the door. The oak was not sported. Master Marlowe was there, but scarcely inside, as if darting through and about.

He grinned when he saw Will, his rival for a patron's purse. 'I know you, Master Shakespeare.'

'Sir.' Aye, like the weasel knows the stoat, or two hedgehogs at the same bowl of milk. 'Where is my lord?'

'I am my lord. Am I thine, Master Shakespeare?'

It was Robert Devereux, Earl of Essex himself, dressed in more cloths and hues than the rainbow has lights. He too was moving wildly about, like a man who had taken wine in moderation enough to stand, but not to stand still.

'My lord of Essex, your servant.' He did what he could for a bow. He had been a player this several years. His stooping was growing sweeter. 'I come here to see your cousin, my lord. William Shakespeare.'

'I know your face, Master Shakespeare. My cousin declares it is worth the knowing.'

'You are kind, my lord.'

'Not so, for I do insist your Henry is right, eh, Kit? He gave me that poem of yours in a book – the lusty one: I forget how you christen it, but I kept my lady in a fever a full fortnight after I perused it.'

'Now you flatter me, my lord.'

'My wife or some lady else.' He beckoned one of the Earl of Southampton's servants to bring Will a cup of wine, then drew him aside from those who thronged about his greatness. All things to all men he might be, but he was clearly determined to be noted by William Shakespeare.

Master Marlowe followed after, wearing that smile of his that Will could scarce separate from his hair.

'You did pen this poem for my cousin, Master Shakespeare.'

'My lord, he was pleased to allow me to place his name before it. The honour was all mine, I do assure you.'

185

'A pox on this honour, Will – I may call you Will? Well, then, a pox on it, for that is what I'm coming to. Answer me straight, yes or no. You did conceive this story of the galloping goddess to act as a spur to him, am I aright?'

'By God, my lord, he's clearly been pricking somewhere,' Master Marlowe said.

'Aye, he's taken you to heart, Will. He's been heated by your whole pitch and sermon to him. He's been pricking as this jester does say, and going into some woman or other as your poem exhorts him.'

Will did not understand.

'He hath a clap, Will, as noxious a dose of crown as Christian gentlemen ever came by; and more chancres than a papist could string on his rosary.'

Will sank his wine like an invalid downing his philtre. 'My lord of Southampton is sick?' he asked.

'Only in some parts. He's well enough in others.'

'Sore between the legs,' Marlowe said, 'and not from his saddle. Saint Julian knows how he'll gallop himself to Bath – for thither he's bound – since everything of him below the waistband is grossly enflamed and inflated. His balls grow bigger than a pig's bladder in a child's mouth a' May Day.'

The other two eyed Master Marlowe carefully on receiving this intelligence.

'Kit has been playing the physician,' the Earl said reprovingly. 'An apothecary might have employed a wiser eye and his tongue been more guarded.'

Will lacked the time to comment.

'He blames you, Will.'

Hal blamed him? How could this be?

'It seems he hath dipped himself deep in some lady of your acquaintance, Will.'

'He spoke of your landlady, Will.' Master Marlowe being as kind as his faded teeth would allow him. 'It seems she is always close after him and large against his eyes.'

Will knew it couldn't be the Mountjoy, though this was scarcely the place to reject such a calumny on her. He knew she was minded. She had a fine rolling eye, and her smile was as gapped as any goat's, but his young patron was never at his lodgings without Will himself knowing. The matter was as simple as that. For the moment he daren't think beyond it.

'You must write my cousin a cure, Will. For the moment I'll leave you with Master Kit.'

Whether to bow, and when to nod and touch a forelock – it was always a riddle. Will did as Marlowe did, which was nothing.

When Essex had gone, or dismissed them by leaving – however one judges where heavenly bodies may be, and what their relation in space – Marlowe seized Will by the cuff and said, 'You've been left with me, Master Shakespeare, and we've verses to think on. Verses of mine, of course. They too are for the Meteor of Southampton, as are both of us. I think you'll find my *Hero and Leander* superior to your *Venus*.'

'That is as shall be seen.'

'That is as it is, Master Shakespeare.'

He was glad Christopher Marlowe did not call him Will, though he felt goodwill to all men. His wits were in a frenzy, that was the truth of it – his patron's alleged displeasure, poor Hal's reported sickness, and then there was the overwhelming question.

Save the gap between this friend and his angel was surely too great an interval. They had only met once, only once. Wasn't it only once, and certainly but briefly then?

Be damn'd to old man Hunsdon for the venom of his tongue. And be damned to all their courtiers and slanderers. He knew his love was clean and unblemished. By the Lord, he did. If she weren't, how had he escaped scalding? There was hope in that thought, salvation there.

~

Will had doubted his lady before. He had thought she was dead, and lo! she was alive. He had thought she was a murderess, then heard her swear otherwise. He had thought she was high and mighty: she had parted her legs for him. He had feared she was given to concupiscence, but she would rather send him into Kent to pick apples. He had guessed she was a sorceress, but she'd confounded his suspicions with moments of sweetest magic. Harry of Hunsdon had sworn she was a whore, but old men are notorious liars. Then there was his story about the clap. Let him prattle onward. Will's wand was as clean as any husband's should be. He had not touched her often, not as often as he'd have liked nor as frequently as she sighed that she'd wanted, if only she weren't with child, or suckling like a milcher, or waiting to be churched, or expecting a call back to Court. But, by all the saints of loving, he *had* touched her, by Mary Maudlin Maculata he'd swear to God he had touched her and entered such of her secrets as love makes a stiff man privy to.

It was about cock-crow the next morning that he woke with his bed in a fever and his jury mizzen braced for a storm. The sheets were furled close all about it, and the member was expanding from his keel with a most peculiar throb. And – by thunder! – the size of it as he lay upon his back, the look of it unwrapped, the feel of it when the linen brushed against it. Even without its halyards and stays it was a full foot long, though he spoke as a man with short feet.

The jakes in the yard was melancholy by moonlight. If the moon chanced to luff behind a cloud, then the whole cess became a horrendous quagmire in which tall women drowned and men perished slowly. Wise men would use their jordan, or not go at all.

He rubbed a flint against steel, and sparked enough tinder to light himself a candle. His member was so long he needed the illumination to reach his cup to the end of it.

He could not ease himself. He simply could not go. He could not release the pressure by so much as a thimbleful. No, he told himself a lie. A little splashed over, midway in volume between a fat gnat's tear and the smaller sort of raindrop.

The pain was impossible. He strangled his spiggot straight away and hammered home the bung. Just to pass the sweat on a maiden's brow was worse than pissing a volcano. He was piddling hot coal. The whole thing was a flame, a flame and aflame and enflamed. It was a fire within a fire. He passed sparks even to think about it. The centre of his being was stuffed with fanged wire.

And yet he had to go. He couldn't lie beneath it all night, or sit upon it or straddle it. The thing would tear his blanket and very likely break the thatch. He went with a horrible effort, his teeth in a grimacing chatter, his head hairs standing on end like life in excrement, to coin a phrase he might find useful with a less painful pen in hand. He felt like Drake bombarding the Armada with red-hot cannon balls, and understood why the Admiral came to decide that fireships were safer and easier.

The colours he saw in his pot. He had to remind himself that his gaze was bloodshot from the agony of production, but he peeped like Abraham into the waters and saw more than the Pharonic legions swimming there. He'd made so many hues that Master Hillyard could have used them to depict Her Majesty's every gown, including the silvers and golds, then paid loving attention to the whites of her eyes, which were yellow; the pinkness of her cheeks, which were not; the cockerel mauve of her wattle, which was invisible; and her miraculous eyebrows and teeth, which though missing were frequently written about.

Had a gnat done all this to his pilicock? A gnat had not, nor any kind of pismire else, so soon into spring. If he'd used foul language in his life, or ever spoken ill of woman, he'd have said he was cunt bitten, as the Scottish poets call it. Feel the proof of it. The Lord Chamberlain had spoken truly: a shark with all its teeth could not have served him worse. A shark would have served him better, or a fat pike in a pool. The thing was best taken off.

Look at Madame Mountjoy's chamberpot. The poor Huguenot lady was entitled to expect better from her jordan than this. If it weren't too far to carry it, he'd have shown the thing to Emilia. Then tipped it in Lord Hunsdon's herb garden.

He could scarcely wait until daybreak. He intended to hear the truth from her. That is he meant to tell her terrible things and have her nod and agree to them. A woman can never speak the truth. She can only hear it, learn what it is, and agree.

189

She had seduced his young earl. She had inveigled that poor innocent into her bed and systematically debauched him. Worse, she had given both of them the clap in all its hierarchies and graduations!

SIXTEEN

Poor sweet Emilia, she was scarcely out of her bed with dear Maria's fingers still plaiting her hair into a winsome curlicue like a pair of matching scallops, when there came a monstrous knocking at the front of the house. Peter was always prompt when he suspected royalty, or at least the young earl, so he opened up much too quickly.

Her much loved Will found her as no woman likes to be. She was not enthroned above, but seated in her kitchen upon a lowly joint stool such as no lady should be caught upon, when settles with shawls look better.

He came storming in, though somewhat quaint in his walk as if newly testing a saddle. Then he nearly fell over, so mistress and maid recovered lost ground by laughing. The poor man had slipped on the wet kitchen floor on which the two women were enislanded while Lisbet scrubbed all about, on her hands and knees at the stones.

The stumble robbed him of speech for a while, as if he were an ancient of three score and ten, and the merest gapping of the legs had pulled his remaining tooth out. When he recovered himself, he was all hiss and spit. He could scarcely bring the words out. 'Mistress, I must be privy with you.' He nodded towards Maria and trod against the kneeling Lisbet. 'There are certain words I must say.'

Maria finished her hair in a phantasy – there was no time for shells. As Emilia rose and led the way towards the parlour, she felt as if she were wearing an elf's ears, not the arrangement she had intended to enchant the young earl, already two days late. She hoped Will wasn't about to fall upon her with a mad declaration of love, lust even worse. The whole edifice on her topknot would have crumbled, and there be an end of it. The poor fellow was clearly in a rush about something, perhaps to ask her to set a song for him, or rescue him from a verse he was stuck in. He lacked her facility with rhyme, her easy familiarity with any of the Muses, though he was loath to admit it.

She held out her hand, but he refused to take it, let alone kiss it, or any part of her else. 'You have given me the clap, Mistress, and my lord of Southampton has gone riding to Bath because of it.'

'I don't understand you, sir.'

'The clap, mistress. Aye, and perhaps the pox, with a chancre or so else, and who knows how many vile bedsores?'

'I do not know of these things you speak of. Are they ailments, perhaps? May I guess they are infirmities of the ear? You speak very loudly.'

'I speak of Lord Hunsdon's affliction of the venereal parts. Young Wriothesley, my lord the Earl of Southampton, is infected likewise; according to his cousin Essex and that catamite Marlowe, he has been forced to Bath in Gloucestershire for a cure.'

She cursed herself for making imperfect provision for her lovers. She was in all ways clean. The great spell had secured her exemption. But she had not protected the visitors to her sweetmeats, so now she would be the talk of all those gossips when they came to Court, including young Essex who had the Queen's ear, if not the rest of her, as some said his uncle Leicester.

'Well, Mistress Emilia?'

'No sir. Not very. How can a poor woman be when her dearest friend bursts in upon her like this, his lips wild with accusation, and sets her head ringing and her heart wild aflutter with talk she scarcely understands concerning matters she has never heard of. So you have contracted a strange disease?'

His silence was explosive.

'And in some fashion I do not comprehend you have transmitted this affliction to your friend the young earl? Will, I have heard things spoken of you both – is this what you are confessing to me? I can scarcely believe it of you. You have furnished me such proof of your strong inclinations otherwise.'

He digested gunpowder. How could he make headway against such a froth of words when he was in a greater torment than anything he had suffered the whole night long?

'You made mention of Lord Hunsdon. I am *not*, I have *never* been, I *could* not be an intimate of such a filthy old man. You know his reputation, Will. He is all talk in the jakes, Will, but nothing outside in the daylight. No doubt he was a man in his youth, but how many reigns ago was that? He has children and bastards to prove it, and apes and monkeys else. In the old King's day, or the King his father before him, I doubt not he was a dirty dog, but his tail has been long since docked. Trust a woman's instinct in such things.'

His balls ached. He could not answer such pain, or get his mouth closed enough to open it. He could swear the tip of his nose was touching his chin, and his teeth down a hole in his gullet.

'Won't you sit yourself, Will? I can see what you have against it, but you look so discommoded afoot, your body would be kinder folded.'

He collapsed himself on to a settle, and wished he had not, save the blood sought another direction, and even a change of agony brought a kind of relief.

'I return to my Lord Hunsdon. He is my protector, Will. My protector and only begetter. It was as Lord Chamberlain he found me as an orphaned girl when I lived with the Dowager of Kent, and recognized my great gifts; he's a brutish old man, but my talents are incomparable, as is widely known. He hath but a foggy brain, yet my genius like sunshine pierces even the thickest cloud.'

Will groaned. He was pierced.

'It is only in the latter capacity – only as Chamberlain – he knows me for one whose undoubted genius must be laid before Her Majesty our Queen.' She wept a little. 'You know my – how can I say it, Will, to you my dearest and only friend? – you know my *body*: I blush to say the word, but my *body* from head to hair hath all been before you, and you have used it lovingly and gently.' She wept some more, and was pleased to see the teardrops freckle his eyes as well, though she was less than certain of their cause. 'Speak to me not of venereal affliction. I have a little son, Will' – Mary, mother of Jesus, where was the little fellow? With Maria and Lisbet in the kitchen? – 'I have a little son, by the blessed intervention of God. And now you have sired upon me another. Am I anything but fresh about those parts a woman dare not mention? I am as free from all such vileness as the Lady Mary, chaster than Eve when the Creator first drew her through a hole in Father Adam's side. You *must* believe me, Will.'

Being unable to answer is very close to belief. 'Lady,' he groaned, 'I know not how to think.' He screamed, briefly, being foolish in the crossing of legs. 'I—' he sobbed. He uncrossed then crossed them again, as if this was the only way to begin, or stop himself, thinking. 'And then there's your living in Lord Hunsdon's house,' he managed at the last.

'*This* house, sir? Lord Hunsdon's?'

'So he did tell me. And said he allows you an income and your husband a dot.' Speaking was painful, but his desire to accuse her overcame everything.

'Sir, I had this house from my father, Baptista Bassano, who had money at Court. My income is principally in the hand of bankers or lodged in the bourse. It derives in chief from my mother's chattels, sir, for she was firstborn of a big estate in Lincolnshire, and brought to my dear father much in the way of dowry.'

'I know your mother's name as a witch.'

'She was maiden as Margaret Johnson, sir, and she is now Queen in Heaven, or more advanced than that.'

'Aye, a witch,' he growled. 'A witch, as I say. I wish she would witch these waters from me.'

194

'My mother is Maid of Heaven, sir, and Mistress also. She'll meddle with no man's waters, nor muddy with them either, not yours, nor any man's!'

'Then who is the father of your child?'

'I have a husband, Will, a good man you have all too frequently prevailed upon me to deceive.' She felt for a cushion, no, a shawl, and dabbed with its corner to a place near her eye. 'Your sin was the greater, Will, in that you stood at the church door with your friend to see me wed.'

'And the child fell out of you not a month of nights after.'

'It happens, Master Will, and not just in Bibles and such like holy writ. Childbearing is a miracle worked upon us womenfold from heaven and on High, by All that is Merciful it is!' She was confusing her religions just a trifle, but that was the problem with worship in secret.

She permitted herself a further tear. God, how funny it was, save it was also a trifle sad, and more than a little dangerous to herself. The Southampton business, she meant.

'Lady, my Emilia, I must take my leave of you. I need borrow some time for thought. I wish I could stay to read out the sonnets the matter has given rise to. I wish—'

We all wish to be spared that, she thought. 'Sweet Will,' she said, glad he would take her hand, though still unable to stoop to it. 'I too need to borrow time.'

Will journeyed to Bath in torment. If he could have stayed standing still he would not have gone, but he had to seek a cure for his barber's pole of an affliction, and the best medical opinion was he should go to Bath or gargle with quicksilver and be cooked in an oven. The latter was the more certain cure for the clap, pox or any kind of consumption including even the buboes. Disease could not abide the quicksilver, especially when the patient was seethed in an additional marinado of brimstone. Men's afflictions fled, and women's also, though lower down the pile. But life often fled as well, and those who survived the roast lived yellow-skinned for years, and croaked from the smoke like frogs. Many died, so it was best endured as a family. One sometimes came through, to be preached about in church, the victim of a horrible jaundice and a dire warning against lechery. Will had a career to fashion, so he decided on Bath, however painful the way.

The problem was how to go there, since mortal man cannot fly, especially with cannon balls bulging his slops – a codpiece and suchlike Icarian equipment being clearly beyond all question owing to the mumpish proportions of its contents.

Walking did not commend itself. He'd have needed to go spread out, with one foot in either ditch, as gappy as a starfish or Saint Catherine on her fiery wheel. Besides, there were footpads to fear anywhere a bowshot west of Westminster Palace, and a lame man is easy meat for a longstaff sixpenny striker or similar lurker in hedgerows.

A carriage was not for him. Carriages did go to Bath for those that had carriages to go in. But the roads were still wet from winter, and wheels took longer than walking. Besides, a man who couldn't bear a settle with cushions above and below could hardly endure the ten million bumps beneath his axle between London and Bath. Some folk died on the way, and others found a cure as they journeyed, their afflictions bubbling and swelling like acid in a flask from the agitation of the potholes until the whole man exploded, and only an angel was left in his stead, or one who could never stoop to error again.

Will was already in an agony from the thing itself, but thinking of the journey made it worse. Then he found further torment in thinking of ways not to think of it, both the thing and the journey.

Yet to Bath he must go. He should already have gone. His mind was already started. The cure was at Bath. More, when he could bring himself to think of it while not dwelling on the rest of it, the *truth* was at Bath. His Lord and Friend and Patron was at Bath, and Hal would tell him everything. Will loved Emilia dearly. He had listened in awe to her account of herself. He believed her but did not trust her. Or was it the other way about?

There was another proviso no lover dared think of: if he'd

caught this fearful torment at her well he daren't dip his bucket in there again.

Will was a countryman. Once he knew he must go by horseback he would have preferred to ride sidesaddle on a pack-frame, or be carried in an ass-hod like a sackful of oats.

As it happened he received a plentiful fist of coin from his friend, the printer Richard Field, for the continuing success of *Venus and Adonis*, his pricksong and spur to his friend the young earl, and now responsible for half his trouble – or so liars told him. With his purse full of angels he found a helpful ostler who hired him both a beast and an appropriate saddle, such was his knowledge of Bath, the rough way towards it, and a man's likely reasons for going.

This was an old-fashioned clap-saddle, high-pommelled and cushioned with eider at the front and snugly supportive at the rear. Once astride this, and lighter in his pouch through the spending of much medicinal coin, Will ambled toward Bath. He went there in a string of fellow sufferers for mutual protection. There wasn't much talking along the way, nor much doing else, though young women were waiting for them at every inn and harbour, and sometimes each coppice and hedge, to earn their progress towards salvation.

Will would have nothing of them. He was a man on fire with love, and he'd already spent too much newly minted coin on his saddle.

~

Bath was what its evil name insisted it was. It was a whoreson Romish style *bagnio*, with all that the label implied; a filthy Italianate *bordello* with nothing to recommend one description above the other save for the saving of letters.

Will was a man of the world but a married man also. He had known few loves because, however great his genital turbulence, he knew he could not do everything. The bard has only two choices: he can write like a poet or he can behave like one.

Will chose to write like one, so he'd found little time for the viler sort of experiences, even though he longed for them often.

197

He was appalled to find all kinds of rooms and snugs served by the hot springs, all manner of kippering and trysting grottos above and below the surface of the world. No wonder the Romans named the place after the British goddess of wisdom. Hell was said to be down there, and the river called Styx. The coming of Sweet Jesus had changed all that, but not this. It was a direct invocation of all those druidical devils whose teeth could be seen glowing deep in the ground. Praise God he could not glimpse Southampton in any of the deeper chasms!

There were places where women could be with women, as was proper; where men could disport themselves with wenches; tiny closets where persons of honour could lie and cook themselves alone; and still he could not find Southampton for vapour. There was a huge steaming pool no better than a sty where man could be with man and gossip of the bourse or the hunting field until his extremities were sufficiently healed by the beneficent waters for him to go and infect them again. He could not find his young friend even here. There were places for lords, places for ladies, and places – judging from appearances, again bleared by steam – that offered shelves for the recently dead. Hal was not in any of them.

Will began to wonder if Essex had lied to him. Marlowe was nothing more than a fleabag of malice, so why should his tongue have been any more strait?

Think of the Devil and straightway hear his voice. Master Marlowe was at Bath days and nights before him, having nothing between his legs to impede his best gallop.

That loathsome catamite and Will's own Hal were romping together in a fountain and twining each to each so close they might have been sharing the same bubble.

'Welcome, Master Shakespeare. You find us in a hedonistic temple of delight.'

Hal said nothing, being more breathless.

Will could not contain his surprise. His soreness vanished on the instant just to contemplate the circumstance he'd discovered them in. They were in a room of bestial and manifest lust, such as was forbidden by all the ordinances of God and Human Justice.

198

He blinked. This was no Temple of Hedonistic Delight. This was a den filled with bum-pluggers and sodomites. Fellows sat here fondling each other by the spring, and several of them were mounted each upon each like bullocks in the pen.

'Come, Shakespeare,' Marlowe said, 'a little water cleans us of this deed. And by all the fountains of Avernus we've water enough here.'

Hal wasn't easy with Marlowe, Will could see that at once. He had fled here and the gossiping spy had followed.

Hal came bounding from the bath and the unhealthy waters of the fountain. He greeted Will like a brother, as they were in spirit, if not in rank or blood. He tried to shrug Master Marlowe aside, but as the horse leech fastens so does it stick. Where it sticks so does it suck, and there's a damnable soreness afterwards.

Now Will must encounter his friend as wet as God made him, though a joint or two larger and much more enduring damp. Will wondered how his lordship could fix back his hair, which in London seemed to have been built by honey bees. Southampton had travelled with serving-men, and he was as unwilling for them to see Marlowe clinging to his arm as he was ashamed before Will.

'My lord,' Will began.

'No "my lords", my Will.'

'Dearest Hal. I must have word with you.'

'I have already brought news of your word,' Marlowe laughed.

'Will, I am ashamed, both beguiled and ashamed.' The earl caught at his hand and kissed him.

'And a shame it is to confess to having such a land wherry as that piece of cargo,' Marlowe shrilled. His teeth were chattering now he was out of the steam, and his tassel was bouncing about like a nag's tail among flies. 'Accounts of her are notorious. She's had whole Armadoes of carracks anchored up her creek to the gunwale, and you beside, Master Shakespeare. So what do you say to that?'

'I say you can't manage a comparison by mouth any better than with pen.'

'Pah, there's not enough spare room in her harbour to float another stick.'

'My judgement holds, sir. Nor can my opinion of any woman be changed by a codling like yourself.'

'A codling, sir. You call me a codling?'

'No, sir, I do not and should not.' Will sought his patron's eye for permission to quarrel just the same. 'I beg pardon of the whole tribe of apples, including the half-ripe, the costers and the crabbies such as you. You are a cogger to abuse a lady so, and were I a man, and free of my lord's bounty, I'd call on you to walk. Now go to, you are a cogger, sir, *and* as mud-mouthed a coystril as I've met in all my years.'

''Fore God, what a bumpkin little start-up the fellow is,' Marlowe screamed, feeling for his blade, which was hard to find, since he was still naked as a trout, and as damp. 'I shall box his ears if I can discover his head!'

'Nay, Master Kit, go to. I would be secret with my friend, and I do count you but an acquaintance in these baths.'

'Aye, and a dozen elsewheres else.' Marlowe bowed low, displaying his bum, and saluted, so exhibiting the rest of him. Then – but whither? – he was gone. Will never saw him again. Nor did many men else.

Two of three serving fellows – his own or the *bagnio's* – had got his lordship dry. He now seized Will's hand again and led him beyond this place of paradox, where men could shed lust's petals even as they plucked its fruit. Outside there was spring sunshine with holes in it for singing birds. Here were trees, horses, houses, and people most of all, attired as God ordained and not naked anatomies as they so unkindly were before. He detected Eve with her tooth upon the apple.

His patron and friend led Will as far as his lodging, which was sumptuous. He was offered and took refreshment there, and was glad to find the steam had wrought a further improvement on his privities, whose cure had been well advanced by the discovery of Master Marlowe being bumptious – and worse – with his young earl among the tendrils of vapour.

Southampton was in a dangerous mood; Will could see that.

He was about to tell all. Friendship can expect no less, and that is why it is always so damnably painful.

'I did deceive you, Will. I did deceive you and I weep for it.' Yes, there would be much wailing and gnashing of teeth, and clasping of hands. 'I did an awful thing to my friend, but you were the less deceived. By God, it was like a rape, a damnable whorish *raptus*. She did besiege me, Will, besiege me, seduce me, and – yes – *rape* me. I think I have come across the exact word in that "rape"!'

'You speak of – you talk to me of Mistress Lanier?'

'Aye, the damned Bassano Lanier quean, the Whore of Babylon!'

They both wept now.

'She did give me the clap, Will. I thought I had it from Master Marlowe or some lad when I was at school, but 'tis but a woman's disease, Will. We young men are clean. We'd never catch it without them!'

'I did love her, Hal. I did love her much.'

'And she betrayed you, Will. She deceived us both.'

'So beautiful as she is.'

'And so delicious to lick at – a taste between fresh oysters and delirium.' It was difficult to know what the young earl spoke of, because a serving girl was buttering cakes before them while a fellow poured ale from a jug, and it is impossible to discuss some things in front of the servants. When they had gone, and with his mouth full of crumbs, he went on, 'A boy has nothing to compare with it, but I must say it takes a deal to satisfy, and there are other ways in which boys, young men and such like bucks are superior.'

They ate and drank in silence, each with his memories.

'I have to thank you, Will.'

'*Thank* me, my lord?'

'Nay, *Will*.'

'Hal.'

'Aye, thank *thee*. Less of this *ye* and *you*. Less of this *my lord*. I am your servant, Will. You have introduced me to *woman*, Will. I shall have to marry one of it someday, for I have to please my

201

Dowager Mum, and there's no marrying anything else. You and that wicked Lanier woman – that wicked lovely Emilia – have taught me it's quite all right with my eyes closed, Will.'

'Words do fail—'

'They failed me, Will. I've been led on to hazardous experiments.' The serving girl came in again, and he nodded towards her. 'I've had the fore-end of my bowsprit be-lee'd in *her* petticoats, I don't mind admitting. But she's not as savoury as the Lanier. Sometimes I think this little one's got a badger on her belly. She stinks like a brock. I should wash her, I suppose.' He licked his fingers for cake-crumbs. 'Or ask her to wash.' He was bred to it, but still slack when it came to controlling his menials.

'You're sure she did give you the clap, Hal? I mean, are you sure it was hers?'

'As I say, she's a woman, Will. She has the afore-mentioned brine-pit. I know no other places to trawl for the disease. My confessor assures me there's none of it in Heaven.'

'But I must have it in back-and-white, Hal, if it be possible such. Did you and Mistress Emilia . . . I do so love her.'

'Barely anything to trouble you. Barely, yes. Only once, Will, with her burr clinging to my berry, and my shaft scarcely entered in.'

'Only once?'

'Otherwise I swear I only had her boy-hole, and that was only offered me with reluctance. Or perhaps it's a boy that I'm thinking of – my memory's so . . . Let's not talk of it, Will. Let us talk of poetry. Let us speak of golden crowns, not guinea-hens and strumpets!'

'Hal, she did lend me the clap as well.'

'Aye, she's free with her lending.'

'I must attend these baths a week.'

'Nay, a month until you're cured. I'll stay with you.'

∾

So Will stayed in the *bagnio* at Bath with his friend, and kept the boy from both kinds of temptation, though from cards and dice and cockerels there was, of course, no holding him.

Will wrote many sonnets, some for his lord and patron to amuse him and please his mother, but most for her, *at* her. Emilia, his deceiving love! She even hurt him to piss. Each time he unfastened the buttons and strings that held up his enflamed heart she was agony, agony . . . oh! oh! oh! *To have ten thousand fiends with red hot spits come hissing in upon her!* . . . that was better, just a little better today. What a flaming firebrand of a pilliwinkle! Stuff it all in a verse, and this awesome *bagnio* withal:

> Cupid laid by his brand and fell asleep,
> A maid of Dian's this advantage found
> And his love-kindling fire did quickly steep
> In a cold valley-fountain of that ground:
> Which borrowed from this holy fire of Love
> A dateless lively heat still to endure,
> And grew a seething bath which yet men prove
> Against strange maladies a sovereign cure:
> But, at my mistress' eye, Love's brand new-fired,
> The boy for trial needs would touch my breast;
> I, sick withal, the help of Bath desired,
> And thither hied, a sad distempered guest,
>   But found no cure. The bath for my help lies
>   Where Cupid got new fire, my mistress' eyes.

Was Hal cured of her yet? Had he ever caught her? Loving Emilia was all hatred now. How the verses screamed and tumbled:

> In loving thee thou know'st I am forsworn,
> But thou art twice forsworn to me love swearing;
> In act thy bed-vow broke and new faith torn,
> In vowing new hate after new love bearing.
> But why of two oaths' breach do I accuse thee,
> When I break twenty? I am perjured most,
> For all my vows are oaths but to misuse thee,

And all my honest faith in thee is lost.
For I have sworn deep oaths of thy deep kindness,
Oaths of thy love, thy truth, thy constancy,
And to enlighten thee gave eyes to blindness
Or made them swear against the thing they see,
   For I have sworn thee fair: more perjured I
   To swear against the truth so foul a lie.

He'd started writing sonnets for Southampton, but not these. These were to her, and he'd written dozens. Written? Nay, wept. They'd come tumbling from his heart. Wept them and now pissed them in anguish.

  He'd take care she read them. He'd send them all – send them? No, *take* them. He'd brandish them before her and burn her with the scalding heat of them. He'd stuff them into her lying heart.

  Meanwhile, when his member was of a size and a sweetness, he'd steal back to Stratford and lie against Anne. How many months was it? He must see how the children were growing – in how many years?

SEVENTEEN

~

Who can tell what a witch sees among the flames in her fire? Or in that fire's smoke, or in her magic glass, whether smeared for ill or clear as quartz crystal? Who knows if what she sees is true, or whether she believes it?

When a lover you love and wish against Heaven to retain has left you, at least for a little, and your half love and beautiful toy has not felt it urgent to return, you consult with the fire at the bottom of the world, you seek Hell itself, and ask questions of the wind beyond the window.

When your husband is away at last and your mind is swollen and perturbed by the new child's fullness between your belly and your heart, then what do you do? You ask the sand in the tray, the little chips of straw, you talk to your women, you seek the wisdom of women, you train up your women and beseech them to teach you in their turn.

So it was with Emilia the lost. She could not help being a vessel for Lord Hunsdon's clap. Nor did she feel any better for thinking it was King Henry's clap before him. There was a clap in Eden; the Goddess Lilith brought it, or the Original Serpent.

Her old Serpent continued to visit. And as he visited her so did he make use of her. Her marriage bed, her private place in her own most magical room, was ceaselessly invaded by the old man's rapes – his body knew its way into hers, and was fond of what it knew. She felt like one of those targets at the butts. His little arrow was always at her, whether

205

at her inner, magpie or bull, his lust would lodge home as it would.

Sometimes her mother's black cat would hiss from the ceiling, or leave fleas whiter than salt on his pillow, and he would miss his strike, and be off in a huff and a sniff, for no man can abide fleas nor a woman's disdain. He would take himself home to his house-women in Blackfriars, to whores he could buy through his host at the ordinary, to all manner of guinea-hens and doxy women who would serve him up tricks. Emilia wouldn't, nor ever did, even when she'd loved him before his misuse of her. She was not a strumpet. She could be ill-used. But she could live to see him gone. He dare not stay, not now there was another child growing. As he left, so did the fleas that salted his pillow, for they were an illusion, though proof of her mother's immortal art even so.

Sometimes she would lie with her eyes closed in disgust at him, while he hung above her like a storm cloud threatening a pasture. She would feel her daughter kick in her wind; the child must be female, she carried so different from little Henry. She would kick, and Emilia would think of the old man's rusty arrow poking her darling's eye out. 'Fleas!' she would call, striking the nearer pillow. 'This room is fusty. I must get the apothecary to smoke it.'

His lordship would cease his onset, and vapour away in the instant, scratching himself from armpit to cod as he stumbled out of doors and halfway up the street.

Sometimes, for the former subject was indelicate, she would sink her mouth behind his less good ear and purr like a cat. 'The old black beast is hereabouts,' she would reflect. 'I think she sits above the tester, bewitched by your bottom's undulant up-and-down, my Lord Harry. You know how those old green eyes love to fasten on anything that moves, and the *claws* . . .' But he would be gone from her by now, without need of a longer sermon. Then Maria would come and lie with her in bed, or Lisbet, who was learning witch tricks, and she and her women would purr together.

Lisbet it was who suggested she keep a bowl of salt near at

hand, on the floor between bed curtain and mattress, just within her secret reach. Simpler to sprinkle a little salt on a pillow, or about the old man's sleeve, and easier than the conjuration of fleas, when the light was bad, now his eyes were fading. But purring was their principal device against him butting his arrow. He could not abide that cat, whether he thought it corporeal or an apparition was no matter. It watched him from places he could not see. It was black. It was full of mischief and fleas.

So the child swelled on and was born out easy in a great bubble of calm among her women. Little Henry was curious, and wanted to be all about her lying in now he was beginning to walk. So Peter Rudkin took a knife and a stick and carved him a boat which they floated in a tub at much the same time as his sister was launched.

They called her Odilla, Emilia and her women, but none of the child's fathers was there as a witness, and Lord Hunsdon dare not be, even though this was a girl, and a second issue, so hardly a menace to anyone.

Whether the old brute was tiny Odilla's father, whether she was the product of Emilia's dallying with the earl, or Lanier her husband's child, or the offspring of her great love Will as she knew the babe was, and as the Lord Chamberlain had insisted to her, her beautiful daughter was out and crying lustily. She was a tiny echo and counterfeit of herself, her own sweetest pearl, not more loved than Henry, but a morsel more intimate than a son.

~

To carry a child asks a deal of a woman's attention, and to birth a child and then suckle it is a considerable skill and art. Neither Lisbet nor Maria had issue, in spite of Captain Lanier's varied degrees of inattention to their protests while they'd helped him wait for his ship to come in – or, as some said, his passage – so no one in the house was in milk save Emilia herself.

Nor would she send Odilla out of doors, or have a nurse come in from among the wives of labouring or indentured persons, still less one of the whores who were frequently excellent sucklers, for it was among the common folk that the buboes most often visited. The Plague never struck in houses like hers where the fleas were but illusions of salt.

So, for a week and then a month of her greatest agony of mind she could not seek the rootsprings of her science for solace. She could consult neither grammarye nor the stars, and Margaret her mother seemed deaf to her call. Doubtless the witch was rebuking her inattention, wherever she dwelt beneath her Crystalline Sphere.

Emilia needed to ask of the sands or stars exactly what had followed between dear Will and her sweetest young bloodlet the earl, and whether Captain Lanier was fully passed beyond the sea, or drowned in the interminable ocean, or in the blood of battle, or even in his own spit, being a musical man who needed too often to clear his throat.

More, she wanted to know what tales they were telling at Court, or at Bath, in the bordels and *bagnios* where all these great jig-a-jigs went for their drubbings. Did Southampton tell great Essex that he had caught a vileness in her bed? Will had told her that he did. And what of the Queen? Was Her Majesty privy to this gossip? Would Harry Hunsdon bring news if she were? Would he care? Was she a story for Kit Marlowe to carry down to Scadbury, to Sir Thomas and Lady Walsingham and their great hive of tattlers? Would he turn her to a ballad and publish her abroad? He was on embassage to the Low Countries each year. Would her fair name be pockmarked even there, and in Calais where he travelled, and in the Parisian Isle of France? Would herself be foul in all men's opinion, her reputation spotted like the poxes in a die?

Worse, what of Will? He had already penned a history of his love for her as part of his rhyming game for her young earl's mother. Would he now endite sonnets to chronicle his hate and disdain?

Then his package came. Peter Rudkin would not say who brought it, save he thought the messenger was a Frenchwoman, large about the mouth and top.

The slut's presence had disturbed the poor man, quite as much

208

as the beloved handwriting disturbed Emilia herself. There was no ribbon this time. She had Odilla to breast, and was clumsy all about her as she tore to open it.

Some verses fell out, sonnets by the look. She could guess at their length as they lay upon the kitchen floor, count the lines even, though read not a word of his blotchy set-secretary. She would peruse them later. They would doubtless scan ill and call for her intervention. It was their likely import that worried her. That, and what other eyes he would lay copies before.

The letter was so bad she came near to smothering Odilla as she read it. By Cock, she was fearful of the poisons the child would be sucking from her. She took her breast from the babe's mouth and gave her to Lisbet.

Lisbet had proved herself clever now she could be encouraged to be clean. She gave the infant thinnings of cow's milk and hot-water-honey, sucked drop by drop from her little finger.

Emilia rushed Maria upstairs, and stood fuming before her day-book and ledger. Will had taken time with his letter. She read it aloud to Maria even so.

'Wicked:
    (Is this the word to address thee by? Or art thou Wick-edness itself, and is thy entitlement superfluous?)
    Emilia, I did love thee. I did not see thee as thou art. I called thee fair and like an Angel in sweetest Heaven. I could not see thee for the blackened strumpet thou art. Thou art Hell's only harlot. My Lord of Hunsdon when he found thee did pluck thee from the abyss.
    Mistress, you have broke your vow to me, even your bed vow, which Ovid says strumpets try to keep. Yet strumpets are cleanness compared to thee. Thou art a monstrous mass of foul corrupted matter, like lugs in a fisher's hooking-jar or life in excrement.
    Thou hast infected me with shame, and my young lord also, whom thou didst infect and seduce, yea other men beside, even unto the North Star. Is there no let in you?

My lord will not speak of this, or not widely, yet this thing is spoken of. I did put him in a play, as thou knowest, and as was widely known, and entitle myself Perowne and thee my darkest Rosaline. It was given before Her Majesty at Westminster, as thou would and cared, and again at Greenwich Palace as thou begged to be. Her Majesty did laugh and clap her hands, and so did many folk else, all knowing how all lovers were, and who such lovers are. Now they do shrill at another clap, for the Earl of Essex hath acquaint Her Majesty of this, thou vilest jest against Nature – yea, now all Loves' labours are lost in deed.

Shalt thou ever forgive thyself?

Thy (erstwhile)

Will'

'Runs not his note like iron through your blood?' Emilia asked, casting it down as if it were a viper among a dish of apples, then stooping to pluck it up and kiss it. 'I kiss thy loved hand, Will.' She threw it down again. 'By all that created me, he has not addressed me once with ye and you. Is he familiar, or does he pour on vinegar after contempt?'

'He is a poet, Emilia, and nice in all such forms,' Maria said. He is also much away from London, you can tell it from his speech.' She picked up the letter, peeped at it timidly, then tucked it into Emilia's book. 'He does go polite on you once, where he calls you "Mistress".'

'He accuses me of such things, Maria. What is this vileness he speaks of?'

'I know not. For your person is as sweet as linen or newly dried bedstraw.' She touched her mistress's shoulder. 'Master Will is a playwright, Emilia. He writes masques, and busks, and suchlike histories which go to men's heads and call for a deal of invention.'

'He's a bumpkin, and I'll have no more of him.'

'A player also by trade, and one who roars scenes in an ale-yard. Such fools are fickle by convention.'

'But Marlowe, he says Marlowe doth bruit me abroad. And this Earl of Essex.'

'Aye, Mistress. Also the Queen.'

'So now, we must log up the fire.'

'Are you cold, Emilia?'

'No, my Maria. I seek retribution. I would see their damnation in the smoke.' She caught Maria with a grip more bruising to the shoulderbone than any that the Lord Chamberlain had ever visited upon herself. 'Revenge, Maria. So shall my capable and wide revenge swallow them up.'

'Who, mistress?'

'Such deeds I shall do – ask me not what.'

This place was no longer her bedroom, no longer the birthing room. It was her own sacred temple where salt could be poured out in earnest, and oil, and the flames fed kindly. She must make it full of her mother's vibrations.

~

No one who knew Mistress Emilia was surprised when she began to lay curses about, and very few blamed her. Those who knew her imperfectly thought she was mad. Others found it convenient to believe so.

For a woman may be mad for reasons peculiar to her. When she is in love she may be mad, when she is with child, and often for a time after she is delivered of it. Then when her months return she can be mad with the moon, and if she lives till they cease she may be in all ways lunatic. Witches have their own kind of madness, and those who are greater than a witch?

'I will have that Master Marlowe dead,' she hissed. 'For his is the tongue that needs a pincer, and his malice towards me an instant stop.'

She spoke for Dingley, or for the Infernal Serpent himself. Yet who knows if either heard, though the Dark One is always there?

She was in a rage, of course, and a curse is better laid cold. Nor did she curse men one at the time. So some of her curses were wild and badly thought, some flew off course, and some harmed

others than the villains she intended, and some hung about her
own head and could easily light on herself and those who were
nearest to her as one did, and quickly. And she forgot the curses
she'd laid long ago, against Lord Hunsdon for instance, till her
mother leant to her ear and told her all such utterances are as
eggs in the hatch of time. 'Their shells are pulsing to break, my
daughter, and who knows what harm may come from them, be
it the judgement of owls or the beaks of vipers!'

'My mother has just spoken to me,' she told Maria sharply,
for the girl was under instruction and like to improve.

'Nay, mistress. It's your own voice you make in your head,
your mother and all such goddesses beside.'

'She told me to be careful who I call to the Cave of the
Dead.'

'And no wonder is it. You tell yourself true there, mistress. So many corpses are lain about the streets and dung-
hills, by Cock they are. Death has no need of you, lady, nor
your curses. Yesterday I saw a naked woman carted, my
Emilia, dead in all ways just like my brother. The buboes
was all about her neck like leeches, and the same deadly
grapes had gone under her groin and made her long-sexed
as any man. There's magic, Emilia. To turn a woman to a
man.'

Lisbet came upstairs and whispered, 'Babe's asleep, Mistress
Lanier, and little Henry too. There came a fellow knocking at
your door just now.'

'A fellow – how?'

'Calls himself by Dingley, he says. Says a certain Saint
Christopher is under arrest and like to be dead if he don't
watch himself.'

Emilia could scarcely contain her excitement. 'This Dingley,
was he missing an eye, or anything strange about the way he
looked at you?'

'I don't gaze at no men, Missus Emilia, not now I've taken
to water.'

Emilia stirred the grate. 'What day is it? I demanded him dead
by the end of the month.'

''Tis the thirtieth of May by the almanac, and a good day for planting mustard.'

The fire was dull now. Emilia could see a room in the darkness between log and log. It appeared to be a parlour in a rich man's house, or a snug in a gentry's ordinary.

Master Marlowe was there. He lay on a bed, feigning sleep, or feigning something. He yawned. Men do not yawn while they are sleeping, but Master Marlowe did.

'He'll not need to pretend much longer,' Emilia said. 'Not now Dingley is at work and my mother is about him.'

There were several men in the room, but they were seated. They had paper and parchments to hand, the remains of a meal. Emilia knew one of them from her days at Court. His name was Robert Poley and he was one of those men busy about those who were busy about the Queen. He seemed to be in charge of an interrogation, but if Master Marlowe was its subject he was having an easy time of it, lounging as he was. She noticed bread on the table, some pie and the carcass of capon or duck. There was wine in abundance, though the two men on the other side of Poley sipped tankards of ale.

She gripped Maria's hand. 'Do you see? Tell me what you see?'

'Nothing, Emilia. I can see hot coals. You can see the forests that burn inside your head.'

'That's him!' Lisbet shrieked. 'There's Master Dingley as was at your door, not half an hour agone, and now walks inside your hearth!'

Emilia couldn't see Dingley at all. She was minded to slap the girl, but then a log fell and she saw even as far as the room's inner portal.

A woman came through it, a substantial person, well dressed, some forty years old. It was then Emilia glimpsed who helped her at the door, though the woman didn't seem to notice him. This was as well, because his eye hung on his cheek, and his ears bled copiously.

She was holding a bill for the food. Poley indicated Marlowe, as if he should pay it.

Marlowe leapt up with a curse. 'Pay the quit? By God, you treat me like a prisoner-in-means, here, and make me pay my own trencher, even though I'm but under day-arrest. Have you not fed off this capon and the good Mistress's pie, Robert Poley? And drunk more than enough of her ale, Master Skeres?'

The others growled and grinned, the way those people do when they're in their cups. They shifted and stretched their arms, but did nothing.

'And you, too, Frizer. Give Mistress Bull's tally to Ingram Frizer, somebody, and let us give the good woman her coin!'

Marlowe was swaggering about now, walking more gap-legged with drink than Will Shakespeare had done with the clap.

The others were still, as if some charade had been planned to follow, but not all of them knew how it would be.

'Come on, Frizer. Sir Thomas hath gone surety for me, and you are my bail-man and companion on his account. Let us see an angel or so, Frizer, or must I feed the good woman groats?'

Frizer flew into a great rage, or pretended so. He jumped to his feet and pulled his dirk out – no, the move was clearly as everyone expected, but it didn't come to pass. His blade was already away from his belt but in Master Marlowe's hand, who had snatched it from thence.

'I did learn that trick from a Hollander in Delft,' Marlowe said, retaining the dirk and his feet by means of a sleight that only drunks can manage. He began to beat Frizer on the head with its hilt, not violently, but nastily enough, pushing at him hard with the pommel.

Frizer was less drunk than he seemed, perhaps nobody was less than sober, and Marlowe the only gull. The others sat forward in anticipation, as Frizer caught at Marlowe's arm, forced it away from his head, and back towards the poet's face, where it menaced his contorted countenance, his blood-shot eyes.

Marlowe shouted in rage, and tried to knock the pommel back against Frizer's skull. They strove together, laughing and panting, amid an awful silence. Then Frizer struck at Marlowe's

214

wrist and a great scream filled the room, transfixing everyone. The scream trembled the jugs in the ordinary, the rafters in Emilia's room. The black cat hissed and leapt.

Marlowe crashed stone dead to the floor with blood leaking through his eyehole from his brain.

'What took you so long?' Poley asked. He sorted through the papers on the table. 'I thought he would slip from you.'

'He did have my dagger.'

'Well, Ingram,' Master Poley said. 'I must restrain you and detain you in the ordinary till Her Majesty's crowner arrives. Thank you, Mrs Bull. I am myself not here, you understand. Not here and never will be.'

'There's a crowner in Greenwich, sir.'

'I speak of Her Majesty's Crowner, the crowner from the Royal Court. He bears the superior warrant and takes precedence in these matters. He shall be here tomorrow, and bring us his experience, which is considerable.'

Emilia stirred the fire again. There was nothing more to come from it, not of Master Marlowe.

'So what did I tell you, Maria? So what did you see?'

'Nothing, mistress. Shall I run to the apothecary for you, and fetch an infusion?'

'But you heard and then did see it.'

'I did hear the shouts that came out of your head, Emilia. And the faces they were painting. And all your panting and pouting. You're like one of those fellows as tells the world what passes when they bait the bear and shouts it out loud for those behind the back that cannot see.'

Emilia did not often strike Maria, but she did. 'So what did you see, Lisbet?'

'In the fire, mistress? In the fire, missus, I saw the flames out of hell, and a cave full of lamps, and a beautiful woman stood there, much like yourself, but with different hair.'

'It was my mother. The witch had red hair. Did she have red hair?'

'This one had burning hair, Missus Emilia. Burning eyes and burning hair.'

''Twas my mother. She showed me that vile Marlowe is dead. He said I did give the young Earl of Southampton the clap! The clap came from him.'

'We'll have to wait for Master Dingley, then,' Maria said spitefully.

Henry Dingley never knocked again. It cost Emilia several weeks impatience before she learned the truth of Master Marlowe's death. Or what passed for truth, when she had already seen it all and knew better than Her Majesty's Crowner.

~

Odilla took a trickle to the nose and died. Emilia wept copiously, but Lord Hunsdon was made of sterner stuff and scarcely shed a tear. 'The child was mine,' he said. 'I acknowledge it freely now he is dead. Indeed, in my sorrow I do willingly profess it. Do you see me weep? Babes and infants die all the time, and I suffer for every one of them: most of the brats in this metropolis are mine own, anyway! But enough of women's weapons, waterdrops, pah! More children die than are born. It's what keeps the world in balance.'

His household-by-proxy, the serving man and women at his Bishopsgate address, had rarely seen the old fellow so moved or heard him speak at such a length.

'Odilla was a girl,' Emilia interrupted at last.

'Aye, my lord.' Maria said. 'And as fair a little maid as ever entered the Kingdom of Heaven!'

'*That* one? The bastard was mine, as I say. And my poor fool is dead. This is hardly the time to put sex before sex and claim one is worth more than another. Odilla? No more? Well, that's one dowry we won't have to find out of your forty pound a year. Woman!'

Little Henry, his undoubted son, was shrieking like a flute, because his uncle Hunsdon always frightened him.

The Lord Chamberlain gave him a squeeze and a kiss before throwing him to Maria, who had not made herself ready for a game of baby-in-the-ring, so missed him. Lisbet was on the kitchen floor, scrubbing it with teardrops as she said, and turned herself most handily and caught the infant before his head struck the ground, so there was no harm done.

Upstairs, Lord Hunsdon became stern and businesslike. 'Do you still gargle, my dear, and practise those dirges you were wont to sing so roundly?'

'Everyone gargles, Lord Harry. There's dust in the sky, and the air is full of greenfly and Plague.'

'Do you practise on the virginal those duets you taught Her Majesty?'

'I do practise daily in my little room along the way.'

They paused for some several minutes while the Lord Chamberlain refused her the least advantage. His implement was like a punting-pole, and got the better of both of them. 'By the Lord,' he said, 'I do not know how it is I go better with me boots on. Perhaps it's because I'm a horse-riding man.'

'I am no horse, Lord Harry.'

'Would that you were, my poppet. I'd keep you hard by me in my stables at Holborn and finger your nose twice a day. Aye, and dock your tail and feed you sugar.'

It was the nearest he'd come to love talk since she'd grown big-bellied with little Henry, so she smiled a suitable smile.

'Fetch me my leg-wrap,' he said. 'Aye, I have to put it straight on. 'Tis what holds this ulcer against my ankle and stops it barking in the street and biting people's legs. I'm obliged to you, Emilia. Mightily obliged. A younger woman would be all nose-up and fastidious, now my extremities are coming on to smell.'

She unwrinkled her nose hastily. 'I am five-and-twenty, my lord.'

'Even so? Well, I can't lie listening to your pillow gossip. I've business to discuss with you, and was a fair way towards doing it till you interrupted me.'

'My lord?'

'I wish to present you before the Queen again. I feel the time is ripe now my son or daughter is dead. Have you written Her Majesty any more of your charming conceits and recitations?'

'Since tasting the delights of motherhood, my lord Harry, and

217

having but the three main servants in my house, I do lack the time.'

'Never mind your own golden words. They'll only serve to irritate my cousin, coming as they do from a woman. Ask young Will when he's next here.'

'He hasn't been near nor by for a twelvemonth, Harry.'

'Forgetful rogue. He's been starting up my own company for me: The Lord Chamberlain's Men. It makes a young man grow forgetful, training the players, acting a bit, doing the sums and writing five long pieces to be given by himself, Master Burbage and the entire company between them – *huge* pieces, Emilia, mostly sad stories of the death of Kings. He has little time left for women – that's why I did advance him so far and so fast. He hath mentioned you to me of late, though.'

Her breast, which was still naked, grew warm. Will, poor dear, Odilla's most likely father, had asked after her at last? 'He hath mentioned my name?' she ventured.

'Yes, now he's finding his feet he hath a little time on his hands for civilities early on Sunday mornings. So seeing that the supervising of the Lord Chamberlain's Men lacks an adequacy of meat for his energies I have designed him a further course. He and Master Burbage are to build a theatre with my help.'

'So how can he find time to pen me a piece for Her Majesty?'

'Because I do own the fellow, Emilia. Young Southampton did merely offer hire and salary – beer-and-skittles money. Oh, the earl did once advance him a thousand guineas, I do hear tell, to purchase an addition to his estate in Stratford – a *thousand* guineas! You can build *four* theatres for a thousand guineas. I could keep three whores like you, in houses like this, for ten years with servants in abundance for a thousand guineas! Save I do not believe you're such a one, believe me, dearest lady. Yes, Lady Lanier you shall be when Captain Alfonso emerges from the cannon's mouth to claim himself a title from Her Majesty.'

'Master Shakespeare, Lord Harry?'

'As I own him, so shall I command him to assist you.'

'And the Queen? Do you own Her Majesty?'

'The Queen is my cousin, Emilia. Ease my other boot for me

and lend me your chamber-pot. I shall go to Court at once. I am in such a buzz at the thought of doing good for you – and finding further employment for Master Will – I can hardly contain my waters with excitement.'

The Lord Chamberlain was gone, then back on the instant. 'Look to your jordan, my love. 'Tis the clap that stiffens me again. That or the pox, for one of them or the other is playing the Devil with my big toe. Read me the truth of it in my waters, witch.'

He had a horse out at door, and a fellow standing patiently to hold it, but in her impatience she knew he would take an age to reach Whitehall. The City of London was so congested a horse was no advantage, what with the barrows, the chairs, the carts and the coaches. A man who rode a horse could waste a deal of time carrying it. But that was scarcely the jest for the day her Odilla died.

Although she had hope at last, she found herself weeping. 'Why is my baby taken from me?' she cried, having no God to ask.

Her mother's answer was firm. 'Because you have littered this house with curses,' she said. 'I told you they'd trip somebody up.'

～

Once you can get a horse at the gallop, people get out of the way. The same with a good little canter, or a ladylike knees-up trot. Nobody wishes to be trodden into the cobblestone by a horse, and in places that lack pavement death among the crevices can be unimaginably fearful.

One fellow caught at the Lord Chamberlain's stirrup with a curse, but the old man did not breast him aside, nor call for his man to whip him. 'Wouldn't you rather be trodden on by a thoroughbred horse,' he asked, 'than die any of the other deaths that await you?'

The fellow who held him by the leathers, being a fellow, spat.

'My poor man,' The Chamberlain felt about himself for a groatsworth of wit to offer with a modest coin. 'Preferable by far, don't you think, to have good clean smithies' iron crushing your cullions and throat than have a crop of buboes in the very same place?'

The man took his pittance and saluted.

''Tis old Henry of Hunsdon who gallops. Not the Earl of Essex. Pass the word.'

Now that remark of the Lord Chamberlain's, tossed so idly over his shoulder, concealed a great rage and bitterness. His saddle made him sore, what with the ague in his bones, the chalkiness of age, and now a grisly resurgence of the clap. (Damn the way these young men of twenty and thirty whined about the disease, which was in other ways such a blessing. It was commonly held to be like pissing hedgehogs – well, a young fellow should be glad to pass anything at all, and what is pain for, save to remind him he is mortal? Do the angels and archangels and such like powers feel pain? They do not, and a devilish dull time they have in consequence.) But be damned to his saddle! It was his grandnephew the pretty young Essex that put him in such a lather. The fellow was all lisp and leggings, just like Leicester his uncle and stepfather. No sooner is one dead than history brings on another, nestling inside Her Majesty's bosom and with his tongue firmly planted inside her ear. Whatever Essex wanted he got. The boy had wanted to be a soldier, and all he'd achieved was getting young Sydney killed at Zutphen just when he was halfway to making a man of himself. Now he wanted to be a sailor, and was whining and wheedling to have a fleet. He'd be another disaster at sea.

Lord Hunsdon arrived at Whitehall Palace in such a terrible rage and fume at the Earl of Essex that he had no idea of how long or how little the interval had been between leaving Emilia's bed and stumbling from his horse. It was raining in the world around him, but he took no thought of that, or that his clothes were drenched. Cataracts and hurricanoes might have spouted in the wind, but his thoughts of Essex overcame everything else.

It was only as he gave his horse to be held that he remembered what enraged him about the fellow most of all. He wanted to be spycatcher-in-chief, now poor Burghley was slackening his grip.

Was there no respect for old men? Nor for common sense? There were no spies to catch in Court, and if there were, Her Majesty's security was Lord Hunsdon's task. Spies – here? Silly Essex. Well, Wisdom and Goodness to the vile seem vile.

That was a fine phrase, plain in its English directness. He must offer it to young Will when he was straining for a simplicity or two. The poor fellow was already hampered by complexities enough.

His head was full of such thoughts as he ascended among the usual hierarchies of sycophants until he neared Her Majesty.

'Ah, Lord Chamberlain – sweetest coz!'

'"Sweet", Highness? Only for the fair, I do answer you. Only for you am I sweet!' He saw why his cousin Elizabeth spoke as she did. Essex, that lisping cot-quean, was already at her side, *advising* her. He had silver stitching on his legs, and kept rubbing his calves together, like a grasshopper attracting attention to himself.

'Here is a foul thing, cousin Harry. Our poor health is in the custody of traitors. No wonder we do dwindle of late.'

'Nay, Majesty, all you need is a romp in the country. Blame not your cooks! You do drain your wits with too great an exercise of Statecraft!'

'Highness, I have never seen you appear more beautiful to men's eyes,' Essex interposed quickly, seeking to silence the Lord Chamberlain with a quick flutter of warning. 'But some Italians in your employ have already been racked. I do beseech you let me follow this home. What do you say, my Lord Chamberlain?'

'To be brief, Lord Devereux, I do not understand you.'

'We shall seek advice of the Chamberlain when we list,' Queen Elizabeth told Devereux of Essex sternly. 'First, let us tell him our concerns. *You* may speak them, Robert.'

'Know that I – I and those diligent about Her Majesty – have uncovered a plot among the royal apothecaries and leeches led by Doctor Antonio Lopez – Italians all – to lead her with their druggeries and chemical arts into a decline and then, when she sickens, to make away with her entire.

221

I do not yet know whether they mean to smother her in her sleep—'

'Impossible!'

'Or introduce a final superflux of poison in a dram or else some philtre they will prescribe and introduce for the cure of her. So what do you say to this, Harry of Hunsdon?'

'If it be true, we shall hang them high. If it be true. But the apothecaries are not Italians, and Lopez is most certainly a Spaniard!'

'Again, do but advise as *we – not* Lord Robert – list to ask thee, cousin.'

The Lord Chamberlain bowed his head at the rebuke. The Earl did not.

'Know several are already at torment and likely to bring down more. Speak, cousin.'

'I do suspect that torment, for I did never see a man stretched on the rack without him uttering.'

The Queen was into one of her prompter rages. 'Then what do you suggest in this case?'

'Gather them into a suitable pound, Royal Lady. Then, when they are all mewed up together, have men with long ears to listen to them. One half of Your Majesty's Court entire would send the other half to the cheats and the block, did you but have them wracked.'

'This is poor advice, cousin.'

'Well, it is mine and it is honest, even if it serves no advancement.'

'So what would advance thee, Harry?'

'Beyond knowing that you are safe, Majesty?'

'Beyond knowing we are safe.'

'To ask a favour of my Queen that shall satisfy an old man's whim. I would have Mistress Lanier, wife of that Captain Lanier, your Majesty's musician, who is now aboard ship with the Earl of Southampton, I would have Mistress Lanier appointed again at Court.'

'Her husband's claim on me is formidable, Harry, I do grant you that. But is she not your sweetmeat and fancy woman, and no better than your kept harlot? Hath she not had children by you and other men, and diseased half my Court? And have we not warned you before?'

'Majesty!' Harry of Hunsdon knelt, and saw Essex smile at how slowly he went down.

'I do forgive thee for asking, Harry, and love you too much, and trust you too far ever to hold this one imperfection against thee, coz. But I'll not see that dark eyed whore at Court again. She hath a damned Italianate name underneath her newer pedigree, and may well be one with those who plot against me. Watch her for me, Harry. I charge thee on my love. But do not watch too closely, if you take me. She is foreign-skinned and halfway to being a damn'd blackamoor, and I'll not have our two mothers' bloods made brackish in her heirs.'

'Agreed, Majesty. You have my entire compliance.'

'May the Earl of Essex, who is ever your friend, be witness to what has been spoken.'

~

He led his retainers off at a gallop, when they could discover his horse. To have the Palace mislay a horse never boded well for its owner. They turned North, on the track across Charing Cross fields, then East along the lane called Holborn in honour of a stream that had died a long time ago. It was the only gallop there was, past the big houses, the stables, the fine ornamental gardens as big as estates, and it gained him a lung full of cobwebs or some such smoke on the evening air, and brought his horse's nose slap against the London Wall in no time at all.

He mustn't see Emilia, and thank God for that, or what would he tell her? His judgement was impaired, his wits gone in the wind. A wise man, a *younger* man, would never have gone so far out of his way to please his secret woman. Was he falling in love with her again – the same sort of love he'd felt for her before she'd begun to crop and farrow? There's nothing like failure to make a man think he's in love, the pains are so similar.

He wished he'd stopped at his house in Holborn. He could have looked in on the keepers of his hawks and dogs. The trouble with

Blackfriars is that it is so near to Bishopsgate, to the dangerous end especially. Still, there was life in him yet. An old fox may be an old fool, yet still survive, providing he doesn't forget to keep his ears pricked for the baying of hounds.

He went inside his Blackfriars house and called for paper, and bad his clerk have ready some wax and his seal.

He wrote to the Queen first:

Majesty. My Cousin Elizabeth,
 I have been turning matters in mind. My sloth in winding up the rack means not I grow slack in your safety's cause. They are vipers. They will stretch too long and too far while we wonder at the forking of their tongues, as they damn all the innocents in the Garden with their poisonous spittle and name themselves but as smooth snakes, snakes of the grass, blindworms even – and not the adders we know they are.
 I tell your Majesty our nephew Essex should be straight-way encouraged to hang this vile physician Lopez, hang him and hang him high, whether Don or Diego. 'Tis the eftest way of stretching your Majesty's enemies, and the warning to others will be plain and manifest.
 Your Majesty's loyal and obedient cousin,
 Harry of Hunsdon

He waxed this with his own signet, then had his secretary tape and seal it with his Great Seal of Office.

'Send a good man to horse with this to Her Majesty at Whitehall Palace,' he instructed, 'and tell off two more to ride with him. This is for Her Majesty's eyes only, so let it be someone smooth enough, and stout-hearted enough, to deliver it in person – my name will be pass enough.'

While his clerk was about this business, he took pen to Essex. The young start-up thought him a fool, so let him be foolish:

Nephew,
 Forgive me that I did this day forget to name you so when I kneeled in audience to Her Most Gracious Majesty.

He chuckled, remembering his Emilia's jest when he'd put his boot into her belly:

> As you will recall, I had need to lie down and wallow a little.

Praise be, Jerson the clerk was not back from his errand yet. Lord Hunsdon found tears rush into his eyes at the thought of her, and the knowledge of her undoubted loss to him. Even his jokes would hurt him now, for she was his only toy. Women he had in plenty, but she was his rest.

> I do most bethink me of those times your youth was fain to be in the charge of my Lord Burghley your attentive guardian, and am mindful of your stepfather Leicester, the noble earl, so forgive me that I did forget – old man that I am – you are the son of my beloved niece Letitia.
>
> Still I do not take to my pen for family's sake, which among us Careys, Boleyns, Devereux, Knolys, et al., is more than a rumour in the blood. I say hang your whoreson doctor up, and quickly. Hang him high – and his apothecary too – by the cods if necessary. But be brief about it for Her Majesty's sake. She doth tremble to think blood. And may all such traitors perish.
>
> You are to be congratulated, my lord of Essex. You have been shown this day to have an excellent nose for wickedness.
>
> Your uncle,
> Hunsdon

Jerson was back now, and confident he had sent the right man. 'Well, send me another right man to search out the Earl of Essex with this.' He signalled for a great seal within and more wax without, so the cylinder looked more important than a proclamation of festival, or a death warrant. 'He'll not need to be such a right man as last time, for Robert Devereux is

225

a spymaster and spycatcher now. He sits lost in a great web, but no door is locked that might lead to him!'

He watched Jerson turn again towards the door and took up his quill again. Three letters, and all by his own secret hand. No wonder his fingerbones began to ache. It was more tedious than rolling dice or stirring up fastidious women before he'd taught himself to come at them quickly:

Mistress,

I did nothing. I made essay. I can do nothing more. I am nothing.

There is a plot, another damn'd plot, which is a Spanish plot if it is anything, but which my cousin calls Italian, so greatly she sniffs a propinquity. You sense how our troubles begin?

Essex was there, a most forward boy, with his brains all over his tongue. He did speak in Her Majesty's ear, of your father's blood, your name, and fill her thoughts with all manner of plagues and poxes I will not endyte in a letter to yourself or any woman.

So whence my cousin's anger? For reasons my tooth is too long to bite back, it is likely she knows the disease herself and in her own person, from the same well-spring and fountain as mine own.

Burn this, or God will not bless you. I can do no more for you. I am no more, though the forty pounds will be annual within my lifetime.

Yours H.

A kinder intelligence is that my cousin did speak fetchingly of Lanier, your husband. May he prosper, and yourself withal.

The clerk came back, and signalled he had found a man who was man enough to reach Essex.

'Aye,' the Lord Chamberlain scoffed, 'thou could'st send a maid, Jerson, or a boy on his hobby. The Earl is as open as a tree in a November sky, and like the tree full of nothing but wind.'

'My lord.'

'Tell me, Jerson. Have you serviced your wife, threatened your children of late? Is your family in good heart? I have an errand for thee.'

'The Lord Chamberlain well knows how I am wed. I am bound only to your employ, my lord.'

'Be bound to no man's employ, Master Jerson, and married to no task mere man can divine for you.'

'Save my lord.'

Hunsdon was touched. He was too easily touched lately. 'Well, sit thyself down, Master Jerson. I've a job for thee, a task that will take thee into winter, so long is the journey. Are you game?'

'Aye, my lord.'

'Pray God I am here when you return, my good Jerson. Now take hold of this letter and fasten it as you will. Do not demean thyself, because thou art a gentleman, but write on its packet such words as you may devise for yourself.'

'My lord.'

Harry of Hunsdon rose and paced about his chair. His back troubled him. His knee ached. His ulcer throbbed in a manner close to barking. He said, as kindly as he could, but no one smiles with toothache, 'I want you to visit my castle in Hunsdon. That's a long ride, Jerson. I have never been less than a week on the road. Take men enough to be secure, and an exchange of horses. Go boldly, and in my livery, not yourself as a gentleman, but see the rest are apparent. Choose a good man – he who sought the Queen perhaps? – to be in charge of them when you are not, but discreet, mind, and privy enough not to mention yourself when you are absent.'

'I cannot understand you, my lord.'

'It shall be apparent. Spend a week in the North. Make a list of my fields, if you like. Take an inventory of my barns, have someone count my does. For all I care, number the cushions in the parlour, the trees in my orchard – have your men check the stones for worm.'

'My lord.'

'Then you shall ride back with a list of items and imperfections longer than a scroll, to leave with your fellow in charge. Oh, and you'll have your little package secured about your person, never far from your own safe-keeping. Do you follow me?'

'I begin, my lord.'

'Come into the city and report to me here. Send my men to Holborn, but not straightway.'

'I see, my lord.'

'Coming from the North Country you'll enter by Bishopsgate bar.'

'Exactly, my lord Hunsdon.'

'Come in, but send your men to Holborn by any alehouse in Smithfield. Tell the fellow in charge they're not to be drunk, nor mention you.'

'My lord.'

'I've a house in Bishopsgate. You'll have counted cushions there in thy time.'

'Indeed.'

'Go straightway past it. Take no notice of it. But go to the gentlemen's ordinary a little nearer the Thames on the Western side.'

'I know it, my lord.'

'Order a meal for yourself. Nay, order a feast. Put yourself about – not in drink, mind. There'll be no coney-catchers there. Master Ribble is a good man.'

Jerson was attentive still. If he was puzzled, he did not show it.

'Call him quietly to you and say you want your packet delivered. Never mention my name. He'll see you're a gentleman. Give him a crown and let him see your embarrassment. Tell him there's a dell there who scrubs for a great lady. Tell him you're smitten below your station. Tell him she's with child. Say it as you will.'

'He'll know the great lady, my lord.'

'Aye, but she'll not answer doors. Tell him to hand the packet to whichever one answers. On it write the name Lisbet Bown. She's the scully, Jerson. I'm sorry to do this. The other letter's inside.'

'Lisbet Bown, my lord.'

'Aye. She'd not disgrace any man, as it happens. She's a proper little primrose for any lord's bed.'

'You are being kind.'

'Not I. Go to, and take money enough. Do not stint thyself.' He pulled Jerson towards him, a gesture that surprised both of them. 'You should be a Knight. You *shall* be a Knight. 'Tis a pity you serve not the Earl of Essex. He's a man who created some thirty knights baneret in the field at Gournay when he was but two-and-twenty. Thirty knights! Twenty seven or so more than Her Majesty found pleasing.'

'My lord.'

Hunsdon no longer needed him as a prop for himself, so the clerk was able to breathe a little air.

'He needs to surround himself with entitlements,' the older man chuckled. 'But he'll never succeed. He's a man who thinks he can grow himself ships-of-war simply by keeping a pocket full of acorns.'

EIGHTEEN

Emilia was in a fury. A fury at waiting a month. A fury at finding a letter thrust inside a scullion's placket by Peter Rudkin.

It did her rage no good to know her protector was in danger and she was in peril more. She'd rather be dead than not at Court, and she'd never been called since the birthing of young Henry, now almost three years old. Everything had happened as Lord Hunsdon had warned her. Nobody visited her, nobody who was an anybody, not even her husband – home and playing for the Queen at Oxford, then away again and at sea without even seeing her, in a vessel commanded by Southampton, if that wasn't a joke. The boy might be beautiful, but he couldn't raise his mizzen properly, as her Hunsdon called it, so how would he ever square a mainsail?

She loathed old Hunsdon. Now the Bitch majesty had forbidden her even the thing she hated. She had no one to insult her, punch her, kick her, be vilely affectionate with her, no one to stink in her bed.

'Mother, I must call down vengeance on the so-called Queen.'

'How, child? Not through me thou can'st not.'

'You are a great witch, my mother. Even Harry Hunsdon calls you so, and I do hear that your dead granddaughter's father does write plays about you which are given before the Bitch Queen. Are you not great enough?'

'Are you not a witch's daughter? So is that Elizabeth.'

A log fell in the fire, an unfortunate yard of ashpole cut with

231

the sap still in it, and black with the buds of that long ago spring when Odilla was born, and Emilia's Will and her sapling earl but scarcely departed. The ash was reluctant to burn, but writhed this way and that like a grey snake, which at last spoke with her mother's voice. 'Queen Anne, her mother, was the Witch Queen, child, as I say – she with her Thousand Days. What a foolish, too mortal husband the old king was, not to see it! She even got him to turn England from the True Religion, too, and only so he would marry her. What witch could do greater than that?'

'The *true* religion, mother? Shadows and Smoke make the true religion.'

'Witches follow the Old Faith, child, and pray to the Horned Head in the Bush. But Rome is the True *Religion*, your dead father's religion, and those who are foolish enough to need a Religion had best follow it. Queen Anne did change that!'

'But Queen Anne, Anne Boleyn, a witch?'

'Aye, with the devil's pap to prove she was chosen by the Shadowy One. She hath it on her left hand, a teat as long as her little finger. She hath a sixth finger. It has both nipple and nail. I can see it now.'

Emilia grew dizzy with the ash smoke, and giddy with the writhers in her fire. She started when the snake crept out and about, touching her all over. Neither hot nor cold, but as comfortable as the sex of a man who makes it worship a woman but forbears to stir her guts with it.

Strange to see it open its eye and speak with her mother's voice again. 'There is no spell I can work against a witch queen, daughter, or the child of such a one, even for my own. Others may fare differently.'

'What others?'

'Essex, perhaps, Southampton certainly, poets and catamites in their circle. Master Shakespeare, your soul's husband, if you will.'

'Aye, I will. He hath abused me in rhyme.'

'And what is verse but a spell? They have abused you mightily – but some are already dead, Marlowe and his bedfellow Kyd, and Greene who did laugh at you for a curse of nature that a

232

man had given you, and a King bequeathed.' The snake left Emilia's lap and crept back into the fire, calling, 'Follow me, child. Follow me with your eyes if you lack faith enough to set foot in my cave.'

Emilia leant nearer and saw a firelit room, with a man asleep with his arms thrown over his head, much as she had seen Marlowe in the last moments of his life. This one had an ashen pallor, and it was only as her eyes grew accustomed to the flames she realized he lay upon a rack.

'Thomas Kyd,' her mother said. 'This is the third time he lay in torment. He was released in a weakened state into your Marlowe's lodgings – and your enemy did perform on him, being his friend, acts he had never been minded towards, but was now too weak to resist.'

Masked figures dropped levers into the cylinders at Thomas Kyd's wrists and heels, anchored them into their holes and leant back on them, tightening the ropes that stretched him. Blood dribbled from his mouth.

'He hath swallowed his tongue,' her mother said, 'swallowed it up or otherwise had done with it – he'll never speak ill of thee again.'

'Of me?'

Blood came down the doomed man's nose, and a bone started from its socket above the knee.

The snake lay across the cave of embers, and Emilia could see no more of him.

'Blame him not – for he spoke no more to his tormentors, and to friends at Court, than your Marlowe taught him to say. That he had a clap from Marlowe who had it from Southampton who had it from thee.'

'Monstrous. My Will did say it was Christopher Marlowe who infected all the catamites in the world.'

'That's as may be, daughter. You have littered the air with curses, aye, and the ground also. You must answer for that!'

'Poor, poor man. My Will did say he was a genius in his time.'

'Will told you many things, when you would listen to him.'

233

'Were we born to listen to men?'

'Only with ears, daughter. Not with our hearts and never with our heads. Shall I show you Master Greene?'

Emilia had supped on horrors enough, but the snake had charge of her will, the snake or the fire.

'Must it always be beds, mother?'

'Most men die on a bed or battlefield, child; most women in bed. Tune your eyes, 'tis a couch at most, a daybed perhaps.'

Master Greene lay in a drowse, with food untasted on the table beside him – a dish of fish, and some bread. There was blood on the board, as if it had been spat from the lungs. Or perhaps not blood, perhaps spilled wine. Could it be that he'd spewed it up? Was he drunk with poppy or poisoned with ratsbane?

'A handsome jack, but he'll sell his soul for anyone's friendship. He did laugh at what Marlowe said of you, and pass it around.'

The sleeper stirred once, or perhaps he was no longer asleep. Perhaps it was the last movement a corpse makes, or the move a fever corpse makes after that.

'There's a story abroad he was poisoned,' the witch Johnson said. 'And another, more pleasing to me, that he died of a surfeit of wine and pickled herring. But look at the so-called wine, child. It is red, and no one could swallow red wine with soused fish, not even Master Greene. Look at his throat. Do you not see the snake round his neck?'

'Snake?' Emilia was amazed. Could England boast a serpent that would strangle a man?

'Is it a snake or a necklace of leeches. Or why not a hangman's ruff? 'Tis black for a snake, child. And look at his groin – did you not see what threw his leg aside, aye, shifted a dead man's leg. 'Tis the buboes, Emilia. He had them at neck and thigh, much as is normal, and deep in his lungs besides. They go on growing even after death, like mushrooms on a heap of mildew, especially when the Creator is displeased.'

'The Creator, mother. You speak of a Maker?'

'Of course I do. You have much to learn. Somebody made us,

One of the Pair of Them did. The question is Which One? That's what will test you, both there and here.'

'Here and Where?'

'Oh, cocks are crowing on merry-middle-earth, but your time is not long to decide which is which. Will you come up or go down? And where are we witches of yesteryear?'

Emilia didn't see her mother, or hear her voice for quite some time, though her black cat came often from the fire as the snake had done.

There was a restlessness in her bed as well, though she more and more surrounded her sleep in a ring of salt. But salt can be brushed aside, by Maria's careless carrying of a gown or Lisbet sweeping the floor.

Then her mother's familiars would come, her long dead puckrels Dingley and Marc Anthony. The one was never more than a sensation in the nostril, but Dingley was there with all manner of monsters more. Herself they dared not touch, whether apes, anthropophagi or crocodiles, but if Lisbet or Maria slept with her, the young would stir and cry, as if with a pleasure that threatened too much pain, and Emilia would know that the shadows were at them and all about.

~

The Thames froze over, and men skated and footed the ball on the ice, or skidded bricks, or played games with nooses and quoits, generally around maids' ankles.

A fire was builded, a tower of driftwood and bavins stolen from poor men's carts and rich men's yards, till it rose as high as St Paul's, then an idiot lit it and a thousand harlots danced all about it under the clear glass sky till they were like to fall through it and drown in the moon.

This fire did not destroy the ice, though it burned a hole in it deeper than the Earth Giant's navel, and was like to touch Hell. So men filled the crater with wood and lit it again, this time under hogs and an ox, and fed roast to the poor, and were surprised how many were poor. Still the frost would not move, for the ice reached down to the bottom, and some said deeper than that.

Emilia was a serious woman and would have none of this ice, till one night Maria and Lisbet drew her out, guarded by Peter Rudkin their man, who lacked the rank for his mistress to allow him a sword, but who could do stout things with a cudgel and be less at risk by it.

So that was the night when Emilia walked in the world again, with Maria bringing Henry to slide on the ice, having less far to fall. She smelled chestnuts roasting, and the sotweed, now planted widely and fogging the air, and dogs and bears and the crotches of men.

The Bitch Queen enjoyed these smells, and perhaps these sights as well, for a carpet was laid for her on the ice from Whitehall Stair.

She came out, with the Earl of Essex bringing her by hand, and bragging about, and Southampton close by Essex; and Southampton commanding musicians to follow as well. Lanier was not among them. He wrote her letters now, complaining of being kept on ships in the Bristol Channel, off Plymouth, the Medway, as if she knew or cared about such places. He spoke of Essex leading them in a great Armada to Spain, of glory at last, or being drowned. Well, he wrote. A husband is better absent, providing he sends her a word or two, or a coin, or a tear.

The Bitch Queen received the applause of the multitude who had walked up river to greet her, and the musicians played sprightly notes while she walked about, though sometimes the horns grew frosted and the viols sounded limp.

Harry of Hunsdon would never allow such a thing even so. He'd have kept all their strings in a warmth with candles and cressets, even on ice, and seen the fiddlers were instructed to stop often and tune. But where was Lord Hunsdon, and why was the Bitch Queen in such an untidy throng of courtiers?

The Bitch Queen continued to circle about, or encourage her people to circle, as if she were an island and her island race a fleet. Her gaze fell upon Emilia, who saw it was full of poison.

It is difficult to curtsy on ice, but no harder than for a man to bow. Grown men and women do neither, whether on ice or cobblestone, lacking the skill, but Emilia was a lady of the Royal Court, if not of the Bitch Queen's Court. She sank down low, and held herself there till Her Majesty walked on.

Mighty is the power of dream, and convenient the recognition that can come by firelight, even if it is only ox-fat that drips on the flame. Emilia recognized the courtier who had overseen Marlowe's death. 'Master Poley!' she called. Did she recognize him from the murder she'd seen done within her hearth, or remember him from Court? Who can tell? She did not curtsy again.

'I do not see the Lord Chamberlain,' she observed.

'Old Lord Harry, 'tis a sorry thing, mistress. I do hear he's unlike to survive.'

Three years she had given him. Had she wished those years to be full of so few days?

'He did not bring out the Queen. She preferred the Earl, but Her Majesty and old Harry spoke very fondly each to each. She told him she'd an errand for him in Berwick, and then in Ireland, and he agreed. Then he did fall upon the ice, the way old bones can, and he broke, the way old bones do.'

She began to move towards Whitehall Stair.

'Nay, Mistress Bassano.'

'Lanier is my husband's name. Captain his rank and gentleman his station.'

'Every gossip knows you belong to old Harry, mistress. He's lying over there, gone in the back and with a thighbone broken in several places. They dare not move him, and he will not shift himself again.' He smiled sadly, then called in alarm, 'I do advise you, for your own sake . . .'

She was already running on the ice, bringing little Henry with her, other people following as they could.

Lord Hunsdon lay beside the stair, never to move again. The heat of his falling had made a puddle on the ice, and he steamed in the midst of it like a peacock in its gravy.

Lady Carey, his daughter-in-law, stood nearby. Half the world knelt around. The lady said icily, 'Who is this woman?'

'Lord Harry,' Emilia whispered in his better ear.

After a time, he opened his eyes. 'Mistress Bassano,' he said. Then, to Henry, 'Little Harry.'

'My Mother's called Lanier,' Harry said. Then, as he watched his father die, 'That is the old Uncle who frightens me. Do you remember him, Lisbet? He was always chasing Mamum upstairs, and in her own house!'

~

Public curses, private griefs. It is surprising how much she could love people once they were dead. Never did she feel such pain or know so much power. She gave torturers employment and sent murderers to work simply by changing the wood in her fireplace. A royal chamberlain – *the Lord* Chamberlain – was dead simply because of women's water spilled from a pot.

Maria was increasingly her physician and guide in such problems of faith. 'It was the dead women's water and I spilled the jordan,' she said briefly, ever the soul's leech. On another occasion she said, 'It was the dead women's stalings, and the old man who killed them. He sowed the whirlwind. Why should you puff yourself up with pride?'

'I do not swell up, nor shall I ever grow large again.'

They were all of them weeping and laughing, and being womanish with one another, and many was the truth that struck them.

'There goes the old man's dot,' Lisbet said. 'There goes forty pounds a year.'

'Yours was the curse,' her mother said sharply, 'and mine was the pot. Though, put another way, the pot was not mine, nor ever was nor shall be. It belongs to the Devil, so it's nothing to do with me. The moving finger writes of she who laid the curse. I see the fiery letters and I note the one he points at, the Darkness in the Wall. Face up to your responsibilities, girl. I told you there were too many curses littering your world.'

'Be silent for my mother.'

'Emilia, I can hear nothing save the wind beneath the door,' Maria said. 'Shall we all begin to purr?' She began to purr herself, until a terrible hissing and scratching could be heard in the fireplace.

Lisbet rose and said, 'I'll go downstairs and put a pan on. We could all use a bowl of hot sherries.'

'Aye,' said Maria, 'enough to sack a city.'

'Follow me into the fire, daughter. There's nothing I can hide from you.'

'Anything within reason, mother.'

'If you're going to mumble away to yourself, then I shall leave the room.' Maria leapt to her feet, a witchlike figure herself, but those illusions come easy to a girl in a working skirt. 'Lisbet's already gone. Sometimes I think there's no helping you, Emilia. A prayer is always cheaper than cursing, and it costs less wood in the hearth.'

Emilia sought her mother inside the coals beyond the flames. She found her sitting among gnomes, devils and salamanders, and all manner of impish wonders else. Little Henry's great aunt was there as a reminder of all the witch Margaret Johnson had spoken of before. Yes, Emilia Bassano-Lanier's kinswoman by breeding if not by blood was there, the great Witch Queen Anne Boleyn, with her third little finger cocked, and she had Sir Thomas Wyatt her lover beside her, whose verses Emilia so much admired – though, just like poor Will's, there was much she could advise him on.

'To bring Essex down and the prattling young earl, you'll need much more than those figures from Hell. I have read their fate in the Scroll of the Years, and all manner of fiery parchments. Why not leave it to time, Emilia, time and the follies of men?'

'Nay, it gives me no power.'

'Time should bring wisdom, Emilia. You're an old woman now. You will soon be thirty years gone, which is ancient for one of our sex, though your flesh is good and I promise you much, much more.'

'I mean ruin to Essex and the Queen, even as I ended young Marlowe. And I need to still Will's pen. He keeps on writing me down – he'll never *speak* ill of me, he loves me and hates me too

239

much to remember me with his mouth. But I need to destroy his poems.'

'It takes a poem to answer a poem, girl. Meanwhile, call back my villain Dingley. That puckrel's still beyond Hell's gate, your tongue hath lent him the key. Dingley only understands death, and he works towards Odilla-my-grandchild's father, even as your malice empowered him.'

'Call him back, mother.'

'Nay, call him yourself, if you can.'

'Is Odilla there? Is she with you?'

'Angels of Fire and Darkness, of course she is not with me. I have powers and comforts here. I bought them all with my Art. I could not purchase the Sphere, just an arc on a line, this hot segment beneath the chord. You must study, girl, and preach to me less.'

'I study you now, my mother.'

'Then know I have no power against your Bitch Queen, for reasons I spoke before. I have propinquity with all the Boleyns through your live child, my grandson, though there your venom must end. As for Essex, and little Southampton, they've propinquity in their way, though thinner far in the blood. To bring them low before their written-down time, you will need more brutish powers. You'll need spirit stolen from a man: I mean not his seed or his blood, still less the breath of his kiss, but he must be alive and in health, and you must steal him away from himself for a festival of your own devising.'

'What manner of man is this?'

'He must be a sorcerer. You will need to enslave a sorcerer, and draw him into your nights so his darkness can be revealed to you.'

'I know no such man.'

'You know Doctor Dee. He is greater than the ignorant think, though less proficient in our Art than he sometimes pretends – a frequent conceit of men. He is potent enough for your needs, and he lusts for you.'

'He is ancient now, and I'm loathe to use his old kindness up.'

240

'What a weakness you show. On the one hand, you hate like a Queen, on the other you're fastidious with those you love. Use the old fool, daughter. He's returned from Bulgaria now.'

'And he's living in Scotland with a shared wife. Where is the strength in that?'

'I did not know he's in Scotland, child.'

'Can't you see down there?'

'I can see a piss-prophet in Lambeth. He reads women's waters for signs, and feels their young bodies for stones. He says he is all for their health, but it's hearts that he's quick to steal, then their honour and virginity after. Yes, he is your man.'

'His name, mother.'

'*Emilia!*' Maria it was who screamed, entering the room and snatching her mistress back from the fire. The Young Witch had followed her mother too far in, so the old lady was near to solving everything for her, but by painful means as such solutions are.

Emilia was too dizzy to scream, too dizzy or too proud. When her mouth flapped open at last, her dress was aflame, its silken stitches dripping like wax down a candle. Maria rolled her on the floor, and called Lisbet to bring water and throw it in her hair which was singed by the fire-damps rising.

By now the whole room was burning, the rushes on the floor at least, and feathers from the bed, and several of Emilia's papers. The bed curtains and wall-hangings were made of sterner stuff, but it seemed best to draw off Emilia's still smouldering dress, and bear her downstairs with her hair still in a fearful stink as if from the curling tongs.

Peter Rudkin had never been up there before, but he'd always longed to be a great one in bedrooms. While Emilia lay shouting and trembling on the kitchen floor, he rushed upwards with a pitcher he'd filled from the alley pump.

'No, Peter,' Lisbet called.

'Not in the Mistress's great chamber,' Maria scolded after. 'Especially not with water from the alley pump.'

'It isn't pure,' Emilia protested. 'Not among my private trophies and hangings, good Peter.'

He obeyed almost at once, coming down three or four steps

at the time, which was clever for a man unused to stairs. ''Tis all afire, missus Emilia. There's flame up the walls, and the rafters are burning like twigs in a forest. Can't you hear them crackle?'

They carried Mistress Bassano into the street, and little Henry beside her. He was still asleep, and slept through it all, just to spite a child's natural curiosity.

His mother lay in a rug, singed about the hair and all manner of other places within and without what was evident, but not enough to sear her, or to fry her or fatten her after.

It's a brave sight to see a house burn down, save when it's your own. The servants enjoyed it mightily, and other people clapped their hands and were in general too busy to throw on much water, what with their finger-faddling and drumming with their palms, and laughing and pointing, until they realized a whole length of their street was catching flame, some of it only thatched, and the whole town very windy. Then they did busy their actions mightily, and call on their neighbours to assist them bringing out their furnishings. But most men ran to help their wives assist themselves, so few sticks were saved, what with the shrieking and swearing and wasting time on children. Stones at most were left standing for a bowshot around – whatever a bowshot is – but Peter kept repeating it, though goodness knows why, after gunpowder's invention, and this a new age when men could hardly walk.

'It's a brave sight once the tiles come off,' Lisbet cried, pointing into the flames. 'And you can see all the skeleton and frame of things. It puts me in mind of a chicken on its back.'

'Chickens is for eating, not burning,' Rudkin grumbled. 'I've never set spark to a chicken.'

'I did lose one from the spit into the fire once,' Lisbet explained. 'So then I saw it burn. My mother boxed my ears for it, but I noted she stood and watched it.'

'It's to be hoped the chicken was dead,' Peter Rudkin queried. 'Had you cleaned it and plucked it? And I suppose someone wrung it by the neck? Or cut into its mouth? Or knocked it still in some way?'

242

Emilia moaned, piteously.

'Well, then, it was dead. What a waste of a chicken.'

'Are you all right, Emilia?' her servant Maria called to her. 'Holla! Emilia, what cheer?'

Just then the Watch went running down Bishopsgate, which only had one side now and was becoming hot to stand in, though kinder to Emilia lying down. The watch was followed by some kind of militia, then some liveries on horseback. Then came the gentlemen of the Honourable Artillery, who are trained to advance slowly behind an Alderman on a horse, so of course could not run, what with the length of their poles, those that bore pikes, and the weight of their arquebuses, those who weren't so fortunate, such weapons weighing heavier than a cannon on a stilt, heavier than a swivel gun on the gunwales of Drake's ships at the least, though now in the command of Essex.

The news came back only slowly. Seemingly, there was a fire down in Blackfriars as well. A spark must have flown over, or perhaps when the winds have the flame in their teeth the Devil will take them anywhere.

Anyway, a playhouse had taken fire, perhaps Mr Burbage's *Theatre* itself, or some said 'The Curtain', others the innyard at the 'Keys'. Whatever the place, there was a play being given.

This wouldn't normally have mattered, being over halfway done, and men only going there for the wenches, and by now fitted up, so a fire would have seemed highly preferable. Unfortunately for discipline and good order, which events became swiftly contrary to, the spectacle being given was by one Master Shakespeare, whose verses were so sweet they'd been known to change whores into nuns, and make even deaf men strain to follow till the very last syllable, of which there'd have been too many if written by someone else.

When Shakespeare's words took fire, and his players' properties besides, some men tried to stay till the end to glimpse and hear the catastrophe. Did Titus fall upon his sword? What happened to Hamlet's ghost, was the Much Ado entirely about Nothing?

Nobody could tell, nor even those that fled early remember

which piece it was. The only cry was 'Shakespeare!' and 'Fire!', the one against the other Then some men lifted fists, and others picked up stones. Women were trampled beneath the gateway, and the militia did fire indeed, though without any balls in their pieces, simply to make things quiet.

This discharge of ordnance, although very slight in volume, occasioned an instant downpour of rain, followed in the end by thunder.

Was this Henry Dingley's doing? Had Will been lost in the flames? Was there some piece of similar good fortune? Her fireplace had disappeared, so her mother could bring no answer. Poor singed, near naked Emilia, a woman half without hair, must take a new dwelling at once.

NINETEEN

Emilia saved nothing in that fire but her jewels, her son Henry and her mother's jordan, which the witch called the Devil's Pot. She also saved her people, Maria and Lisbet and her man Peter Rudkin, though they – in the way of their ignorance – claimed to have saved her.

'Well, each to his belief,' Maria said.

'Mistress is a her,' Peter Rudkin said.

'My belief is greater than yours, and on firmer foundation. For I did walk inside the fiery cave.'

'Nonsense, Emilia! You fell asleep by the fire and were nearly a cinder.'

'I tell you I walked in Hell with my mother at my side and talked of little Henry's aunt who is Anne Boleyn. So what do you say to that, Peter?'

Peter was very much a man, so easily led. He said, 'I think anyone but the Queen had better be quiet about Her Mother's blood. If not, you'll get your throat chopped, missus, or would if you'd rank enough. As it is, they'll hang you up high, a very disrespectful way to treat a woman, but I've seen it with witches in Smithfield and very long legs they had, from all that dancing with the Fellow in Black, or some say Green.'

'Thank you, Rudkin.'

'They were dancing while I watched them, as it happened. And danced for a long time after.'

'Enough should be enough, good Peter.'

'*You'll* not dance, Missus Emilia, not if you're done by the Queen.'

'I should meet my end with dignity, and in all ways befitting a woman of my station, and the brave Captain's wife.'

'Doubtless, missus. If the Queen has you done they cut all your tripes out, and worse if you're a man. All your bumps and lumps and pipings, too. It's a very pretty sight, missus, and pleases the crowd, but of course they sees no dancing after, and that's a disappointment.'

Emilia had her grand house now. She had taken it with rent deferred, as a great lady can. In what ways was she great? She was great because people spoke of her. They knew who she was. She was the late Lord Chamberlain's thing, she had crouched by him at his death upon the ice; she was a warrior's lady. She was great above all because she felt huge in herself, in spite of singed hair. When a house burns down in the Bishopsgate fire, then a lady needs a place of similar dimension, say four times as big, a solid tower of stone.

She took a place in Longditch, next to Canon Row, which was full of earls and similar folk who were more to her liking. The City was in all ways too hot to hold her. There were those who knew her as the Great Witch who had started one of its greatest fires by summoning a serpent from her hearth, or some said a cat with its tail aflame. Peter Rudkin was the discreetest of men, but he had a stomach for a tankard of ale and the tongue to follow it. Whatever men said of this sort, including aldermen and knights of the nearer shire, only served to increase her sense of herself.

She came to the City of Westminster, close to Whitehall Palace, not to be near that merely earthly monarch, Elizabeth, her own Bitch Queen – Elizabeth was seldom there of late – but because it was only one of Peter Rudkin's bowshots away from Lambeth across the tide, and the soon-to-be-captive astrologer quack who lived there. She sent Maria by water to make an appointment as soon as she was settled in. So when the iron knocker sounded on her door she thought it was Maria back before time.

Alas, it was another that Rudkin showed in, better dressed

than she remembered him, but older now. Age is never pleasing in a man, even if he does own half of Stratford. What was Stratford to her, or she to Stratford? He might as well be Lord-of-the-Manor of the Cheese on the Moon.

'Mistress Emilia.'

She spent some little time looking Master Will over, her disappointment at what little had become of him plain for him to see.

'Mistress,' he faltered again. His voice trembled with an emotion hardly defined. It was easy to gaze him down.

'Mistress Emilia, I came to share with you a parcel of my sorrow at hearing your ill news. However,' – he gazed around in wonderment at all her leasings, and hirings and chattels-upon-payment deferred – 'I see you are a great lady now. My late Lord and Patron of my Company must have remembered you well, or Master Lanier done well from his voyaging. Did the Earl of Southampton's vessel capture a prize?'

She wondered whether to answer such a libellous inquisition. She was, was she not, a woman who made miracles alone? A fellow who scribbles but to sell his wares is hardly more than a costard monger, or any such seller of crabs in the market.

The soft brown eyes of his saw what she let him see of her mind. She could see he thought what she meant him to think.

'I am sorry for your fire, my Emilia,' he said.

'Nay, sir – is it *Sir* Will? Have your patrons not bought you a knighthood yet? Well then, my Will, let Not-Your-Emilia offer you condolences instead. She is told your playhouse burned down that self-same night. She wishes she could express her grief in a tear, but her own conflagration has left her dry-eyed. As hath the furnace of her supposed friends' use of her.'

He brightened at her patchwork of insult. There's nothing like a little venom on a pretty woman's tongue to make an actor sparkle. 'Nay, Emilia,' he said, but offered no more.

'I think a tiny sprite flew from my own conflagration with a spark in its mouth?'

'Nay, Emilia. Do not fret yourself. You bear guilt enough for more things else, but do not fret for our playhouse burning. It did not burn. It was the play that burned, just the one performance only. We gave it in the Keys Inn yard. It was the Inn that burned. Nor was it your sprite, for a firebrand did it. I did see the arsonist myself. 'Twas a vile fellow with a locket hanging by his ear.'

She breathed a little happiness into herself and said, 'Not a locket, and not by his ear. Was it not a rogue with a fallen eye, that hangs on his cheek, like a locket in a chain? An eye, not a locket, you see, even if it seems like a locket?'

'Very like. But only if you like, my Emilia. Methought it as a locket by his ear. But it might have been his eye. 'Twas very like a locket in the firelight. Do you know the rogue?'

'My mother died. If only I could ask her, but—'

'Nay, "if" me no "ifs" and "but" me no "buts".'

Men are such nothings, she mused. They are the whoreson zed, the unnecessary letter. So easy to string by the nose. She decided to fetch him by a different tack. 'Will you not love me, Will, and let us be friends? Not a love such as lovers use, but such as may be betwixt friends?'

He answered nothing to that, as if surprised at being so quickly forgiven. She must try again.

'Will you not love me for old time's sake?'

'Do you still have Lord Hunsdon's clap, Emilia? That must be the first question.'

'I spoke of the love between friends, such as Plato mentions.'

'Do you have the clap, I say?'

She swallowed just a little, but her voice was firm.

'I do not have this vile disease you speak of. I had no notion on the subject until you accused me all those years you've let gone. Then I stole a look at a learned treatise, full of etchings and painting so vile you'd have thought a butcher made them, or a devil in torment.'

'Lord Hunsdon gave you the clap. You gave it to me. The old Chamberlain – God rest his generous soul! – gave everyone in London the clap. It's a fact for alehouse gossip even now. He gave it you when he gave you young Henry.'

'He never gave me young Henry. Do you wish to see me

hanged? I had young Henry from Heaven, and doubtless you caught the clap in Hell.'

'Yes, your Hell, lady. I did say so in a poem.'

'And printed it vilely about.'

'I shall never print it, Emilia, or any of my sonnets else. My love for my lord is too great.'

'And his purse too deep. You do show it men, though.'

'No, his mother hath all the text, both my fair copy and my old foul papers. You have whatever I sent to you. There are no more. On my life, I do promise you that.'

She yawned at him then. He was worth a yawn. He'd made no move to touch her breast or kiss her ear. He did not by a nod or half a wink suggest he was thinking of creeping near enough to part those legs of hers, or even feel about to find what legs she had, so she had been denied the entertainment of refusing him. So where did his interest reside? Certainly not in his speaking. He spoke more and more like a character in a play. Touch enough pitch and . . .

'This I do say, Emilia, and believe me 'tis a tribute I pay you. That singeing in the fire hath leant a little lightness to your skin, and bleached a trace of gold into your hair. I give the Good God my blessing for that.'

He had found himself a speech and made it, so was now clearly going. He had not been invited to sit, so he need not rise. He allowed himself to bow, the way players will, still with too much wrist and his leg half across the room as she remembered from before.

'Well, all you ladies seek an alternation, my Emilia, and God hath whitened Mistress Lanier till she looks more like the Queen than Her Majesty does Herself.'

The Bitch was a hundred years old, and he was ageing almost as fast.

'Poor sweet Will,' she told him. 'I have to tell you that your child has died.'

'Aye. I thank you for your grief. Little Hamnet is dead. But his twin and his older sister continue well.'

'I do not mean your Stratford child. I mean your babe by me.'

249

'Your children are by God, mistress. You always said so. Let us find a subject on which we can agree.'

Having ended on a couplet, albeit in long measure, the lesser poet was gone.

~

Maria was returned from Lambeth at last, bearing no message but a letter. She seemed flushed, and bothered like a lass newly escaped from a romp in a summer haywain, not one who has just been boated across the Thames with the wind blustering hard from the East.

'By Cock, Mistress Emilia, your Doctor Simon hath sly hands, and quick to fasten on a maid where there's money to be earned! Know what he did say? He did feel me all about and tell me I am not with child, then feel me again and say I could be if I wanted to be!'

She handed over a letter, fastened with a seal done in the fashion of an astrolabe, and almost as big:

Mistress Lanier,
I shall see you at eleven o'clock, Tuesday forenoon. I can grant you one hour.
Simon Forman

Emilia went to place the note in her day-book, then remembered she no longer had it. She enjoyed that 'shall'. She showed the letter to Maria, as used to be her wont with Master Will's, before she allowed him to think he loved her. 'We shall see about that "shall",' she said.

'He's a powerful caster, Emilia. He hath a magic hand with a magnet in his fingerbone. He did half frighten the waters out of me, I do warn thee straight.'

''Tis his profession, my Maria. My mother calls him a piss-prophet. Let us see what he may tell from them.'

Tuesday was only a day away, less than a whole day by the dial's point, so it was false of him to announce it so grandly.

So he did reside in Lambeth, her charlatan astrologer, and no wonder he did. She found everyone in Longditch knew of him, and half the great names in Canon Row as well. Yet Lambeth was where only Archbishops lived, a little way along from the great bordellos and the baiting of the bears. Not even common players would dwell there. Yet Maria told he had a great house, with all manner of rooms for scrying and casting, and fondling rooms as well.

Emilia would not be fondled in any room in Lambeth, and certainly in no chamber. She went attired all in black as a widow, for she felt she had been a widow to many men, and she still mourned her child.

She arrived on his doorstep early to test him, and was surprised to be shown in by a man. She hoped Doctor Forman did not keep catamites, though the fellow was a big and sweaty thing too bristly for comfort and bushy about the ears, for if he played with boys it would make matters harder for her. Still, nothing was impossible to her. She smiled, remembering Southampton, and smiled again when she found his parlour. It was full of chained up silver, locked from his maids, who were plentiful about the kitchen, and who did not seem in the least locked away, though surprised to see her step in.

Upstairs, as down, she found all manner of chests and caskets with every sort of hanging, some with naked weavings and stitchings of Satan with Eve, and Eve about Adam, and a fiery serpent with a smiling face. There was all manner of Spanish armour too, as though he'd taken a pleasure fleet in tow. She considered for a moment having him properly to be her own instead of Lanier, he was so great in movables, but decided to inspect him first as well as his few thousand pounds of chattels, although they would have bought up half the guilds in the City of London, or at least matched them spoon by platter about.

One thing she disliked was the number of his seats, settles, and other furnishings that concealed commodes. It was part of his profession no doubt, but it encourages the servants to be sloppy however encouraged to scour and sand them, and it gives vent to fusty smells. Any chamber or lower room she looked in had some kind of pot concealed in some sort of joint

251

stool, as if this was all mankind including woman was about. Where, for example, were his charts and starsigns? Worse, she had not yet uncovered a library, not even for pretence, no matter where she looked.

'Mistress Lanier, I have been hunting you high and low.'

'The morning is well advanced, sir. I thought it best to search you out.'

'Know, Mistress Lanier, I do not normally grant myself to be available at such an hour of the day, but your woman said the matter was urgent and I took you to be a householder of substance, judging from the fact you reside in Longditch.'

'I never walk abroad, sir, and certainly not to places like these.'

All this time he had been climbing the stairs or stalking along the landings and galleries, talking in that calming voice of his, like a snake or lesser devil twisting from its place in the shadows, and all this time she had spared him any glimpse of her, treading through room after leading-off room, so he panted after her and felt as Narcissus must have felt when seeking the bewildering nymph-maid Echo.

At last she turned back on him, and found him planted in a priestly posture hard by a copper bowl which was burnished bright and full of his image, mostly his eyes that glittered strangely. So she did approach him by his pretty bowl.

The bowl, and his image in the bowl, could not contain his hands which leapt out at her, and began to circle her as if they were moons and she their sphere.

She grew quite giddy watching them, as was his practice no doubt, and listening to his voice, which was full of distractions. But she disliked hearing any man's voice when she had so much to say herself. She could match any fellow's talk if she had to. 'I need to know my future and my husband's destiny.'

'Are you not a widow? You wear the weeds.'

'He is away in a command under the Earls of Southampton and Essex, sir. He has been gone too long for a woman to contemplate. My waters trouble me. I have heated blood. I will

not talk of my menses. They are like the Battle of Cadiz, sir. Or
Sir Richard Greville's action in the Azores.'

'I shall need to take notes, mistress.'

'Aye, but not in a chamber. Bed feathers frighten me, in case
they catch aflame from the fire, or take a spark otherwise. So
below, by your desk, sir. No, I can find the way.'

So she did lead him down his stairs again, examining more
rooms as she went, then dictated the poor fool notes about her
history, her phantasies, her dreams, her relatives, the dreams of
her relatives, and the dreams of all the notables she knew, for
upwards of an hour.

She could see he felt he was losing the advantage, but it was
ever thus with men. She let him put his notes away, and start
talking again.

'There are stratagems, madam, philacteries, manipulations.
Some you would blush to hear of are so efficacious . . .'

'We are short in the blush, sir.' Indeed there were stratagems,
and strategies. Master Forman must be shown that she was the
better admiral in any combat. 'Stratagems, sir. I look forward
to them.'

'I work miracles nightly, mistress, I and my art. Methinks I
know your eyes—'

'I am like that philosopher's toad, sir. Beneath my lap sits the
mystical stone. Aye, and I have the unguent aplenty. But a man
must be bold, sir, if he would transmute . . .'

'Fore Heaven and Hell, was it greed or lust she was using to
draw him on? She clearly desired him. He could tell from the
way she held her hands.

She rose and left him abruptly. She left him with a hole in
the air. And a silence too. She left him with his notes, and his
quills and endless paper.

∼

He wrote for several hours after she had left. It took him this
length of time to set her down completely, or to set down what
she had revealed of herself, which took her so long he thought
she'd told him everything. And the lies:

'My child, 'tis from Heaven, sir. You must have read a like tale in the case of Jesus and Adam, one being born of a handful of dust, the other of a star.'

Several times he had to break off from recalling her. She made him sweat to think of, break out in hives, and all his juices swim at once. One glance at her and he was as a boiling pot – no, never, this would not do. He was remembering somebody quoting somebody. Was it not the mother of the Earl of Southampton, Lady Heneage, who had spoken of her son with some dark woman, and the poet Shakespeare? Could this be the lady? By heaven, he must try her and see.

He finished with his notebook, and drew out his magic parchment. On it he wrote:

I longed to hump and halek with the lady, to rut hip to hip, belly to belly-part, aye, and to enter my member into her soul's undoubted cave and join us completely as the double beast, the five-legged monster. I intend at once to be so, and so shall I scheme.

How I lust to go two backed with her, or even to sit upon her shoulders like a hump or a cockerel on her perch, providing she lets me come home to roost inside that nether nostril of hers . . .

He was interrupted in these droolings by a visitor at his door. Pretty woman again, no pretty women.

It was that Lanier woman's maid, the delicious Maria, whom he also intended to halek, but he couldn't do it now, she found ways to stop him.

'I've brought another servant, master Forman, to see you don't go feeling my water again, or any other part of me, since my mistress intends us for a convent. This is Lisbet Bown, who'll see you mind your hands.'

He let his dark eyes roam between them, saucy eye and saucy eye, sweet little lips, and breast and breast about.

'Mistress Lanier tells you to leave off your staring, sir. She is watching through a spyglass brighter than Galileo's from just across the river, and she likes her men pure, at least for such evening as promises. You are to come straightway to Westminster. There are capon's a-cooking, and crabs in a pie. Our little boat is waiting below the stair.'

'Certainly not, you pert girl. Tell Mistress Lanier – tender her my apologies – tell her I've another command to supper tonight.'

'Our house is full of women, sir, she most particularly bids me say. And its cellar is stuffed with all manner of surprises. There's stuffing in the chambers as well.'

'Assuredly no. As I say, you must acquaint your gracious mistress . . .'

How was it he found himself shivering knee to knee with them, not five minutes later, and being poled and then back-skulled across the Thames in a boat?

~

What a strange supper they had, with the young women all about, and her fellow called Rudkin playing his nose flute, and then the lady herself singing to herself on the virginal, but not like a woman, like a damned sick monkey boy similar to those the Arabs used to keep in their harems in Cordoba. He would remember everything about the meal except the capons and the pie stuffed with crabs. Everything. Was there mandrake in the wine, or some other kind of gallowroot? Or was it the Spanish Fly?

Then after supper, on that great tasselled settle, did he even open his mouth?

He once again stated his wish to lie with me, and about me, upon me, and through me (to make his meaning as plain as it had been since this morning). So I told him 'no', or 'fie no', or 'nay' (to make my own meaning manifest, as it had been also since this morning). He had a sharp eye, good legs, and a hugely ornamented lump at the front of him that I knew was not entirely filled up by tennis balls nor taylors, but I had to keep him out of me for my Art's sake.

255

'You may share my bed,' I told him. 'And hold me in discourse or sleep with me the whole night long, but there at this time – *there* must be an end of it.'

'Nay, mistress—'

'Added to which,' I enjoined, 'you may touch me all about, but only with what is soft, your hardest parts to brush me being no more than your finger ends! I'll not lay a sword between us, or bend a chain and padlock about your waist, but there'll be a grand curse between us if you presume to digress.'

Then I led him above, and took all my garments off and lay upon the bed consecrated to my Art.

He felt me here and there, there more often than here, in an entirely expert manner, bussed me by the lips, I mean his lips on mine, and swept me head to foot with his beard, which was nearer lambswool than besom and brought several of my particles, and principally the entire estate of my skin, into a most delectable buzz, as if I were blistered by a swarm of bees or secretly growing freckles.

Then he took my breast in his mouth and nearly sucked out my heart. Then he began to dampen my entire body with kisses before fishing it with his tongue.

Now a man's tongue is an overstiff thing – and for many a young blade the stiffest thing about him – especially if he desires to be witty. Well, I gave Master Forman a deal of licence with his tongue and nearly lost my Art to his insistence with it down under, such was its shifting, its fiddling, its hither and thither sawing and bowing. I nearly began to howl like a whole case of viols with a nose flute in countertone, but I would not cry out, in spite of the intensity of my pleasure, both there and in my fundament which he several times licked into for a simple change of view.

After about three hours of this, I mean the tonguing (we'd had three hours of touching earlier, him of me, me not of him, because I could afford the brute no encouragement), he came up from my lower back and belly the better to find himself some breath and spit out a mouthful of bedfeathers. ''Fore God, my lady Emilia,' he said, when he'd got his croak back (his beard lay as limp and unattractive to his neck as the hairs on a plasterer's brush). ''Fore God, you do taste well. I've tasted several score of young ladies in my time, virgins and other females, including some of the highest in the land, but none of them compares to your bouquet. I must write to the King of Bulgaria about you, though mentioning no names!'

'Tell me,' I said, then wrinkled my nose as I said it. 'I don't think I should like to sample a woman for bush, be she ever so quaint and privy.'

'Fish is what most readily springs to mind,' he said, 'not so much in your case alone as in the quainter comelies of all young women, but I mean nothing unwholesome or unsavoury by that. I mean the clean fish of our moon's or in Venus's oceans, perhaps those sweet salt sea oceans themselves, or the tears of the moon's mad eye.' He took a chestful of air and tasted me again, like a manciple testing Rhenish wine. 'In your case, Mistress Lanier, I do not think fish or oceans are midway appropriate, though I once took a trout straight from the stream and cooked it on an ember with honey, and the memory of that delight comes close!' He closed his eyes and tried again. 'Oyster,' he pronounced, 'a fresh live oyster under a squeezing of lime and pomegranate and yet more honey – that would be near.' Again he dived beneath me, this time not finishing till I swear he nearly sucked the bones from my back, and certain of my privities almost inside out so I had to reassure myself with a finger to make sure he hadn't left me hanging behind like a cow's udder. 'Now I bethink me of fruit and honey,' he whispered, but this time speaking through me as if my secret underparts were a pair of doe's ears, and the particles of my spine all fashioned into a speaking trumpet. 'You are a nectarine damp with the dews of heaven!'

All of this, and the breathlessness most of all, had

rendered his member very stiff. He could have hung a hook on the end of it and used it to catch sturgeon, it was so bonny, or those dolphins that jump across the poop, but I dare not let it enter me, not so early in our acquaintance when I scarcely had the mastering of him, nor his mastery from out of his pocket.

Fortunately I noticed his licking about my charms had brought his cups close to running over. He already wore a droplet of moon juice at the top of him, as white as a pearl or the oozings of a freshly cut dandelion stem.

Even as he groped and shifted about me, I flung myself upon this cannon with my one hand and tickled his belly with the other. I did not tickle loosely, or allow my concentration to wander, but marked out King Solomon's greatest seal, the sign of the endless pentagram, between his wishbone and his gastrium. The pentagram did it. He discharged all over my fingers and quite filled up the cuff of my nightgown, which I'd somehow slipped about me to keep my back warm while he'd been truffling below. He emitted a great sob as he did so, pumping out soul dust and seed in perpetual broadside till he'd lost more of his essential oils and magical fluid than would saucer a cat – nay, he wasted enough to make up the white of an ostrich's egg, or an elephant's if it laid one. And as embarrassment had proceeded his pleasure so did I take care with my busy little hands that his pleasure kept on rushing after his embarrassment, pinning him there beneath the weight of my body on his lower half until his ecstasies were unravelled, his wick entirely barren of oil, and now at last relenting, and relaxing, and creeping back towards the gun port of his belly, till it rested like a moist nosed little spaniel on the paws of his balls. He had not come into me, nor at me, nor about me. My Art was intact, and he would certainly remember the service I had done to him. Great Magister that he was, I do believe he became at that moment entirely mine.

It was now about the hour – I do not jest – of the first

cock. Like many an animal in such a circumstance, be he shrimp or stallion, the sluggard thought he would slink towards sleep.

'Fair is only fair,' I said, 'and quits are best requited. You've had many a sip at my nectar, and I not even a sniff at yours.'

Poor, sweet punchinello, little browbeaten Puck and then Punch! The tiny brute, now no bigger than a sparrow, shrank down and away from me. But I took its head between my lips, prized its tiny beak apart with my tongue, and the moment he so much as began to gawp at me sucked him with tremendous violence into the back of my throat. Oh, how he stiffened and lengthened then, as I guided him from thence into the hole in my bolster's end, which Lisbet had prepared for me.

He was too far gone in the head to notice. He did enter as far inside as a fire-eater's brand or a sword swallower's blade. He shouldn't have tried, but his member couldn't help itself. It took so much pain in his pleasure that – whether or not having a hole in my bolster made him sore – it would be several weeks before he would belong to himself or any other woman again, in spite of his boast of doing it with several of us several times a day.

He did stop abusing my bedclothes at last, though each clung to each completely exhausted, as such lovers will. 'Oh, Emilia,' he moaned, 'my love, my love. Such love it hath been, such ecstasy it is, and ever more will be,' speaking in his sleep, you understand, as he was accustomed to do to many women or their fourposters else. Then, in a troubled dream, he found my lips and kissed them.

You can't keep writings like these,' Maria said to her. 'They'll burn you as a manifest witch, Mistress Emilia.' She was ever stern and forceful was Maria, though obedient to every command. 'Besides, I don't know why you bother to boast. Master Forman didn't stay overlong. It's all in your wicked head.'

'No, it's in the bolster's end,' Lisbet said.

It was then that Margaret Johnson's cat paid the first of many visits to the Longditch house. It came walking from the fire and cleaned all his leavings up.

She keeps on commanding me. Her women come often to my dwelling, but never her. I swear I am given a salted or otherwise seasoned drink each time I go there. 'Fore God, my brain is abuzz with nutmeg and mummy oil, if not with other more drowsy syrups.

Where am I to put such a witch? I speak of this testament of human weakness and woe! I make my casebooks in code, but her name refuses every cipher. She tells me – her daemon *commands* me – to set her down in my fairest secretary hand but with the seed of my loins in place of ink. This is pure necromancy, the blackest art! I have no seed. She has lit a furnace at my root that blasts my every leaf. My whole tree of man does waste and wither. Were I a man I should castigate her evil in my own water, and endite her name lefthanded to scry myself of her, but she infects me even to my last fluid drop.

The devil calls for me now, not her woman. I had thought him first to be her man. She hath a most wholesome man, tall and good of thew, a simple fellow called Peter Rudkin. This man, this devil, is from the grave itself. He names himself Dingley, and his eye is put out and his ears still bleeding from the pillory. I know not how he makes the blood. He hath bled for me a fortnight now, and behold my case. I have Charon for a boatman, be it night or day.

She dines me at table, with this brute Dingley sitting at large, and another, who is called Marc Anthony, also doth share our feast. She tells me he is not alive, but was drowned in exile at sea. I do believe her. I do see the water within his chest, and the food that he eats swim inside him. What manner of woman is this that sits with dead men at her table, then takes me unto her bed whether I will follow or not, but no longer to halek with her.

I write this down, vile though it is, and not fit for anyone's eyes, because I am like to die of her. She hath poisoned my soul.

The world knows I have entered her. I did enter her on our first evening, and was busy within her several hours without end. She now does deny all this. Listen to how she says:

'Sir, what I do desire of you – what I will *admit* you to – is Satan's kiss.'

She turned her bottom towards me, and I saw her Devil's pap, she had grown a mole on the cheeks of it, like the spot on a hawk moth's wings – aye, the image is apt, she did so flap her bum about, like a harvest of butterflies.

'Madam, that's a vile injunction, to ask what the Devil demands, to bless your fundament.'

'Sir, it's my last and only command. Everything about me is scented and oiled – would you know me otherwise? My most secret parts taste of pomegranate and cucumber, as you yourself have noted, and the least nothing of my nethermost corner is sweeter than cherry honey.'

'But to put my tongue to that gate, mistress.'

'Sir, my other way leads directly into Heaven, and you are not ready for such a place.'

So I did oblige her, and begone my soul. She did anoint herself, she claimed, with some witches' ointment she had from her mother. It tasted well, but is principally aconite, and bane diluted by poppy. Once I had tasted, I did fly all right. I did fly all night, with Lisbet, Maria and those other witches, but I landed in Hell.

Let me write what followed.

There were no women now. I was naked and alone in her bed, bound in the form of a Saint Andrew's cross, like any saint on a Catherine Wheel, and spinning, spinning.

261

Dingley stood by me, but with his eye bandaged back into his head, and wearing an apron such as surgeons wear. He had no knife, sword or saw – praise be! – and he needed none.

This Dingley – first name Henry (boatswain or bastard, they are all copied after the late King!) – put his fist into my navel. I had always taken this to be a solid affair, as stout as any ship's hatch, being the last part of my *corpus* to be stitched by my old mother, but the brute entered with a whole bunch of fingers as easily as a needlewoman's feeling into the neck of a nether-stock or stretching the heel of your old hose.

I swear he entered my belly up to his wrist, if not his elbow. Once he was truly inside, he began to finger a devilishly ticklish tune on the ivories of my backbone. This did not amuse him for long. With a cry of triumph, he began to pluck out my visceral organs, beginning with my kidneys, of which he found several, and my liver, of which he stole a lot. I have scarcely been able to swallow any breakfast since.

Then the witchwoman came. I mean Bassano-Lanier, my harpy possessor.

'Master Dingley hath made me a present of your parts,' said she.

'That Dingley is a liar and a devil.'

'Several of your parts, at the least. I did ask him for your cullions and your kneecaps, and he promises to oblige me the next time you drift towards slumber.'

'Mistress,' I pleaded, 'I'll not be able to walk if he steals off my kneecaps.'

'Nor your cullions, either,' she scolded. 'I've seen you step on those a time or two once your breeks were off, but that's only to be expected from a man of your age. Old scholars like you should only creep between the sheets in the cold weather. You can surprise your loves with your goose-pimples if nothing else.'

The impudence of the woman. What a naughty lady!

'For the rest of the year you should get your washer-women to peg you up by the heels. It's the only way you'll avoid treading on yourself.'

I woke back here, in my own bed. I saw her no more. She hath used me completely up, like scraps of rabbit in her pie.

'So, my child,' Margaret Johnson said. 'You have it all now. You have stolen another man's power, not a negligible villain as wickedness goes, yet you have taught him a lesson and bent him to your will.'

'Thank you, my mother.'

'Enough of this "my"! I am your sister's mother too.'

The two women sulked for a time, both the living and the dead. Emilia became impatient. She tapped the arm of her chair, then a piece of the wood that waited by the bedroom fire.

'So what will you do? Will you be wise, or will you be powerful?'

'I am wise in having you for my mother. I would be power-ful.'

'You frighten every man who sets eyes on you. Is that not power enough?'

'I would do those things you promised me.'

'Throw that branch upon your fire.'

The bedrooms were taller in the Westminster House, with their rafters half hidden in the ceiling, for each dwelling in Longditch was its own little palace. Even so, the fireplace was meagre.

Emilia regarded it with suspicion just the same, and was careful with the piece of wood, which was beech and bone dry.

'Sit where you will, daughter. I want to show you a picture.'

The log burned at once, and straightway began to plead and moan to the fire that burned her, and those who had lit the fire. Then the log began to pray. It prayed for many minutes in a soft low voice, a country voice as befitted such a tree, but unmistakably a woman. The voice continued in prayer until the log was consumed.

'Who was she praying to, and in whose name did she pray?'

'I do not answer such questions. Watch the embers closely.'

The woman was about Emilia's own age – no, a year or two younger. It would be reasonable to say she was young. She was quarrelling with her husband, who occasionally beat her, and then with other men, who scoffed at her and beat her as well. Emilia wondered if she was looking at an image of herself, but the woman was fair. The woman left her home, bruised as she was, and walked a great distance on foot. Church bells began to ring from Emilia's hearth. The woman frowned and halted.

'She's walking to London,' Emilia's mother said. 'You have heard of Dick Whittington.'

Emilia nodded eagerly.

'She isn't Dick Whittington.'

The fire fell apart, and Emilia lost the picture and began to curse. There must be a better way of seeing things. She poked the embers into shape and at once saw a room, with the woman outstretched on a bench.

'A pity you grew talkative,' her mother said. 'You nearly lost the best bit.'

The woman groaned, again very softly. Emilia realized she was stretched on the rack. Whenever her mother showed her anything there was always a bed or a rack in it. She began to feel her ancestor's limitations.

'Don't watch the woman. Look at the man.'

The man was in young middle-age. He was dressed in a stiff black doublet and wore black clerical leggings rather than hose. He didn't wear a ruff. His face was extremely striking, and it reminded Emilia of someone.

'He was the Lord Chancellor, some fifty years ago. A fine upright man of extreme moderation in everything. And yet he personally racked this woman, turning the screws with his own hand, then burned her in Smithfield as a heretic.'

'What for?'

'He thought it right and proper. She was full of religious nonsense.'

'He's a cleric himself.'

'A scholar but not a priest. They do like to argue, those church-given men. I won't show you the end of her. It's much too horrid to mention. She was so stretched by the rack, she had to be carried to the stake in a chair. She made a great impression on people, so as a special act of mercy they hung her about with bags of powder and turned her into a firework. Her name is Anne Askew.'

'I've never heard it before.'

'She's hardly your sort of woman, Emilia. I think you ought to meet her, just the same. Her tormentor was Thomas Wriothesley, the First Earl of Southampton. The Southampton's are all most noble men, each of them generous to a fault. But their bloodline has this enemy other than yourself. Surely you may have need of her?'

'I'll not build a wall of smoke to summon her, never again, nor play with your fires. Where is she laid to rest?'

'No known burial place. She was burned to a cupful of dripping, then the wind took her atomies all away before the pigs could eat her last gobbets up. You had better go seek her at Smithfield.'

～

Emilia was amazed at her new-found power, which was much like her old power, or any other power which ordains the destiny of things.

News kept coming from the New World islands and each dispatch was full of disasters. No Spanish treasure galleons were encountered, and scarcely an island discovered. The seas were a-gnash with storm, and the men eaten up with scurvy. (Would she be able to tolerate Lanier if his teeth dropped out and that magnificent nose fell in?) Hawkins was dead. Drake, who was held to be immortal, had been buried at sea in a hammock.

The disaster was Essex's fault. Even the crowds, who loved him, said that. Even Lisbet did, who had seen him walk on the ice.

Then Rudkin announced a visitor, who anyway walked in unannounced. It was her sweet young earl, four years older than young, weatherstained but still full of dash and flair. He'd changed from his seaborne gaskins into magnificent Sunday hose.

'Lady Emilia.' He bowed almost as deeply as Will had bowed. When he straightened up, she counted the teeth in the front of his mouth, still anxious about her husband's health. 'Lady, for such you should be called! Alas, my cousin Essex refuses to make a single knight, because the Islands have been such a failure.'

'My lord, what is your pleasure?'

'You, Mistress Emilia. May I sit down? Know your husband Lanier is well. I have hurried towards you from Plymouth, in order to be a few weeks ahead of him. He shall be at home and in your bosom, I promise you, just as soon as the fleet has sailed to the Thames. With the winds full in the East, this should require a month. Then he'll have himself to make ready, his viols and such matters to look to, his sword to polish, and some ropes to make fast.'

'Lord Henry.'

'One question I ask you, before I – ah! – ask you my question. Are you still inhabited by that affliction a man may not mention to a woman, but only joke about among men?'

'The clap, sir. Master Shakespeare made similar inquiry.'

'Will – Will Shakespeare. I hear he does well for himself. Sweet Will.'

'I never had the clap, my lord. Nor the pox.'

'Good, very good. More than good. I am to be wed, do you see. And I – not to put it too fine – I need to practise.' He blushed. He stammered. 'You – I – my mother . . . You three are all I know and understand of women, Lady Mistress Emilia. You made it so easy for me. May I try again?'

'My lord Henry.' God, how many of them there were. 'My lord Henry, will you, as you ask, sit down?' How she despised the impudence of the fellow, yet she had a question to ask for herself. 'Why do you need to be wed, sir, given that your tastes are largely held to be backward, or at least the other way?'

'Because I am an earl, Mistress. My mother expects it. Also my cousin Essex says I keep on getting his cousins with child, and must marry one quick, if not marry them all.'

'His girl cousins, my lord?'

'Young women to a man.'

'Then how do you get these young women with child, may I ask, if you don't see your way to being in bed with them?'

He thought for some time, then beat on his forehead with the flat of his hand. 'Essex does bully me so.'

'Perhaps you should seek answer from him about just which cousin is getting the ladies with child, sir. I take it they are creatures of pith and ambition, these young women of noble birth? It must be from suitable suitors they desire increase?'

'I shall think upon your words, sweet Emilia, and fret no more.'

He was gone. He left an agreeable aroma behind him, like a man who had painted himself with a woman's unguents several hours at the time. And now his face showed traces of hair, and the Carib sun had grizzled his head just a little . . .

'Will you still kill him, Emilia?' It was Maria calling from the chamber door, then Lisbet also. 'I hope you will do way with him soon.'

Emilia had no time to frame an answer.

'He hath learned some wicked tricks while seaborne, the young earl. On his way through the servants' parlour, he did clap Lisbet and myself upon the back. Then he did kiss Rudkin's hand.'

'It is but a dumbshow,' Emilia answered. 'He doth not do such things, save out of conceit and as an act of deception. He has given you a message which he knows will be reported back, that's all. Yes, I think he must die. It's the idleness of the man that teaches me that!'

Her servants were her friends. More, they were people whether friends or not. His lordship the earl had taken no thought of that.

Then how doth Gentry come to rise and fall?
Or who is he that very rightly can
Distinguish of his birth, or tell at all
In what mean state his ancestors have been
Before someone of worth did honour win?

Had his grandfather won it for racking and burning a woman?
And what for? Expressing a belief? Or simply for being a
woman at all?

TWENTY

Smithfield at dawn was a daunting place, though mercifully it was November and dawn was late.

Emilia had never felt so strong, so sure of purpose than when she went there with her three servants, her only friends. She knew that if she found the place she could summon the dead.

At the same time, she looked towards Maria standing a short way off, with her head bowed and shivering, and realized there were things that she could not do. Maria was right. Her magic was in her head. She would take a house she could not afford. She couldn't take on the people such a big house needed, because to take them on would be to owe them their keep.

There were several gibbets. There was a tumble-down post and strut. There was a straight bar. There were two of the new three-legged triangular frames. The condemned could be given society there. They could choke to death among friends.

It was one thing to gull a rogue like Master Forman. To rob him of the pride which was the essence of his soul. But to cheat the people who depended upon her?

There were four brick hearths for the burning fires. No stakes, merely slots in the hearths to accommodate them. If more than four were condemned, then they planted more stakes.

Four were to burn when Anne Askew was burned. Poor sweet Anne, now she knew her story. A woman just like herself, married against her will, and churched against her every inclination. A woman with two children by a father she did not love and whose mind she did not respect.

Only three had actually reached the flames. One had recanted. How awful it must be for the others if one recants and exemption beckons. Wriothesley pleaded with Anne to recant. He had prayers said beside her beseeching God she would recant. Her knees and hips were out at the joint because of what Wriothesley did to her by turning the screw with his own hand and too far. She did not recant. She was burned in a chair.

'Do you seek Lady Anne?'

The woman appeared beside them only slowly. It was her voice that led their eyes to her, above them in the freshening breeze.

'I seek Mistress Askew, yes. Is this the place of her burning?'

'Call her Lady Anne. She cares not for the title. But call her that. Her married name appalls her. She was nobly born.'

The woman was about twenty-five years old and dressed in black. She had walked across the great expanse of Smithfield from the open land towards the north. She walked towards the London Wall.

'Lady Anne was burned when the wind blew from the south. It was not a friendly wind. It flattened the flame, nor let any smoke rise up to stifle her.'

'Was she not strangled from behind?'

'Not once the wind had flattened the fire. Wriothesley said "No", so they did not strangle her.'

'She was very brave.'

'She bore her pain. Wriothesley wished to spare her only to torture her again.'

'Where can I meet with Lady Anne?'

'She will see you in Church. She approves of no Church, but she'll meet you in the Church where you were wed. She feels for those places where women are wed against their will.'

The wind began to blow. It had backed from north west to south. The woman had come from the north. Now she disappeared.

270

Emilia turned to her companions. 'She told me to go to Saint Botolph's in Bishopsgate.'

'*She* told you?' Maria scoffed. 'We saw your face move. We heard you talking to yourself.'

'We saw you talk to a young Bedlam girl,' Lisbet said. 'A whey-faced virgin as loony as snow.'

'The wind has backed towards the south,' Emilia explained.

'She's a witch,' Lisbet told Peter Rudkin. 'She notices winds.'

~

They entered the City of London and walked to St Botolph's. It was scarcely a mile away.

Lady Anne did not appear. The young Bedlam-mad woman from the Bethlehem Hospital, if such she was, certainly did not appear. Emilia knew no ghost may stand in a church.

This is because only witches may summon them, witches and wizards and such like poor students who steal the gifts brought by lesser gods when the Christ child lay in his infant cradle.

All else is a trick, and a treachery against Heaven. Paltry men may do it, hermaphrodites and half men with their coddling boys – actors like Will, but only on stages. These men may make apparitions or such things seem.

'Nothing here,' Maria muttered.

'Only dead sunlight and a few blown leaves,' Lisbet said.

Peter Rudkin crushed the silence with his foot.

Their tricks are done with smoke, or a pumpkin behind a gauze, or a whole man – beloved hated William again – illumed by a candle and made to shine in an ingle of blackened glass.

So it was that no ghost but an old woman of five and seventy stood by Emilia's side as she waited facing the altar. 'I remember Anne Askew,' the old woman said. 'I was there to see her burn.' The old woman's teeth were long and strong, like a young skeleton's teeth. It was only her gums that had receded. 'I was five and twenty then, the same age that she was. Today I have the years you will have when you die. Think of poor Anne's pain. Then think of poor Will's.'

'I do not mean Will such harm.'

271

'But you have sent him harm. He and Southampton, your beautiful boy, they'll both go to ruin with the Earl of Essex. There's no stopping that one. He'll ruin himself. But you don't need young Wriothesley to lose his head, not Lord Henry the beautiful boy you wound in your bedsheet.'

'I want him dead.'

'I want no Wriothesley dead, and I have cause. Yet the old man unstrung my ligaments, drew out my joints, and denied me my middle years and this, my old age.' These were bitter words, spoken without bitterness. The old woman gave them time, then said gently. 'If Southampton goes down, Will will go down. You will see. The charge will be treason, and you know what that means for a commoner?'

Emilia shuddered. Peter Rudkin had told her.

'They'll burn his entrails before him in the fire, and only then hang him up.'

Emilia said she would think. She hated to have other people's fiends come whistling in on her.

'You could pray,' the old woman said. 'Not to the Church. Not to the building itself and its chains. I do not worship in churches, not for myself, not in any such place – and so they did roast me. But I worship the God of these churches, even if not as men demand of me. And I love His sweet Son in my own way.'

Emilia tried to walk from all this, but she could not. The old woman caught her by the little finger, and held her still as death, bone to bone. 'I'll tell you directly, Madam Lanier, there are no miracles to be had elsewhere, save by Him. Miracles? Nay, nor no changes, neither. True you may be swallowed by the Infernal Serpent, and the juices of his entrails will change you. They will change you to *cac*, Madam Lanier, and leave you no better than a serpent's excrement, which is mostly dribble and easily wiped away by a slim blade of grass. Is that your idea of a miraculous transformation? Or do you seek to be grilled on the Everlasting Bonfire? You've a liking for fires, so the ballad-makers and their harlots do scream at me.' Her fingers knitted with Emilia's so tightly now it was like a change of bones. 'You needs must pray, and pray hard, Madam Lanier. And never mind the terror in it – that's a gall too bitter for Margaret Johnson's daughter to stomach. Or for one with a pride like yours, it is. So no terror in it. Let it all be praise, your prayer.'

'Pray, you say?' The old woman was hurting more than her fingers. 'Me *pray*? Pray how?'

'Pray *Salve Deus Rex Judæorum* – what a title for a poem such praise would be!'

Emilia did not see the old woman go.

'We saw you talk to an old lady,' Lisbet said. 'A fine old crow with more chins than scarves.'

'There's always old women in church,' Peter Rudkin added.

'They come here to wait for Heaven,' Maria agreed. 'It's out of the wind, whichever way it blows.'

~

'Well, daughter?'

'Mother, be quiet. I am chewing on the costard. When I've eaten the core, I shall spit the pips into their eye.'

'All this for so little?'

'I'm chewing, mother. I can think with an apple, just like the Queen.'

> These high deserts invites my lowely Muse
> To write of Him, and pardon crave of thee . . .

'Granted, child.'

> For time so spent I need make no excuse,
> Knowing it doth with thy faire Minde agree
> So well, as thou no Labour wilt refuse,
> That to thy holy love may pleasing be:
> His Death and Passion I desire to write,
> And thee to read, the blessèd Soules delight.

'It's better than your Will's verses. He was never one for Heaven.'

273

'Maria says I talk to myself, mother.'

'I can't answer that. Shouldn't you be in bed? Your husband's back home at last, and husbands are always quick to want a good wife with her deed-boxes open, and her entitlements on show – *and* to scribble their names on her nether parchments.'

'I'm cutting another quill, mother.'

> Long mai'st thou joy in this almighty love,
> Long may thy Soule be pleasing in his sight

'I don't intend to stop till breakfast time.'

~

Lanier was approaching ecstasy – not that transient tremble a man experiences when he kisses his wife's naked body, but that much greater, almost religious joy he knows when he has a stroke of good fortune.

'God be praised,' he said, 'and this Jesus you keep on writing to all these titled old ladies about!'

'Amen,' she said. She could feel his breath on her ear, but it wasn't lust, only good news.

'I am Captain,' he cried.

'You have been a Captain since you fell down drunk on my kitchen floor in the Bishopsgate house.'

'I mean I am made Captain of the Queen's music. The Earl of Southampton wants me to lead them in a great *concierto* at the opening of Master Shakespeare's new theatre.'

'The Earl of Southampton?'

'And the young Lord Chamberlain who is the new Lord Hunsdon, your old man's son.' He did kiss her now. It was less flamboyant than kissing himself. 'You shall see. You shall come there and see me.' He paused, as if lacking the English, or wondering whether what he had to say was tasteful. 'Isn't it a gracious thing, to know that all the men who have loved you – save one, and he will be represented by his son – all of us will be gathered together with you in one place?'

~

274

Will was knocking on her door the next instant, with the Earl of Southampton – or the Earl of Southampton with Will, according to who was most famous.

Southampton wanted to see the musician. Will needed to see her.

'Ways of the world,' he cried. 'Hearken, my Emilia. You know we have built this playhouse on Bankside? Well, Her Majesty will be there, your husband will be there, blowing and scraping his woods and beating his drum . . .'

He'd run out of breath. He was doing less acting of late. 'Thing is, Emilia, we'll be giving one of my plays, my company the Lord Chamberlain's men and me. I don't know which one, but it will be the usual patchwork of stuff I've written, stuff that actors have scribbled, stuff I've borrowed, and half a thousand lines I'll have stolen.'

'I am not your confessor, Will. You had best go to Church.'

'What I mean is, you might care to scribble something for me, my dark Rosaline.'

'Emilia.'

'I'm alluding to *Love's Labour's Lost*. Do me a prologue or so. You won't be paid. Your words will be swallowed up, but you'll know they are there. And I'll take care to mention it to Her Majesty.'

How she was glad she'd taken Lady Anne's advice, and called Dingley back from killing the poor sweet fool.

The galleries were too far above the ground, taller and much more giddy than anything at the Tabard, and the pleasure taverns of Southwark. Not so high as St Paul's across the river – she thought not so high, but in truth she could not see it; and if she could she dare not look! – yet far too lofty to dare a glance at the clouds that raced overhead in the little chimney of sky.

So that's how the Globe was built, more like a tower than an inn, more like a well than either. It had a roof on top of the walls, but nothing to keep rain off its middle. A well expressed it exactly. She was growing dizzy with the height, and her only thirty years old! She daren't tell herself she was older than that, even by a season! She mustn't look up or down, lest the sight of her own toes giddied her.

The musicians were far too remote above her. They had their own little perch and nest on top of the slender turret that rose at the back of the stage. She could just see Lanier there, his head and not much else. He'd told her he didn't mind heights. He'd lived many years on a ship, and had sometimes gone up the mast. The mast grew taller each time he told the story. She felt proud of him just the same, proud to know what he was, and what he was doing up there.

It had never been easy to call herself Mistress Lanier. Lady would be a better title. While she was waiting for him to go back to his war across the sea, she had taken to calling herself Wife of *Captain* Lanier, Servant of the Queen's Majesty. That's what he also had been, but Captain was what made the difference. He would earn them a title one day.

Now came a beat on the drum. Master Shakespeare strode down the stage and began to speak her magnificent prologue. She made her way downstairs to enjoy her own poem to the full. At the third or fourth step she fell.

She lay among men's feet and swooned into a kind of daze. This scarcely lasted a minute. She could still hear and see Will. The legs made a balustrade all about her.

It was Poley who helped her up – praise God she fell among gentlemen. The Queen and the important nobles were seated on the stage. The groundlings and other rabble were standing in the pit. Here, in the galleries, there were gentlemen.

Poley helped her to a private place just as Will thanked the crowd for the applause and told them the Prologue had been written by Mistress Lanier, a gentlewoman. The Queen had shifted on her stool at this, but at least she had listened to it.

Mr Poley began to feel Emilia all about, as soon as he was able, pretending to see if her heart still beat, or if her limbs were broken. What he discovered was what she could have told him at the commencement, namely that she was a damned pretty woman who had fallen downstairs.

He did pat her for some time, did Poley, until she told him to desist or her husband would chop him into cutlets.

'I merely wish to reassure myself, Mistress Lanier.' He put his hands away at last, or folded his arms, and said, 'I have to tell you this. You would have been next in line for my inquisition after young Master Marlowe, if the Lord Chancellor had not protected you, then the next after Doctor Lopez, if the Lord Chancellor hadn't died.'

He seized hold of her again. 'By God, I'd rather stretch you than any number of varlets like that pair!'

She saw little more of the play, as Master Poley became brutally indelicate with her.

She tried to yawn. She tried to pray. She tried to see the sky beyond his ears, or even to count knot-holes in the ceiling. There was no pleasure to be had from him, so little joy she began to wonder if she hadn't tripped over one of her old stray curses as she came down the stairs.

～

Nothing could save Essex from his own destiny, not even Emilia's reconversion, and Southampton fell with him as a result of her original spells. Or so her pride told her, for the job was well done. Will nearly lost himself to the executioner's knife in consequence.

Essex bullied Southampton to bribe the Lord Chamberlain's Men to give a performance of Will's *Richard II* . . . oh, what folly, with its

> Let us sit upon the ground
> And tell sad stories of the death of Kings

As the Queen's own Majesty so neatly put it, 'I am Richard II.' And she was, except for the inconvenience of a whisker or so.

Then Essex and Southampton got some three hundred knights and gentlemen drunk and went rushing to the City of London, to raise the Mayor and Citizens against all manner of indignities. The Mayor was faced with a moral problem much like Will's, only Will did not know that his play was being acted. Here's how the Mayor saved his own skin. He locked Essex and Southampton outside his city.

The gentlemen and knights were all disarmed. The Earls of Essex and Southampton were arrested, as were Master Shakespeare and some of the players.

That great Jehova King of heav'n and earth,
Will raine downe fire and brimstone from above,
Upon the wicked monsters in their berth
That storme and rage at those whom he doth love:
Snares, stormes, and tempests he will raine, and dearth,
Because he will himselfe almightie prove:
   And this shall be the portion they shall drinke,
   That thinkes the Lord is blind when he doth winke.

But Emilia, having been well converted by Anne Askew, had called her curses off from her Will, who was released almost at once, and, more reluctantly, from the Earl of Southampton.

Essex and Southampton were arraigned before the Star Chamber, and condemned to death.

Emilia lit a great fire in Longditch just a few days later. Before she gazed into the flames, she said a prayer for Southampton, who was reprieved.

Inside the flame, she could see the Tower yard, and Essex walking bravely, led by his personal chaplain towards the block.

He died unflinching from the first blow of the axe, which did noble work on his neckbone but did not sever his head. The executioner had to adjust his mask before finishing the job to the witnesses' satisfaction.

A cinder fell at this point, but Emilia swears she saw what had caused the botch. The executioner could not see his mark. His mask was awry, because one of his eyes was malformed, and half hung out beneath it.

'It's only inside your head you see all this,' Maria scolded. Maria had been a failure as a witch, and as a visionary Christian was slow to take example.

He shall within his Tabernacle dwell,
Whose life is uncorrupt before the Lord,
Who no untrueths of Innocents doth tell,
Nor wrongs his neighbour, nor in deed, nor word
Nor in his pride with malice seems to swell,
Nor whets his tongue more sharper than a sword,
　　To wound the reputation of the Just;
　　Nor seekes to lay their glorie in the Dust.

Emilia lit no more fires in Longditch. She was evicted shortly afterwards. She had never paid any rent. Christian lady or not, she was much too great to pay rent.